THORNS
OF LOVE

To my daughters, husband, family, friends, and my readers.

Please skip over the sex scenes and focus on the plot. You DA best!
Love ya!
To everyone else, thank you for reading my stories.

THORNS OF OMERTÀ SERIES

Each book in the Thorns of Omertà series can be read alone with the exception of Thorns of Lust and Thorns of Love, which is the story of Tatiana Nikolaev.

If you'd like the preview of the next standalone book in this series, Thorns of Death, keep reading after this duet ending.

THORNS OF LOVE PLAYLIST

https://spoti.fi/3mp6fBl

AUTHOR NOTE

Hello readers,

Thorns of Lust is the first book of a duet and is NOT a standalone. Tatiana Nikolaev's story completes in *Thorns of Love*.

Furthermore, please note that this book has some dark elements to it and disturbing scenes. Please proceed with caution. It is not for the faint of heart.

Don't forget to sign up to Eva Winners's Newsletter (www.evawinners.com) for news about future releases.

BLURB

My husband.

His secrets.

Our tragedy.

I thought I knew him. I didn't. I thought he was trustworthy. He wasn't.

But nothing in this world is as it seems.

I caught the attention of the most notorious man in the underworld.

Konstantin wasn't the type to be ignored. He commanded his criminal empire with an iron fist but he had secrets of his own.

But I was Tatiana Nikolaev. I'd never bend to a man's will or be used as a pawn. Not again.

The moment I tempted the fates and played with fire, life spiraled out of control.

My only way of survival was to trust again.

But could I?

ONE
TATIANA

P*ush me, moya luna, and I'll snuff out that pretty blue inferno in your eyes.*

The words played on repeat in my mind. Was that a threat? All I had to do was utter a single word to Vasili and the war would be back on.

Except my brother intended to use me as his "*peace*" offering.

My fingers trembled as I attempted to tug the zipper. I stared at my reflection in the long mirror. I couldn't recognize myself. My light blonde hair, cascading down my shoulders. My eyes were clear, a turquoise so blue that people sometimes labeled it its own color. The freakish Nikolaev pale blue.

The beautiful dress, the color of palest lilac, swallowed my frame. The dress's neckline fell off my shoulders, accentuating my collarbone. I was slowly gaining back the weight I had lost over the months since Adrian's death. My curves were slowly filling in, the little life growing inside me still unnoticeable.

Nausea hit me suddenly, it had been coming and going. I clutched my stomach, but I knew all the contents of it were about to come out.

Spinning around, I rushed to the toilet. My dress hung half

unzipped, falling off my shoulder as I grabbed the toilet and threw up. Except this time, there were no strong hands stroking my back. Violent heaves wracked my body.

"Tatiana." My name sounded far away, drowned by the buzzing in my ears and ugly sounds my body made. A hand landed on my back, roaming it with soft strokes. "It's okay. Just let it all out."

A painful moan fell from my lips as I sat back on my knees. "I'm not going to make it through Sasha's wedding," I whimpered, my stomach feeling queasy.

Although I wasn't certain whether it was the pregnancy or the thought of Sasha and Branka's reception at The Den of Sin. So many fucking memories there.

It was where Adrian finally caved in. I thought back to that night. It seemed like a different lifetime. A different me.

I caught my reflection in the mirror. A sexy maid costume barely covered the round curves of my ass. Dark black material was stark against the white lace, my long blonde locks making me look like a porn star. Or maybe it was the built-in push-up bra that gave me excessive cleavage. My cheeks were flushed, probably the result of the shots we had before even leaving the house.

Shifting my weight back and forth between my feet, I let my gaze travel over the room. My oldest brother had a weird sense of humor. He learned the name Isabella and I assigned our dorm room and decided to name his bar in its honor. The Den of Sin.

"There is Adrian," Isabella whispered and I followed her gaze. My heart fluttered in my chest. The dark-masked man. Sophisticated. All dressed up. James Bond at its best. The suit hugged his muscular body perfectly and not even his ink could ruin his clean-cut look.

I wanted to go to him but it didn't feel right to leave Isabella behind. As if she read my thoughts, she said, "Go ahead. I'll be around. Text me when you are done, and we can meet by the bar."

I grinned and rushed to the man of my dreams. I was so damn ready for the repeat of our last rendezvous. Sex, lust, and alcohol saturated the air. I walked through the large room, coming to stand in front of Adrian.

"Mr. Bond," I greeted him. "What are you drinking?"

"Vesper martini."

My lips curved. I wasn't into James Bond movies but I knew what the fictional man drank. The Vesper. Shaken, not stirred.

"In that case, Mr. Bond, you gonna buy this girl a drink?"

He signaled the waiter and the drink appeared in front of me in no time. The waiter slid it across the bar and I caught it without spilling a drop.

"Impressive," Adrian commended.

I shrugged. "I'm an impressive kind of girl."

Those green eyes studied me and I wished he'd discard the mask. It was easier to read him without it. Somewhere along the way, Adrian became hard to read. Distant.

It was a girl's worst nightmare. Sleep with a man and suddenly they became cold and distant. Each time I tried to get closer, he put walls up or gave me vague answers. Frustration bubbled up my throat and I quickly swallowed it down, by downing my fancy martini.

I waited for him to say something. Anything.

Then I couldn't keep it in anymore. I needed to know. I had been hung up on this man for years—fucking years. I was Tatiana Nikolaev, damn it. Boys and men chased me all through high school and college. And here I was saving myself for this man who I couldn't even tell if he wanted me.

"Adrian, if you're regretting the gazebo, please be honest and say so," I blurted out. "It's not right to keep me hanging. I'm an adult," I rattled. "I can handle rejection. Just say your piece and we'll both move on."

Adrian stood up, his chest brushing against mine. His eyes were on me, simmering with an anger that confused me. My cheeks grew warm, but his fury cooled my heated skin.

One second we stared at each other, the tension stretching and wrapping around my lungs. I didn't understand it. It felt like there was a key piece I was missing, but I just couldn't grasp it. That night in the gazebo was everything and so much more.

3

His gaze descended down my body. My throat squeezed and my breathing labored.

"Let's go," he said.

I blinked. He snatched my hand and, confused, I followed him. My skin lit like a beacon, aware somewhere deep in my mind that if this was a normal scenario, I'd punch the guy in the face and tell him to explain himself.

And here I was, following like a blind puppy.

We were outside the club now, Adrian's black Maserati parked in the alley. My heels clicked against the pavement. Click. Click. Click. *Until we came to a stop in front of his car.*

He removed his mask, revealing his beautiful face.

"So you've been thinking about the gazebo?" he asked, his voice almost bitter.

I faltered. Something about the way he watched me nagged at me. My heart beat fast and hard. Alarm bells rang inside my brain. Except the warnings made no sense. This was Adrian Morozov, my big brother's best friend. The boy who'd been around me my entire life pretty much.

He opened the passenger door to his Maserati, signaling for me to enter. My brothers always warned me to listen to my sixth sense. Always. This time, my sixth sense went way off the rails.

He grasped me by my nape, then swallowed my next breath in his mouth, along with all my common sense. I hadn't had sex since that night. My body tingled, fire spreading through me, all-consuming. My blood sizzled and my stomach flipped.

"Get in, Tatiana," he drawled against my lips.

His hands felt different than I remembered. His kiss felt different. "Did you change your cologne?" I breathed against his lips. He nodded. "Go back to that citrus and sandalwood," I murmured, wrapping my hands around his neck.

The heat of his body seared against mine. I rubbed against him. Abstinence was a bitch now that I knew what I had been missing. I wouldn't last long. In the back of my mind, I kept comparing it all to the gazebo. But in the haze, my lustful brain didn't process it.

4

His fingers glided up my legs, his touch rough. I rose to my toes and kissed him. A rumble resounded in his chest and I pulled away.

"What?" I questioned, my tone breathless. He stilled, the look in his eyes torturous and conflicted. "What is it, Adrian?" I repeated, my cheeks hot.

He pulled my hair to one side and pressed his face into my neck. A shudder erupted beneath my skin, cold from the volatile energy emanating from him. Maybe he'd abstained from sex since that night too and he was barely holding on. His lips pressed against my skin, skimming over my flesh.

"That dress." His tone was rough. His gaze caught fire as it traveled over my body. Heat bloomed between my thighs. "It makes you look so fucking hot."

Goosebumps ran down my arms. A tremor rolled through my body.

"Car. Now," he rasped.

I listened to his command without a single objection. I listened to it, ignoring the feeling that kept nagging at me in the back of my mind.

As soon as he pulled the door closed, he shifted me over him and I straddled his hips. Our mouths met. His fingers dug into my hips, pulling me closer to sit on his erection. It was new. Different. Unfamiliar.

I rocked myself against him. "Why did you make us wait so many years?"

My eyes, half-lidded and hazy, met his.

"You're my friend's little sister," he stated. "I should have never touched you at the gazebo."

I should be disappointed that he let my brother keep us apart. I wouldn't have let anyone keep me from the one I love. But that was the thing with infatuation. It made you stupid and crazy.

I pulled his bottom lip between my teeth and kissed him. He even tasted different from what I remembered. I met his eyes, pushing his suit off his shoulders. Then I undid the buttons on his shirt, eager to touch him. The last time, I didn't get to touch him. Last time, he gave me pleasure. This time, I'd give him pleasure.

Pressing my fingers into his skin, I scraped my nails down his chest. Ink marred his flesh, revealing the casual Adrian I'd come to know over the years. I shifted on his erection, rocking my hips and grinding, desperate for release.

This was so much better than all the nights over the years I had to get myself off. I was starved for a man's touch. Delirious with the need for it.

In one swift move, a shredding sound filled the air. A shaky breath escaped me as I met his gaze.

"The gazebo was nothing compared to this, Tatiana," he growled.

The claim made no sense. I wanted to tell him that night in the gazebo was my fuel that kept me going. But before I could reply, he pulled the straps of my costume down and captured a nipple in his mouth. A white light shot behind my eyes. His hand squeezed my breast, while he sucked the other.

My eyes rolled back into my head, my pulse throbbed and I knew I'd orgasm soon. A seductive echo of a zipper. Crinkle of a condom. And he slammed inside me with a hiss.

I gasped, my eyes burning with tears. It felt different. This time it hurt. More than last time. Maybe after so many years of no sex, my virginity was back. Stupid thought. Stupid everything.

My thighs quivered. Our eyes connected.

"No more endearments?" I rasped breathlessly. I needed to adjust, remain still so the burning would ease.

"We're both too old for those. But maybe you'll be my rose."

His grip tightened on my hips and then he started thrusting.

I panted. He groaned. I gasped. He growled.

As if he was proving something. He gripped my hips, bouncing me on his erection. My eyes burned. It wasn't comfortable. I thought he might have confused my whimpers with moans. I needed him to go slower, he went faster. Confusion at the vast difference between my first sexual encounter with him and this one flabbergasted me.

He finished. I didn't.

Disappointment.

Why was there disappointment that night? I finally got the man that

I had been swooning over and dreaming about for years, only to be left with disappointment.

It had felt so different from that night in the gazebo. But I'd finally gotten my wish that night. Adrian finally chose me. Married me a few weeks later. I was happy. Was he happy? Why was I questioning everything now?

I let out a heavy sigh. I couldn't deal with the memories. I couldn't deal with the triggers of this club. But my brother wanted me there. For him and Branka. He deserved his happiness.

"You have to tell Vasili you're pregnant," Isabella whispered softly. "That the baby's father is—" She trailed off. God, if she picked up on who the baby's father was, then Vasili was sure to figure it out once he learned I was pregnant. "He's important. You know it as well as I do, Tatiana. I don't know if we'll stand a chance against him."

That was an understatement. Konstantin had the resources and backing to tear down several empires, never mind our families. Would he kill me like that woman in the video? Maybe he'd take my baby and then kill me. And then there were Illias's words haunting me. *You forgot me, Tatiana.*

He sounded so mad when he uttered those words. I gasped at the images forming in my head, picturing him killing me right after taking my baby. Bile rose in my throat, threatening to empty my stomach again. Would he find another woman to raise my child? Jesus, hormones made me paranoid instead of mellow. I didn't know which was worse.

"I—I…" My voice cracked.

Illias wouldn't be so cruel. Would he?

"Tatiana?"

I swallowed hard, words failing me. The back of my eyes burned, but I blinked hard. Once. Twice. Three times.

No time for crying, Vasili's voice whispered. It was never time to cry.

I inhaled, then exhaled. Crying was useless anyhow. It didn't make anything right. The tears I spent on Adrian didn't bring him back and they certainly didn't save me. Adrian might have pulled me out of the car, like my brothers stated, but he left behind the whirlwind of secrets and danger. And no warning.

I couldn't help but think back to the accident. If Adrian saved me, then why didn't he save himself.

Images from the accident danced in front of my eyes. Adrian's dead eyes. He pulled me out of the car, so how did he die?

Distorted voices. I heard whispers that night that kept me going.

I'll be back, moya luna. I'll be back when you're ready for me.

That voice. Deep. Dark. It reminded me of Illias's voice, but it couldn't be right. I didn't trust my mind. My memory was unreliable when it came to that night. I was still missing key parts of that night.

Betrayal. Bullets. Blackness.

Sometimes a villain turns into a hero. That would never be the case with him. Illias Konstantin was a different breed of monster. Yet, it felt like I had sold my soul to the devil and he delivered what I had desired the most.

A baby.

Something Adrian refused to entertain. Over and over again.

Adrenaline hit me like a tsunami, washing through me until emotion withered away, leaving nothing but emptiness in its wake.

I started trembling again. My fingers, shaking like a leaf against the wind, came to my forehead. There was nothing there. Not even a scar. There should be something left from that night.

Yet, it was a blank canvas. Emptiness. Darkness.

Breathe through the nose. Exhale through my mouth. Repeat.

A sardonic feeling pulled in my chest. At least I had about seven months to get it all sorted out—baby daddy, his demands, my brother's demands. I could say fuck them all and then hide somewhere where they'd never find me. I had resources and funds.

"Tatiana, please talk to me." Isabella's soft voice pulled me back. For a second, I forgot she was here. Her furrowed brows and gaze full of worry refused to let go.

"There's nothing to say." My voice portrayed nothing of the

turmoil inside me. My brothers and Illias would learn if they'd fuck with me, their temper would pale compared to mine.

"We love you," she rasped in a low voice.

"I love you too." But I love my baby more, I thought as I pressed my hand softly to my lower belly.

I'd raise hell on earth to keep my little one protected.

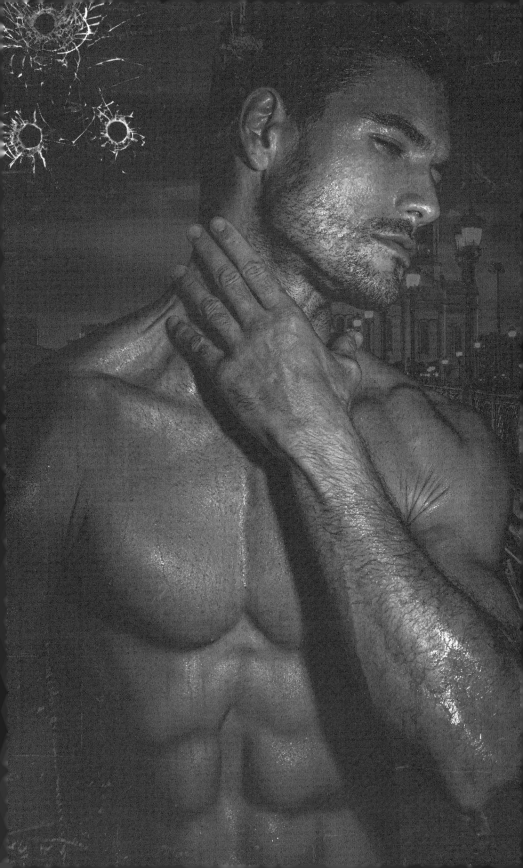

TWO
KONSTANTIN

T atiana Nikolaev was bound to me for life, whether she liked it or not.

Now, I just needed to make her my wife. We were always meant to end up here. The two of us, married with children running around us. Maybe I should have gone about it a different way but fuck it.

I was done waiting. My plan was unfolding. The goal was always to knock her up and see her swell with my child. So she'd be mine.

I had been planning this since Adrian's death. Watching her. Biding my time. Truthfully, the Yakuza did me a favor because it only sped up my plans. Maxim attempting to kill Nikolaev's brother and getting himself killed wasn't part of the plan. But truthfully, I'd use that to my advantage too.

The Nikolaevs knew they fucked up when they killed Maxim. If I had to, I'd kill her brothers to get Tatiana. Although, the thought of seeing pain in her eyes caused a twisting in my gut. Just like it did seeing it the night Adrian died.

That shattering pain that tore at her crystal blue gaze and her voice as she tried to save her late husband.

I wanted to shield her from all the pain, even the pain that her late husband caused. From the Omertà. Everyone. And the only way I knew how to do that was to bring her under my protection. As my wife and mother of my children.

She'd become a target, but as long as I had her in my sights at all times, I'd be able to keep her safe. My love for her knew no bounds. And it was love, not just need or obsession. I didn't know that I was capable of that and knowing I loved her should scare the fucking hell out of me. But it didn't. It just made me want her more. Whether she knew it or not, she was fucking mine. Her moonlike hair was the only light in my darkness.

Nobody had ever gotten a second chance in my book. Except for her and her family. But only because I had given my faith to *her*. Not even my twin brother got that much from me.

A fact that should have been alarming. I had always believed another human being, family or not, couldn't be trusted. It was a waste of time, energy, and faith. Only to be disappointed at the end. Just look at my mother.

Yet I couldn't fathom a day on this earth if she wouldn't walk in it. She was my anomaly. My desire. My destiny.

I couldn't fully grasp the extent of my obsession, but it has been there from the moment I first saw her. It stared at me with wide eyes of the bluest skies, inviting my raging, insatiable beast to own her.

A dark obsession clawed at my chest, insisting I take the woman now.

But I'd let her have today. To celebrate the wedding of her beloved brother.

Then she'd be mine. Fucking *mine*. Forever.

Another building acquired.

I sat in my new office, the scenic French Quarter view spreading in front of me. Waiting. Expecting. Anticipating.

My phone buzzed with an incoming message. Amon's name

flashed on the screen. I slid it open to read it. **Yakuza will be moving on Tatiana. At her brother's wedding.**

This would be the fourth attack in the span of a year. It wasn't a random attack, but everyone else followed my lead and kept away from her. The Yakuza, on the other hand, just kept going after her. Even in the motherland, on my turf, which was stupid. It showed the Yakuza's desperation to get their hands on that chip.

If Tatiana wouldn't have killed that bastard, I would have, and my methods would have been more tortuous than a bullet.

The body that was left in the Moscow hotel room was no effort to dispose of. After all, I owned most of the city, including the police force. Though I had to say I was impressed. The photo of the corpse showed the bullet lodged into the man's chest with precision. Straight through the heart.

I tightened security around Tatiana because my sources, namely Yan and Yuri who were now on my payroll, related that Tatiana instructed them to keep all the attacks on her a secret from her family. If her brothers didn't know, it left her vulnerable. That was unacceptable in my book.

Commotion in front of my office came right on time. The three Nikolaev men stormed through the door, muscling their way through my men. It wasn't much of a struggle since I was expecting them and instructed my men not to put up too much of a fight. I knew Vasili wouldn't be happy with my expansion in his city.

So fucking predictable.

Nikita just waltzed in behind them, not even bothering to hinder their way.

"I'd say come in, but you're already in my office."

Not that I expected anything different. Not from the Nikolaev brothers. Tatiana was their protected sibling. Now more than ever. They'd connect my property acquisition to their resistance to give me their sister.

"You motherfucker," Sasha hissed. "I'm going to shred your fucking body to pieces. What the fuck are you doing in New Orleans? What's the matter? You can't have Tatiana, so now you're poaching our territory. No matter what, you'll never have her. I'd rather see your pretty face in the coffin next to your fucking brother."

I let out a sardonic breath. "I'm glad you brought my brother up."

I'd had enough of the Nikolaev men. The only reason I let them live was for their sister's sake. It was that simple. I leaned back in the chair, studying the three brothers. Vasili's jaw was about to crack if he didn't ease up. Alexei was his usual blank mask. And Sasha was his normal impulsive, unhinged self.

"It's a woman for a woman in our world and you know it," I said, bringing my drink to my lips.

We held our gazes and Vasili rubbed his jaw, a pensive look in his eyes.

"Fuck a woman for a woman," Sasha snapped, his usual temper flaring. He and Tatiana were similar in that regard. "Your crazy brother just about killed my wife."

My brow shot up. "I thought you were getting married today at the courthouse. And then a party at The Den of Sin, nonetheless." I snickered at the odd name. According to the rumors, Vasili's wife and Tatiana named their dorm room The Den of Sin. It remained to be seen just how much sinning they did in that place.

Sasha flipped me the middle finger, the mature motherfucker. I didn't bother returning the favor. If I did, it would be in the form of his pretty face smashed against my wall. And I wasn't ready to stain my walls with blood quite yet.

"Back to the topic at hand," I continued in a bored tone.

"Tatiana isn't for sale," Vasili growled. "I told you I'd run it by her and her answer was clear. She won't marry you."

"Her wants don't matter here." Fucking lie. I wanted to fulfill all her wants, desires, and wishes. But her brothers didn't need to know that.

"We don't want trouble with you, Konstantin. But if needed, we'll go to war." Lovely, again back to the war topic. A war that they cannot possibly win. "Your brother shot Branka, almost killed her."

"And her father killed Maxim's woman," I replied coldly. "You killed my brother. Somehow the scale is tilted to the Russos' and your favor. My brother and his woman are dead."

"I killed the old Russo," Sasha admitted, hoping that would somehow exonerate them for my brother's death. "Take that for your payment. Eye for an eye. And be gone."

His oldest brother's expression turned murderous as he shot a warning glare at Sasha.

"Tell us why you want her," Sasha demanded to know.

It would seem their little sister kept secrets from her brothers. Pregnancy being one of them.

"She has something that belongs to me," I responded calmly. The chip was only a small piece. The baby in her womb was the bigger piece and the only one that mattered to me now. I sat up, straightening my sleeves and signaling the meeting was over. "I expect your final answer by the end of today. My men will see you out."

My men started to escort the brothers out when Vasili stopped and turned around. "I'll be right behind you," he told them. "I want to talk to Konstantin alone."

Sasha grumbled something but headed out. Nikita's eyes flitted my way for permission and I nodded.

With everyone gone, Vasili narrowed his eyes on me. "What does she have that is yours?" he questioned.

The chip. My baby growing in her belly. My fucking heart. *Take your fucking pick.*

I sat down behind my desk and leaned back, studying the brother who raised his siblings while his father roamed this earth looking for his next lover. I couldn't help but notice similarities and differences between us. After my mother's death, my father went off the deep end and I had to navigate Maxim through the years. Then when Isla was born, I had to raise her.

I guess the only difference was my father killed my mother. His father didn't.

"Vasili, you and I both know the road has come to an end," I answered him vaguely. His sister obviously withheld information from her big brothers, but Vasili was a smart man. He had to have guessed

15

she was pregnant. He had a few kids of his own. "I don't know whether you're blind or just choosing to be." The fucker growled. Like that would help his sister.

"I promised her when she was a little girl that she'd choose her own husband," he said tiredly. "And that she'd never be part of an arranged marriage. I cannot break my promises to my little sister, Konstantin."

"It's not exactly an arranged marriage, is it now?" I noted sarcastically.

"Let me talk to her again," he tried. "If she's pregnant with your child—"

"There are no ifs about it," I growled. If he even insinuated she slept with someone else, I'd cut his throat and dig his heart out of his chest.

He shook his head. "I still don't understand how that happened." I let out an incredulous breath. He didn't actually expect me to explain to him that I fucked her and got her pregnant with my semen. Did he? He pushed his hand through his hair. "Honestly, I don't like that she's keeping secrets from me, and I don't like that she got involved with you."

"But you were okay with her getting involved with Adrian," I spat out. "The guy that put her on the radar of every fucking powerful crime family on the planet."

"Frankly, I didn't want her getting involved with him either," he admitted begrudgingly. "I don't think I'm good with my little sister being involved with any man."

"She's carrying my child." There was nothing else to be discussed. Of course, I wouldn't admit to him it was my plan all along to put a baby in her belly. Hence, fucking her without a condom.

I rocked back and forth in my chair, studying him. His jaw flexed, signaling he was pissed.

"I won't force her to marry you," he finally concluded and turned around, heading for the door. "And I won't let you force her either."

He disappeared through the door and my thoughts instantly shifted to the woman I was about to marry. Whether they agreed to my terms or not, Tatiana Nikolaev would be plucked from her natural habitat and forced into my world and my life. Permanently.

It was only a matter of time before she remembered the whole incident. Before someone got their hands on her or she found that chip.

She might wither under my rule, but she no longer had the luxury of her freedom.

Sooner or later, it would get her killed. And if the feds got their hands on that chip, she'd pull the entire underworld into it. And the woman didn't even know it.

I had given her time to heal after the accident. I pledged for her. I understood the risks. I understood the danger. Did I care? No, I didn't. The Omertà had my oath, but she had my heart. It was about her life and our child's.

I had let her go once, this time nothing would save her from me. We were two souls that stupidly passed each other, multiple times, only to end up here. Or rather, where we'd soon be.

In my kingdom. In my country. In my home. In my bed.

Exactly where she should have been all along.

She had been mine for almost a decade, but fate pulled us apart. Now, it was me who controlled our destiny.

It was time to make Tatiana Nikolaev remember who she belonged to.

THREE
TATIANA

A nd my last brother wed.

I watched Sasha and Branka, standing by my car. Hugs and kisses were plenty. Whispers of promises and love. Then those two would ride off into the sunset together.

Or the tattoo parlor.

It wasn't my idea of romance but they were happy. It was all that mattered to me. Sasha deserved his happiness and so did Branka. The two of them looked good together. There was no doubt that Branka loved my brother—not after she took a bullet for him.

I envied their love. I envied their connection. But the bitterness was nowhere to be found. Yes, I wanted what they had, but I also had a bundle of joy that I'd created all on my own that eased any sense of sorrow.

Okay, technically it wasn't created on my own but those were minor details. I already started to picture our life together. Maybe we'd have to hide, but I'd keep my baby happy and protected.

The October sun shone bright, warming my skin. New Orleans had always been home. Until it wasn't. Now wherever my baby was would be my home. My brothers were always my rock in the storm. Until they weren't. Maybe it was a natural way of life. Growing up and all that.

It came late for me because they'd always sheltered me. Though there was nothing and nobody on this planet to shelter me from Illias Konstantin. I wasn't exactly sure that I wanted to be sheltered from him. I'd have to handle him on my own.

Ironic really! A whole year after Adrian's death, I learn of this new life growing inside me. There was uncertainty but joy outweighed it all.

I sensed Vasili's presence behind me. Protective. Warm. Sheltering.

Except, he couldn't help me with my current predicament. Not with Illias Konstantin. I'd never forgive myself if my family got hurt because of me. So this time, I'd protect them, like they'd always protected me.

"Getting on Konstantin's bad side is a bad move, Tatiana," Vasili warned. "The whole crime world, in fact anyone who ever crosses paths with him, doesn't want to get on his bad side. And we are already on tenuous ground with him."

I shrugged, not acknowledging him with an answer. Okay, maybe I feigned my nonchalance a bit. Fake it till you make it and all that. While I had this baby in my belly, I was untouchable. And so was my family.

For now.

"Are you listening to me, sestra?" Vasili grumbled.

"Yes."

"Konstantin has the ability to inflict irrevocable damage on all of us," he warned. It wasn't anything new. "He might seem silent but his wrath is lethal. He learns your weakness and exploits it. Trust me, Tatiana, right now we have plenty of those. In our children. They are a blessing but they also make us vulnerable. More than ever we need allies."

My gaze strayed to the streets, watching the city buzz with life. For the first time in forever, I could breathe. Hope and love bloomed in my chest and in my womb. I'd have to tread lightly and ensure my baby was safe.

My baby and our family.

I squared my shoulders, my decision was made.

"Nothing will happen to you," I told my big brother. For the first time ever, it was me who'd protect my family. "Nor our family. Especially not my nephews and niece."

I turned around and faced my brother's dubious face. He was used to playing the protector, but now it would be me protecting them.

"Do you trust me, Vasili?" I rasped.

Our gazes locked, and for the first time, I didn't feel like his little sister. I was his equal, playing chess with one of the most ruthless men in the world.

"I trust you with my life and my children's," he declared.

Pride and love for my family swelled in my chest. No matter what came down the road, I'd always love them. I'd always be there for them as I knew they'd be there for me.

"Then trust me to protect you." I wrapped my arms around him. "To protect us."

Vasili sighed. "The only way to avoid war with the Pakhan is to agree to his terms. For you to marry him."

I watched my big brother who had been so much more than just my eldest brother my entire life. Sasha had been my protector and my brother, but Vasili was everything. And he took the responsibility seriously. I had never lacked thanks to his protection and love.

"You want me to be the pawn," I murmured.

"Pawn today. Queen tomorrow."

I nodded. "Except I have something he wants," I declared. "So how about we skip the whole pawn shit, and I just go straight to queen status."

Vasili's lips curved into a smile and pride entered his expression. "There is my sister." I wrapped my hands around him.

I was a queen. The most powerful piece on the chessboard. It was time I started acting like one.

FOUR
TATIANA

My bravery must have been left on the sidewalk in front of the courthouse where Sasha and Branka got married because as I neared The Den of Sin, so many emotions stirred inside me. Dread among others.

It was the first time I'd stepped foot anywhere near this place since Adrian's death. My fingers reached for my necklace, twisting the thorned-rose pendant nervously. I never took it off anymore. I didn't know whether it was to remind me of my husband's love or betrayal.

It had been a year since that fucking accident. Since the explosion that wiped out everything. Traces of his body. Traces of his car. Traces of my memories.

I was left with an emptiness. A fractured mind. Suffocating feelings that I couldn't understand.

My hand fluttered to my stomach.

It was ridiculous to feel this dread as I neared The Den of Sin, the club Vasili named after Bella's and my dorm room. Our wild days when things seemed simpler. Bella hooked up with Vasili the same night that Adrian finally caved in.

It was the night when our story finally began. Officially.

That last year of college, he called a mistake. I didn't. I called it the best night of my life.

Yan opened the door of the car, waiting for me to exit. I sat unmoving for two heartbeats too long. I inhaled a deep breath and slowly let it out. I forced myself out of the vehicle and stepped onto the busy street in the heart of New Orleans. The buzz of the city hummed. A drop of sweat ran down my back. The sun burned hot and heavy. For once, the laugher of the locals and tourists didn't make me want to claw at my brain.

I was about to take a step when I felt eyes on me, watching me. I paused and peered around me. There were tourists, families, my brothers' guards. Everybody was talking in rushed, happy tones. Nothing out of the ordinary.

I was about to chalk up the sensation to my state of mind. But my skin prickled again, sending a visible shudder down my spine.

My eyes traveled across the street. The oldest surviving building of New Orleans stood there. A local pub. Men smoked and talked. Each one of them had a drink in their hands.

Except for one.

A familiar dark shadow stood silently, taller than all the other men. He didn't exactly blend in, nor was he trying to. He wore a black shirt and pants, matching his hair, giving those businessman vibes. God, his face was beautiful. It belonged on the billboards. Sharp angular features. High cheekbones. Thick-stubbled jaw.

And those eyes that could send you spiraling into their darkness.

He watched me, taunting with promises of what was to come. Like he was decrypting me, piece by piece, before he'd tear me apart.

A shudder rolled down my spine. My ribs dug into the flesh of my lungs, or possibly heart, making it hard to draw air into my lungs. He wouldn't try something here. Would he?

My phone buzzed in my purse. A text from Illias.

You're ready for me, moya luna.

FIVE
KONSTANTIN

Everything was in place.

Tatiana would be mine after this event.

My eyes conveyed there'd be no more delays. Then to ensure there were no misunderstandings, I sent her a message. The words I'd given her when I left her in the hospital. I promised I'd be back when she was ready for me.

She was ready for me!

Her body was rigid, her graceful back in full view as she entered The Den of Sin. The dress fit her perfectly, her frame was no longer too thin. It enhanced her elegance. Her beauty. And the way she moved befit a queen.

Yes, she was a pawn in Adrian's revenge, but she came out of it a queen.

Once she disappeared inside, I caught Amon from the corner of my eye. His eyes weren't on me, but on the building next to the wedding reception. He started walking, his eyes never wavering on the building while I kept mine on The Den of Sin.

Amon just about reached me. He stopped in front of me, kneeled, then pretended to tie his shoelaces. He never glanced my way as he muttered under his breath, "They're going after her when she comes out."

Over my dead body.

"Make sure it doesn't happen before," I hissed.

Tatiana deserved this moment with her brother. Sasha might be an arrogant, psycho prick but the two were close. This was her moment with her family. Were my feelings hurt that I didn't get an invite?

Fuck no.

Would I crash the event so I could have *moya luna* in my sights? Fuck yes.

Amon rose to his full height, leaving a single ticket on the ground. He left without another word as I typed a message to my men to ensure all the shit was in place. Then I picked up the ticket off the ground and headed to the event.

I entered the venue, dropping a million-dollar check as a gift to the bride and groom and signed it as Illias and Tatiana Konstantin. It'd lead the Nikolaev brothers straight to my door but fuck it.

Once my ring was on her finger, there was nothing they could do.

Vasili spotted me first. Keeping his smile on his face, he marched toward me. He could fool most of the people that he was being a happy host right now but the ice in his pale blue eyes was a warning to anyone with a brain.

"Konstantin, I don't—"

His wife must have picked up on Vasili's vibes because she rushed to us with her baby girl in her arms before Vasili could even finish his statement.

"Hey, babe, can you help me with Marietta?" Before her husband could even respond, she pretty much shoved the little girl into his arms. Vasili's eyes lowered and instantly the ice melted. *Interesting.*

His wife smiled smugly, then flicked me a cautious look. "You're welcome to stay, but let's all keep it civilized. Including you, Vasili. Okay?"

I didn't peg Isabella Nikolaev for the manipulative type but clearly she knew how to handle her husband.

"As you wish, Mrs. Nikolaev," I agreed. I didn't care about

anything but keeping my eye on Tatiana and keeping her safe. Yes, she'd be safe inside The Den of Sin, but the fact of the matter was if Amon was able to secure an entrance ticket, so could the enemy.

"I'm too old for this shit," Vasili muttered. "Right, Marietta? You won't be giving Papa a hard time like your mama and aunt."

Isabella snorted, but she smiled softly at her husband. "You know our kids will be even worse than we were, right?"

He sighed, pressing a kiss on little Marietta, who looked about a year old. The kid looked like a rag doll in Vasili's arms but she grinned wide, clearly content to be in her father's arms. I wondered if my child would look at me *that* way.

My father was my hero until he wasn't. After the day he executed my mother, he was the Pakhan and only that. It was hard to form and maintain a bond with a man who was never there for you once he took your mother away. He whored around, made every woman—whore or not—pay for the sins of the woman who betrayed him.

So while he wallowed, I observed and studied. I'd learned what technology worked and what didn't. I'd learned the enemies' weaknesses and exploited them. I expanded our territory and portfolio until it became one of the largest ones.

I sought out Tatiana, thankful I towered over most guests and found her standing with her brother and his bride in the far corner of the room. She smiled while the newest Mrs. Nikolaev spoke animatedly, then pointed to Sasha's chest. She mimicked something that looked like stabbing her husband.

Would our baby look like her mama? I hoped so. I couldn't decide whether I'd dreamt of a boy or a girl first. Maybe a boy so he'd keep everyone away from his little sister. Although it was tempting to see Tatiana with our little girl. She'd dress her in the latest fashion and parade her all over the world.

"For fuck's sake, Konstantin." Vasili's growl pulled me away from gawking at my favorite woman. "I swear if you force her to marry you or—"

"Vasili, babe, can you go check on the kitchen staff?" Vasili's eyebrows shot up to his hairline. I'd imagine he never had to check on kitchen staff before. "Please, babe. Then let's check that back room to ensure it is intact."

She winked and Vasili already turned, heading to wherever. Then as if he remembered something, he narrowed his eyes on me. "I mean it, Konstantin." His gaze darted to Tatiana, then back to me. He gave me a hard look. "She's off-limits."

I leaned back on my heel. "I see that's worked out with you and your brothers," I retorted dryly. "If I remember right, you bribed your wife's boyfriend, then chased him out of the city. Your brother kidnapped his bride."

"Maybe I'll just marry her off today," he baited.

"You can try." My voice was dark and I clenched my teeth. "And you'll see how fast your empire crumbles."

Vasili opened his mouth but his wife stopped him before he could say another word. "Vasili, not today." Her voice was soft as she nudged her husband forward.

She stayed behind though and I cocked my eyebrow, waiting for her to say what she clearly wanted to.

Once her husband was out of earshot, she turned to me. She tilted her head as she studied me.

I held her gaze. It was peculiar that she and Tatiana were best friends, considering how different the two women were. But then, maybe that was what made it work for them.

"You're inviting trouble," Isabella said softly, tilting her head. "But then, you already know that."

My gaze flickered to the blonde hair. The group around her grew larger. She must have been entertaining with a story because the crowd grew louder and rowdier.

"She's always been the social butterfly," Isabella remarked. "Miss Popularity. She even won the title at Georgetown."

"Remarkable," I noted wryly. If only the men would clear away from her. I pondered whether it would be going too far killing any man in her vicinity with the exception of family. I didn't think so, but my thinking might be skewed when it came to the woman carrying my child.

"How is her pregnancy progressing?" I asked her. "Is the baby healthy?"

Isabella stiffened, then gave me a cautious look. But the truth lingered in those brown eyes.

"I have no idea what you're talking about," she remarked slowly. "And even if I did, doctor-patient privilege and all that."

A corner of my lips lifted and satisfaction ran hot through my blood. My chest grew full as I thought about becoming a father soon. Fuck, it couldn't come soon enough.

I smiled. "Thank you, Isabella."

"For what?"

"You just gave me all the answers I needed."

SIX
TATIANA

I stepped outside, my eyes flickering to where I'd seen Konstantin last. He was no longer there. Not that I expected him to stand there all that time.

Shaking my head at my idiocy, I took a step forward and noticed a black Land Rover driving by, and from the corner of my eyes, I spotted the window lowering. The barrel of a gun was aimed at me. My heart stopped. The world ceased to turn for a fraction of a moment.

Bang.

The nearby glass window to my left exploded, blasting shards of glass everywhere. I froze, so stunned that I didn't even feel the glass digging into my bare arm. The screams reached my ears first. Adrenaline flooded my veins as my brain finally started to function again.

They are shooting at me.

Then I saw him. The head of Yakuza. Jesus Christ! This chip must have some serious shit on it if he was coming for me personally. Another black car, an Expedition, stepped on the brakes behind it. I watched in horror as its window lowered, but much to my relief, the bullets were aimed at Yakuza.

My feet reacted and I started to run just as another bang sounded behind me. It had missed me by the width of a hair. Terror flooded me. It tasted like blood and copper. Did I get shot?

My heartbeat drummed in my ears, like the roar of a loud engine. Screams, shouts, and the screech of tires all sounded like a distant noise. But I was alive. I could feel the burn in my muscles as I continued to run. It was harder to run in my five-inch heels, but I'd be damned if I'd slow down.

I was finally pregnant, and there was no chance in hell I'd let anything happen to my baby.

My fingers gripped my dress, uncaring how much leg I was showing. My life was worth more than a glimpse of my bare legs. I had to stay alive.

Making a sharp right turn, I sprinted down a narrow side street where I knew Vasili kept his spare vehicle for emergencies.

Well, this was a bloody emergency. Over my shoulder, I caught a glimpse of two men running after me at full speed. They had the advantage over me, not wearing heels. My lungs screamed for air, the muscles in my legs trembled, threatening to give out, but I ignored it all.

Pushing myself harder, I sped up down the street and dashed into a side alley. At the end of it, a six-foot-tall chain-link fence separated me from Vasili's getaway car. Uncaring of my Chanel dress, nor shoes, I quickly kicked them off, picked them up—it'd be a blasphemy to ditch Christian Louboutin heels—and climbed up and over the fence. Adrenaline rushing through my veins was making me fast, strong, and agile.

Once over it, I had to choke down a sigh of relief, a sob suffocating me. *Run, Tatiana. Run. You can do it.*

Each step echoed those same words over and over again. Desperately sucking in air, I sprinted down the street and towards the inconspicuous car. A simple black Honda Pilot. Every normal family's kind of car.

My fingers frantically punched in the code on the door handle. It was Nikola's birthday. But my fingers shook so badly, I kept pressing the wrong digits. And just as I got the right numbers, a hand wrapped around my mouth.

"Let me go." My voice was muffled. I didn't even know if it came out clear enough to be understood. I struggled against the grip, but my strength slowly waned. Then I bit into his palm. Hard.

A grunt. Vibration against my chest. "No more playing games, moya luna."

I stilled. Konstantin? That sounded like Konstantin's voice. My body relaxed, I fell back into a hard, male chest, and his arms folded around me like a steel band. A chained rope. His scent slowly seeped into my lungs—citrus, sandalwood, and spice.

With the last feeble attempt to show him my defiance, I attempted to jab my elbow into his stomach and bucked against him.

His warm breath tickled my earlobe as he chuckled.

"Are you coming willingly or would you prefer I force you?" His lips met the edge of my ear. "Either works for me," he purred, nipping at the edge of my earlobe.

God, something had to be wrong with my body because it went up in flames. My nipples tightened and my thighs quivered knowing exactly how good his mouth was when it wanted to be. Something deprived in my brain screamed, "I'm coming willingly," but I opted for something more reserved.

"You dicktwat," I hissed, pissed off more at my reaction than anything else. The guy was threatening me and I was getting turned on. Bad move.

I attempted to push away against him again but failed. Two of his men stood behind him. One bulky and blond and the other dark, something about him off. I'd seen him before.

When I didn't make a move, he gave another soft chuckle. "Or I can throw you over my shoulder."

"Caveman," I muttered. "At least let me put my shoes on," I added begrudgingly.

As I did, a black G-Benz Mercedes pulled up, stopping in front of us. Illias ushered me inside, then slid right next to me and the car left the alley. I stared out the window, trying to see if the Yakuza were still out there. Or if my brothers learned of the attack outside The Den of

Sin. But there were only frantic tourists, broken glass, and damaged stores.

A relieved breath left me. There were no wounded or dead on the street. Maybe I should have run back into my brother's club when the shooting started. Except, I wasn't thinking. My first instinct was to run; so, I ran.

"Have you found the chip?" Illias's calmly spoken words pulled me out of my observation, and I turned my head to meet his gaze. He watched me with curiosity and interest.

"No, I haven't. You know my life doesn't revolve around that fucking chip," I snapped at him. "Besides, I didn't start this. I don't usually get involved in mafia affairs and now I feel like I'm neck deep in this shit. And I don't even know what shit it is. Not all of it anyhow!" It was the truth. Aside from my brothers, I had no part in the underworld. "Anyhow, you can drop me off at Vasili's compound. I'll be safe there."

I knew the answer before he uttered it. "I don't think so. You're coming with me."

I gasped at his response and my eyes widened. "Are you... Are you kidnapping me?"

He faced me with an exasperated look. "Think of it as our little vacation. We're overdue."

"Are you out of your fucking mind?" I hissed. "If you don't want the full wrath of my brothers, you'll take me to Vasili's place and I'll tell him you saved me. That might get you some brownie points."

He took my chin between his fingers and brought my face close to his. "Your brothers need brownie points if they want to live. Not the other way around. Don't forget. I'm the Pakhan here, not them."

He might have had a point, but the stubbornness in me refused to cave in. So I just let out a "pfft" sound and shrugged my shoulders, our faces still close to each other.

Then he smiled, something dark and menacing about it. "Consider this a payment for all your family's mistakes. To the Pakhan, and guess who that is?"

"A dicktwat?" I asked innocently, blinking my eyes. He didn't

34

react, but the touch of his stare made me want to squirm. I held my ground, although my tongue decided to taunt. "The Pakhan sounds like such a boring title, if you ask me. It equates to an anal-retentive asshole," I deadpanned. The corner of his lips tipped up. "I mean, what the fuck does it even mean?"

"It means I can crumble your brothers' empire within days," he drawled lazily, but the undertone of threat didn't escape me.

"What's stopping you?" I breathed, my heart beating hard against my chest. "Maybe the fact that my sister-in-law works for the FBI and she'll come after you."

I sounded like a brat and my threat fell on deaf ears. Konstantin didn't seem concerned at all. If anything, a challenge flashed in his gaze.

"No, Tatiana," he answered. "You're the only one stopping me."

Sure enough, the Pakhan was kidnapping me. We weren't even staying in the city.

I watched the city disappear behind us and a small private airport appeared out of nowhere. A plane already sat there, ready for takeoff. I studied the area, the small building where I'd probably find security guards.

The car came to a stop and the door opened. "After you," Illias drawled, signaling for me to exit the car.

"You realize I haven't packed," I remarked wryly. "I won't wear this for the duration of my imprisonment. I have a reputation to keep."

A half-smile pulled on his kissable lips. There was nothing more I wanted to do than to lean over and trace my tongue over them. Or feel his tongue on my skin. A shudder rolled down my spine.

I'd have to keep my wits about me. I'd have to keep reminding myself that Konstantin wasn't like my brothers who kept a certain code of honor. Never hurt women. Never hurt children. No human trafficking. Oh my gosh, did he participate in human trafficking?

"Whatever you want and need, we'll get on the way."

I narrowed my eyes on him, while the question lingered on my mind. "I'll be sure to give you a long list of the most expensive items I can think of."

Illias grinned. "I'm counting on it."

I shook my head and was about to exit the car, when I couldn't hold it in anymore.

"Do you have whorehouses?" I blurted out. Surprise washed over Illias's expression. "Do you participate in human trafficking? Force women into your whorehouses?"

"Yes and no." I narrowed my eyes on him, demanding elaboration. "No, I don't have a whorehouse. No, I don't force women into anything nor participate in human trafficking. I have an associate or two who own whorehouses and we're working on getting rid of them."

"Let's give him a medal," I muttered under my breath. Immature behavior on my part for sure. Although it was a small relief in that aspect. While I fought him, I knew that this baby would eventually change the dynamic between Illias and me. Assuming he didn't kill me and kidnap my baby.

He can try, but he'll fail.

"Now, let's get going before your brothers show up and I have to shoot them."

"You wouldn't dare," I hissed.

A flicker passed through his eyes that told me he totally would. His next words confirmed it.

"I would. It'd make my life easier, but I know how much you love your brothers, so I'm letting them live. For you."

We stared at each other in silence. Electricity played in the air, and each breath I took sent little tremors through me. The fact he'd say something like that should be alarming. Yet, I thought it so fucking sweet. That he'd keep my brothers alive for me.

Someone had to slap me so I'd get my senses back. Enemy. *He's the enemy.* It was what I needed to remember, but it was so hard when he said such sweet words.

"But if they think to take you away from me, I won't hesitate to put them six feet under," he added. He **had** to go and ruin the moment. The man was infuriating.

I exited the vehicle without sparing him another glance. He was right behind me, his hand on my lower back and nudging me forward toward the plane. I knew if I climbed into that plane, the chances of escaping him would be slimmer.

I had to try to escape. I refused to be a meek prisoner. Or a prisoner at all. Even during some ludicrous vacation.

So, remembering how he easily anticipated my move back in D.C. before I even had a chance to run, I kept my body relaxed and strutted towards the private plane like I was on the catwalk. I even swayed my hips a bit, hoping he was staring at my ass.

Another two steps and I saw my chance. The pilot approached Konstantin and I wasted no time. I ran, kicking off my heels on the go as I sent a silent farewell to my pretty shoes. A string of curses sounded behind me and footsteps followed close, but I didn't stop to look. I didn't bother glancing over my shoulder. It'd cost me precious time.

My lungs burned. I wasn't a jogger like Aurora. She was a nutcase to put her body and lungs through this madness. *God, if I make it, I'll run every day,* I lied to him and myself. *I'll go to church too. Every Sunday.*

The building was within my grasp. Just a bit more and I'd be there. I reached the building, my palms landing flat against the glass and I started banging on the glass.

"Let me in," I shouted breathlessly.

The men looked at me like I was crazy, then shared a glance among themselves. Slowly, one of the guards stood up and walked to the door. One step. Two steps. He was so fucking slow, I'd wager I ran the distance from the plane to here faster than he walked from five feet away.

Finally the door opened. "Let me in," I begged. "That crazy idiot is kidnapping me, and I have to call my brothers."

His eyes flickered behind me and he smiled. What-the-fuck… "Mr. Konstantin," he greeted and my heart sank. "You lost your cargo."

I slowly turned around, like living in a dream, or rather nightmare, and saw Illias casually walking over with a smile on his face and his hands in his pockets. It was like Mr. Rogers strolling through Central Park, for fuck's sake.

"Hello, Daniel," Konstantin greeted him pleasantly. "You're right, I did lose my cargo. She's a bit on the wild side and we had a little premarital dispute. But we'll resolve it before the day's over."

My mouth dropped. *This motherfucker—*

"Fuck you and your premarital shit," I snapped. "You are crazy if you think I'll marry you."

I gritted my teeth. Couldn't a single fucking man get down on his knees and ask the right way? Adrian's proposal, possibly even less romantic than this, flickered through my mind in snapshots, mocking me.

Illias dismissed the security guard with a nod and he promptly disappeared inside, the door closing behind me with a firm click putting an end to my feeble plan for escape. *Traitor.* He was certainly not a hero to a damsel in distress.

The two of us stared at each other in silence. Illias slipped his hands in his pockets and took a step toward me, the scent of citrus filling my lungs. That alone was enough to make my thighs quiver. I could blame my hormones, but it'd be a lie. This man had a way of reeling my body to him, then commanding it with a simple look.

"We'll marry, moya luna." His eyes trapped me, promising dark pleasures and my pulse fluttered. "Sooner than you think."

My jaw clenched. "No."

"Yes."

"Konstantin, take me back to the city," I warned, my voice low.

"I told you, it's Illias." His voice was rough as he took another step forward. The slightest muscle tightened in his jaw and I took a step back. "Or your beloved." A soft snort escaped me. "Your husband. Your love. Your soulmate. Take your fucking pick, but stop calling me Konstantin."

He took another step forward. I took one back. "Make me."

Dark eyes pierced me, then without warning he scooped me up into his arms. "You're lucky we're expecting, or I'd put you over my shoulder and carry you like a sack of potatoes."

My hands wrapped around his neck instinctively. My traitorous fingers pushed into the short hair at his nape.

"Who says I'm pregnant?" I challenged. My pulse beat wildly as his eyes darted to me briefly. The crazy, possessive look that lingered in those dark depths was enough to make a woman lose her panties. Or maybe her mind. "Maybe it's someone else's?"

His expression turned cold and he stopped in his tracks. "Let's get something straight," he growled. His words were rougher than usual. "Let another man touch you and I will destroy him. Once I'm done with him, there won't be a trace of his line left on earth."

My bravado slipped and he must have noticed it, because his next words were spoken softly. Vehemently. "I will ruin you, Tatiana. Break you. Then put you back together."

The air escaped me in a rush as he brought his lips an inch from mine. "Do you know why?" he rasped, that Russian accent thicker than I've ever heard before. I shook my head. "Because you're mine. You've been mine for a very long time."

With that, he resumed walking towards the plane.

"Besides, moya luna," he purred softly. "I know nobody has touched you because I've been in your shadow all along."

Now that was a way to shut me up.

SEVEN
KONSTANTIN

The second we stepped into the cabin, Tatiana's eyes landed on the priest with Boris and Nikita by his side.

It was hard to miss a Russian Orthodox priest in their elaborate priest clothing. Why he needed to parade in those clothes, I had no idea. No matter though. The only thing that mattered was that he was here and he'd perform the service.

"No, Illias." Tatiana's eyes stayed glued on the priest while shaking her head. "No, no, no." Then her gaze darted my way. The shocked expression in her eyes didn't sit right with me, but I still intended to proceed with it. "Absolutely not. I mean it, Illias. We're over."

Gripping her chin, I pulled her closer to me. "You and I, *moya luna*... We'll never be over."

I closed the distance and sealed my words with a fleeting kiss. Her body was tense but her mouth molded to mine. Her response to me was exhilarating. I'd never understood addiction until I crossed paths with this woman.

"You can start the ceremony," I told the priest. "As soon as you wed us, one of my men will take you back to your rectory."

"And the check?"

41

A sardonic breath left me. The priests loved their checks. "And the check."

His eyes flickered to the bride-to-be. "Do you wish to change into a wedding dress?"

"Fuck no," Tatiana hissed, glaring at him. "Are you deaf? I'm not marrying him."

The priest chuckled. He heard her but he didn't care. "With that little bun in the oven, you have to marry. You don't want your baby burning in hell, do you?"

Tatiana's eyes flashed like blue flames and she took a step towards the priest. "Married or not, my child will not burn in hell," she hissed, glowering. "But you might, if you don't take those words back."

"The Bible says—"

"That's enough," I cut the bullshit. "Tatiana, there is a dress in the back of the cabin." My eyes traveled over her. She looked beautiful in her dress, but I wanted her to have a special dress for this day.

She folded her arms in front of her chest, pushing her boobs up. "I'm not putting it on."

"Either you put it on yourself or I will put it on you," I said coldly. Her jaw clenched and daggers shot from her eyes. If expressions could kill, I'd be dead. "Think of your brothers as you change. If you refuse to marry me for our child, do it for your brothers."

I'd make her *mine*. Both the mother and child. This was where we should have been seven years ago. I could see her pulse beat quickly, her eyes stubborn on me. I took a step forward and wrapped my hand around her slender neck.

"Last time, Tatiana. Don't fucking push me. Go put that dress on or I'm going to do it for you. And I won't be so nice about it."

"That is not how you treat your baby mama," she retorted in a bored tone, but at least her feet started moving towards the back of the cabin where the bedroom was. At least she admitted she was pregnant. *Baby mama.*

It sounded fucking perfect.

"Two minutes, then I'm coming to *help* you," I drawled after her.

She flipped me a middle finger over her shoulder, then shut the door of the bedroom.

"The bride seems willing," the priest remarked.

I gave him a cold look, knowing exactly what he was hinting at. More money. Greedy motherfuckers.

"How much?" I asked in a chilled tone.

"Two hundred thousand." *Motherfucker.* That made his check four hundred thousand just to read a few paragraphs from some scripture and proclaim us as husband and wife. The door from the back of the cabin opened and I swore she stole my fucking breath.

My gaze coasted over her long, blonde hair, smooth pale skin, and ruby-red lips. There was even a hint of a smile there. Her hands smoothed down over the soft silk threads of her dress.

"It's the Oscar de la Renta," she murmured softly, her eyes lowering to the dress as if she wanted to ensure it was real. The dress fit her perfectly. It was elegant but simple. Yet, unforgettable.

The strapless dress was made of white, Italian silk faille and delicate silk poppy buds that cascaded across the bodice and skirt. Individual petals and stamens lifted up and off the dress here and there to add dimension, while the strapless top resembled a full scalloped flower.

"The material is so soft and elegant." Her voice was almost reverent and my lips curved. Tatiana Nikolaev had expensive taste. One just had to look at her.

"I thought you'd like it." She rolled her eyes, but her smile was still there as she kept touching the fabric. "Now, let's get married. I'm eager to get to the wedding night."

I watched red creep up her neck and onto her cheeks. Fuck, it was such a turn-on to see her blush. It'd never get old. But the look she gave me told me I wouldn't like her next words.

"I don't want to get married." The stubborn tilt of her chin was cute.

"Yes, you do."

"No, I don't," she argued back. "I refuse to be a pawn in your schemes against my brothers."

I let out a sardonic breath, hating that she wasn't excited about marrying me as I was about marrying her. I had been dreaming about it for over seven fucking years. I had a priest. She had a wedding dress. We'd get married if I had to speak the words for her.

"Firstly, you and pawn don't belong in the same sentence."

"I agree," she muttered under her breath.

The woman certainly knew her worth. "Secondly, you can marry me willingly. Right here. Right now. Or I could phone one of my men and tell them to pull the trigger they currently have aimed at one of your family members."

"You motherfuck—"

"Watch how you finish that," I drawled. "Now, which path do you want to take?"

Lightning flashed in her blue eyes. "Let's get one thing straight, Illias." Determination crossed her expression, her attention on me. "You want me to marry you, fine. You're the Pakhan." Before I could even relish in the sensation of victory, she shut it down. "However, let's not forget one thing. Actually several things." I cocked an eyebrow. Tatiana had some balls on her, I'd give her that. "It seems to me, I have greater power than you do currently, Mr. Pakhan."

Her sassy mouth needed some punishment and my dick immediately took over while images flashed through my mind. Tatiana naked on my bed, on her knees, looking up at me with those beautiful eyes. It sent a rush of heat to my groin and made my ears buzz with adrenaline.

"And what's that?"

Tatiana's eyes were filled with defiance, her pulse in the vein on her neck throbbing. I wanted to wrap my hand around her neck and feel her pulse on my fingers. See her eyes haze over with lust. Maybe with love one day.

"I have the chip," she reminded me.

"Except you don't know where it is?" I remarked. "Unless you do know."

She waved her hand, dismissing me. "Minor obstacle. I'll eventually find it. And don't forget, I'm the pregnant one here. Not you."

God, this woman. She'd cost me my sanity. "Without me, no baby and no chip. Seems to me, you should do what I say."

"Tatiana," I warned in a low voice.

"However, I do realize there are benefits to marrying you. You can provide safety from the Yakuza." She paused and dread washed over me. "And I want you to tell me who killed Adrian."

"What makes you think I know?" I questioned her calmly.

"A lucky guess," she remarked. "I want to know what happened."

I shouldn't be surprised. After all, she wasn't a meek woman. Regardless of what she went through, she came out stronger than ever before.

"Vasili warned me not to share information with you," I lied. I didn't feel guilty. If I told her, she'd rather take this plane down than marry me. "Your doctors indicated you have to remember on your own terms."

It was a semi-truth. Vasili didn't say jack crap, but I obtained her therapist's notes. It was clear that Tatiana's memories from that night were too traumatic to recall. She'd remember them when she was ready.

"That's bullshit."

I shrugged. "Doctor's orders. And your brother's."

She scoffed, letting out a frustrated breath. "Like you listen to either one of those."

"When it's time to remember, I'll help you through it," I told her seriously. "I'll tell you everything you want to know." Surprise flashed in those eyes of pale sapphire skies. "Now, no more delays."

Tick. Tock. Tick. Tock. "Fine," she muttered.

She lifted her dress, revealing her red Christian Louboutin pumps. Fuck, it was kind of sexy seeing red pumps under that white dress. It wasn't planned, I was so focused on wedding rings and the priest that I fucking forgot the shoes.

"You forgot to buy the matching shoes," she hissed, then stepped over to the front of the plane. And the whole time the priest looked back and forth, almost amused. I bet he'd come up with another few hundred thousand to add to the price tag.

The moment she was within my reach, I wrapped my arm around her slim waist and pulled her chest to chest with me. Her eyes flashed with defiance and I swore I got a hard-on. There was no doubt our marriage would be lots of push and some pull, but we'd always meet in the middle. She'd be mine and I'd be hers.

My eyes bore into hers, getting lost in those depths and my heart thundered under my chest.

"Stop looking at me like that," she whispered under her breath.

"Like what?"

"Like I'm yours. There's some crazy carnal possession lurking in your eyes. I'm nobody's possession."

My lips curved. "Fine, then, I'll be your possession." But she'd be mine too; she just didn't know it.

Without glancing at the priest, I ordered, "Start."

The priest's thick Russian accent filled the cabin as he started to talk about marriage and the value of vows. I bent my head down, my lips brushing against Tatiana's lips.

"I'll protect you and our children. I'll cherish your body every day and night," I murmured low so only she could hear me. My lips brushed against her earlobe, the scent of roses overwhelming all my senses. I watched in delight as a shiver rolled down her body. "I'll give you pain and make you scream, but always in pleasure. From this day forward, I'm yours and you're mine. It's my vow to you."

Her delicate neck bobbed as she swallowed, but she tried hard to keep her mask on. Too late. It was slipping with each day. I'd shred that thing to pieces. I only wanted the real her. All her happiness. All her sorrows. All of her.

"Do you, Illias Konstantin, take Tatiana Nikolaev as your lawfully wedded wife to live together in holy matrimony, to be with you always, in sickness and in health, forsaking all others, for as long as you both shall live?"

"I do." My answer came swiftly and firmly. I'd known it was her I wanted all along. After all, I've lingered in the shadows for years until I could claim her again.

The priest turned toward Tatiana, his eyes on her and I wanted to claw out his eyeballs. Fucker! I should order him to look away and then just make her say "I do" so there wasn't a chance of her changing her mind.

I clenched my teeth, controlling my possessiveness and the urge to kill. After all, he was a priest.

"Do you, Tatiana Nikolaev, take Illias Konstantin as your lawfully wedded husband to live together in holy matrimony, to be with you always, in sickness and in health, forsaking all others, for as long as you both shall live?"

She stared at me, the promise of defiance and retaliation in her pale blue gaze, but she knew there was no way out of this. The baby in her belly only sealed the deal.

"I do." She gritted the words between her clenched teeth. But the promise of making me regret this danced in her furious expression.

I smiled, totally up for the challenge. She had yet to learn that I always win. Unlike my father, I'd never give up on our family.

Turning to Boris, I retrieved two small boxes. I opened the first one revealing the Blue Nile eternity diamond white-gold wedding band. I took Tatiana's hand into mine and slipped the ring onto her graceful finger.

"It's a perfect fit," she murmured, her eyes on the elegant piece.

"Because we're the perfect fit." Her eyes flickered to me, something in them I couldn't quite read. Almost as if she was pleasantly surprised. Though knowing Tatiana, she was probably trying to get me to lower my guard so she could pounce and then get back to her brothers.

Never. We were one final sentence away from being husband and wife.

I placed the other ring, a simple white gold band into her palm, then watched her slide it onto my finger.

"I now pronounce you husband and wife," the priest said. "You may kiss the bride."

Before he even finished the announcement, I pulled her against my chest and grabbed her by her nape.

I pressed my mouth against hers, the softness of her lips always surprising me. I fucking loved kissing her. Her little sighs and moans could drive a man wild.

"My love knows no bounds, Mrs. Konstantin," I murmured against her lips. "Remember always that I'm yours, but you're mine too."

"Love!" she snickered. "This isn't love. It's lust. You should be able to recognize it."

"Touché," I retorted wryly.

"Besides, kidnapping is not love," she continued, her lips curved in disgust. "And first chance I get, I'm leaving you in the dust. Asshole."

Anger washed over me that she'd even consider leaving me. Years of obsessing over her and all she could talk about and think about was leaving me.

"Want to run?" I asked. She nodded her head, her eyes watching me suspiciously. "Do it. I'll love every second of hunting you down." I grinned savagely. "And catching you will be the best part."

Her glower followed.

"You're a monster," she rasped in a shaky voice, her lips swollen from my kiss.

The corners of my lips tugged. "If I'm a monster, you're my prey. And guess what, *moya luna*?" I brushed my lips against hers, then sunk my teeth into her lower lip. "I just caught you."

Twenty minutes later, I had finally gotten rid of the priest and was five hundred thousand dollars lighter, having charged me another hundred grand for the inconvenience.

But it was fucking worth it. I tapped the inside pocket of my suit where the marriage license lay securely. In my eyes, it was the most valuable piece of paper I owned. Fuck everything else. I could rebuild my empire, but I couldn't get another one of *her*.

The steward set the table with our wedding dinner feast, then disappeared. Nikita and Boris did the same, leaving me alone with my wife.

My wife.

That sounded so fucking right. She was mine. Finally! I was bound to her and she was bound to me. For life. God help any man who'd tried to take her away from me. There wasn't a corner on this earth they could hide that I wouldn't find them.

I studied her, sitting in her seat like a queen and glaring at me. I might as well be her subject. She acted like it.

Although I was under no illusion that she had fully accepted this marriage. She probably schemed as we sat here how to get out of it. But sooner or later, she'd realize there was no way out.

Marrying her was the best way to keep her protected. There was no fucking way anyone would dare take her away from me. I had already sent a notice to the underworld that she was my wife, even before we said our vows. Her last name alone would keep certain people from coming after her.

I'd keep her and our children safe. Yes, children, because I planned on having many with her. Hopefully, she'd be on board with it. But at least two would be nice.

"How many children do you want to have?" I blurted out, like some damn teenager swooning after his first love. Fuck it. I told her I was all in.

She was my wife. Fucking *mine*.

A dark obsession surged through my veins. The lust and love intertwined and urged me to rip off that dress so I could thrust inside her tight heat and claim her. Over and over again. Yes, that dress was beautiful on her, but she was even more beautiful without it.

"I'm surprised you even bother asking." She snickered derisively, reaching for the glass of water and bringing it to her lips. "I mean, you forced the wedding on me. Why not force children on me too?"

I stiffened. "You don't want kids?"

"I didn't say that," she snapped.

"Then how many kids do you want?" I asked again, keeping my tone even.

She took another swig of her drink, then landed the glass on the table with a loud thud. That strength that was part of her DNA had her spine straightening up and staring at me head-on. It always intrigued me her lack of fear of me. Women usually cowered in front of me, kept their heads lowered, and rarely met my eyes.

Tatiana always met me head-on. In the bedroom she'd turn into putty under my touch, but outside it, she was a fierce woman ready to go toe-to-toe with anyone.

"Illias Konstantin, I will not entertain children with you until we get certain things straight," she stated with a clear voice and thunder in her eyes.

"But, my love, we already have one child on the way," I pointed out.

"That is one child," she remarked. "I'm speaking of children. Now, until you fix some of your wrongs, I refuse to have any more babies with you."

"What wrongs exactly are you referring to?" I inquired curiously, admiring the way her hair reflected the light. Her hair was so light it almost gave her an angelic look, blinding me. But her mouth and brain fascinated me even more.

"Fucking men," she hissed, as a few strands of hair fell down her forehead. "Figure it out if you're so smart."

I waved my hand. "No matter. We have the rest of our lives to work that out." My lips curved at her thunderous expression. "Now eat, moya luna. Remember you're eating for two. And I ensured the cook prepared only the healthy food that agrees with you."

"And how do—" She stopped, the look in her eyes full of stubbornness and indignation. "You goddamned stalker."

It was time to teach my wife her first lesson.

EIGHT
TATIANA

My expression was murderous.

Sometimes a villain turns into a hero. Like my brothers. That will never be the case with him.

Fucking ever!

Somehow it didn't surprise me that the fucker was my stalker, but the knowledge still managed to piss me off. The silence that followed was almost suffocating but also charged with so much sexual frustration that I could just touch myself and get off within a fraction of a second.

Nothing beats whiplash like two completely opposite types of feelings—kill him or sleep with him. Well, honestly, I had to admit to myself that there wouldn't be much sleeping going on.

He removed the top from the tray and the smell of food drifted through the air, making my stomach promptly growl. At Sasha's reception I couldn't stomach anything due to the smell of meat. But true to Illias's words, he only had foods that agreed with me—fruits, veggies, crackers, vegetable-based soup.

Without asking, he made me a plate with a little bit of everything and set it in front of me. Then he did the same for himself. We ate in silence, Illias vigorously typing on his phone and not giving me the time of day.

"I'd like my phone back," I said, breaking the silence. He had taken my little clutch when he snuck up behind me.

He barely spared me a glance. "We'll see," he answered cryptically.

Anger boiled inside me and I clenched my teeth so hard, my jaw hurt. I forced myself to take a deep breath, then slowly released it. I'd have to be smart if I was to win my battles with him. So instead of arguing with him, I threw a fresh carrot into my mouth, relishing in the crunching sounds of it as I chewed it and imagining crushing my husband the same way.

But not to murder him. The idea of Illias dead didn't sit well with me. Maybe he'd get on his knees and beg me to forgive all his offenses. Yes, I liked that. Him on his knees.

Immediately another image followed and this one was a lot more X-rated. Suddenly the dress felt too heavy. My thighs clenched and, to my horror, arousal rushed through me, drenching my panties. I rubbed my thighs together, shifting my hips, which only made it worse.

Or better. Depending how you looked at it.

A tiny moan slipped and Illias's eyes snapped up to me. His eyes gazed down my body and the warmth of it seared through the material as if he'd touched me.

"Did you eat enough, *moya luna*?"

I shouldn't cave into this carnal desire. This damn lust was bound by thorns that would eventually make me bleed. But I found myself nodding, and the next thing I knew, he lifted me up and carried me to the back of the plane like it was the threshold of his home.

He placed me down on the bed almost reverently. I watched him yank his jacket off his broad shoulders and throw it on the nearby loveseat. His cufflinks followed. Then he unbuttoned his shirt and, with each flick of a button, more and more of his muscular chest came into full view.

Goddamn him, his chest was ripped and his abdomen cut, making my mouth water. His physical beauty drew you in until you were so deep inside his web, you couldn't get out. It should be illegal to be so damn hot.

I could blame all this attraction to him on my hormones, but deep down I knew it wasn't. I shamelessly watched as he removed his belt, then discarded his pants and socks, leaving him only in silky black boxers.

"Turn around," he ordered.

"I don't like you ordering me," I said dryly but I was already halfway to obeying him.

The sound of the zipper filled the back of the plane in a seductive echo, sending maddening anticipation through my veins. God, I had never wanted sex so much in my entire life. And I wasn't the shy nor reserved type. Sex with this man—my husband—was on an entirely different level.

He pulled my dress off my body, leaving me in heels and my undergarments. The latter was soon ripped off my body and discarded right along with the wedding dress, but when I moved to kick off my heels, he stopped me.

"Keep them on." The deep rasp of his voice and that Russian accent liquified my insides.

He wrapped both hands around my waist and pulled me up onto my hands and knees, his warm body against my back. When he put distance between us, I glanced over my shoulder to find him discarding his boxers.

He was fully erect already, pre-cum glistening at the tip of his cock. His fingers wrapped around his cock while his eyes were locked on my backside.

"We still haven't talked about the butt plug issue," he said nonchalantly, his gaze on my ass making me even more turned on. "We'll discuss that tomorrow."

My pussy clenched although I was unsure whether it was from his words or the way his gaze burned as my pussy and ass clenched.

He took a step closer and kneeled onto the bed, right behind me. He dragged his cock along my wet slit and I gasped, pushing my ass against him so he'd slide inside me.

Then remembering his butt plug comment, I felt obliged to say something back.

"I'm not discussing the butt plug with you today... tomorrow... or ever," I breathed, my moans in between my words ruining the effect.

He chuckled darkly, fires burning in his eyes melting everything in their wake.

"You and I both know you'll like it. You want to be mine to fuck in every way. Your body craves my cock in all your holes." My body shuddered in betrayal, but he seemed to like it rather than mock it. He dragged his palm down my back, his fingers tracking my spine like he was playing a piano. "You want me to own you and control you so you can fall apart." He grabbed my hair and tugged it back in a merciless grip. "But only with me. I'll murder any man who sees you like this, never mind touches you."

Then his calloused hand landed on my ass on a sharp slap as if he needed to punish me for something I hadn't done yet. *Slap.* The burn exploded on the skin of my ass and zapped straight to my core.

There was no point in complaining because a gush of juices trickled down my inner thighs and a moan shattered the air. This chemistry was mind blowing. The kind that you only read in books. Yet, here it was. In this room. On this bed.

Illias knew how to own my body. His every touch, every word never failed to turn me on. But I'd rather die than admit it to him. It'd give him ammunition against me. Although I feared he didn't need it. The evidence of it was trailing down my legs.

My pants and moans mixed with the loud hammering of my heart that I feared it would crack my ribs. However, it never occurred to me to ask him to stop.

His hand slowly parted my thighs as far as they could go, and the second his fingers brushed against my soaked pussy, a violent shudder rolled through my body.

"That's my good wife," he purred, then lowered his face to my core from behind, and to my horror, he inhaled deeply. "Fuck, you smell so good. You..." His hot tongue swept through my core, from my clit to my back hole. "You are my addiction."

I buried my face into the pillow, every inch of my skin burning. From the lust speeding through my veins, threatening to break the dam.

My breathing was hard, like I just ran a marathon. Fractured breaths. Chopped heartbeats.

"Are you ready, moya luna?" His voice was hoarse. Deep. A hint of control tethering on the edge lacing around his Russian accent.

He wrapped a hand around my throat and pulled me up, so his chest was against my back. Then he forced me to turn my face over my shoulder. The haunting darkness and possession in his eyes were daunting, leaving me panting and my heart drumming like a hammer against my chest.

"I'm going to fuck you now." His words vibrated through his chest and against my back. His lips brushed against mine, then he took my earlobe between his teeth and nipped it. Hard. "I'm going to fuck you as my wife, sealing our marriage. And you... you'll scream my name."

He planted his knee between my legs and thrust into me from behind without a warning.

"Ahhh..."

My head fell back, resting against his shoulder. He pulled out, only to slam inside me again as he reached around my body to twist my swollen clit.

"Ohhh... yes."

"That's it. Give me all your screams," he murmured against my ear. My eyelids peeled open to a painting that hung over the bed of the airplane cabin. I couldn't distinguish a single thing about it because all I could do was stare at the reflection of us against the dark glass that protected the painting.

Illias's eyes were hooded, the expression on his face one I had never seen on a man. His pace built up. His teeth on my neck. The slap of flesh against flesh. The slick sounds of my arousal echoed in the air and fragranced the room.

Then his eyes darted to the painting and our gazes locked.

He owned my body, thrusting harshly at a fast pace bringing me closer and closer to the peak.

"My wife has such a needy pussy," he growled into my ear. "I'll take care of it."

And he did.

Illias pounded into me and I feared he'd tear me apart. Break me. But he promised to put me back together. His thrusts were so rough, my body threatened to fall forward but his hand held me in place. His other hand reached up to play with my sensitive nipples—rolling them, pinching them, and kneading my breasts.

A tingling sensation blossomed deep in my belly. My breaths came out in short pants. My moans in a louder symphony.

I was so freaking close... so, so close.

"Illias, I'm going to—"

A ring of an incoming call interrupted the moment and our erotic mix of grunts and moans.

"Konstantin."

My eyes flew wide open. I looked over my shoulder and gaped. He actually answered the phone. The hooded, carnal look in his eyes was replaced by a murderous expression.

"What the fuck," I mouthed. We were in the middle of having sex! He couldn't be answering calls while buried deep inside me, especially since I was so damn close to an orgasm. So I took matters into my own hands.

I got back into doggy position, baring every inch of me to him and started rocking my hips back and forth, grinding against his erection. Satisfaction curled in the pit of my belly when his sharp intake of breath filled the air.

"Yes, I'm here."

I glanced over my shoulder to find his flared eyes on me, but he didn't stop me as I pushed my ass against him, his erection thrusting in and out. His fingers dug into my hips and he thrust harder. My eyelids grew heavy and my pussy throbbed. Lust spread through me and he started fucking me all over again.

In and out. Hard and deep. His harsh breathing. My panting.

His thrusts picked up. My breasts hung heavy and full while I was on all fours, and all the while I watched Illias over my shoulder as he fucked me like a god intent on proving a point. I reached with my one hand to play with my nipples, my pleasure building up.

"Tatiana's safe," he said, his keeping his tone even. "In fact, if you want to talk to her, she's right in front of me."

A brutal satisfaction passed his expression while panic flared inside me. I scrambled to move away from him but his hand tightened around me, not allowing me an inch of reprieve. His cock was still hard, deep inside me and I watched in horror as he put his phone on speaker.

"Please say hello to my wife," he drawled, keeping his voice cool. He threw the phone on the mattress, faceup. "Or we could even do FaceTime if you want to be convinced she's safe. You'll see I'm taking very good care of my wife."

I shook my head in panic, only for another whimper to slip through my lips as he thrust deep inside me hitting my sweet spot. I bit my lip, then turned away from him only to find the reflection of me staring back at me which was even worse. A wanton and flushed woman stared back at me. My long hair looked like a tousled mess giving a good indication of what we've been doing. Although my naked body and breasts flapping with his each thrust were proof enough.

"Tatiana?" Vasili's voice was laced with worry while I fought lust with Illias's each brutal thrust.

"Y-yes."

Illias squeezed my ass, while with his other hand he kept plummeting in and out of me. The flames of desire burned hotter. My hips meeting his thrusts of their own free will. I buried my face into the pillow and bit into it, muffling my whimpers.

Sasha's voice filled the air. "Are you okay?" *Never better.* "I swear to God that fucker will pay if he hurt you. Pakhan or not."

Illias's tempo increased to a maddening speed. He fucked me like a rag doll. He hit that spot that caused my mind to blank and my back to bow.

"Tatiana?"

Jesus, I couldn't think when Illias fucked me like this. He fisted my hair and tugged my head back until his chest was against my back again. He bit my earlobe. "Tell them all is good, and I'll give you the pleasure you want."

His words were so low I could barely hear them.

"Y-yes." I hoped my voice didn't portray anything. "I'm good. All is good."

"Want me to kill him?"

"No!" *I need to finish first and only he can give me an orgasm right now.* "Not yet," I added because I couldn't let Illias get away with it all. His hand wrapped around my throat, squeezing in punishment. But it only enhanced my pleasure. I arched my back, pushing my neck into his grip and he muffled his groan by biting into my shoulder blade.

"Where are you?" *In heaven.*

"Moan for me," he murmured against my ear so only I could hear it. "Fall apart for me."

Illias's hand reached around and rubbed my clit, smearing the wetness around. My body shuddered as he twisted my swollen clit. He kept thrusting inside me, the friction and carnal type of pleasure threatening to overwhelm me.

"Don't worry about me," I breathed. "I'll call you."

I begged Illias silently to hang up. I needed more of this. His thrusts increased in speed, he kept hitting my G-spot, and with the tightening of his rough hand around my throat, I was so fucking close to screaming my orgasm.

"You heard my wife." Thank God for small mercies. "Don't call us, we'll call you."

"You—" *Click.*

Then he started moving at a maddening pace, fucking me harder, deeper. The mattress screamed with protests right along my moans and pants.

"You take it so fucking good, Tatiana," he praised and a sob of pleasure came from my lips as an orgasm shot through me. My body shuddered with the force of it. Illias pinched my nipples, one, then the other, eliciting throaty moans from me.

"Are you mine?"

"N-no," I panted, desperate for more of this amazing feeling as my husband started fucking me harder, deeper and faster. But just because I loved the feel of him, didn't mean I'd just roll over and tell him I was his.

His hand came around my throat and my traitorous body actually leaned into the damn touch. Like what-the-fuck!

"Wrong," he rasped, his lips against my ear. Thrust. "You are mine." Thrust. "Your pussy." Thrust. "Your ass." Thrust. "Your everything."

"Oh my God," I moaned.

"That's right." My knees gave out, but that didn't stop Illias. He kept fucking me, the pace pushing me towards another orgasm. He pulled out of me, only to slam into me with such force a scream tore from my throat. He was hitting a spot so deep that I'd agree to anything, just to feel this pleasure cruise through my veins. "Don't ever forget you're mine. You feel how your pussy clenches around my cock?"

His groans and my pants danced in the air as we both shuddered against each other, tumbling toward the edge of release. I lost all sense as I relished in seeing my husband lose control.

"We're going to have many babies," he growled against my neck. "Because I'll never have enough of this. Of you."

His hold tightened on me and he stilled as he shot cum inside me. The warm liquid trickled down my thighs and exhaustion pulled on my muscles. Both of us breathing heavily, our hearts beating as one.

With my husband still inside me, his strong heart beating against my back, I let myself relax as his lips trailed over my skin. Gentle. Like feathers. So different from the roughness of his fucking. His hands roamed every inch of my skin, petting and holding me, until I started grinding against him. Needing him again. And again.

The carnal lust we shared filled the skies until both our bodies gave in to exhaustion. With his arms wrapped around me and soft Russian words in my ear, sleep pulled me under.

The scent of citrus and sandalwood wrapped around me like a protective blanket.

NINE

TATIANA

A warm chest cradled me.

We were moving. Words in a language I didn't care for. Then the heavy shifting of doors and cool air washed over me and a different kind of shudder rolled through me. My eyes opened and landed on the landscape of snow-covered ground that stretched for miles.

My eyes darted around in confusion.

"Where are we?" I rasped, my throat dry from sleep. "And why didn't you wake me?" It had been the running theme lately. Every time I turned around, Konstantin had swooped me up, carrying me like his cherished bride.

He stood at the top of the staircase landing on his plane, readying to depart the plane.

I glanced down and found myself wearing Illias's dress shirt and someone's long black wool dress coat.

"It's my coat. I figured it'd cover your body and keep you warm." The deep timbre of his voice warmed my chest. When he ran a thumb across my cheek, that warmth crept into my heart. "I didn't have boots that would fit you." The cool against my toes registered and I wiggled them. I was barefoot but Illias managed to tuck the hem of his coat under my feet. "I ordered you new clothes and everything is being delivered to *our* home." He accentuated the word and somehow it related the message that I wasn't sure I was ready to hear. Not until I learned exactly the story behind the killing of the woman in his video and behind what happened to Adrian. I let it go for now, but I needed to uncover the mystery there.

Then I remembered he didn't answer my question.

"Where are we?" I repeated.

"Home."

I frowned. "Your home is California. Los Angeles. I don't think L.A. has ever been covered in five feet of snow."

"Russia."

I attempted to pull away from him but he wouldn't have it. "Russia?" I hissed, pissed he'd bring me here. I hated winters in Russia. I hated the bitter cold. Period. And this guy brought me *here*.

This had to be a nightmare. I fell asleep with bliss in my bones and soul and woke up in the freeze-your-ass-off motherland. This was what happened when you played with the wrong person. You woke up married and thoroughly fucked in Russia, better yet, freezing hell. Chained to the devil.

Jesus Christ!

"This is your idea of a honeymoon?" I shook my head. "I fucking hate Russia. Especially in winter."

He didn't pay attention to my protest as he descended the stairs towards a Land Rover waiting for us.

"You were born in Russia."

"Yes, but I grew up in New Orleans. Warm climate." A shiver rolled through me. I hated the cold, and in my book, high forties was too cold. It was in the negatives here, for Pete's sake. "I demand you take us back. I can deal with California. But not Russia."

He ignored me as he continued towards the car.

"Konstantin!" I protested. "I'm serious, take us back to the States. Or Fiji. Anywhere, just not this frozen tundra."

The door to the back of the Land Rover was already opened by the time he reached it and he slid into the seat, sitting me on his lap. I went to slide off his lap, but his grip on me tightened.

"No."

"I'm not a kid," I muttered under my breath as two of his men got in the front seat. "You don't get to tell me what to do."

"Thank fuck you're not a kid," he responded wryly. "But you're my wife, and I want you close to me."

I rolled my eyes but kept my mouth shut for the rest of the drive. If there was one thing I learned growing up with my brothers, it was never argue and dispute the head of the family in front of his men.

So I focused on the landscape. Or lack of it.

The white powder stretched on and on for miles. Illias didn't say a word during the ride through the back roads, keeping his attention on his phone. His men kept their postures stiff and their gazes trained forward, although I caught Nikita's eyes flicker to the rearview mirror once or twice, but he'd immediately trained them forward.

My brows furrowed. I tried to spot any kind of landmark that would give me an idea of where exactly in Russia we were, but there were none. At one point, we passed a stone wall with a tall iron fence on top of it with a metal gate that slid open with a loud creak. The car slowed down and I thought we were home.

Home.

It felt strange saying that word in a foreign country. Unlike Vasili and Sasha, I never considered Russia my home. Even Alexei spent more time in Russia, but his hatred of the country matched mine.

Was it right?

I didn't know. But I associated my home with happiness and I was never particularly happy in Russia. In New Orleans, I was very happy. I loved the people. I loved the cuisine. I loved my brothers with me there. Papa was rarely there with us when I was a little girl, always chasing after Marietta Taylor, his lost mistress. Isabella's mother.

Yes, our family was complicated.

My attention returned to the white landscape. It felt like forever until the car slowed to a halt outside a large mansion. No, not a mansion. A freaking honest-to-God castle.

My mouth parted as I stared at it. I'd seen my share of luxury, but I swore I hadn't seen anything like *this* before. It looked like one of those luxurious palaces from the eighteenth century that belonged to the Russian imperial family. The Romanovs and their fall in the early twentieth century was known to every girl of Russian heritage. I was no exception.

"You live here?" I asked, my voice awed.

"I have a place closer to the city, but this is safer," he remarked. I tilted my head and shifted my body so I could see his face.

"Are we not safe?"

"*Moya luna*, we are never too safe."

"You think the Yakuza will still attempt something?" I questioned. I had a lot more to lose now. We both did. It wasn't just about my life anymore. It's about the baby's life too.

"The Yakuza will attempt shit for as long as the head of their organization remains the same."

And with that, he shifted out of the car and swiftly picked me up into his arms. I opened my mouth, but he quickly stopped me. "I am carrying you through every threshold of our home. So get used to it."

I didn't protest. I couldn't help it. My heart fluttered and warmth seeped into my soul and made its way into my heart. My hands wrapped around his neck, my fingers pushing into his thick, dark hair, as he passed the threshold of his home.

"Welcome home," he murmured, his mouth on my cheek. "We'll spend more time in California, I promise, but this is home too." I smiled despite everything. "I don't want my young bride to freeze to death here. I sent a text ahead and instructed the staff to light up fireplaces in every room so we can keep you warm."

My chest cracked. Butterflies erupted. It was such a simple thing to do for me, yet so thoughtful. If he kept this up, I might be in danger of falling for him. I couldn't let that happen.

My childish notions and romanticism led me astray with Adrian, and I'd known him for a lot longer than this man. There were secrets surrounding Illias, not to mention that damning video of him executing a young woman spoke volumes against him.

Therefore, I couldn't give in to these feelings. I sold my soul to the devil, although I fought him at every turn. But I lost the game. I married him, even if I really didn't have a choice. But there was an upside to that. We didn't sign a prenup, so half of everything he owned was mine, including half of my soul. Right?

Half of everything you own is his too, my mind whispered. I immediately shut down the reason. There was no reason for negativity in my life right now.

"Oh my gosh," I whispered, my mouth parting as I titled my head back to stare at the ceiling. I stared at the centuries-old mosaic decor painted on the ceilings. "Vaulted ceilings have nothing on this."

A loud squeal shattered the air. Illias's and my eyes followed the sound.

What the heck—

The young woman Illias executed stared at us with a wide smile, her eyes darting back and forth between Illias and me in excitement.

"Isla, what are you doing here?" Illias asked, his brows pinched. "I thought you were in Paris, attending your friend's fashion show."

Isla? Who in the fuck was Isla?

An attractive blush colored Isla's cheeks while questions burned my brain. She was beautiful. Petite frame. Her soft ginger curls were in such contrast with her creamy complexion, but I swore the faint freckles on her nose matched her hair color.

"That was last week," she replied, her eyes curiously on me. Who was this girl? The video showed Illias executing her. It looked too real to be fake. "If you want me to go, I can leave though," she added teasingly.

My eyes darted curiously to Illias. His gaze was soft on the woman and a slither of jealousy flared in my chest. Confusion overwhelmed. I didn't like being jealous, nor bitter. I shifted away from Illias, attempting to put some distance between us, which was hard considering he carried me.

"Where are you going?" he growled at me.

"Put me down," I demanded.

"No." God, I hated that word.

"We're inside. I can walk now," I protested, pushing against him to no avail. He only pulled me closer to his chest, holding on to me like I was his most precious cargo.

Illias returned the attention to the red-haired beauty, ignoring my protest. "Isla, meet Tatiana. My wife." The girl's eyes widened, practically bulging out of her head.

"Oh my God," she squealed so loud I just about jumped out of Illias's arms. "I'm so happy for you, brother. When did you get married? Where? Why wasn't I invited?"

Wait. What? Did she say brother? So the rumors were true! Holy shit! Illias had a sister. But... my brows furrowed. She looked nothing like him. I stared at her, studying every single feature of her face.

Maybe her nose, I thought to myself. I shook my head. No, definitely not the nose. *Forehead?*

"We got married right before my plane took off," Illias answered her, while the two of us kept staring at each other. Now that she was closer, I could see she wasn't quite as young as the woman in the video. Maybe he staged that when she was younger so he'd kept her hidden. There were crazier things that happened in the underworld. "You would have been invited, but it was an emergency."

"I could have dropped everything and come to you," she remarked, slightly hurt.

Illias pulled her into an embrace, while still keeping me in the arms, so it turned out to be a slightly awkward three-person hug. Her face an inch from me, I could see her freckles even better. Fuck, she was gorgeous—freckles or no.

"Don't worry," I said softly. "He kind of kidnapped me, then forced me to marry him, so it truly was an emergency."

She blinked in confusion. Illias groaned.

"You kidnapped her?" Her voice pitched high and her face twisted with panic. "Oh my gosh, we're going to go to jail." She glared at her brother, then threw me an apologetic look. "I'm so sorry. W-we can still fix this. Illias didn't mean it. It's probably because you're so... s-so beautiful."

I waved my hand, feeling sorry for her. "Don't worry about it. My brother kidnapped Branka last summer. In the middle of her walking down the aisle to marry someone else. Happens more than you think."

Awkward silence followed. Her gaze darted to her brother, the look in her eyes clearly stating something was wrong either with me or her brother. Okay, maybe my answer wasn't the best. Illias's stiff posture alerted me that there was no *"maybe"* about it.

"It's nice to meet you though," I added, trying to at least end our conversation amicably. "I hope you won't leave because I'm here. I hate being stuck in Russia in the winter."

She blinked again, and it would have been comical if a suspicion didn't form in my chest. Konstantin kept his sister in the dark about his status. How was that even possible?

Illias pecked his sister on the cheek as he headed for the grand staircase. "We'll talk to you tomorrow, sestra." She opened her mouth but he immediately added, "Tomorrow."

Her eyes flicked my way, back to her brother, then back to me. I offered her a comforting smile and nodded. "Tomorrow," I mouthed.

"Uh-oh... okay."

She remained glued to her spot as Illias took long strides up the stairs. Once we were out of her earshot, I hissed under my breath.

"She doesn't know you're the Pakhan," I whispered angrily. His shoulders tensed. His jaw clenched and his eyes turned murderous. "Please don't tell me you left your sister in the dark about the underworld." He remained silent. A muscle in his jaw tightened. "I know you are smarter than that. You left her vulnerable and clueless."

His eyes darkened. "She's not clueless." I gave him a pointed look. "She knows I don't want her around my business. She has a normal life and normal friends." My eyebrow shot up to my hairline. Did he really just say that?

"Pray tell how anything about being born into a family that belongs to the underworld is normal?" He kept striding forward, down the elaborate hallways. Left. Right. Left.

So I tried a different approach. "Does that mean my... *our* child will have a normal life too?"

It was the first time I referred to my little bundle of joy as ours. But I wanted to drive the point home.

His step faltered and he took my chin between his fingers. "Our child will be raised to take over all my businesses."

My eyes flashed victoriously. "Then why are you keeping your sister in the dark?"

He gritted his teeth so hard, I could hear his teeth grinding. "She's my half sister. Illegitimate. It puts her in a completely different category."

I couldn't exactly argue that point. Alexei and Isabella were illegitimate children. Alexei wasn't hidden from the underworld, and it cost him his childhood. Almost his entire life. Isabella didn't know for her first twenty-five years that she was the illegitimate daughter of Lombardo Santos. The old Santos didn't know he had a daughter for the longest time. It saved her from the underworld. So maybe Illias had a point.

"You know very well that illegitimate daughters are often kidnapped," he said coldly.

"Sometimes legitimate daughters are kidnapped too," I retorted dryly.

"And they're dragged into whorehouses to be used for flesh selling and trading."

I nodded. Unfortunately, he was right. "I promise I won't tell anyone about her," I vowed, surprising even myself. He had forced me into this marriage, but it'd be cruel to use her to get back at him. Isla *was* innocent. "Not even my brothers."

His eyes found mine, something soft in them, sending my heart into overdrive. He trapped me into his depths and I held his gaze.

"Thank you."

Two simple words. One simple promise.

TEN
KONSTANTIN

I'd burn the world and anyone who'd try to get near my wife and our child.

Her vow meant more than she would ever know. I didn't need her vow to know she'd protect Isla like she was her own and she'd only met her. That was who Tatiana was down to her core. She was as protective of the people she cared about.

"Our bedroom," I told her. "Welcome home."

She pushed herself off me and slid out of my arms. Then she discarded the coat onto the ground and stepped over it as she studied the room.

Her bare feet padded silently over the hardwood and onto the rug. Her sparkly red toenails caught light every so often as she moved across the floor as she moved around.

"Not our home," she remarked, her eyes traveling over the large room. I had the rooms redone last year. My parents kept separate but adjoining bedrooms. I had no intention of keeping separate bedrooms with my wife.

"Our home," I said.

Just the thought of her leaving had me turning into a fucking crazed beast. It was my fear that Tatiana would get so far under my skin that

69

I'd become my father. I didn't want that. It'd be a bad ending for both Tatiana and me. For our children. For our family.

My wife glanced over her shoulder playfully. "So everything you own, I own." I nodded and her lips curved with that smile that promised trouble. "That's good to know."

Tatiana knew as well as anyone else in our world. Marriage was for life, hence no reason for a prenup. Besides, it wasn't exactly as if she was penniless.

"Where is the closet?" she asked, then followed my eyes to the corner of the room. She padded to it and pushed the door open. "Oh, a walk-in closet. That's good." She strode in and I followed. "Kind of small," she remarked.

"We can make it bigger."

She met my gaze. "I was being sarcastic," she teased softly. Fuck, I loved when she was soft. Pliant. I loved every single side of her. I had yet to find something I didn't like about my wife. "Wow, I see you weren't joking when you said you'll have everything here."

Her graceful fingers trailed over the clothes. Chanel. Burberry. Armani. Valentino. Hermès. Dior. Gucci. Prada. It should be all her favorite brands.

"I rarely joke around."

"Yeah, you're not exactly the comedic type."

"Whatever is missing, you can order. The top drawer on your side has a black Amex with your name on it. And some cash."

She slowly turned around, then casually leaned against the cabinet, resting her elbows on it.

"You know, I have my own money. And my own black Amex. All you have to do is give me my purse back."

A sardonic feeling pulled on my chest. Any other woman would be falling to her knees and thanking me. Not Tatiana. She'd rather point out she had it all.

"From now on, you'll use my money for your needs."

Her fingers tapped lightly against the flat surface of the cabinet that her elbows rested on. Her French manicured nails clicked against the wood. The vein in her neck showed her pulse beating wildly. She held her mask in place, keeping her cool. But she was nervous.

I didn't like it. I wanted her trust. Her love. Her devotion.

These feelings surrounding her were visceral. Carnal. A hunger that roared in my chest grew with each taste of her. Unknowingly, she fed my obsession.

"Or what? You'll punish me?" Her voice was sultry. Slightly breathy. Sassy.

In three long strides, I closed the distance between us and scooped her up.

"Both of us know you get off on punishment," I drawled as I carried her through the bedroom. Tatiana's delicate fingers grabbed on to me, a knowing smile on her lips.

"And so do you," she purred. "So why deprive us both of it?"

I entered the bathroom and kicked the door shut behind me. Tatiana's eyes instantly hazed with lust and her cheeks flushed. The blue of her eyes was notably starker against the black marble of the bathroom.

"Let me down," she demanded softly. Her lips were only a few inches away, tempting me. I wanted to draw a bath for her and then let her rest tonight. But her lips were impossible to resist. I took her mouth and her lips parted with a soft moan spilling from them. I lost all semblance of control.

I claimed her lips like it was the last thing I'd do before the world exploded. Her body molded against mine, her fingers pushing into my hair and her fingernails scraping against my scalp. Satisfaction ran hot through my blood.

And determination.

I'd make my wife love me. Then when she learned the truth, she wouldn't leave me.

ELEVEN
TATIANA

Illias watched me with a peculiar look in his eyes.

I caught a glimpse of the two of us in the mirror. Me, only wearing his shirt and my bare legs on full display. Him, suited up, looking every bit the Pakhan he was. My hair was a disheveled mess while my husband's appearance was pristine.

He set me on the counter, and I watched him move swiftly around the bathroom. He turned on the water, the sound of it filling the bathroom. Illias reached over and retrieved a bath product.

Just as he was about to pour it in, I stopped him.

"Whose bottle is that?" I asked, motioning to the bottle in his hand.

"It's yours." He shook his head as if amused by the display of jealousy. I wasn't jealous but damn if I'd use another woman's product. "It was delivered along with the clothes. Everything is new—and yours, Tatiana."

"Well then. You can pour it in." I started unbuttoning my shirt, discarding it onto the floor. Heat in his gaze flared and my body instantly responded.

"You must have been a queen in your previous life," he muttered, dumping its contents into the tub. The scent of roses drifted through the air. Several faucets filled the large tub that could easily house ten people, and the two of us watched in silence as the water filled the tub.

"Aren't you going to take your clothes off?" I asked shamelessly. I realized it made me sound slightly desperate. Oh well. I might as well enjoy the benefits of being married.

"No."

I didn't care to evaluate the sinking feeling in the pit of my stomach. So I just slid off the counter and swayed my hips as I made my way to the tub.

"Your loss," I murmured as I passed by him.

His hand lightly tapped my ass. "Tease. Get in the tub."

He helped to lower me into the tub, and the moment I was submerged, a deep sigh left me.

"This feels good," I exhaled. He leaned over and for a moment I hoped he'd join me, but he just reached behind me and shut off the tap. Then he sat at the edge of the tub while I soaked in the bubbles.

The silence after the constant rush of water was sudden. Somehow overwhelming. But not uncomfortable. After months of pushing and pulling, it still seemed odd to find myself here. In his home. In Russia. Freaking married to him.

Somehow the idea of our marriage wasn't repulsive. It had to be the great sex. Not the best basis for marriage, but it was at least something. Well, there was also a child growing in my belly.

My chest warmed. Our baby wasn't exactly planned, but I already felt a connection with her. Or maybe it was him. It didn't matter, as long as he or she was healthy. I placed a palm on my lower belly and rubbed it gently. I had already purchased pregnancy books and started reading up on anything and everything about pregnancy and the first year of our baby's life.

Illias removed his jacket and hung it on the towel hanger, then undid his cuffs and rolled up his sleeves, exposing his forearms. Gosh, I loved Illias's hands. They were so strong and veiny. Rough, yet they could bring so much pleasure.

He lowered down to a crouch beside me and slid his hand in the water.

"What are you doing?" He didn't answer as his fingers started massaging my shoulders. His strong fingers rubbed circles down my back, then up again, loosening muscles on my upper back and shoulders.

I tilted my head to the side to give him better access, a low moan filling the air. With horror I realized it was mine, but I couldn't help how good it felt.

"I read that a massage is good during pregnancy," he remarked, his voice deep.

I sighed in pleasure. "I certainly agree," I murmured. "Where did you read that?"

"American Pregnancy Association." My eyes fluttered closed as my muscles loosened with every passing second his fingers expertly worked on me. "They warned about massaging the belly, but indicated prenatal massage therapy can help reduce anxiety and stress."

He rubbed long circles with a tenderness and sure, firm movements. "Well, Illias. If you ever want to give up your career as the Pakhan, you will succeed as a masseuse."

I watched him through my heavy lids and caught the corner of his lips tipped up. He was gorgeous when he half-smiled. I feared when he actually smiled, he'd send me into a spiral.

"I'll keep that in mind."

"What else did you read?" I inquired.

"You need a lot of sleep in your first trimester." His hand came around and slowly trailed down my neck. "No stress." He flattened his palm over my racing, hard-breathing heart. "No alcohol."

I stiffened, meeting his gaze fully. "I haven't had any for months."

He nodded. "I know."

"I forgot you're a stalker," I muttered under my breath.

"Only with you," I thought I heard him say, but I couldn't be certain. My eyes traveled over the luxurious bathroom. Black marble was stark against white walls and white fixtures.

"When will we go back to the States?" I asked, still studying every corner of the bathroom. There wasn't much to see, but maybe I avoided drowning in Illias's darkness. It was slowly pulling me under, and I feared where it'd take me.

There were still many secrets between us. As fucked up as it was, I was okay with certain morally gray methods of our world. But I wasn't okay with killing innocents. Killing women and children. Vasili always said there was somewhere where we had to draw a line.

"We just got here," he responded as he got to his feet. He pulled out a clean towel and dried his hands on it with firm movements.

My brows furrowed but then I remembered what I'd asked him. I didn't expect him really to give me a concrete date but a general time-frame would be nice. No matter. He wouldn't succeed in keeping me captive—wife or no wife.

"The woman in the video... is that your sister?" I changed the subject, addressing the elephant in the room. We had to talk about it eventually. Might as well do it now. "Did you stage it for some reason?"

"No."

The one-word answer grated on my nerves, but it was his expression that concerned me. I could practically see his walls going up. The calmness and coldness in his expression would shake a newbie to this world. I was well aware Illias was dangerous, a ruthless killer.

But he wanted our baby. He wanted me. For now at least.

"Do you know that the spousal testimonial privilege precludes one spouse from testifying against the other spouse in criminal proceedings?"

His darkened eyes held mine in a cage.

"I did know that." Of course he knew that. "But that video was never meant for your eyes."

"And yet, I've seen it." Frustration welled inside me, but unlike Sasha, I wasn't always impulsive. Once in a while, I chose my words carefully. "If we are to trust each other, we should start somewhere. Shouldn't we?"

That *pop* from the video when he pulled the trigger played in my mind. I could almost hear it in this silence between us.

"She was Isla's mother." I held my breath and my heart thundered against my ribs. "My father took her from somewhere. Some whore-house. She was barely sixteen. He brought her here because she was pregnant with Isla. One night, he went to her room, ready to beat her, then rape her, and I lost it."

"You killed him?" I rasped, my ears buzzing.

"I did," he admitted, leaning against the column that stood closest to the tub. "You're the only person alive who knows it. Boris suspects it, but he doesn't know for sure. Since my mother's death, he hasn't been right up here." He tapped his temple, then folded his arms across his chest. "Well, Isla's mother wasn't right up there either. I don't know if my father broke her or something else."

"Jesus," I muttered.

"When she gave birth, I hoped she'd focus on the baby," Illias continued. "She didn't. She didn't bother giving her a name. She didn't bother feeding her. But she did try to kill my sister." I gasped, my heart clenching at hearing those words. It made me feel for Isla more. No wonder he kept her protected and sheltered. "Once, I caught her trying to smother my baby sister. Another time, she tried to drown her. It got so bad that I couldn't leave her alone in the room with Isla. My tipping point was when she took Maxim's gun and tried to shoot the baby."

I leaned over the tub and took his hand into mine. "No wonder you killed her."

"I killed her the same night."

The story shook me up. But there was a relief that came with it in the knowledge. It was a testament to Illias's code. After all, he saved his sister. While my brothers didn't kill our mother, they certainly didn't save her either. In fact, I had no doubt that if Vasili was the one who caught our mother trying to kill me alongside herself, he would have killed her too.

"Does she know?" I whispered the question, but deep down I knew the answer. He had been protecting her from everything. I was certain he'd protect her from this knowledge too. Just as Sasha protected me from mine.

"No."

His admission filled the air.

"I got a cell phone delivered a while back," I started quietly. "I don't know who sent it, but when I opened it, a video started playing."

Illias visibly stiffened. "What was the video about?"

His voice was slightly off. Almost worried. But his expression never changed.

I swallowed. "The video showed Sasha killing someone. Strangling a man. No clue who that guy was but it freaked me out." I took a lungful of air and then slowly exhaled. "That wasn't the worst part. At the end of it, Adrian made a comment about erasing the video. Yet, there it was. The damn video playing right there in front of me." I shook my head. "I don't think he erased it, but I don't know why. He and my brothers were so close."

Our admissions weaved through the air, pulling us closer by invisible ties. And slowly my trust in this man grew another notch. At least as far as protection went. I knew Illias would protect our family at all costs. All I had to do was look at Isla and know it to be true.

She owed her life to her big brother. Just as I owed my life to my big brother. Sasha saved me from my mother, but Vasili and Sasha gave me life. A stable and healthy childhood.

I rose up to my feet, water dripping down my body, then swung one leg, then the other to get out of the tub. He watched me, his eyes running over my body with that dark lust I'd come to expect from him. A lust that, if I was honest with myself, excited me. But he only reached for another plush towel and wrapped it around me. I kept my hands in the air, then turned slowly until we were face-to-face.

I wasn't a short woman, but I wasn't exactly tall either. Next to him, I felt like a fragile little thing, yet protected. I reached up to Illias's chest, having to crane my neck to keep eye contact.

His silence touched my skin. His darkness tempted. His obsession overwhelmed.

And slowly invisible strings pulled us together, weaving through the thorns of our world.

My thighs quivered. My pulse rushed. My ears buzzed. I waited for him to touch me. My pussy throbbed in anticipation. Every cell in my body lit up, waiting, as my heart thundered. Maybe it was the fact that our baby grew in my belly that weaved this connection or maybe something else entirely. I wasn't sure. All I knew was that I had never felt anything like this with Adrian.

"Go to bed," he instructed softly, brushing his knuckles against my cheek. "You need sleep."

Sleep was the last thing I needed right now.

"What about you?" Fuck, I needed him to touch me. Get me off. My whole body was on fire, tingling with sensations that I feared went beyond the physical attraction.

"I'm going to get in the shower."

With that he turned around and strode to the opposite side of the room where the glass-enclosed shower was and turned on the water.

"Maybe I should watch you take a shower since you watched me take a bath," I half-teased. "Tit for tat and all that."

He didn't answer, but those kissable lips tipped up, tempting me to go to him.

Oh, well. Maybe he's spent.

I turned around, reaching for the new toothbrush, while still sneaking in a few glances at my husband's gorgeous body as he stripped. Jesus, he had the body of a Greek god. The tan hue of his skin covered his muscles and displayed his strength.

Quickly done with my teeth, I whirled around and left the bathroom with one last glance over my shoulder at Illias. Once in the bedroom, I padded to the walk-in closet in search of some pajamas.

"Maybe some sexy lingerie," I mused out loud.

There was none though. So I fished out a pair of lacy light blue panties, and just as I was about to pull out a T-shirt, my eyes landed on Illias's organized row of shirts. I reached for one and slipped it on, leaving it unbuttoned. Then I searched through the rows and rows of ties until I found the perfect one. Silky. Blue. Matched my panties.

I put the tie on, letting it fall loosely between my breasts.

The water still ran in the shower, so I climbed on top of the bed and got myself comfortable. I waited, the cool air brushing against my sensitive nipples. My bare thighs. My barely noticeable rounder hips.

My fingers trailed down my collarbone, over my nipples and

pinched them. Hard. The way Illias does. I arched my back as my eyelids fluttered shut. A soft moan slipped from my lips. Then I pinched my other nipple, giving it the same attention.

"Fuck," I rasped. This felt good.

My pussy throbbed for the same attention. My thighs quivered. Wetness pooled, ready for my husband's cock. *Except he wants me to rest*, I thought wryly. My hand trailed down my body and into my panties. The moment my finger touched my clit, a shuddering breath left me. Blood rushed through my veins and buzzed in my ears, lighting up every single inch of my skin.

I rubbed my clit, sending shivers through my body. I spread my slickness to my entrance, then pushed one finger inside me. A disappointing shuddering breath left me. It felt nothing like when Illias fingered me.

So I returned my attention to my throbbing clit. I rubbed it, grinding my hips against my hand. I pretended it was my husband's rough hand. Circling my clit, I applied pressure on it. Pinched it. My back arched off the bed. My movements became erratic. Still stroking my clit, pure bliss bloomed in the pit of my stomach.

I remembered how it felt to have Illias ram into me with those powerful, ruthless thrusts. His groin slapped against my flesh with savagery, punishing me and giving me pleasure at the same time.

Illias's dark, filthy words echoed in my brain.

My walls clenched. My pussy ached. An electricity built deep in my core and slowly spread to my spine. A moan traveled through the air, but I only heard it as if I were submerged in water.

I was so close. Almost there.

My heart beat vigorously. Erratically. Rubbing my aching pussy desperately, in chase of that ultimate pleasure, until a hand wrapped around my wrist and stilled it.

My eyes shot open.

My husband's dark eyes, full of flames of lust, stared down at me. He was wearing only boxers and the ache between my thighs intensified tenfold. We stared at each other, my cheeks flushed, but I wasn't embarrassed.

There was no point in it.

His taut forearms and those graceful, thick fingers were so close to my aching pussy. And I knew what pleasure they could bring.

"You couldn't have waited for me?"

My eyes widened. "You said to go to sleep. I assumed you weren't interested in sex."

The soft light from the bathroom came from the corner of the room. His strong, almost harsh features spoke of dark lust. The look in his eyes was one of possession and obsession.

He inhaled deeply, letting the scent of my arousal deep into his lungs. He watched me through his half-lidded eyes.

"Who were you thinking about while touching yourself?"

"You."

The answer seemed to please him, because the disarming smile had my heart thundering against my rib cage in a whole new rhythm.

"Good girl." Holding my wrist, he pulled my hand out of my panties, then grabbed my other wrist, holding them both together in his big hand. "For that, I won't put a belt to your ass."

Oh, fuck.

My arousal thickened. My blood pumped faster.

I should be appalled at his words. Nobody had ever spanked me, never mind put a belt to my ass. Then why in the fuck did it sound so goddamn hot. Maybe it was time to visit a doctor.

He pulled his tie over my head and calmly wrapped it around my wrists.

"My dear wife, this is your first lesson," he drawled, his voice rough. Deep. Dark. "Nobody... nobody gets you off, but me." A shudder rolled through me. This was beyond crazy. I fucking liked it. He effortlessly bound my wrists in front of me with the silky blue tie. Then with one hand, he spread my legs.

"You're soaked," he groaned, his eyes lingering on my covered pussy as if he could see through my panties. I followed his gaze and saw the wet stain on my panties from my arousal. Okay, that was slightly embarrassing.

Slap.

His hand slapped my pussy. A tingly sensation pulsed through my core and spread with a need for more.

"Your arousal belongs to me, Tatiana," he growled. *Slap.* Fuck, I might orgasm and I didn't think he'd like that. He was punishing me, not rewarding me. Yet, it was stimulating, sending a tingly sensation throbbing through my core. "Do you understand?"

Closing my legs, his hand trapped between my thighs, I nodded frantically. One more slap and the pleasure would burst through me. I had no control over it.

Shifting my upper body towards him, I brought my face closer to his. His hand between my thighs burned, tempting me to grind myself against him. But I ignored it. I wanted to bring him pleasure. Then I'd beg him to fuck me.

"Let me make it up to you," I murmured, against his lips. I traced his bottom lip with my tongue. His mouth parted, letting me in, and I took the opportunity to slide my tongue in. Our lips molded. I moaned against him, my hips arching without my permission against his hand still between my thighs.

Our kissing was frantic. Desperate. Needy. Fuck, it was so hot, I feared I'd melt.

He broke the kiss, both of our breathing labored. His eyes were like dark, black pools with the promise of pleasure there would be no returning from.

"Take off your boxers," I begged, sliding off the bed.

He looked at me puzzled, slightly sardonic. "I make the rules here, moya luna."

I slid down to my knees and realization hit him. "Please, Illias. I want to taste you. You can do whatever you want to me. To my mouth. To my ass. To my pussy. My whole body."

His hand reached for my cheek, his thumb brushing it gently. Almost reverently while a look in his eyes was the one of utter devotion.

Was I just imagining it?

Either way, I realized my power while on my knees in front of him. I *was* his queen.

TWELVE
KONSTANTIN

My wife knelt in front of me, her eyes on me begging me for my cock.

Jesus H. Christ.

I had to be dreaming. When I came out of the bathroom, I just about spilled into my boxers seeing her in nothing but my shirt, tie, and those skimpy little panties. Her hand inside them as she pleasured herself.

For a moment, fury overwhelmed me, thinking she imagined someone else between her legs. In that tight cunt. But it was me she thought of. She begged for *my* cock.

A growl spilled from my lips and a carnal sense of lust hardened my dick. It was so much more than lust though. It was fucking obsession. Love. Devotion.

She was mine and I was hers.

Standing up and pushing my boxers down my legs, I watched Tatiana's pale eyes darken a shade and haze over with desire. The only time she had sucked me was that day in D.C., and I had been fantasizing about it since. It was a constant battle not to push her onto her knees and make her take my cock to the back of her throat. I loved her mouth and her sassiness, but I fucking loved her sucking my cock even more.

But I needed her to want it. To want me.

"Please, Illias, give me your cock." Tatiana's soft voice was a melody to my ears. Like she read my thoughts and knew exactly what I wanted.

Her tongue darted out, licking her lips while her eyes were level with my rock-hard cock. She leaned over and swept her tongue over the tip of my cock, licking the pre-cum.

My fingers dug into her blonde hair, gripping it roughly, as I groaned deep in my throat.

"Fuck, moya luna."

"Is that okay?" She stared up at me with those eyes, like there was nothing more she wanted to do than please me.

"Fuck yeah."

She swirled her tongue around the crown, lapping at the droplets of pre-cum. But it was her noises that were my undoing. Like sucking and licking my cock was the best thing for her. Like she loved it as much as I did.

"Mmm. I love your taste." *Holy fuck.* I might fucking spill into her mouth before I got to deep throat her. "Fuck my mouth, Illias."

I was on the verge of coming then and there. I fucking loved my wife. I had loved her for so long, I knew there was no turning back from Tatiana. And now I finally had her. The look in her eyes and her words could bring me to my knees and she didn't even know it.

She opened her mouth wider and took me to the back of her throat. She moaned, her eyes fluttering shut and it was the strongest aphrodisiac that had ever hit me. The fact that she enjoyed doing this. That she *wanted* to do this.

The dark corners of my mind and soul filled with light that only she could give me.

Fuck the chip. Fuck the Omertà. They had my oath, but she had my heart. She'd always come before anything and anyone. No matter what.

"Look at me while sucking my cock," I ordered her hoarsely. Tatiana opened those pretty blues, watching me through her heavy eyelids. Her head bobbed, sucking me and taking more and more of my cock in. My hand fisted in her hair, and I thrust to the back of her throat.

She gagged slightly. "Relax your throat. Let me own it. Like you own all of me."

She obeyed. My little rebel wife had something to say about everything, but she was meek and obedient in the bedroom. She relaxed her throat and let me use her hot mouth. I drove in and out of her wet heat. Tears welled in the corners of her eyes, but she kept sucking me in.

She accepted my thrusts, my slaps against her pussy, my slaps against her ass. The trust in her eyes gutted me. It was as if she trusted me blindly to break her, then put her back together.

My wife moaned with my cock deep in her throat, her softness in these moments stealing every single piece of me. My roughness perfectly matched her in the bedroom. But to the outer world, she would always be the queen fit to rule by my side. To level punishment to those who dared come after us.

Pulling out of her wet heat, I gave her reprieve. She sucked in a deep breath, but then darted her tongue licking the cum dripping from my cock. Fuck me. She wanted more. Gripping her hair tighter, I pounded inside her without mercy, my rhythm increasing.

"You want your husband's cock?" Thrust.

"Mmm," she sputtered around my hard dick, her eyes hazy.

"You like having your mouth fucked by me?" She let out another seductive "mmm" sound, rubbing her thighs together. "You like being mine?"

She nodded frantically, her head bobbing and her knees trembling. Her gagging sounds were music. Her eyes were notes. And her body was an instrument.

"Are you wet because I'm using your mouth this roughly?" Her moans were my answer. "Take me deep."

Her tits bounced with each thrust, her jaw widened and her tongue swirled around my painfully hard cock.

"That's it," I crooned. "Eyes on me, moya luna."

My dick pulsed. My hips thrust, tunneling deeper into her throat.

Tears glittered like diamonds on her long, pale lashes. It was the most beautiful sight. My wife. I could feel the orgasm building, my balls growing tight and heavy. I held her by her beautiful blonde hair, ramming my cock down her throat. In and out. Deep and fast.

She swallowed. Once. Twice. Sucking on my dick like her life depended on it. Even if hers didn't, mine fucking did. I fucked her mouth roughly like a man possessed, all the while her tongue rubbed the underside of my shaft.

"You'll swallow all of it," I panted. "Every single drop."

She nodded with yet another moan in her throat and the sound vibrated along my shaft. My control snapped and my balls exploded with the orgasm.

Pulling half of my cock out, I fisted it as cum spurted out. True to her word, she swallowed and kept swallowing, the drips of my cum on her chin and corners of her mouth.

"Fuck," I rasped with an animalistic groan. "You belong at my feet, my cum dripping off your chin."

Grinning, her tongue darted out, licking her lips, and true to her word, she swallowed every single drop. It was the most erotic sight I had ever seen.

"Only in the bedroom and because I want to," she replied smugly.

With a snarl, I lifted her to her feet and slammed my mouth against hers. She broke the kiss, both of us panting and I threw her on the bed. She landed on her back with a delighted squeal, her tits bouncing. She still wore my shirt, her tits on full display. I loved seeing her in my clothes, wrapped in my scent.

She turned and struggled crawling on the bed, giving me a full view of her ass, and I regretted those fucking panties blocking my view. She swayed her hips, then positioned herself on her back against her pillows.

I ripped her panties off her swollen pussy.

"My turn for dessert. Spread your legs," I ordered.

Tatiana didn't even hesitate. She parted her legs wide, letting me see her glistening pussy. The flesh was swollen and pink, tempting me. I'd eat her until she screamed for release.

Her wrists still bound with the silky blue tie, she brought the tip of it to her pussy and let it drag along her wetness. The silk brushed against her throbbing, pink folds and her back arched, but her eyes remained locked on my face.

My eyes flared. My cock was already starting to harden, eager to be inside her tight heat.

"What did I tell you about touching yourself?" I growled, ready to punish her.

Her smile was pure smugness. "I'm not touching myself. Your tie is."

The little minx. I took her tied wrists, ripping them away from her pussy. "My tie can't touch you either," I bit out, jealousy lacing my voice.

Chuckling, her eyes lit up mischievously. I fucking loved this side of her. Playful. Sexy. It reminded me of the girl in the gazebo. Before Adrian. Before all the shit that separated us.

She looped her tied wrists around my neck. "Then, Mr. Konstantin, you better get to work," she suggested seductively. "And make this honeymoon memorable."

A dark chuckle vibrated in my chest. I didn't know whether to punish her or make her scream my name.

Kneeling on the mattress, I stared at her cunt, open for my taking. Tempting me with her scent and juices that made my mouth water.

I cupped her pussy harshly. "Whose cunt is this?"

"Yours." No hesitance. No resistance. "Now will you just fuck me. Hard." Fuck, maybe my wife was just as depraved as I was.

"That's right," I purred, her arousal coating my fingers.

Wedging myself between her thighs, I lowered myself until my stomach met the mattress and then proceeded to lick her from her entrance to her clit. She shuddered, arching her back and grinding her pussy against my face.

"I love the stubble of your beard against my pussy," she breathed, burying her fingers into my hair and that fucking tie at my neck. I'd have to buy better bondage equipment. I sensed a lot of lessons for my wife in the future.

Without mercy, I feasted on her pussy, laving her harshly. Hooking her legs over my shoulders, I buried my face deeper into her cunt where only she existed and that scent of roses. I nipped her clit, punishing her for making me lose all semblance of control. With her, it was pointless to hold on to it.

She crept deep into my soul and under my skin. She became part of my heart and my bones. There was no extracting her. She was intoxicating, the scent of her arousal making my mouth water. My chest heaved, my mouth on her soft skin.

I ravished her pussy, teasing her throbbing clit. Her fingers threaded through my hair, gripping my strands. Together we were fire. We both wanted this. The question was, when the truth came out, whether we'd burn to ash.

Thrusting my tongue inside her, her back arched off the mattress and her tits pushed up. Fuck, they were perfection. It might be fucked up, but I couldn't wait to see them fill with milk for our baby. To see her belly swell with our child. If I had to, I'd keep her pregnant so she'd never leave me.

A satisfied growl vibrated through me and against her pussy.

"Fuck, Illias," she moaned. "Yes, yes. Ohhh…"

I nipped her clit again, massaging it with my tongue, then I drew it into my mouth and sucked on the swollen sensitive nub. Her thighs trembled. Her hips ground against my mouth, her movements jerky. I thrust my tongue in and out of her, tongue-fucking her.

"Oh my God," she breathed. "Don't stop, please. I'm going… Oh, oh, oh…"

Her scream of pleasure pierced the air, pushing her pussy into my mouth while her fingers gripped my hair. If there was a way to go, this would be a perfect way to die. Being smothered by her pussy.

The gush of her juices soaked my tongue and I licked her clean and she trembled while her slim, long legs wrapped around my neck. She shuddered, those small tremors telling me this impacted her as much as me.

I rose over her, positioning us in the missionary position.

"Ready for another round, moya luna?" I groaned against her lips, my dick painfully hard.

Without giving her time to answer, I shoved inside her in one powerful thrust.

"Ahhhh..." She struggled to breathe and I stilled.

"You okay?" I stroked her face, those eyes glimmering like sapphires. She opened her legs wider, the soles of her feet digging into the backs of my thighs.

She arched off the bed, her lips seeking out mine. Fuck, she felt so good. Her cunt gripped my cock, and it felt like heaven. Every single piece of her felt like home. "Don't stop," she breathed against my lips. "I l-love y-you..." My heart stilled. My chest swelled. My ears buzzed. "...inside me."

Disappointment rushed through me, like a rapid river. It tasted bitter. But I pushed it away. It was too soon. In time, it would come.

So I made love to my wife. Her slickness welcomed me. Her hips arched against me. I moved in and out of her tight heat, strangling my dick. I kept my pace slow and unhurried. Each thrust inside her was like coming home.

"Oh, Illias..." Her eyes hazed. Her lips parted.

I powered into her body with deep, long thrusts. I rolled my hips, letting her feel my every stroke, hitting her G-spot. My hands were all over her. Squeezing her tits. Grabbing her ass. Digging my fingers into her soft hips, I pulled out, leaving the tip of my dick in her hot entrance.

Our lips brushed, my tongue slid inside her mouth. I kissed her with the same rhythm of my thrusts, my tongue sliding in and out of her mouth. Then my mouth trailed down her chin, nipping and marking. I kissed her delicate neck, sucking on her tender flesh.

I feasted on her tight nipples, thrusting in and out of her. Her sexy, throaty moans encouraged me forward while her inner muscles milked me, strangling my cock.

"Illias... oh, God..." She panted. "Please untie me. I want to touch you."

In one swift move, I removed her bindings and her hands wrapped around me. Her nails clawed at me. I pushed inside her, losing control. Each thrust was rougher than the last. I powered in and out of her while she throbbed around me.

My blood rushed through my veins, relishing in the feel of her heat as she milked me. Her eyes shut, her mouth parted, and she cried out as she came undone. The rush of hearing her cries of pleasure had my blood rushing through my veins and down to my groin.

Her nails clawed at my back, drawing my own orgasm out. My groan reverberated around the room as I spurted cum inside her. It filled her pussy, the overflow dripping all over her. The buzz spread through my veins, entered my brain, and had me out of my mind with this animalistic sense of ownership.

Tatiana was the only one who drew this out of me. The connection between us was deep, dark, and so fucking overwhelming that it shook me to my core.

A deep, contented sigh slipped from my wife's lips and she snuggled into me, my dick still buried inside her.

It was where I was meant to be all along.

I watched my wife sleep as the first rays of dawn flickered through the windows, shining over her golden hair. She looked like a soft angel when she slept, but when awake, she could be a vengeful queen.

Tatiana understood the family unit.

She'd lived it. She'd breathed it. It was part of her DNA.

Maybe it was those invisible strings that connected us. Yes, there was physical attraction, but it went beyond that. She might be the Nikolaev baby sister but she had that strength about her. Underneath her rebellious nature. Underneath that slightly unhinged Nikolaev way.

Even surrounded by guns and men who caused most adult people to piss themselves, she'd threatened them as she tried to revive Adrian.

The night of Adrian's death played in my mind as I watched her sleep, that light blonde hair spread on my chest like a halo. She was the most peculiar combination of an angel, fighter, and rebel. Sometimes it fucking hurt to look at her, especially like this. When she slept. It reminded me of the night I took her to the hospital. When I thought I'd lost her.

In my entire life, I had never experienced that kind of fear. I witnessed my own mother killed at six and that didn't scratch the surface of the fear I had of losing Tatiana.

I remembered how each heartbeat felt like a knife in my chest as the car sped through Louisiana to where I tracked Marchetti.

"Speed up," I barked at Nikita in a cold tone.

The dark streets of New Orleans's suburbs were ominous and reminded me of another fatal night so many years ago. The night that started it all. Adrian's hate for us.

If Marchetti got to them before us, Tatiana would be dead right alongside Adrian. Just for being with him. Marchetti never left loose ends, and regardless of what Tatiana knew or didn't know, she was a loose end.

Nikita pressed harder on the gas, the engine roaring louder as we sped down the highway. Not even the moon was our friend. It was a perfect Halloween night.

The first flicker of lights in the distance had my pulse leaping.

"There." I pointed to the side of the road. Fuck, Marchetti was here already. The car was upside down. Where in the fuck was Tatiana?

The car came screeching to a stop, and I was out before the engine even stopped.

"Kill him," Marchetti ordered. Adrian stood all bloodied in front of him, but alive. Just surface bruises. Then whose blood was it. My eyes frantically searched around until a glimpse of light gold strands against the car window caught my eye.

"They both have to die," Marchetti commanded in that unemotional voice, his expression dark. He valued his work from the shadows above all else. It kept his family protected, although for generations Marchetti's women ended up dead.

"No," I gritted and his eyes finally came to mine. "You touch her

and I'm out." His eyes narrowed on me. It was a risk, but I'd take it. For her, I fucking would. "And don't forget her unhinged brothers."

"You can control them," Marchetti answered, putting his hand in his suit.

"But I won't," I said coldly. "If you kill her, they can go hunting you for all I care."

Adrian laughed. Maniacally. Sardonic.

He spit on the ground, blood and saliva mixing in his mouth. "You fucking Konstantins always have to get your way."

"And you, fucker, should have never come after us," I growled. "You had to drag your wife into it."

"My wife," he hissed. "Remember that."

Red mist worked into my vision. My blood roared in my ears. I reacted and punched him in the face. Hard.

"End him," I hissed.

Bang.

It was that simple. Adrian's body fell to the ground, blood seeped through his shirt, spreading like a red lake.

"I fucking vouch for her, Marchetti." The anger vibrated through my voice, my veins electrified with it. If I had to kill every member of the Omertà myself, I'd do it. For her, I'd do anything. "If she has the chip, I'll retrieve it. If she was part of it, I'll handle it."

Adrian bled on the ground. He might already be dead, I didn't give a shit. Tatiana Nikolaev was my only concern.

"Fine." The invisible rope around my chest eased up and oxygen flooded back into my brain. Thank fuck. Fighting Marchetti wasn't on my agenda. I had to get Tatiana to the hospital.

I rushed to the flipped car. I'd done my share of killing. Blood was never an issue. But seeing the blood staining Tatiana's pale blonde hair from the open split on her forehead was something else entirely. I was ready to lose my fucking mind seeing her in that state.

Kneeling on the dirty gravel, I extended my hand and reached for her.

"Grab my hand," I urged her.

The look in her eyes, full of trust and desperation, was like a punch in the gut. The fighter and rebel vanished in front of my eyes, being replaced by fear.

She shifted, reaching for my hand. She strained against the airbag.

Losing her strength, she slumped, her face stained with blood, dirt, and tears. "You can do it. Don't you fucking give up."

It was one thing this woman never did. She wasn't the type to give up.

I leaned closer and growled, "Give me your hand, moya luna. Don't you fucking give up."

Her shoulder was fucked up too. Goddamn it. She was in a bad state. She reached out again for me. She kept trying, a frustrated cry leaving her lips.

"I don't want to die," she whimpered.

The words sliced through my chest. Her pain felt like my own. My fucking heart and soul were so attuned to hers. Yes, I barely crossed her mind, but she was always on my mind.

"You're not dying," I hissed with determination. I'd hunt down God if he dared take her away from me. "Just another inch and I got you."

She pushed herself, wincing as she tried. She looked fucking battered and fury swelled in my chest all over again. I wanted to punish Adrian for putting her in that position. He should have left her and then gone after his fucking revenge.

Our fingers brushed and her exhale shattered through the tension in my bones. I wrapped my fingers around hers. Then I held on.

For her. For me. For us.

Because it was always meant to be us.

"I'm pulling you out," I said with determination. "It might hurt. Whatever you do, never let go. Understood?"

She nodded, gritting her teeth. She was in pain, but I had to do this before the car went up in flames.

"You're doing well," I praised, gritting my teeth as a piece of glass sliced into my forearm. I tried to shift my arm to ensure it didn't cut into her.

"You're bleeding," she murmured.

"Don't worry about that," I hissed. "I'm fine. Let's get you out."

I let out a string of curses as I saw a piece of glass cut into Tatiana's arm. There was too much of it everywhere to keep it away from her. It cut into her flesh, blood gushing out of her forearm. Or was that my blood dripping down on her? I hoped it was the latter, but the way she clenched her teeth, stifling her whimper of pain, told me it was her cut and her own blood.

"Come on, moya luna," I ground out, pulling her body. It terrified me that she might have fatal internal injuries that I couldn't see. I had to get her to the hospital.

She crawled up, glass cutting into her knees but it gave me just enough access to her. I put my hands around her waist and lifted her out of the burning car.

The scent of roses and ash filled my lungs, mixing with the terror of almost losing her. I wrapped my arms around her. She buried her face in my chest, the mixture of pale golden hair stained with blood brushing against my three-piece suit. Her fingers curled into my jacket, gripping it tightly.

"Thank you," she muttered against my chest. Her body shuddered and my palms roamed her back, hoping to soothe her. It gutted me to see her so shaken up.

She pushed her face away from my chest while her hands remained on my chest, gripping my suit like it was her lifeline. Slowly, her eyes darted around. Marchetti. Agosti. Our men. Nikita. Boris.

Then lowered to the ground. "Adrian!" she screamed.

I took her chin. "Don't look."

She pushed me away with so much force, she almost stumbled back and would have fallen if I hadn't caught her. She slapped my hand away, taking another step back.

"Don't you fucking touch me," she hissed, her eyes on Adrian's body on the ground.

Then she fell down on her knees. Her bloody fingers shook badly as she crawled over the gravel, reaching for Adrian's dead body.

Her fingers searched frantically for his pulse, pressing against the vein on his neck. Then his wrist.

"Adrian, please," she cried, and fuck if it didn't hurt seeing her like that. I didn't like to see her upset. Yes, the bastard deserved death but she didn't deserve the pain. She leaned over him, her lips pressing on his. I fucking hated the sight of it. My hands clenched into fists and it took all my control not to yank her from him. "Please, please, please." Her voice was a raspy whisper. "Wake up," she pleaded, cupping his head. Her tears, a mixture of blood and dirt, stained her face. "Wake up."

She shook his body, but there was no waking him up. He was dead. My father's words swept through my mind as the wind picked up.

Boys grow up to become men. They come back to find you, and suddenly, the hunter becomes the hunted.

He was right. If I had let my father do what he needed, Adrian would have never come to be. It would have saved us all this bullshit. And Tatiana her pain.

She leaned over and started performing CPR. One. Two. Three. She breathed air into his lungs. One. Two. Three. "Breathe," she screamed. She repeated the procedure. Over and over again.

Her eyes lifted, darting around desperately. Frantically.

"Please, help me," she screamed her plea. "Please. Just one breath and then I can save him."

She sobbed, pressing her palm on his chest where he had been shot mere minutes ago. She attempted to stop the bleeding. It was pointless but she refused to give up.

"Adrian, please wake up," she murmured, pressing her forehead against his. "P-please wake up. P-p-please. Come back to me," she choked.

It was for naught. The fire from the car was expanding, but when Tatiana lifted her eyes, it had nothing on the inferno burning in her gaze. She screamed, devastation vibrating through her and traveling through the air. She raised her bloodied hands and gripped her hair, ignoring her injured shoulder.

I took a step towards her but the hate in her eyes stopped me. There was raw rage there and it was aimed at me. At us.

She rose to her feet. Her body was in bad shape. Cuts, bruises, and *who knew what else had her unsteady on her feet. I closed the distance and took her elbow, holding her up. She jerked away, then her small fists came to my chest. She hit me. Then another punch landed. Her small fists started pounding on my chest. Over and over again.*

"You killed him," she shouted, tears streaming down her beautiful beaten face. "You did it."

I grabbed her forearm and shook her, pulling her to me. She didn't seem fazed, her rage feeding her actions and her next words. Her fists curled into my jacket.

"I'm going to kill you for this," she vowed with such calmness I feared she meant it. Her gaze traveled over all of us. Her eyes were unfocused. She blinked hard. She was losing her strength fast. "I'm going to kill you all for this."

Her body slumped and I scooped her up. The fire surrounding the car spread.

"We have to go," I ordered. "The car is about to blow."

We all rushed towards our respective vehicles. Mine was parked right next to Marchetti's, and as Boris opened my door, Marchetti's voice stopped me.

"Are you sure it's smart to keep her alive?" he asked, his voice casual. "I don't doubt she meant her vow."

In that very moment I realized, even if she worked with Adrian against me, I'd protect her.

Life without her would be abhorrent.

A warm body pushed into me, almost snuggling, and pulled me out of the memories. I watched her, taking in her soft features when she slept. Her full lips were relaxed, a small smile on her lips almost as if she were happy.

Was she happy?

It was hard to tell with Tatiana. She was a contradiction through and through. Strength and kindness. Rebel and diplomat. I intended to dissect every single inch of her and understand everything that drove her.

Her flushed cheeks tempted me. I loved seeing that color against the paleness of her skin. The scent of roses became a permanent association to her. It no longer represented betrayal. It no longer represented my mother.

Only Tatiana.

Since my mother's betrayal, the boy was forced to grow up and become a man. Truthfully, I wasn't ready but the choice was taken away. One thing I had that my father didn't have was a cool head. I lacked the irrationality and impulsiveness of my father.

Until Tatiana.

My eyes traveled over her soft curves. My child grew within her belly. That alone drove my dark obsession into madness.

Taking a soft strand of her hair between my fingers, I inhaled it like it was my own aphrodisiac. The scent of roses slammed into my lungs and carved a permanent place there. She and our child would forever be part of me.

Our child.

Simple two words, but they had the power to make me and break me. There was only one other statement that would hit me as hard.

Hearing Tatiana utter those three little words that made the world turn.

THIRTEEN
TATIANA

Bright light filtered into the room, a streak of white reflecting against the snow waking me from my deep sleep. I checked the time against the red digits of the clock and was shocked when I noted the time.

Eleven a.m.

But then I remembered. I was in Russia. It always took me several days to adjust to the time difference. Unlike my brothers.

I rolled onto my back, every muscle in my body sore, and reached for Illias, only to find an empty bed. The sheets were cold. I sighed, slightly disappointed. But then, I'd wager that Illias wasn't a man to lounge in bed for half a day.

Sighing, I stretched out my hands and studied the ceiling. The same one that royalty studied for centuries. How many princes and princesses stared at the same ceiling?

Excitement rushed through me. I couldn't wait to explore the castle.

I jumped out of bed, then headed for the shower. Twenty minutes later, I was dressed in a La Perla bra and panties and a white wool dress. Slipping on a pair of black Chanel flats, I made my way out of the room.

The castle was quiet. The chill in the air present.

It didn't matter how many fires burned and how good the central heat system was, there was no warming up a Russian home. Especially one this size. I'd experienced that in our own home in Siberia. Even in Russian hotels. It was just the way it was.

I slipped through the corridor, studying the paintings. Aivazovsky. Repin. Malevich. Only to finish it with Leonardo da Vinci, Michelangelo, Monet, and...

My step faltered and my eyes widened. A ten-by-ten-size painting of a family portrait. I recognized the twin brothers, both resembling their father. But it was the beautiful woman who captured my interest. Blonde hair. Sad green eyes. I'd seen her before. With a different family.

It was the same woman from Adrian's picture that I dug out of that parking lot. What-the-fuck! Maybe I should be asking myself how the fuck that was even possible? I dug through my memory, trying to remember what I knew of the late Pakhan's wife.

The answer was nothing. I came up empty.

I stared at the woman, the unexpected connection. I'd have to believe that woman was Illias's mother. Otherwise, why the family portrait? Shit, maybe that other photo that Adrian left me wasn't his family. But that man with her was the spitting image of Adrian with the exception of the eyes.

A gasp left my lips and I leaned closer to the painting. Adrian's eyes were green, the same shade as this woman's. My brows creased and my temples throbbed. *C-could it be...* I shook my head. No way. No fucking way.

Pushing the thoughts away, I headed for the grand staircase. But the painting never left my mind.

The smell of baked pastries entered my lungs as I started my descent with my hand on the rail and my mind on the strange revelation.

My stomach growled. I was starving and prayed Illias had enough sense not to have his cook make traditional Russian dishes. Those usually involved meat and it was something I still couldn't stomach.

The sound of voices traveled through the air, distracting me from food. Straying to the left, the voices got stronger and louder.

"Are you fucking blind?" Illias's voice boomed. "The Yakuza must want to take over. Amon could be the solution to it all. You allowing Dante to marry that girl will push him away from the Thorns of Omertà. We'll lose his support, Marchetti."

My brows furrowed. Why would Enrico Marchetti care about Yakuza? Or anything Omertà related?

"My approval has been given." Marchetti had to be on the phone. "The wedding has been set."

No fucking way. Marchetti was involved in the underworld? Well, that was... unexpected.

"Fuck that shit, Enrico." Illias was majorly pissed from the sound of it. "Have his other daughter take her spot."

"He wants Reina. You should have told me earlier Amon had eyes for her. How in the fuck was I supposed to know?"

"Goddamn it, Marchetti. Then end it," Illias growled. "The Yakuza have tried to take us down way too many times. With that chip, they'd succeed." Illias's tone was low and dark. Deadly. "With Amon, they'll succeed."

Amon Leone? Did he work for Illias? I really needed the structure of Illias's organization. It was way too confusing.

"What's done is done," was Marchetti's response. "No more of that." It was clear by the equally dark tone of his voice the conversation was over. "Speaking of weddings, it was good thinking on your part to wed Tatiana Nikolaev. I bet you planned to get her pregnant. Tatiana knocked up gives you leverage with this latest discovery and over her psychotic brothers."

My chest cracked and an unbearable ache slashed through me. A burn ignited somewhere deep in my heart and spread wide, until it had nowhere else to go. Until it seared those fragile, invisible threads that had started weaving between us and left nothing but thorns.

Leverage. Planned to knock me up.

The words echoed in my brain on a broken loop. He used me. *Leverage.* My ears rang, drowning out my heartbeat. My skin flushed hot, then cold. My soul ached but tears didn't come. I refused to mourn a deceitful, lying, son of a bitch.

I'm going to murder that motherfucker. Just wait and see.

All I had to do was call Sasha and he'd help me take Illias down. Pakhan or no. Yet, the idea of Illias dead didn't sit well with me. The thought of seeing the life leave his eyes sent a cold chill through my veins.

Fuck!

Maybe some torture. I'd have to think of something good. Maybe I'd bite his dick when I sucked him off. I snickered. Now, that would be funny.

A loud thud vibrated through the air, waking me out of my stupor.

"Hey, Tatiana." A cheerful voice came from behind me at the same time and I whirled around to find Isla coming down the stairs. "You looking for the dining room?"

No, I'm looking for a way to kill your traitorous brother. Thankfully, the words remained unspoken.

"Actually, I was thinking about taking a drive," I managed to answer, hiding all my emotions. "Maybe pick up something from the nearby bakery. Want to come along?"

The look she gave me told me she thought it was crazy to want to go out driving in the snow when there was perfectly good pastry in the castle.

"Sure." Her answer surprised me, but I didn't show it.

"Lead the way to the garage, then."

We walked in silence down the elegant hallway. Both of us grabbed a coat, then continued down the hallway. It seemed we walked for miles with a lot of twists and turns, although it was mere steps. I was so desperate to silence the words I overheard. They kept playing on repeat in my head, but I couldn't think of a single question to ask Isla to distract myself.

"How was your first night here?" Isla inquired as we strode down the hallway. My eyes traveled over her. She looked even younger wearing jeans and an oversized emerald sweater that made her eyes stand out even more.

"It was good, thanks." I threw her a side-glance. Her smile was soft, but there was silent strength about her. Yet, my mind whispered not to get too close. Her brother manipulated me. *Leverage.* That fucking word. "You live here?"

She chuckled. "God no. It is so cold in Russia during the winter months and those months are damn long. I split most of the time between Paris, London, and California."

It was too bad. I already knew I'd like her. There was a warmth about her that kind of reminded me of my best friend. Isabella was so caring and thoughtful, but underneath it all, there was a quiet strength that was hard not to notice.

"Don't care for Russia?" Isla asked curiously. She still wasn't sure what to make of me, and I couldn't blame her. She probably never even heard of me and then boom… I was her sister-in-law.

Not for long though.

I shrugged, keeping track of the turns so I'd know how to get out of this castle. "I was born here but raised in New Orleans. I prefer to stay there. It's home."

She nodded. "Have you and Illias known each other for a long time?"

"Depends on what you consider a long time," I remarked automatically. "We crossed paths many years ago." Silence followed as I remembered that fleeting moment in California when I joined my brother for lunch. He and his brother left minutes later. "He didn't leave an impression."

It was a lie. Yes, I forgot him, but I remembered that first moment I locked eyes with him. His eyes penetrated mine for a few seconds, full of intense darkness.

Isla chuckled. "Yet, here you are."

"Yet, here I am," I concurred. Fuck, did my voice sound a tad bit bitter. "Your brother is persistent."

"That he is," she agreed. "Although I'm surprised it took him years to leave an impression. Usually women fall at his feet."

A memory came. My steps halted and my brows furrowed as

confusion rushed through me. That was Adrian's memory. My first time with my late husband.

Yet, why was I thinking about it and associating it with Illias?

Adrian disappeared through the entrance gripping the twins by their collars. Frustrated, I scribbled a note on a piece of napkin and handed it to the waiter.

"Can you give this note to the gentleman when he comes through the door?"

And with that, I whirled around and headed out the patio door and out to the gazebo that stood on the far end of the property, overlooking Patapsco River.

It was my last year of college. If I didn't get a man now, I never would. I loved my brothers but they growled when a boy even looked at me, never mind anything else. It scared them all away.

So, I'd demand what I wanted. What I needed! I'd never been shy and I knew Adrian could give me what I'd been missing my whole life.

I decided that I'd seize the moment. I should feel bad that the twins got in trouble, but truthfully, they weren't my type. And letting both of them kiss me at the same time had done little for me. It should have turned me on beyond my wildest dreams, yet I found my panties dry.

Adrian was probably still busy roughing the twins up, but I hoped he'd see the message.

Soon.

I kept pacing around, impatient to get our evening going. Heavy footsteps sounded behind me and I stilled. I stared at the only closed part of the gazebo, my heart thundering wildly. My nipples tightened. My thighs clenched and arousal trickled down my inner thighs. God, he hadn't even touched me, and I was drenched.

A hand came over my bare shoulder and I tried to turn around when his other hand wrapped around my waist and pushed me towards the wall.

"I'll make you moan. Follow my rules."

A shudder erupted beneath my skin, warm from his touch. His hard body pressed against my back and his hot breath against my ear.

"Do you consent?" His voice was accented, dark and heavy. I never heard Adrian's Russian so prominent.

"Yes." Anyone in their right mind would consent to such a sensual, seductive voice. He was already binding my hands with something soft.

His scent enveloped me. He must have changed his cologne, because his scent of leather was replaced with the unique, probably custom-made cologne. It smelled of citrus mingled with spice and sandalwood.

It was like there was an aphrodisiac in it. It kicked up my desire several notches, soaking my panties with my arousal. His hand on my waist gripped the skirt of my dress and yanked it up. Goose bumps broke over my skin as the cool air touched my flesh. My thong left little to the imagination.

His groan vibrated against my back and as his fingers cupped my ass and squeezed it hard. His touch was dominant and confident. It felt so good.

I felt his lips against the curve of my neck, marking me. I turned my head, wanting to see his face but he wrapped a hand around my throat and pressed his chest against my back. His scent washed over me and his length pressed against my back. If that was any indication of his length, he was big.

My breaths came out in small pants. Moans and whimpers. Releasing my throat, his fingers gripped my hair and forced me to bend over a few inches, then his foot nudged mine.

"Open for me, moya luna."

He barely finished the sentence and I spread my legs for him. Eagerly.

"Please," I moaned.

He let go of my hair and his hand slid between my thighs. "So soaked," he grunted, sending a shudder down my back.

In one move, he shredded my thong off my hips and then traced his finger over my pussy drenched with my slickness. When his fingers brushed over my clit, a violent shudder tore through me.

"Ahhhh." We barely got started and I was ready to fall apart. His expert touch kept teasing me with slow circles over my clit before

plunging a thick finger inside me. "Please. More," I breathed with a desperate edge to my voice.

"You want me inside you?" he demanded to know with a growl.

"Yes," I moaned. "I need you inside me. Please."

His growl of satisfaction vibrated against my earlobe as he continued finger-fucking me, teasing my clit while his finger thrust in and out of me. The imminent orgasm only stoked the fire inside me.

He removed his hand as my body still shuddered but only for a second. The crinkle of foil reached my ears as he tore open a condom. My skirt still bunched around my waist, he poised the tip of his cock at my hot entrance. In a single thrust, he plunged forward and buried himself deep inside me.

A scream tore through me. My virginity gone.

I sucked in a ragged breath as he stretched me, pain overtaking my pleasure.

"Fuck," he grunted.

"Don't you fucking dare stop," I hissed. I could feel his surprise in the way he tensed. "Make it good."

"Your wish is my command," he rasped.

Slowly he pulled out, only to plunge inside again. Initially he moved slowly, letting me adjust to his size. My insides clenched all around his shaft, greedily taking him in. I wanted more of him. I wanted his unleashed desire. With each thrust, my moans turned louder. He released my waist and brought his hand over my mouth. He fucked me hard and fast. Each thrust allowed him deeper inside me. A scream bubbled on my lips and I muffled it by biting into his hand, my teeth digging into his palm.

His teeth scraped the soft skin on my neck, then sucked to ease the sting. Pain and pleasure mixed, blurring the lines and I no longer knew where one ended and the other started. The orgasm shattered through me like an avalanche, but he didn't stop fucking me. He kept thrusting through my orgasm, my cries turning into screams as he fucked me harder and deeper.

My inner muscles clamped around his thick cock and he shuddered with a grunt, finding his own release. This was fucking incredible.

Fuck virginity and fuck everything. I wanted to marry this man and have sex like this for the rest of my life.

"Mine," he rasped. "You'll always be mine."

Simple words. Simple claim. Simple truth.

I always wanted to be his. I leaned against the wall of the gazebo, my legs slightly unstable as he pulled out of me. It took me a few minutes to put myself back together, but when I turned around, he was gone.

"Tatiana, are you okay?" Isla's voice pulled me away as the memory danced before me and something nudged the back of my mind. A thought I couldn't quite grasp. "Tatiana?"

Isla shook my hand lightly, squeezing my fingers.

I blinked, catching her worried gaze. I forced a smile to my lips, not wanting to worry her.

"Yes, I'm fine," I assured her. "I'm sorry. I just remembered something, and it caught me by surprise."

Her gaze studied me, and suddenly, I knew this girl saw and knew more than her big brother gave her credit for. The question was how much more.

We took the last turn and arrived at the end of the hallway and Isla pressed a button. "Elevator?" I asked incredulously.

She rolled her eyes. "I know. Like he didn't have enough space to make a parking lot. He insisted on the parking garage."

What Illias wants; Illias gets. Apparently.

The elevator door opened and we both stepped into it. She pressed another button and swiftly we were taken two floors below. The doors opened, and the two of us stepped out. I shook my head. All the men in the underworld had one common trait.

They all loved their stupid cars.

Rows and rows of parked cars. Maserati. Range Rovers. Land Rover Defenders. Mercedes G-Benz. Bugatti.

"Does he realize snow and sports cars don't go together?" I muttered.

"He has one of these on every continent," Isla grumbled. Apparently she wasn't a fan either. She led me to the Land Rover. "This one has bulletproof windows," she remarked.

"Well, I guess we'll be safe getting pastries," I remarked dryly.

Just as we reached the vehicle and my hand came to rest on the handle, a voice startled both of us.

"Where are you going?"

The voice had both of us turning around. Two guards were leaning against the wall on the far side of the wall. My eyes shifted around, wondering where they came from.

"That's where the elevator is that leads to the other side of the house," Isla remarked quietly. "We're going to pick up something and we'll be right back," she shouted to the guards.

Two of the guards shifted off the wall and strode over to us. I studied them, surprised to see they looked to be of Asian descent. Maybe Mongolian. I couldn't quite distinguish. Somehow I found it surprising. So far, I'd only seen Russian men surrounding Illias.

"Boss said to wait for him," one of them remarked. A cigarette dangled from his mouth and moved as he spoke. "Nobody is to go anywhere without him."

I watched the cigarette move up and down, his eyes traveling over me. Then he did the same with Isla. She shifted uncomfortably, glancing my way while the guard kept leering at her. I didn't like it.

Narrowing my eyes on him, I took Isla's hand and shoved her behind me. "We are not nobody. We don't need your boss to dictate what we do," I told him coldly. Then because I couldn't resist, I added, "Don't forget we are your boss's boss. And you better watch yourself, or you'll lose your eyeballs."

He sneered, then advanced further, each step bringing him closer to us. It would seem the "boss's boss" card didn't seem to impress him.

"Who is this fucker?" I hissed quietly.

"I've never seen him before," Isla muttered under her breath. "Usually they are never so rude."

Blocking the view of Isla with my body, I kept my eyes on him. I could take him. He was lean, as tall as I was. High cheekbones. A scar across his left cheek. Hair as dark as midnight. But his eyes kept throwing me off. They were blue.

With each step he neared us, I sensed something was off about him.

"Let's get you to the boss," he ordered, grabbing my elbow. His fingers dug into my skin to the point of pain. The expression on his face was murderous. Like he blamed me for something, and I didn't even know what.

"You can't touch her," Isla scolded him, trying to maneuver herself around me and get in front of me. I blocked her way. The other guard muttered something low, but I couldn't understand the language. It almost sounded like... Japanese? No, it couldn't be.

"Move it," the fucker growled, shoving me. I attempted to shove him back. Unsuccessfully. God, he might be thin but he was strong. All muscles. His looks were definitely deceiving.

"Let go," I hissed, attempting to jerk my arm out of his grip.

"Or what?" he scoffed.

I was just about to open my mouth when a voice lashed through the air.

"Take your hands off my wife." Harshness and the cold tenor in Illias's voice sent a shiver down my spine. Goose bumps rose on my skin. My eyes flickered over him, but he kept his gaze locked on the two guards. "If I have to say it again, your death will be very long and painful."

The two guards shared a look and I acted on instinct. One reached for Isla, the other already had his hands on me. I pushed Isla and she stumbled out of the way, her eyes widening in horror that I'd do something like that. The guard that went after her only caught empty air.

But it gave Illias enough time to act. *Bang.*

The next thing happened so fast but my brain processed it in slow motion. Isla's scream filled the underground garage. The guard fell on the ground with a grunt, blood pooling around him. He was wounded, not dead. The other guard pulled me closer to him while I fought him, his chest flat at my back and his gun at my temple.

More guards came swarming in. Illias's gun was trained on the man holding me hostage. He took a step forward, my captor took one back.

"You're not getting out of this alive." Illias words were colder than the temperatures outside. My heart beat hard against my ribs, threatening to crack them. My hands covered my lower belly instinctively worried for the baby that had barely reached a few months of life inside me.

My husband didn't look at me. His dark eyes were trained on the man behind me. His face was a brutal, cold mask that I had never seen before. This was the Pakhan that men feared. This was who Vasili warned me against, but I had never seen this side of him.

Not until now.

I stood stiff, waiting for a sign. Any sign. There was no chance in hell that I wouldn't get caught in the crossfire if Illias and the idiot behind me started to shoot.

So I took matters into my own hands.

First I said a prayer, even though I wasn't particularly religious. It didn't hurt to get a little extra help from up above. Sasha had taught me self-defense since I was a little girl. Of course, the last time I used it against the Yakuza guy in the alley, it didn't work out that great. But I just needed a little window, and Illias would take care of the rest.

Locking gazes with my husband, I tried to convey a wordless message. I blinked, swallowing the lump in my throat with a barely noticeable nod. I relaxed my body, keeping my breathing even. I needed to hit his ribs with enough force and his grip on me would loosen enough for me to get away from him. A deep breath. Exhale.

With all my strength, I elbowed him into the side of his ribs, then kneeled down on the ground, protecting my stomach with my knees and covering my ears and squeezing my eyes shut.

Bang. Bang.

Two shots. Warm liquid splattered over my face. I kept my eyes shut, stiff in my position. Scared to move.

"Moya luna." That deep, familiar voice was close. A pair of warm hands on my face. "Open your eyes."

I did, the world seemed red, so I blinked. A drop of blood dripped off my lashes and trickled down my cheek. Suddenly I wondered if our story maybe didn't start with blood. The question was whether it would end with it too.

He held my face between his palms, worry etched on his beautiful face made of granite. I was unsure which side of him was true anymore. The one who made my body fall apart at night. The one who saved me—twice now. The one who stared the enemy in the eye. Or the one who used me for leverage?

"Are you okay?" he asked. "How are you feeling?'

"Fine," I muttered, pulling away from him and rising to my feet. I couldn't look at him. Not yet. Not after hearing those words between him and Marchetti. Not after what had just happened. He brought me to Russia to keep me safe, and he had enemies in his own home.

How could he possibly protect me and our child if he couldn't trust his guards?

As bad as it sounded, I didn't care that he shot someone. In our world, it was kill or be killed. Isabella struggled with it. I never did. However, I struggled with being used and being manipulated.

I smoothed my dress down, blood from the dress staining my fingers. My white wool dress had blood splashed all over it. My breathing was high-pitched, but strangely my mind was calm. Or maybe that was the shock.

My eyes darted to Isla who stood five feet away with two men next to her. Her face was pale and her gaze slightly frantic.

"Maybe no outside pastries today?" I said, my voice strange to my own ears.

Isla swallowed, then nodded. Flicking a glance at the two men on the ground, I strode to my sister-in-law without another glance at my husband.

I knew what he'd do next. After all, he wasn't that unpredictable.

FOURTEEN
KONSTANTIN

He held a gun to my wife's head.

It was all I could think about as the doctor patched up the intruder that wasn't killed. They didn't work for me. I knew every single one of my men, and these two were not my men. Which brought me to the only conclusion I could come to.

I had a traitor among my men.

My knuckles were bruised and bleeding. I didn't feel the pain. Maybe it was the adrenaline running through my veins. Or maybe I was so fucking numb from the realization that I could have lost her.

One fucking day after wedding her.

I rolled up my sleeves, hiding the bloodstains on my shirt.

"You're a mess and getting blood all over me," I said coldly while my insides boiled. "Now, I want to know who let you in and what your plan was."

One guy was already dead, but the guy that held the gun to Tatiana's temple had the honor of having his life extended. I'd make him regret ever stepping foot anywhere near a Konstantin.

Each time I pictured his gun against her head and Tatiana's hands covering her lower belly, protecting our baby, rage overwhelmed me. I had to punish him more. So I hit him again. And again. And again.

Boris and Nikita stood behind me, leaning against the wall. They knew this was my punishment to extract.

"Who let you in?"

He glared at me, his expression furious beneath all the blood and bruises. He was tied to a chair, his arms and legs bound with rope. Underneath my garage, I had a special place for those who attempted to hurt my family. It hadn't been used for a long time since nobody dared.

"For the last time, who let you in?" I gritted.

Blood hit the concrete floor in a steady *drip, drip, drip*. There was a lot of it, ruining my suit and my shoes. Isla would be terrified to see me in this state, but Tatiana probably wouldn't bat an eye.

I was so fucking proud of her. The way she protected Isla. The way she fought this asshole to give me a chance to shoot him. As this fucker held a gun to her head, I couldn't pull the trigger. I was an excellent shot, but knowing that one move and it could even scratch her skin sent cold terror through my blood.

"I will never tell." The guy spat out a mouthful of dark red fluid. I ran a check on him. No identity. But his tattoos told me plenty. He was part of the Yakuza. Soon, he'd be a dead Yakuza.

I was so sick and tired of these fuckers coming after Tatiana.

"You know, I believe you," I said, smiled, then hit him again. "Nobody, my guards or not, is allowed to touch my family. Fucking ever!"

Nikita and Boris nodded. They'd ensure everyone got the message, loud and clear.

His head snapped back, and a pained yelp filled the air. The scent of copper and sweat drifted through the air. It had been hours of this and the fucker refused to crack. I itched to go and check on Tatiana and my sister. The doctor was here to check her out and ensure the baby was okay.

Of course, the stubborn woman refused to see him and slammed the door in his face.

"You know what happens to people who hurt my family?" I drawled, while a tsunami of rage rolled through me. The rage was fresh and burned like a fucking inferno. "I deliver their heads back to their masters."

His eyes widened, and a second later, a howl of agony ripped through the air.

Medieval torture had nothing on my wrath.

"I told you already, I don't need a doctor. Tell Konstantin he can have a doctor check his fucking ass over."

Tatiana's voice came clear through the door after I knocked on our bedroom door. She locked herself in it. I had showered in a spare room and changed into clean clothes to ensure I didn't alarm either one of the women with the amount of blood that soaked my clothes.

Although from the sound of Tatiana's voice, she was out for my blood.

I cleared my throat. "Do it for me, then, *moya luna.*"

Silence followed. *Click.* The door unlocked, I pushed on the door handle. I almost expected an outburst to greet me. Yet, there was nothing. Just silence. I glanced over my shoulder at my doctor who was watching me warily.

"Give me a minute," I told him. He nodded, almost looking relieved.

I entered to find Isla in the sitting room, both her and Tatiana on the couch, cuddled together. My wife held Isla, murmuring something I couldn't hear, but neither one of them bothered to acknowledge me.

The coffee table in front of them had platters of fruits, veggies, and pastries, half eaten, which was a good sign that Tatiana was eating. Silence stretched, heavy and thick, until both of them finally gave me their attention.

Unsure who'd be easier to handle right now, I started with Tatiana. Bad mistake.

"I assume you told Isla."

Her eyes met mine, anger and something else in them I couldn't quite read.

"Why would I do that and make it easier for you?" she snapped.

Yeah, it would have definitely been easier to start with Isla. My sister's gaze narrowed on me too.

"And you kept the fact that I'm going to be an aunt from me," she accused.

Fuck, if both of them were ganging up on me, I'd never win.

"You're going to be an aunt," I told her.

"I know now!" I had never seen my sister furious before. "And I know you're not a normal businessman." So Tatiana had told her something. Before I could say anything, Isla continued, "And no, she didn't tell me. I suspected it for years. I mean, who has guards with guns surrounding their house. Or on their tail at all times. The only time I had freedom was in boarding school and college."

I sighed, suddenly feeling tired. Maybe I should have left my bloody clothes on so my sister could see exactly who I was. A killer. A criminal.

It didn't mean I'd stop it.

"I just don't get it," Isla murmured. "The clothes you wear. The way you handle yourself. It's like you are a normal businessman and then... bang. You kill a person without a second thought."

"That's right," I told her. "And I'd do it again. If it comes to them or my family, I'd kill all of them without a second thought."

Isla shook her head. "I really don't know what to think of all of this, brother. Illegal business. Racketeering. You left me in the dark and I'm not sure how to process it all. I need time."

And with that, Isla kissed Tatiana on the cheek, then stood up. My heart clenched in my chest. Somehow I had a feeling it'd come to this one day. And if she learned I killed her mother, Isla'd hate me even more.

She marched past me but then stopped just as she put her hand on the door handle and glanced over her shoulder.

"I still love you, brother," she said, her eyes softening, and it was as if a heavy rock had been lifted off my chest. She might be my sister but I raised her. She was part of me, just as my future child would be. "No matter what."

"And I love you, sestra." She nodded, the green emeralds shining against her pale complexion. Today was stressful. For both of them. "Please send in the doctor."

Isla's eyes darted to Tatiana, asking for her permission and the latter gave her a terse nod. I let out a sardonic breath. I could already sense the two would gang up on me a lot. But I was up for it. As long as I had them in my life, I was up to any challenge.

My wife's eyes finally met my gaze. The stars I vowed all those months ago I'd put back in her eyes were there yet duller somehow. There was something else there too. *Loathing.* I didn't think it had anything to do with what had happened in the garage. Tatiana had seen and heard her share of stories where the Nikolaevs spilled blood.

"What is bothering you?" I demanded to know. The flash in her gaze could spark a flame on its own. She was pissed off. "Don't tell me it's about the doctor?"

Her lips thinned.

"You're not known for holding back," I said, taking a step closer to her. I needed the scent of roses to assure me she was here and safe. That she was mine. "Spill it, moya luna. We might as well discuss it and resolve it because I intend to be inside your tight cunt later."

She rolled her eyes. "You're an asshole."

Lowering to my knees, I took her chin between my fingers. There was no more blood on her face and she had changed into another dress. Black this time.

"Careful." I leaned closer to her, my mouth an inch from her lips. "Your mouth gives me a hard-on." I tilted my head pensively. "Unless you want me to fuck you now."

I wouldn't. Not until the doctor examined her and ensured she and the baby were okay.

The door opened behind me and I stood up to my full height. I trusted my doctor, but I never left my back open for anyone to stab me in it.

"Mr. Konstantin. Mrs. Konstantin," he greeted us with respect.

Tatiana stood up stiffly, her hands behind her and studied the doctor. "I have a doctor back home," she told him. "I'll let you check me over once because this guy"—she tilted her chin my way—"is a pain in my ass, but it won't be repeated. Understood?"

The good old doctor's eyes darted my way in surprise. I was too fucking tired to argue, so I just nodded. We'd only been married for a day, and I felt like we'd been at it for years.

"Very well," he acknowledged. Truthfully, I'd have preferred a female doctor to check her, but I didn't have one I trusted on my payroll. So here we were, a man would touch my woman. At least he was old.

The doctor's eyes roamed the room, and when he spotted the bed, he instructed her to go lie on it. She kicked off her flats, then headed over to the bed. I followed right along. Fuck if I'd let even a sixty-year-old doctor see her without me present.

She lay down and glared at the doctor. "Now what?"

"We're going to listen to the baby's heart first," the doctor started explaining, holding Tatiana's gaze. "Nothing invasive."

She nodded. "Let's get this over with."

FIFTEEN
TATIANA

Illias's gaze burned on me.

He took my hand into his, I assumed it was his way to comfort me, but I was still pissed off, partly because someone just tried to kill me. Mostly because it seemed that my husband had used me. I wasn't sure I wanted him near me at the moment, much less touching me.

It annoyed the hell out of me that my chest still warmed at his offered comfort. Something was seriously fucked up here. A small, innocent touch and I was putty. Where was my feminism?

In my vagina, that's where.

But I'd be damned if I let Illias get away with manipulating me. I was going to beat my heart into submission if it was the last thing I did. I would not be used by anyone, least of all by a man who knocked me up intentionally for *leverage*!

The doctor opened his black bag, then slipped on a pair of latex gloves. He retrieved his instruments and started his exam.

Truthfully, I wanted to hear the baby's heart again. I wouldn't mind listening to it every day. After finally being pregnant, it was hard to keep the paranoia at bay. If Konstantin had gotten me knocked up on purpose, I couldn't even say that I hated it. Not even close.

119

A baby of my own was all I ever wanted.

But the least he could do was be upfront about it.

The doctor asked me to pull down the top of my dress so that he could check my own heartbeat before the baby's. A growl vibrated through the room. It belonged to Illias. I gained a degree of satisfaction knowing he wasn't happy about this. I shifted around and offered my back to the doctor, smiling smugly.

"Do you mind unzipping my dress?" I asked sweetly.

The poor doctor paled a few shades even before another growl vibrated against the walls. It appeared I married a wolf, not a man.

"I'll do it," Illias growled, his eyes promising retribution to the doctor if he even attempted to touch my zipper.

I blinked my eyes innocently while part of me relished in making my husband suffer. At least a little bit. It would seem he wasn't the sharing type, regardless of the reason he married me.

The sound of the zipper replaced the growl.

The doctor listened to my heartbeat, took my blood pressure, and then drew my blood. And all the while, Illias's hands never left me.

"Wow, I've never had two men touch me at the same time," I remarked casually, keeping my tone light. I knew it was a lie but Illias didn't need to know that. After all, I'd had two men kissing me the night Adrian took my virginity.

A hiss sounded and Illias pulled me closer to him with a murderous expression aimed at the poor old doctor. The doctor's hands immediately left my skin and he turned his back to us, fumbling with his bag. I almost felt sorry for him. I shouldn't be using him to get back at the son of a bitch who forced me to marry him.

"What about the twins at the party that got kicked out?" Illias asked. I frowned, wondering how in the fuck he would even know that. But the doctor's words chased all the thoughts from my mind with his next words.

"We'll listen to the baby's heartbeat now," the doctor declared, his hand firm but his voice held a note of tremor. I sighed. I couldn't do that to the poor old doctor.

He took a small box with a tiny microphone attached. He handed a gel tube to Illias.

"Would you please put that on your wife's lower belly?" he asked him.

Illias snatched it out of his hand, then pulled up my dress to find me wearing red, lacy panties.

"Why are you wearing such revealing panties?" he grumbled.

Oh, he didn't! There wasn't a single pair of panties in the stack that he bought me that was less revealing.

"Sorry, I forgot my granny panties at home," I remarked dryly, shifting up to rest on my elbows so I could glare at him better. I needed him to see my wrath. "You know, I didn't have a chance to pack since you kidnapped me, right outside my brother's wedding reception."

"I saved your ass," he bit out.

"And then you kidnapped me," I snapped, glaring at him.

The doctor cleared his throat. "Th-the gel on her belly," he stuttered.

I flopped back on the bed, knowing I probably looked like a brat to the doctor, but, at this point, I couldn't have cared less. Maybe I was. Maybe my brothers had indulged my whims a bit too often in my life. Or maybe my husband was just an asshole. I was choosing option two.

Illias removed the top of the tube, then spread a generous amount of the cold gel on my belly. His fingers firm and rough, he rubbed the cold thick liquid over my skin, and I managed not to respond to the sensation of his fingers on me. A woman scorned and all that shit.

A clearing of the throat cleared my head of the multiple ways I was thinking of how to kill my husband and get back home... alone.

"May I?" the doctor asked, but he wasn't asking me. He was asking Illias, his eyes locked on him with a slight hint of fear. He should be asking me, not that Neanderthal. It was my body, after all. Men, in general, were really starting to piss me off.

It didn't matter that I wanted this man. My husband. For what reason, I had no fucking idea. But my body wanted him inside me, on top of me, behind me. All over me. But even more than that, I wanted a partnership. I wanted to trust him and for him to trust me. I was by no means a fragile flower or an innocent woman. I was raised with my brothers, knew what they had to do—although not in gruesome detail —and what they'd done to keep us protected. It didn't make me respect them any less, nor love them any more.

Illias clenched his jaw and nodded. A few seconds later, we heard the rapid whoosh of the baby's heartbeat inside me, and I let out a relieved sigh. I knew the baby was still inside me, but there was something so emotional about hearing that heartbeat, reassuring me that it was still beating.

Without thinking, I took Illias's hand and gripped it tightly, emotions swelling inside me. The moment I heard that proof of life— whoosh, whoosh—something inside of me shifted. My heart raced excitedly every time I heard it. I would never grow tired of it, but to hear it with the baby daddy by my side, it was emotional on a whole new level. I needed to start rethinking this whole "kill Illias" thing. Maybe I could just maim him a little bit.

"It's a strong heartbeat," the doctor uttered with a smile.

Then he stiffened and my eyes widened in fear. "What?" I demanded to know, panic lacing my voice.

"I—I'm not sure—" he started and my eyes darted to Illias, letting him see fear in my gaze. I wanted him to fix it, whatever it was.

Illias's eyes betrayed nothing of his worries. His face was a cold mask. But his hand gripped mine and I knew, just fucking knew, he wanted this as much as I did. He worried as much as me.

"Speak," he ordered him, his voice a cold whip.

I glanced at Illias in confusion, then at the doctor. "Huh?"

"Two heartbeats," the doctor repeated, smiling. "You're going to have two babies."

His words thundered through me like wildfire. My mouth parted. Blood rushed through me, making it hard to think.

"Two babies," I repeated.

"Da," he confirmed in Russian. "Two babies with very strong heartbeats."

A burst of brilliant happiness rushed through me. I grinned, unable to believe it. Two babies! Illias and I shared a look. The smile he gave me just about blinded me. He looked as happy as I felt, and suddenly, I wondered if he'd really used me like I heard him say. He seemed way too happy for this to be just a means to an end.

I wanted to ravage him. Fuck everything else, but I wanted to thank him for this. These babies.

Whatever leverage he wanted, I hoped he got it because I got so much more.

He returned his attention to the doctor, thanking him. Then the doctor left our bedroom, a soft click sounded behind him and I just about jumped on my husband.

"Two babies," I exclaimed.

I could feel dampness between my legs. An ache pulsed in me and throbbed, demanding I get relief. No fucking idea if that was normal after the events of today. I didn't give a shit.

All I knew was that I'd be a mother. To two beautiful babies.

I straddled him and slammed my mouth on his. "I'm so horny," I murmured against his lips, grinding myself against his hard erection. I leaned forward and kissed his throat. He still owed me an explanation about that phone call but, for now, I just needed him. "You and I have some shit to talk about, but right now, just fuck me."

"Fuck," he ground out.

His hand cupped the back of my head, his fingers lacing through the strands and gripping them tightly. And all the while, I kissed his throat, licked his skin, sucked on his neck.

My nipples were sensitive, brushing against the thin material of my bra, sending sizzles of pleasure lower. I ground down on his erection and my forehead fell forward, resting on his shoulder as the pleasure spread through me.

Grabbing a handful of my hair, he pulled my head back and took my mouth, devouring me. I parted my mouth, welcoming him. He slid his tongue inside and I was lost to him. The wetness and heat. The feverish desire.

The sound of my panties being ripped filled the air. Our mouths drifted apart, and in one swift move, he pulled my already unzipped dress over my head, leaving me in a bra, which disappeared in my next breath.

I pushed his vest off his shoulders, then struggled with the buttons, only to rip them. The buttons went flying all over the room, landing with little clicks.

"Fuck, I need to be inside you," he said roughly.

My hands reached for his belt but he was faster. The jingle of his belt. A seductive echo of the zipper and he slammed inside me in one forceful thrust.

Two groans. Two shudders. Two heartbeats.

He leaned forward and captured my top lip between his, kissing me. Seducing me all over again. A tremor ran through me as our tongues danced together. I licked inside his mouth. He sucked my tongue. Our moans and groans mixed. His hands tightened on my hips and then he slapped my ass.

Breaking our kiss, he rasped, "Fuck me, wife. Show me how you get yourself off with my dick inside you."

I rolled my hips, slow and lazy. He felt so big and deep inside me. I wrapped my arms around his shoulders and held on as I rode him. I wouldn't make it long. A shiver rolled through me. My pussy throbbed with each thrust he took control of. His hands gripped my ass, pulling me harder against him. Making me ride him faster.

I rose an inch and slid back down. Then again. His groans guided me. He was losing control. The sensation of him deep inside me was intoxicating.

His teeth nipped my top lip. Then his mouth moved lower to my neck. Kissing. Marking. His lips ran up my neck, then pressed to my ears. "I'll kill anyone who tries to take you and our babies away from me."

"Yes," I breathed, crazed with lust.

He kissed me hard. Possessive. Wild and rough.

His hands gripped my hips and started to control my movements. He started to move me up and down. Hard and fast. Deep and rough. I moaned into his mouth. Pressure built. My chest rubbed against his.

But when his head lowered and sucked a nipple into his mouth, a shudder rolled through me and my head fell back. He turned his attention to my other nipple and he bit the sensitive peak.

I moaned and the pressure boiled past the point of no return. He rocked me against his hard length, hitting all the right spots. Shudders rolled through me like waves crashing against a shore.

An orgasm slammed into me, and I moaned his name like a prayer. My walls clenched around his length and he kept fucking me through my orgasm until he sank so deep inside me, I didn't know where he began and I ended.

He spilled inside me with a loud groan and his mouth on mine.

His heart thundered hard in his chest, threatening to crack my own. His fingers intertwined with mine, holding me as if he feared I'd disappear.

"Mine," he rasped. "You've always been mine, Tatiana."

It was then that realization sunk in. Illias's words about me forgetting him finally sunk in and made sense.

Illias Konstantin had fucked me in the gazebo, not Adrian.

SIXTEEN
KONSTANTIN

My hands roamed her bare back, her skin soft under my rough palms.

Her hair was like silk brushing against my knuckles. That fucker could have snuffed the life right out of her, and it made my throat tighten.

I'd been in love with this woman for almost a decade.

It wasn't lust. It was love. Devotion. She was my lightning. My rain. My sunshine. My moon. She was someone I couldn't live without.

I was buried deep inside her and the fear of losing her made my blood burn hotter, searing the word *mine* into my chest. I wanted to blast it to the entire world so they'd know whose wrath they'd incur if they came close to her.

The Yakuza knew I married Tatiana. Yet, they still came after her. That chip had to be found or they'd never stop trying. And if Amon lost his allegiance to our organization, we'd lose all leverage over them.

Marchetti was a fool to let the wedding proceed.

Goddamn it!

We hadn't made progress on that chip for weeks now. It hadn't exactly been a priority. I was too focused on Tatiana and stalking her. But now, I had to get my head in the game. There were more lives at stake. My wife and our children.

"Illias." Tatiana's soft voice stopped my thoughts. Her breath was like a caress against my neck. My fingers ran through her hair. Her fingernails pushed into the hair at my nape and I could feel them against my scalp. "We need to talk."

I stiffened. The words *"We need to talk"* never boded well for anyone. In our world, someone was usually shot. And knowing my wife, she probably had a gun handy somewhere.

"Talk, wife."

"I need you to start being honest with me." She shifted, locking her gaze with mine. "I'm not a tool for you to use. For *anyone* to use." She accentuated the word. "Hurt me or the babies or use us in any way, and you'll see what being a Nikolaev means."

A sardonic breath left me. Somehow it didn't surprise me that she was threatening me. The truth was I wouldn't want this woman any other way. And if I ever turned like my bastard father, I knew she'd kill me to protect our children. And fuck it, I'd hope she succeeded.

"Duly noted, wife," I acknowledged. "And I agree. You and our babies are most important."

Her expression softened. My fierce queen needed reassurance too.

My hands lowered to her hips that would soon widen to allow her to give birth to our babies. Twins. Warmth and love flared, spreading through my chest.

"Hmm." Then because I couldn't wait to hear it, I asked, "Are you happy?" Her eyes sought mine in confusion. "About the twins?"

She smiled and the stars in her eyes shimmered like the brightest diamonds. Seeing them hit me in the chest. I wanted nothing more than to see her happy.

"Yes," she whispered, leaning back studying my face. "So happy."

My dick began to harden inside her at the sight she gave me. Her perfect breasts, already growing bigger with the pregnancy.

"How many children do you want?" I asked her the same question she refused to answer yesterday. I nipped her bottom lip. "I want to know."

God, I couldn't wait to see a little blonde angel running around her mama, wearing a matching Chanel dress.

Her gaze came to mine, a little crease between her brows. "That depends on you, Illias."

I tucked a piece of hair behind her ear, trailing my mouth down her cheek and tracing it along her jaw. "Many, moya luna. I want many children with you."

She tilted her head, giving me better access. Her soft moans drove me mad. I thrust my hips upwards, feeling her insides clench around my shaft greedily.

"You misunderstood me," she murmured, still straddling my lap and rocking her hips shallowly.

Fuck, my dick throbbed, eager for another round of her tight, wet pussy. My cum dripped down her thighs and I ran my fingers upward and brought it to her lips. Like an obedient wife, her mouth parted and I smeared my cum over her lips. Her tongue darted out, licking the tip of my finger, then nipped it gently. But watching her lick the cum off her lips drove me to the edge of insanity.

"What I meant, Illias, is that unless you're honest with me and we're partners in this, I won't have any more children with you. And these"—she rubbed her stomach affectionately—"will be born to separated parents."

A growl vibrated in my chest. "Over my dead body. I told you, Tatiana, you're mine. For life. There is no other man for you nor our babies. Not even your brothers."

She shook her head and her lips quirked. "I know you're Pakhan and all that. But don't forget I grew up in this world. And my brothers can give just as good as they get."

Sardonic amusement escaped me. Her brothers had unconditional loyalty and irrationally, it made me jealous. I wanted all of her—her loyalty, her love, her passion. Fucking everything.

"What do you want to know, Tatiana?"

Her pale blue eyes met mine. We were such opposites. Lightness and darkness, despite both of us growing up in this world. Some women in our world were timid, bowed their heads and minded their business, pretending ignorance of our world.

That was never meant to be Tatiana. Regardless of what world she lived in.

I took her chin between my fingers. "What do you want to know?"

She swallowed with a soft gulp. "When did we meet?"

Silence morphed between us. Her fingers played with the rose pendant on her necklace. A thorned rose. She reminded me of a rose full of thorns in a way. She bloomed and shined, but when threatened her thorns came out.

"When did we meet, Illias?" she asked again.

My gut feeling warned she had started to unravel some things on her own. My eyes fell on the unusual necklace around her neck. She always wore it. It was unusual. Not exactly her style.

"Your last year of college. Halloween night." She closed her eyes for a moment, and when she opened them, they were the darkest blue I had ever seen them. "A waiter gave me a note. From you."

Her mouth parted. "He gave it to you?"

I nodded. "You caught my eye the moment you strolled in with those boys," I admitted. "So when I got the note, I couldn't resist but oblige you."

Her cheeks flushed a deep red and I stared at her in disbelief. Fuck, she was beautiful when she blushed.

She buried her face in my neck. "Oh my gosh."

My lips pressed against her ear. "You don't seem surprised."

Her hands trailed down my shoulder, forearm, until our fingers met and interlocked. Her graceful fingers traced mine.

"I started to suspect," she remarked, her breaths fanning my neck. "Something you said last night."

"What did I say?" I cupped her head and made her look at me.

A shiver rolled through her and her eyes shimmered, like the sun rays over the Caribbean Sea.

"That I'm yours. That I've always been yours," she whispered softly. She brushed the tip of her nose against mine. "During all the years I'd known Adrian—" I stiffened, hating the fucker's name on her lips. " —I heard it only once. That night in the gazebo."

She pulled her bottom lip between her teeth, then asked, "Did you know who I was?"

"That night, no," I admitted. "I tried to find you, but your information was impossible to trace. It wasn't until I saw you approaching your brother in my L.A. restaurant that I learned why."

"Why didn't you say anything?"

"Maxim went through some shit that I had to deal with," he grumbled. "By the time I came to New Orleans, you were already married. It left me with two options. Kill him or let you be happy. I didn't want to repeat my father's mistake."

A gasp filled the space between us. I watched her neck bob as she swallowed and a tear rolled down her cheek. I caught it with my thumb.

"What do you mean?"

She paused, like she was considering telling me something. I grabbed a fistful of her hair and pulled her head back. Her lips were swollen, her cheeks flushed and her eyes shining like stars.

"Tell me," I demanded. "There's something else that's on your mind."

"Illias, I found something." She went silent for a moment, studying me. I waited for her to continue. "Adrian left a picture behind." I tensed at the mention of her late husband. If I could erase that whole period of her life, I would.

She took a deep breath. "The woman in his photo was in your family portrait," she blurted out. "I think Adrian's mother is your mother."

SEVENTEEN

TATIANA

Illias shook his head and let out a sardonic breath.

"No, Tatiana," he uttered. "My mother had an affair with Adrian's father." My shocked gasp filled the air. "It's what got her and Adrian's father killed. I was there that night, I saw it."

I stared at Illias in shock. His revelation was unexpected. It would make sense why my late husband would have a picture of his father with Illias's mother, then. But my gut feeling warned there was more. Green eyes were very rare, like only 2% of the population had them, so, what were the odds that Adrian's eyes were the same color as Illias's mother.

"How old are you?" I asked him. I knew the irony of not knowing my husband's age, but it wasn't as if our courting-slash-dating was normal.

"Forty."

Adrian would have been forty-two. Maybe Illias was right and his mother had an affair with a married man.

"What happened that night?" I asked him quietly.

Illias's jaw clenched and his eyes darkened to black pools.

"My mother woke my brother and me up in the middle of the night, to run away with her lover. We met them in a parking lot outside Moscow. The guy had another kid, but my father knew her plans. He showed up there with his men. They killed him, then her. When it was time to kill the little boy, I begged him to spare his life."

I swallowed a lump in my throat. "If you remembered it, so would Adrian." In fact, I had no doubt he remembered it. He took me to that parking lot after we eloped. He left me a clue there. Except, I had no idea where it went from there. "He came after you."

Illias nodded. "He did."

I searched for something in my mind when a headache nearly split my temples open. Distorted images of the accident flashed, but they made no sense. None of them were connected. Faces were unrecognizable.

In the back of my skull, the headache intensified by the second. I closed my eyes, desperately searching through my memories, but it made the ache in my skull multiply tenfold.

When I opened my eyes, I found Illias watching me. The unnerving darkness and answers I wasn't sure of lurked in his depths, frightening me.

"Why did you marry me?" I asked, shelving the memories that refused to come forward for now.

"Because you're mine." His voice was cold. Dark. Possessive. The tenor of his voice was calm, but there was a harshness to it.

"Not for *leverage?*" He remained silent and then realization fell into place. The wedding dress he had ready for me. It was tailored. It was fucking tailored. "How long did you plan on marrying me?"

Our gazes clashed. There were secrets there and something akin to carnal possession. Although as I stared at him, I watched his walls build up and his features slowly close off.

"How long, Illias?" I demanded, keeping my anger at bay.

"Since the gazebo." My mouth dropped. It wasn't the answer I expected.

"B-but... But that's like seven, eight years." I swallowed. I got to my feet and wrapped a sheet around me. "Have you been stalking me for all those years?" I narrowed my eyes on him. "That's not healthy."

"If you say so."

"Jesus, it's like I'm talking to my brothers." A strange look passed in his eyes. It flickered and disappeared before I could decipher it.

"That's it," I said. "Nothing else to say?"

Without warning, he stood up. "Get some sleep."

I tossed and turned for hours, expecting Illias to come back to bed.

He didn't. It was almost midnight, Moscow time, before my eyelids started to droop and sleep pulled me under.

Adrian's hands grasped the wheel in a steel grip as we drove away from Vasili's home. It was their traditional Halloween-slash-anniversary party. It was my favorite time of the year too. The holidays were right around the corner, yet I couldn't muster the energy to be happy about it this year.

My eyes darted my husband's way.

He was in a strange mood.

Something had pissed him off. He was irritable, and by the way his jaw pulsed, he wasn't in the mood to talk. Was it my comment about wanting a baby? He didn't want kids. It was another thing he kept from me. So many damn secrets, I started to feel like I didn't even know him.

Or maybe there was something bigger going on?

I saw Vasili, Sasha, and even Alexei get into a heated discussion with Adrian, but the moment they spotted me, the four of them abruptly stopped talking. There was only one thing my brothers didn't share with me—Bratva business.

Adrian stuck more to legal businesses, but every so often he ventured into the illegal side. I'd be a hypocrite if I held that against him considering where my family came from. But there was something amiss, and I couldn't put my finger on it.

I studied my husband's face.

His expression was dark. His jaw clenched. His knuckles white as he clasped the steering wheel.

"Are you still mad about the baby comment?" I demanded to know.

My heart clenched remembering how fast he shut me down when I first mentioned it a month ago. It had slowly progressed from there—the anger simmered, the bitterness swallowed, and the betrayal grew.

Ironic really. It only took one major topic and only a month for our differences to manifest.

But I refused to cower or accept defeat. I'd been honest with Adrian from day one. I wanted a family. If he never had any intention of having children, he should have told me before I pledged my life to him.

He flicked his eyes my way, then returned them to the road. I waited for an explanation. For another argument. Anything.

Instead, I just got silence that felt heavy and thick, suffocating us both.

"I just want a simple family," I rasped, my heart fluttering with broken wings. "A simple life. I don't need all the fancy stuff." He scoffed, throwing me an incredulous glance. "I totally would," I protested.

"You'd give up your wardrobe? Your jewelry? Your Gucci, Chanel, Dior, Hermès?" he asked with a snicker.

Okay, so I liked nice stuff. I couldn't help it. It made me feel good when I was down. Whenever I was sad or upset, my brothers would take me shopping. They hated it, but it was the only way they knew how to compensate. Sasha would hug me, try to talk to me, then drag me out to the fanciest store within our vicinity. Vasili would just grumble about hormones, then drag me to the store. He'd find a corner where he'd brood while working and order sales ladies to satisfy my every whim. Father was rarely, if ever, around.

Hence, my brothers created a monster. A stylish monster.

"I would give it all up," I claimed. There was no doubt in my voice. No second-guessing. I just wanted us to have a family. A child. Maybe two. A boy and a girl.

"No." One word, but it had so much power to hurt. Pain sliced through me. Anger followed. He had no right to take that away from me without an explanation.

"Why not?" I snapped, but as the last syllable left my lips, Adrian floored the gas and my body flew back into the seat. I shot him a glare to find him peering into the side mirror.

"What the fuck are you doing?" I hissed.

No answer.

Worry furrowed his eyebrows. The vein in his neck pulsed. I opened my mouth to say something, but it was like the switch was flipped.

My head hit the passenger window. Again and again.

Adrian said something. His lips moved. He said something else. I couldn't hear it. I tried to focus on the words. "Tatiana, I'm so sorry. I shouldn't have used you."

Smash.

The world was turning. We tumbled, the car rolling over with a loud thud. Until silence came over us. Until the world settled the wrong way.

I shifted, trying to reach out to Adrian. He wasn't in the driver seat.

My eyes darted out the window.

Men in suits surrounded him and they all studied Adrian with disdain. A disgusted look on their faces.

"Meet Marchetti, stronzo." He had to be a bodyguard.

My heart leapt into my throat. Something about the name, Marchetti, sounded ominous. Dangerous. I had heard the name somewhere, but I wasn't sure where.

I studied him, unable to peel my gaze away from him. He was handsome. Older. Slightly older than the other devil with a deep voice. Marchetti had thick dark hair and piercing eyes. The kind that could shred your soul into pieces. By just snapping his fingers. Silence stretched, ready to snap like a fragile rubber band.

It was Marchetti who broke the silence.

"Adrian Morozov, we finally meet." His voice was smooth. His words rolled off his tongue with a smooth Italian accent. "Do you know why we're here?"

My husband nodded once. No words.

"Then you understand there is no escaping this alive," he said *softly. Yet, there was nothing soft about his words nor the look he gave him.*

"Where is it?" Marchetti demanded to know.

Adrian's eyes flickered my way as I watched the whole exchange with wide eyes. I had no idea what they were talking about.

Adrian. My mouth moved, but nothing came out. My throat was too dry.

He turned his gaze away. "It's no longer here."

Then as if Marchetti read my mind, he snapped his fingers and one of his men slammed his first into Adrian's chin. His head snapped back from the force of the impact. I tasted blood in my mouth and realized I bit into my tongue. Another fist came at my husband but he didn't fight back. It was hardly fair, five against one. But why wasn't Adrian fighting back?

The man in an expensive Italian suit kept his hands clean, tucked in his pants as he watched dispassionately as one of his men beat Adrian.

My fingers finally found the button and pressed it. The seat belt came undone, hitting the door with a loud bang. It sounded like a gong going off and instantly everyone outside stilled.

A quick burst of shots rang through the air. It felt like they went on for hours, when in fact it was just a few seconds.

Instinctively I ducked down, although I was already crammed down, and I placed both hands over my ears to block out the loud noises. It reminded me of the crescendo of a bad opera piece. The pitch got louder and harsher, piercing my brain.

Then it stopped. A deafening silence. I should be relieved but it felt even more ominous than the sound of gunshots.

My heart squeezed in my throat, the pulse choking me slowly.

More words in a foreign language. The voices were high-pitched, angry, and not holding back.

Russian.

One of those was Russian. More words. It was hard to hear them over the buzzing in my ears, but I recognized it. I was certain it was Italian. Russian and Italian.

"She dies. No loose ends," one of them replied in English, and

instinctively I shrank further back into the car, although it was burning, coming closer to becoming an explosion.

"No." A cold voice. A hard tone. But it wasn't Adrian's. Was he even alive? "She knows nothing."

"Are you sure?" The deep masculine voice filled the air. A pair of expensive Italian leather shoes filled my vision. "Are you willing to stake your life on it?"

I had to be in utter shock. Because I registered the brand of shoes. Santoni men's shoes. My husband and I were about to die and all my attention was on the shoes, staring at a pair of five-grand Italian shoes.

"The woman doesn't know anything." A voice sounded vaguely familiar. I couldn't place it. "I'll take full responsibility for her."

"If I find out she had anything to do with her husband's agreement, I'm coming for her." A light Italian accent. Deep voice. Another set of expensive shoes entered my vision. Prada.

"She knows nothing. If she does, I'll handle it." Another pair of expensive shoes. Art. 504 shoes. Even more expensive. Dark suit pants. Perfectly fit. Expensive material.

I shook my head. Snap out of it, Tatiana.

Smoke filled my lungs. Bile rose in my throat and I inhaled deeply to stop myself from retching. The one pair of shoes left. One remained. My heart raced. My vision swam. My ears buzzed. My lungs burned.

"D'accordo." Definitely Italian. What the fuck did that mean? "Don't make me regret it."

Bu-bum. Bu-bum. Bu-bum.

I thought I heard Adrian's voice, but the buzz in my ears was too loud, drowning out all the words.

The next words I heard were, "End him."

Bang.

The last bullet. It felt like a final bullet before it was my turn.

A body hit the dirt with a loud thud. Adrian's dead eyes met mine. The terror was still etched on his face. The last expression before he died. Staring back at me. Blood covered his clothes. A bullet hole in his chest was marred with gun powder, blood seeping out of it like tomato juice.

A gasp left me, and my heart stopped. "A-A-Adrian," I choked out, my voice broken. He didn't move. His stare blank, fixated on something I couldn't reach. With each heartbeat my life slowly faded, following him.

Until something inside me snapped.

"Nooo!" I shrieked and my world as I'd known it ceased to exist.

A man, a familiar face, pulled me out of the car. He kept saying something but my ears rang too much to hear a single word that left his mouth. Our gazes locked, I held on to his strength as he pulled me out of the car.

My knees weakened, failing me. He caught me before they'd hit the gravel. I buried my face into his warm chest. The familiar scent of citrus and sandalwood soothed. Then it reminded me of my husband. My eyes darted back to Adrian. I couldn't look away. Adrian's dead eyes, staring somewhere I couldn't follow.

"Nooo!" I shrieked, pushing the man away from me and falling to my knees.

Adrenaline pumped through my veins, giving me just enough strength to crawl over to him.

"Adrian, please," I cried, pressing my lips on his and tasting blood. "Please, please, please."

Tears wet my face, tasting like the bittersweet goodbye.

My hands cupped his head. "Wake up," I begged. "Wake up." I shook his body, but it was all dead weight. He refused to budge. Images of our life together flashed through my mind. What we had. What we could have had. "No, no, no," I muttered.

This couldn't be the end.

CPR. I had to do CPR.

I leaned over and started pushing on his chest. My shoulder hurt so bad but I ignored the throbbing ache. I gritted my teeth, each move shooting a piercing pain through my shoulder blades.

"Breathe," I shrieked. One. Two. Three. I prayed to God I did it

right. I put my mouth on his, tasting copper, then blew air into his lungs. One. Two. Three. Again my lips on his.

"Please, help me," I screamed, looking frantically at the men who took him away from me. "Please. Just one breath and then I can save him."

A sob suffocated me as I pressed my palm onto Adrian's wound, trying to stop the blood from seeping. It was pointless, but I couldn't give up. I shook my head furiously. His skin was cold.

"Adrian, please wake up. Please wake up," I murmured over and over again, pressing my forehead to his.

Blood lined his lips, his gaze lost in a space that I'd never reach. He left me.

A gasp left me and my heart stopped.

"P-p-please. Come back to me," I choked out before raising my eyes to the men who took him. Fury unleashed in me and spread through my veins like wildfire. It was freezing cold, then it burned. It unleashed something I never knew I had inside me. Madness. Hate.

I let out a scream. Then another and another. I screamed until my throat turned raw. My hands gripped my hair pulling on it. My heart bled and mixed with rage, pulling me under until I was fully submerged in it.

I stumbled to my feet. Illias's hand gripped my elbow, steadying me, but I jerked away from him. Then I fisted his chest, hitting him. Over and over again.

"You killed him," I screeched, hot tears streaming down my face. "You did it."

His eyes blazed with fire but it didn't match mine. His hands grabbed my forearms and shook me. Not hard but my head whipped back and forth, like a rag doll.

Shaking my head, I gripped his suit. "I'm going to kill you for this." My gaze traveled over all of them. "I'm going to kill you all for this."

Pain clawed at my chest. I couldn't tell if it was real or I was dreaming. I couldn't breathe. I was suffocating. So I screamed again, hoping this anguish inside my chest would ease.

"I'm here, moya luna." It was a deep voice with a slight Russian accent and husky tenor that pulled me out of the nightmare. It was the same voice. It was the same scent, but I couldn't think about that now.

As the pain dulled, the scent of sandalwood and citrus rocked me back to sleep.

EIGHTEEN
KONSTANTIN

A weight pressed on my chest as the first ray of the sunrise flickered through the serene landscape. More snow fell last night, so it appeared peaceful. Yet, there was no peace to be found. Not in my body and apparently not in my wife's dreams.

Tatiana had been thrashing in her sleep, plagued by nightmares, while something else entirely plagued me.

The picture Tatiana claimed she found.

Why would Adrian hold on to a picture showing my mother with his father rather than his parents? Yet the idea that Adrian could be my brother was incomprehensible. How many times had I heard my father brag about having a virgin bride? And Adrian was older, so that would have meant my mother would have given birth before she married my father.

And then there was the whole issue with the Yakuza.

Reaching for my phone, I messaged Bitter Prince. No fucking wonder he was bitter, every time he came through, he got fucked.

I typed a quick message to meet him. The reply was instant, except he demanded a meeting on his turf. Smart fucker.

I sent a quick agreement, then headed towards the bed where my wife slept. She mumbled something unintelligible in her sleep, her brows furrowed and her breathing harsher. I smoothed her brows softly and her breathing evened out. She even pushed into my hand, as if she received comfort from my touch.

I'd rather stay here and fuck her day and night, but unless I took matters into my own hands, we'd be looking over our shoulders for the rest of our lives. Tatiana and our children's lives would be constantly in danger.

So the Yakuza had to be handled and that fucking chip had to be found, then destroyed.

For the interest of the whole of Omertà.

Two days later, I was in the Philippines.

A weight had been pressing on my chest and I knew it had everything to do with Tatiana. I fucking hated leaving her. But bringing her could be risky. Especially since the Yakuza controlled a lot of this territory.

I was doing this to save her and our children.

We headed straight from the airport to Amon's. It could be a trap, but I was inclined to think he'd have something to gain from our meeting as well as I did. Boris and two other guards were with me. I'd left Nikita behind with the women.

Boris and Nikita had been with me the longest, so I trusted them more than the others.

"Make sure Nikita is ready to follow through if something goes wrong," I told Boris. "No matter what, she's to be handed to her brothers if things don't go well. They'll keep her protected."

"You had to marry a mafia princess," Boris remarked sardonically. "Her past with Adrian made her a liability all along."

"Adrian was using her to get to me. Believe me, she was just Vasili's sister until he figured out she was something to me. It was the only reason he used her. To get back at me."

He released a deep sigh. When all this was over, I'd have to give him a long vacation.

"So now what?"

"Now we bargain with the Bitter Prince and help him become the king. It's better if we get on his good side now and help him get there. He's on that path anyhow."

"How in the fuck do you even know that?"

A small smile graced my lips. "Because I've seen Amon and Reina Romero together. And trust me, I know he will never let her go. He'll start a war with his brother to keep that woman away from other men."

The driver came to a stop in front of a large property. We were on one of the southern islands of the Philippines, Jolo. I fucking hated islands, but here I was, meeting Amon on an island.

My eyes traveled over the horizon. The crystal blue waters shimmered under the sun, reminding me of my wife's eyes. Well, if I died today, at least it would be to a good fucking view. Although I had no intention of dying today.

The large gate at the entrance slid open and the driver restarted the car, passing the statues of Shinto gods—Amaterasu, Susanoo, and Tsukuyomi. The rest of the driveway had cherry blossoms on both sides welcoming us all the way to the large manor on the edge of the earth.

Amon stood, looking grim and tall, like one of the samurais, ready to extract revenge. There was no shortage of guards around either.

Fucking lovely.

I'd rather have ten feet of snow than cherry blossoms and samurais right now. As the car came to a full stop, Boris and I exited it.

"Amon," I greeted him.

"Konstantin."

His jaw was pressed tight. His eyes were darker than midnight. Fuck! He was beyond pissed. He was furious.

As we stepped forward, Amon's eyes flickered. "Just you."

Boris immediately stepped beside me. "I'm coming too."

"No."

I always knew Amon would be a force to be reckoned with. Little did people know, but over the last two years, his wealth, ports, and empire had become vast and significant. His net worth was right up there with Marchetti and me.

Not that his brother cared one way or another. Dante always got what he wanted. Amon fought for everything he got. He earned it and that made him even more dangerous.

Boris reached into his holster, to bring his weapon out, but I stopped him. "Stay here."

Amon turned around and headed inside, without waiting for me. A sardonic breath left me. It was rare for me to follow any fucker, and here I was, dependent on a prince over a decade younger than me.

Maybe I was getting too old for this shit. Amon was much younger than me. Hungrier too. It was that which made a man more lethal. I really hoped he wouldn't pull some shit because I'd hate to kill him.

"If I wanted you dead, I'd have seized your weapon," Amon remarked, as if he read my thoughts. "And you wouldn't be standing behind me."

"Good to know," I retorted dryly. "Although, I don't have a habit of shooting people in the back."

Yet, I didn't regret a single moment that led me to this. To here. Because I got my wife. And our babies grew in her belly. I'd dig my own grave, over and over again, if it meant their safety. I'd do it all over again if it meant having her.

My only regret was that I didn't take her sooner.

Three of Amon's guards followed behind me. We made it to the opposite side of the house and sat on the terrace. The ocean surrounded the house from three sides, ensuring you'd never forget you were on an island.

"You have yourself a paradise here," I said.

"Yet you hate it," he responded wryly.

I shrugged. "What can I say? I prefer snow and Siberian temperatures." Especially when my woman was there.

The two of us sat down. Amon's face betrayed none of his feelings nor thoughts. He could contemplate mass murder on everyone in the Omertà and there'd be no signs on his face.

"I can't help you with the Yakuza," he said, breaking the silence. My eyes flickered to his hand on the armrest and noted his knuckles turning white.

"Maybe we can help each other."

His piercing stare turned to me and his lips curved into a cold smile. "And how do you figure that?"

I could taste the fury on my tongue. He was steaming, despite his cold exterior. I recognized the signs. I lived through this same moment when I learned of Tatiana's identity, only to find her married to Adrian. Except, his woman wasn't married to his brother. Yet.

"How about we cut the bullshit?" I said. Amon watched me silently, his face a cold mask.

"Be my guest," he drawled, annoyance flaring in his eyes.

"I got my hands on the agreement Leone and Romero drafted, to tie their families together." If I thought his face was a cold mask beforehand, it had nothing on the expression that stared at me now. "I found a loophole and I have a plan B that will ensure Reina never marries your brother."

A sardonic breath left him. "Really? And let me guess, in the midst of it all, you'll get me killed. If not by Marchetti, then by my cousin."

I locked eyes with him. "I'll kill your cousin. You'll take over as head of the Yakuza. You're aiming for it anyhow. I'm probably speeding it up by a few months." His expression remained impassive. I'd wager none of it meant anything to him without the youngest Romero daughter. "Romero is dying. I'll make his passing more bearable and expeditious. You'll take his seat at the table."

It was that easy. Kill your enemy. Kill your partner. Save the woman you love.

"If Marchetti hears this, you'll be dead before you get back to Russia."

I let out an amused breath. We both knew very well this conversation would never make it back to Marchetti.

"He's never going to get wind of it because thanks to me, Reina Romero will marry you, not your brother." I pulled out an envelope and slid it across the table. "And this is the reason that will make Marchetti change his mind."

I watched him open the envelope.

His mask cracked. His eyes flared. And I feared the Bitter Prince might have turned into a wrathful king.

NINETEEN

TATIANA

It had been days since I'd seen my husband. Almost a week since I remembered that night.

The memories filled every single second of the day since I awoke that morning. Konstantin should have told me. I gave him every chance to come clean and he hadn't.

I felt played. Betrayed. Bitter.

My mood reflected the winter storm that raged outside. It had been snowing since the morning I woke up to Illias gone. As if he knew I'd be trapped with the memories and no way out of this place.

The air was chilly inside the castle. The wind whipped against the windows, a constant reminder that going outside in this weather was a bad idea. Not that I had anywhere to go but home.

The damn chip was still a mystery. So was the next clue.

"You hate being trapped inside, don't you?" Isla's voice startled me.

We'd gotten to know each other well over the last week. There was nobody else to keep us company but the guards, and they had a clear order to keep their distance from us.

"I hate being cold and trapped inside," I remarked dryly.

Thank fuck she was here. Otherwise, I'd have gone nuts alone.

We'd binged all the seasons of *Game of Thrones*, *The Originals*, *Emily in Paris*. I hadn't watched that much television in all my years of life put together.

But the part that irked me the most was not having my phone. I was a grown-ass woman and he'd get a piece of my mind when he returned. The. Worst. Honeymoon. Ever!

Isla's phone pinged again and I found myself irritated even more. She and her friends were like a group chatting 24/7. Who even wanted to type that much?

"If y'all talk so much, why don't you just move in together?" I grumbled, slightly bitter.

Isla gave me a sympathetic glance. She tried to break into Illias's safe for me. Unsuccessfully. She wasn't exactly the *B*-and-*E* type of girl. I still liked her.

"We shared dorms," she explained. "We probably talk on the phone too much."

I rolled my eyes. "Ignore me. I'm just cranky and miss my family."

She looked at me with understanding.

"You could call them from my phone," she suggested for the hundredth time this week.

I shook my head. I wouldn't want my brothers tracing the phone and accidentally exposing Isla. "I don't know their number by heart," I muttered my excuse. It was a lie. I knew every fucking phone number my brothers ever had.

Her phone pinged again and she glanced at it. "Oh my gosh!"

Her exclamation piqued my curiosity. "What?"

"Remember the fashion show I told you about." I nodded my head. She raved about her friend's designs so much that I blindly ordered two dozen outfits by her. Isla swore her friend was amazing and her fashion would surpass Chanel one day. It was a steep comment, but I couldn't help but be influenced by Isla's enthusiasm. No matter how subjective it was. "Reina got the video. Now I can show you her designs and you can see you got a good product for your money."

I chuckled. My sister-in-law's enthusiasm was worth what I'd paid sight unseen already.

"Okay, show me," I said, smiling. She scooted closer and put her phone screen between us. Our heads bent, she pressed play and the show started. It took the first model to strut halfway down the runway and I knew Isla wasn't lying. Her friend's designs would be all the rage.

"Tell her I want to invest in her company," I told her.

Isla's eyes widened. "Are you serious?"

I nodded, my eyes on her screen. "Absolutely. These are stunning."

The grin on Isla's face was priceless. "Oh my gosh, just wait until I tell her. She's going to die!"

"Don't let her die," I teased. "I want to make my money back first."

The two of us giggled. Isla's face beamed, her green eyes turned even lighter. Her eyes reflected her moods. We returned our attention to the video, then watched the rest of the fashion runway. Her friend even had designer clothes for children.

"So you were part of the band?" I asked curiously.

She shook her head. "No, we all went to the same school and had some connection to music." I studied them on the screen. They were good at it. Isla with the violin had the hair on my arms standing up. Seeing her play it, her eyes half closed. Like she forgot about everyone and everything in the room and the violin was her lover.

"This is Athena." Isla pointed to the girl sitting on the screen. "Her mother is a famous opera singer. She insists on her becoming a singer too, but she's not too keen on it. She prefers to write. This is Raven. She plays guitar but one day she'll be a famous painter."

I smiled. "Make sure I get one of her paintings before they blow up too." Another excited squeal. "You're like my dealer or something," I mused.

She chuckled. "I'll ask her to send me pictures of her paintings and you can have your pick."

I tapped my chin pensively. "Maybe we can help her get some exposure. New Orleans has these wonderful venues where paintings are sold. I know a few people and we can see if they'll host her work there."

Isla's eyes lit up like emeralds. "That would be so grand. Oh my gosh, you're gonna hook us up, aren't you?"

"Okay, you're making me sound like a pimp."

"A pimp needs a phone," she noted. "We're gonna have to do something about that." Then a mischievous smile curved her lips. "Phoenix and Reina might be able to help. They're the criminal minds in our group."

I shook my head. "Well then, I'm glad we're friends and you're hooking me up with your criminal gang." The two of us giggled. "Okay, back to this fabulous fashion show that you'll invite me to next time. Who hosted it?"

She returned her attention to the screen.

"Enrico Marchetti." Isla's face turned bright red, her freckles more pronounced than ever and I stared at her in amazement. She knew Enrico Marchetti?

"You know him?"

"Mmm." She swallowed, keeping her eyes on the screen. "Not really." Oh, there was something she wasn't telling me. Something big. Huge... if her blush was anything to go by.

I wouldn't push it though. She'd tell me when she was ready. I returned my attention to the little group of friends she had. They seemed extremely close. You could tell. A shared glance and it was as if they knew what each one of them was thinking.

"Have you known each other very long?" I questioned her.

"High school and college," she answered.

"How did you bond?" I couldn't help the curiosity.

"Murder." The word seemed to slip past her lips without thinking. She immediately stiffened and I held my breath. Murder per se didn't shock me. I mean, hello. Look at my brothers. Her gaze met mine. A mischievous smile played on her lips, but it didn't match the panicked expression in her eyes. "Just joking."

I didn't think she was but decided not to push it. Her spine was so tense, it might break in half.

"Do you know where Marchetti lives?" I asked casually, keeping my posture relaxed and my eyes on the phone.

"In Paris, I guess," she muttered.

"For some reason I guessed Italy," I remarked. "He has a lot of luxury brands in Italy."

Isla's brows furrowed. "Hmm, it could be. Reina mentioned he owns half of Italy, but I assumed she was exaggerating."

"Any chance you'd be able to find out his address?" If Illias refused to share details, then Marchetti would give me answers.

Isla shrugged her shoulders. "Maybe. It's not like I've been to his place."

I stifled a snort. It didn't even cross my mind that she was in his place until she made this comment. Now, I was fairly certain she had been to Marchetti's place.

"Duh," I replied, storing this for another day. "Now tell me who the rest of the girls are? And how do you know Enrico Marchetti?" Her cheeks reddened again. Interesting. "He's only one of the most desirable men in the world," I remarked. If Isla knew anything about him, I needed her to spill it. The man was responsible for Adrian's death, and I'd use every piece of information I could get on him.

She chuckled nervously. "Right! Like hello, hot daddy, where have you been all my life?"

An awkward heartbeat, then I burst into a fit of giggles. I laughed so hard that my eyes stung with tears. Illias had no fucking idea who his sister was. I bet underneath that innocent face and shimmering emerald gaze, she was a downright freak.

Yes, I definitely liked her.

"You know, I'm happy you're my sister-in-law," I noted. "You and I will teach Illias a lesson." She had no clue how literal I meant that.

She shook her head, smiling. "I have to keep my troublemaking on the down-low. I get the sense you set the streets on fire as you drive down them."

"What an adequate description of me and my family," I joked. Isla was perceptive, more than her brother gave her credit for. "I'd bet Enrico Marchetti wasn't far off the crazy mark."

A heartbeat passed.

"Here. Let me show you who's who so you know them when you

meet my friends," Isla remarked. The change of subject didn't escape me, but I'd table Marchetti for now. Certain questions have to be asked delicately.

"Okay, tell me everything about your friends," I agreed, then added softly, "And about Marchetti." It was time to dig for information.

She let out a sigh as if she knew I wouldn't let it go.

"Okay, this is Reina," she started explaining, pointing to the pretty blonde with wild curly hair. "Her sister is at the piano," Isla continued. Every so often the view was obstructed by another model wearing Reina's designs. My eyes followed her finger. The girl with dark brown curly hair played the piano, a serene smile on her face and with a face that was almost identical to her sister's. "Phoenix is incredible at playing the piano. Reina is amazing too, but she loves her fashion more."

"I thought you said Reina's sister is deaf," I remarked curiously.

They all looked to be Isla's age. About twenty-three or so. Except Reina. She seemed to be younger.

"She is." Her eyes lifted off the screen, her green emeralds pensive. "Phoenix was rejected when she initially applied for the music program at our school. So Reina applied on the caveat that her older sister would be accepted. I think she knew all along Phoenix would need her, and it was the reason she worked extra hard in high school. She finished high school two years ahead. She's twenty-one, Phoenix is twenty-three." That confirmed the age. "Anyhow, Reina took double majors, fashion design for herself, and music for her sister."

I raised my eyebrows. "That's impressive."

"Phoenix is impressive too," she retorted. "It's just that nobody would give her an opportunity to flourish because she was deaf. So Reina took it into her own hands."

"I think I want to be Reina when I grow up," I muttered, suddenly feeling lacking.

Isla chuckled. "Yeah, me too."

My eyes returned to the screen and my mouth dropped. The screen switched from the fashion show to the after-party. And to say Isla and her friends danced like strippers would be an understatement. Bruno

Mars's "Bubble Butt" played and the girls were smacking their asses and dancing like their whole purpose in life was to seduce men.

Mission accomplished because all the men had their eyes on them. My brows furrowed. Holy fuck! Was that Aiden Callahan? His eyes narrowed, displeasure clear in them. The question was at whom it was aimed.

With Marchetti on the other hand, I didn't have to guess.

Isla danced seductively, her eyes flickering to Enrico Marchetti. He was stoic but the way his eyes burned on Isla and the murderous looks he sent the other men in the room betrayed him.

There was more going on with my sister-in-law than she let on. She might be harboring some secrets of her own. Although one thing I knew for sure. My husband might be withholding information from me but I'd get them on my own.

Isla would be my ticket to get close to Enrico Marchetti.

"Ne, ne, ne."

The chef shook his head in disapproval as Isla and I minced rosemary and garlic. There was something about cutting up vegetables and the repetitive motion that was relaxing. Well, it would be if the chef wouldn't utter "*ne, ne, ne*" every three minutes.

The two of us shared a look and rolled our eyes. "Pavlev, we want Italian food, not Russian today."

The look of blasphemy he gave us was comical. Both of us held our grins in, trying not to burst into laughter. The cook waved his hands in the air, then stormed off.

I reached in front of me where a veggie tray sat and picked up a cucumber, then threw it in my mouth.

"I don't know why he gets upset whenever I suggest Italian food," Isla said as I chewed on my veggies. "He has the personality of an Italian."

I chuckled. "You know any Italians with that flamboyant of a personality?"

Both of us burst into laughter.

"I know some hot ones," she remarked, giving up on mincing the garlic.

"Like Enrico Marchetti?" I teased. Her cheeks flushed. It was killing me not to know. Besides, I wanted to see if there was a way I could get in touch with him. If there was something with her and Marchetti, which I was certain there was, she'd be able to hook me up with him. "Or is there a hotter Italian than that daddy?"

She giggled softly. "He is a hot daddy, isn't he? And I don't even know if he has kids."

"That's not the kind of daddy I'm talking about."

Isla's eyes gleamed and laughter floated through the kitchen. She padded over to the little stereo and started flipping through the channels. She settled on a classical music channel. Definitely not my first choice, but I let her have it. For now.

"Want some wine?" I offered.

"Oh, yes. Pour it in." So I poured her a glass of wine, then readied to pour myself one. My movement paused, a bottle hovering above the glass. "Shit," I muttered.

"You okay?"

"Yep." It was such a habit to pour myself a drink. But I kicked that habit to the curb. For my babies. For my well-being. "The question is whether you're okay?"

Her brows furrowed. "What do you mean?"

I shrugged. "Well, you get so red every time I bring up Enrico Marchetti. I worry your cheeks might remain stained forever."

"My fucking complexion sucks," she muttered.

"I think it's beautiful." She just rolled her eyes, then took a sip of wine. Both of us gave up on Italian food, but not Italian men. "Now, about Marchetti—"

She reached across the table and grabbed a piece of broccoli. When my eyebrow rose, she just muttered, "It goes good with the wine."

"If you say so."

"I do," she muttered. "And there's nothing about Enrico Marchetti to tell." I studied her, refusing to believe that. I was certain there was plenty to tell. She sighed. "Okay, it was just one night."

One night. With the hot daddy. Jesus Christ. Illias would blow a gasket. Whatever the business partnership the two had going, it'd go up in smoke.

"Does your brother know?" I asked while a plan started to form in my mind. Nikita was on me like a fly on shit while Illias was gone. However, when he was around, he usually stayed away. It might be my chance to get out of here and search out the answers.

Marchetti would have them since it was clear he'd wanted Adrian dead.

Isla snickered. "God, no. My brother still thinks I'm twelve." Well, that sounded familiar. I got wild in college, dragging Isabella with me into trouble. My first taste of freedom and I flew like a bird. No regrets.

"You don't think your brother would approve? After all, Marchetti and Illias are friends," I remarked dryly.

And partners in crime, I added silently. I needed to know exactly what Adrian's crime was.

Her eyes flickered to me, watching me strangely. "They don't know each other."

She grabbed a piece of carrot and bit into it. The sound of her crunching filled the kitchen. Tension seemed to grow with each crunch, reaching high levels. There was something off and Marchetti was the connection. At least it seemed that way.

"What makes you think they don't know each other?" I couldn't force myself to lie to her. It was obvious at Maxim's funeral that they knew each other. And then there was the phone call. And my memory. Marchetti and Konstantin weren't just mere acquaintances.

A freaking year! It took a whole goddamn year to get to this point and remember that night. The therapist knew what he was talking about, after all. My memories from the accident came back when I was ready to handle them. Yet, I couldn't shake off the slight taste of betrayal that Illias had left me in the dark.

He should have fucking told me.

"What makes you think they do?" she asked, studying me curiously. I'd have to be careful with her. She was too observant.

I shrugged. "Bad assumption, I guess," I answered vaguely and filled her glass back up.

At the other end of the kitchen, Nikita watched us. He couldn't hear our conversation. I was never fond of bodyguards lurking like dark shadows around me. Well, Nikita seemed to be determined to become exactly that. It drove me fucking nuts.

"Hey, Nikita," I yelled across the kitchen. "Want a drink?"

His expression remained unmoved, but something flickered in his gaze. Annoyance maybe. He was probably pissed to have to stay back and watch over us women. Isla said he usually traveled everywhere with Illias, but this time, her brother insisted he remained behind with us.

He didn't trust anyone else to keep us safe.

"Don't taunt him," Isla whispered, downing her drink. "He'll get mad."

I snickered. "I think it might be too late for that."

"I don't think he likes watching us," she muttered.

I shrugged. "Well, he's free to leave anytime," I remarked as I refilled Isla's glass.

"You're going to get me drunk," she complained, her speech slightly slower already. She was well on her way. "Then take advantage of me."

She was funny. How did Isla have such a serious brother? Probably the same way I did. Vasili was all bossy, serious, and no fun. Sasha was special. A bit on the crazy side. And then there was me. A perfect angel.

"You have to drink for both of us." I put the bottle down, then rubbed my belly. "And I promise my hands will never touch you," I teased.

She waved her hand, then winked. "You can watch but cannot touch." She put her hands on her cheeks and her eyes turned hazy. "I cannot think about that right now." My sister-in-law was funny when tipsy. "I'd have to ravish a man and that would be inappropriate."

And apparently she was horny.

"Totally inappropriate," I agreed, then lowered my eyes. "See what happens when you do inappropriate things."

She giggled. "Get knocked up?" I nodded. "Two babies, huh?"

I grinned. "Two babies. I still can't believe it. I've wanted to have children for so long, and now, it's happening."

"I bet you never thought it'd be with my brother when you met him all those years ago," she remarked.

I let out a sardonic breath. There were many things I never thought would be with Illias Konstantin.

"Life works in mysterious ways." I leaned conspiratorially across the table. "And I have a feeling, it'll work that way with you and Marchetti."

"Tatiana," she scolded, but her giggle ruined it.

I groaned. "I'm dying here," I admitted. "His luxury-brand empire fascinates me." His connection to the criminal world and Adrian's death even more, but I left those words unsaid.

The cook came back through the kitchen door, muttering and glaring at our half-prepped meal.

"We don't know how to cook," I lied. "Come and make us Italian pasta. Gelato. Italian dick? Anything Italian, we'll take it."

He whirled around like a prima donna and left the room again with a string of Russian curses behind him. "He just has to curse in Italian, and there'd be nothing convincing me he's not an Italian deep down."

Isla giggled. "You're incorrigible. Illias isn't the type to like anyone with opinions. He must love you so much."

Her comment momentarily stilled me. My heart tugged in an unnatural way, followed by a raw wave of warmth that flickered in my chest. It was different from anything I had felt before.

Love me?

Sardonic amusement mixed with a hint of bitterness filled me. I was getting ahead of myself. I loved Adrian, but he had never uttered those three little words to me. I had said the words plenty for both of us. Yet somehow it fed the resentment and bitterness.

Love and marriage were a two-way street. At least I thought so. It seemed to be the case with Vasili and Isabella. It wasn't as if I'd model my marriage to what little I heard of my own parents' relationship.

So here I was. Married again and clueless on what I should and shouldn't tolerate from a partner.

Pushing the ridiculous notion of love out of my head, I stood up. The feet of my chair dragged against the tiled floor, breaking the sounds of music with a loud screech.

"We need a better song," I told her. I switched through the stations, my motion pausing. "No freaking way," I muttered under my breath.

The very same song by Bruno Mars. "I love that song," Isla chirped, jumping to her feet.

She shook her ass like Beyonce, or maybe even Shakira, and I shook my head amused. I'd wager all my money that Isla and her friends were wild, keeping their innocent, sweet expressions in front of their families.

"Want me to tap your ass like your girlfriends in the video?" I asked loudly when she bent over, twerking her ass.

For the next four hours, I saw a completely different side of Isla.

TWENTY
KONSTANTIN

Almost a week since I'd touched my wife. Fucked her. Heard her moans. And fuck if I'd go another day without her.

Each night without her was agony. Every day felt like a year without her. The Omertà could go to fucking hell. It got my vow but not my dick and certainly not my heart.

And here I was, meeting the goddamn Italian in Mongolia. Brussels Belgian Beer Cafe in Ulaanbaatar, Mongolia. Leave it to the Italian to find a bar like this in Mongolia. I refused to meet him in Italy. It wasn't on my way to Russia. So it was going to be Mongolia or nothing.

"Eager to get home to your wife?" Marchetti mused.

I didn't bother answering him. He wanted this meeting. He got this meeting. So he better get it over with before I walk out of it.

Marchetti lounged on the couch opposite me, his eyes cool. We discussed security and business, but there was something else on his mind. And it had nothing to do with business nor my wife.

"Romero wants an expedited wedding," he remarked offhandedly.

I shrugged. He knew I didn't agree with that approach. "I don't need a wedding invitation," I remarked dryly. Not that the wedding would happen. Amon was going after his queen—whether she wanted it or not. "Unfortunately, my wife and I must decline since we're busy."

Judging by Marchetti's expression, he wasn't happy about it. He liked the members of Omertà to show their support during events like that. We eliminated threats together. We grew wealth together. We got married together.

Amon was never meant to take a seat at the table. His father's background gave him a foot in the door. His mother's background kept a foot out. The opposite was true when it came to the Yakuza. But our empire would stretch all around the globe if Amon Leone took over.

"You went above me to Amon," Marchetti declared calmly. "I'll be sure to return the favor. Maybe with your bride. Or maybe your sister?"

Something dark and unwanted snaked through my chest.

"How in the fuck do you know about my sister?" I growled.

Marchetti's chuckle filled the space. "I have my ways, Konstantin. You're not my only tech guy." Giovanni better hope I never get my hands on him. I might strangle him. It had to be him. He was the only other tech guy in the group. Smart fucker.

Learning about my meeting with Amon probably wasn't too difficult. Although, it seemed incredible that Giovanni would be able to dig that up. When I initially erased all Konstantin connections to Isla, I had Maxim attempt tracing her back to us. He wasn't able to. How in the fuck was Agosti able to?

It was pointless to ponder on it now. Enrico knew about her. Tatiana and Isla were my biggest strengths and weaknesses. He knew it. I knew it. But I also knew his weakness. One in particular and I wouldn't hesitate to use it if he attempted to hurt my family.

"Did you know I've met her?" he asked, amused.

My jaw clenched. "No, that's fucking news to me. And how in the fuck did you meet her?"

"She and her friends held a fashion show at one of my venues," he explained, his tone bored. God, he could sometimes irk the shit out of me.

"My family's off-limits." The burn inside my chest flared and spread like an inferno. Marchetti watched me with an amused gleam in his dark brown eyes. He looked like an Italian, which women seemed to fall all over themselves for. "Glance their way and you'll regret ever hearing the Konstantin name."

"Oh, we both know you wouldn't drag your sister into a messy war with me," he said curtly.

Ice crept into my veins. This was the second time he mentioned my sister. The one he wasn't supposed to know about. Unless—

"Did you get another video?" I asked while uneasiness vibrated beneath my skin.

"I did," he confirmed while blood drummed in my ears. I've kept Isla off everyone's radar. She didn't even carry the same last name. I ensured every connection between us was concealed so nobody would ever find her.

Yet here we are, my mind mocked.

Part of me wanted to strangle Marchetti. Eliminate the man who knew of my sister's existence. "Who else knows about her?"

"Just me," he said mildly, disinterest in his voice. But he was trying too hard to keep it there. "Since you enjoy fucking with my plans, I figured I'd return the favor and fuck with yours. It was either your sister or your wife, and I wasn't quite ready for this planet to burn."

He smiled but it lacked any hint of humor. My gut twisted and my anger boiled to a full-blown rage at the thought that he entertained doing something to my wife.

"Don't ever mention my wife or even hint of her again," I said, my voice deadly calm despite the inferno raging through me. "And Isla's off-limits or I'm done with the Omertà." He seemed animated by my response. We both knew the only way out of the Omertà was death. But I'd be sure to take him along for the ride.

"She's a lovely young lady," he remarked casually and a cold blast of fury ignited in my chest. I could have choked the life out of Marchetti without skipping a single heartbeat.

That *fucker*. Red dotted my vision. Rage coiled in my chest. I wanted to smear his blood all over the walls and floors.

"Trust me when I say you won't like my departure from the organization if you so much as look my sister's way," I threatened. "And I'll be sure to drag you along with me to the depths of hell where neither my wife nor my sister will be of your concern."

A knowing smile played on his mouth. A smug expression passed his eyes as if he were satisfied I had just confirmed something for him.

"I look forward to it, Konstantin."

I stepped inside my home, greeted by walls that thudded and glass that vibrated by the loud music that blasted through the whole first floor. It was so fucking loud, I was surprised an avalanche didn't follow from the nearby hills. Heck, even a mountain.

The music blasted with some old song that I even recognized. I couldn't believe my sister would listen to Brother Louie from the '80s. Or was it the '70s? Fuck if I knew.

The familiar song thundered through the air and I almost expected a disco ball somewhere. Brother Louie seemed to be the theme. If I saw someone in those fucking shoes with double platforms, I'd start shooting.

I turned the corner and found my guards filling the hallway.

"What the fuck is going on here?" I barked. They all crowded in front of the double doors to my living room. Two of my men had their ears pressed against the doors, listening. I must be hiring idiots because there'd be no chance in hell they'd hear anything over the loud music.

"Why aren't you in there watching them?" I demanded to know, my eyes on Nikita. "Instead you're out here holding each other's dicks."

Nikita stepped forward, an implacable expression on his face. "That blonde angel of yours shot one of the men."

A growl vibrated through my chest. She shouldn't have to feel the need to shoot someone in my home. If someone had attempted to hurt her, I'd shoot all these motherfuckers myself.

Red dotted my vision. "What happened? What did he do?" My voice was like a whip of cold air.

Nikita shook his head. "Did it occur to you to ask what she did?"

Tatiana was wild. And impulsive. But she was my woman and I wouldn't allow any man to question her or her actions. That was only my prerogative.

"Watch yourself, Nikita," I warned in a low voice. "She's my wife."

His lips thinned in displeasure. "Your wife instructed us to remain outside. She and your sister are having private dance lessons and Mrs. Konstantin threatened that her next bullet would pierce someone's heart."

Okay, Tatiana could be wild. I knew that. But fuck it. I'd prefer her wild side to her sad one. Although I worried about the influence that would have on my baby sister. Isla was timid and shy around strangers.

"Why didn't you cut off the music by shutting down power to the room?" Boris questioned, appearing behind me.

"That sounds like a better approach," I agreed.

Nikita's jaw clenched and his expression turned darker. "Fuse box is in the room," he remarked. "Inside." He tilted his chin towards the closed doors. "You said if anyone lays a finger on her, you'll cut their hands off. She played on that."

I didn't know whether to be proud or mad. Definitely proud. Queen through and through.

Leaving them all behind me, I pushed the doors open and strode through it. The doors bounced against the wall, hinges protesting at the violence. Of course, not a sound came through since the music blaring through the speakers drowned all other noises.

Hence neither my sister nor Tatiana noticed me enter. But I noticed them. They danced like they were professional strippers and Isla was drunker than a Russian sailor. My jaw flexed. My sister never touched alcohol, not even at Christmas.

And barely a week with Tatiana and my sister was hammered.

Tatiana wore black leggings that hugged her curves and an over-sized, light blue sweater that came down to her mid thighs. My sister wore some shorts and a tank top that barely covered her ass. In the middle of fucking winter!

Okay, my proud moment might have diminished under that revelation. Anger simmering under my skin, I strode to the power outlet and yanked the cord from the wall.

Music came to a halt in the middle of a verse. Both had their hands on the support column, their asses jutted out. It looked like they were competing for the gold medal in pole dancing. If that was a category at the Olympics, the two of them would win it.

"What—" Tatiana's undignified voice filled the silence.

Two sets of eyes met my gaze. One drunk and one surprised. Her expression quickly turned smug. Deafening silence followed as my wife and I had a stare down. She won it.

"What in the fuck are you doing?" I roared.

She smiled, smugness still filling her expression. But she didn't lose her cool. In fact, she seemed to be extremely pleased with my reaction.

"My dear husband, you've finally come back to your wife. I have missed you so much. I cooked and cleaned, filled my days with sewing and knitting, but nothing quite pleased me. I prayed and counted the days when my beloved would return home to me." Her eyes flashed with the anger she hid under her pale blue gaze. "To the wife he knocked up."

Jesus Christ.

She was pissed. And I was fucking rock hard.

TWENTY-ONE
TATIANA

Illias's eyes simmered with lust.

They were darker than midnight, and despite my anger, my hormonal body responded. Yes, it was immature to blame it on my hormones but whatever.

"Isla, go to your room," he barked.

I glared at my husband, frustration bubbling in my chest. "Don't talk to her that way."

"It's okay," Isla assured. She looked mortified to have been caught by her brother shaking her ass.

"No, it's not okay," I snapped. "Newsflash. You're a grown woman. He doesn't get to tell you what to do. Especially when he's the one with so many fucking secrets."

Isla's eyes darted from me to her brother, then back to me. She didn't know what I was talking about. But she was smart enough not to ask. She might have been sheltered, but she had good instincts and an excellent sense of self-preservation.

"Go to your room, sestra," Illias ordered. He was a picture of remorselessness. Shocking. The guy was used to getting what he wanted. "You and I will have a talk tomorrow about your fashion show at Enrico Marchetti's venue."

Both of us stilled, shock waves rolling through us. We shared a glance and I gave her a barely noticeable shake of the head. There was no sense in denying it. Whatever he found out, he was certain of what he learned. Hopefully, it was purely platonic information. Isla happened to be at the venue that was hosted in Marchetti's building. That was a story I would stick to. Either way, it meant I'd have to expedite my plan.

I'd kidnap my sweet sister-in-law tonight. It'd be more subtle than my own kidnapping, but kidnapping nonetheless.

"Now, Isla," he barked and she startled which earned him a glare from me. "To your room."

She sent me a worried glance and I gave her a reassuring smile.

"Don't worry, I have three bigger, scarier brothers than him," I assured her. "Illias is like a big pussycat."

A groan filled the space. "Don't call me a pussycat, wife."

I shrugged. "If the shoe fits."

Isla's eyes darted between the two of us, unconvinced I could handle her brother. He was a force of a man. But she hadn't met my brothers; otherwise, she'd have more faith in me. I could have all four of them for breakfast if I wanted to. Even if I had to resort to playing dirty.

"It's okay," I repeated. "I'll check on you later. Grab two Advil before you go to bed."

With a nod, she swayed on her feet as she left the room and headed upstairs. The moment the door clicked shut behind her, Illias was on me in one long stride.

My back hit the wall. His body pressed against mine. His hands grabbed my thighs as he forced them open. "You are wrong to compare me to your brothers," he purred, too dangerously soft. "Because, Tatiana, my angel, your brothers would never do this."

In one swift move, his fingers slid inside my pants and under my panties. He pushed a finger inside me and a moan slipped through my lips. God, it felt so good having his body against mine. To have his thick finger inside me.

"Ah, moya luna," he purred. "Your pussy missed me."

I scoffed. "Don't fool yourself." He thrust his finger, followed by a second, into my clenching entrance. "You left without a fucking word," I hissed, my tone breathy as he plunged in and out of my greedy sex. "I'm mad at you."

He chuckled, his mouth skimming my cheeks. My jaw. My lips. "You can be mad at me while I'm eating your pussy."

My mouth parted, but I couldn't find it in me to deny him. Did it make me weak? Maybe. But fuck, if I wanted it too, why not take advantage of it. He slid his fingers knuckles deep inside me and my eyes grew half-lidded from desire.

My hips arched into his touch.

"Where were you?" I rasped, curious if he'd give me an answer.

"I met with Marchetti," he responded, his mouth back to skimming my jaw. "He says hi."

Surprise flooded me that he answered honestly.

"About?" I asked hopefully. Maybe we could work together. Maybe Konstantin could tell me everything that led us to that night of the accident. I'd help him with that chip and he'd help me understand what exactly Adrian did.

"A fashion brand deal." Okay, maybe not. Disappointment flooded me. Obviously, he wouldn't tell me anything. Fine. It worked both ways. If he refused to share information, I'd do the same. His thumb found my clit and my head fell back. Gasps and moans traveled through the air.

"I can smell your arousal." My clit throbbed. My vision blurred. My ears buzzed. "I'm starved and I'm going to feast on this pussy all night."

"Maybe this pussy doesn't want you," I replied nonchalantly. "Maybe she's in the mood for another man."

My breathy voice might have ruined my intent, but the result was perfect. Suddenly, Illias grabbed me by a fistful of hair. His gaze locked on me full of turmoil. His gaze burned, revealing currents underneath his darkness that would pull me into oblivion.

"Don't ever joke around about touching other men." The venom in his voice had my heart racing. He pulled his finger out, then slammed two back in. "I'll murder a man for just looking your way."

"Th-that might be a problem," I breathed, my pussy grinding against his hand. My blood thundered in my ears. Lust drowned all other noises, leaving me alone with him. "Because if I murder every woman just looking your way, it will leave only the two of us in this world."

"I'm fine with that."

His gaze burned hot. Obsessive. Possessive. Madness. Those were the three words I'd use to describe my husband. And all of it was aimed at me.

His hands left me. He took a small step back. Fuck, nobody looked as good as Illias in a suit. Broad shoulders that his custom-made suits hid. The tanned skin I knew it hid. A savage and ruthless man packaged in a sophisticated suit.

I wanted him naked. I wanted to feel his hot skin against mine.

"Take off your clothes." Something about his commanding tone sent shudders through me. I obeyed quickly. Too eagerly. But a week without him inside me had been agonizing. My clothes discarded on the floor, I stood naked in front of him.

His fingers traced my lower belly, his touch gentle and reverent. "How are you feeling?"

The reverence in his voice sent a fever through me. Shower me with money, fashion, diamonds… that was all great. But this… the reverence in his voice for our babies was what made me fall to my knees.

"They missed their papa," I murmured. He took a step forward, closing the space between us.

The darkness in his eyes flashed with the light. Time suspended. Our breaths intermingled. Then his mouth crashed down on mine. Effortlessly, he scooped me up, my legs wrapping around his waist. He held me tightly as he walked across the room.

I'd leave him tonight. I'd go searching for answers. But he'd come for me. Without a doubt, I knew he'd find me. I just didn't know where we'd be at the end of it all.

He sat down on the couch, my knees straddling him. His heavy gaze caressed every inch of my body. My mouth. My breasts. My stomach. My curves. His hands followed the path of his gaze, a rough and claiming touch leaving marks behind. As if he wanted the entire world to know I was his. His mouth latched on to my breast and a shot of lust rushed through my bloodstream. His touch was rough and urgent, mirroring my own. He fed my fire. I ignited his.

My hands buried in his hair as he sucked on my nipples, each graze of his teeth against the sensitive flesh sent tremors through me.

His hand slapped my ass. "Stand up and sit on my face."

He barely got his command out before he jerked me upward. I squealed softly, but it quickly turned into a moan as he pulled me down on his face. His stubble was rough against my sensitive flesh. I groaned. He groaned. I braced my thighs on the back of the couch and my hands in his hair while his face was buried in my pussy.

He sucked and licked. My hips rolled and ground against his mouth. My moans filled the space. In the back of my mind, I worried about suffocating him, but the moment I tried to shift away, his hand came down on my ass.

Slap.

I yelped, gripping a fistful of his hair.

"Get back on my face," he growled. "I want to suffocate with your pussy on my face."

His fingers dug into my hips and he slammed me down back on his face. The groan vibrated from him and straight to my core. He swirled his tongue in circles, lapping my juices. Then he nipped my sensitive, swollen clit and pushed his tongue inside my entrance. My hips bucked. I gasped. The orgasm shot through me, stealing my breath away.

I had no fucking idea when he'd unfastened his pants, but he was pulling his dress shirt from his pants and I pulled him out, my movements eager and frantic. He was hot and heavy in my hand, and so hard. Then without warning he grabbed my hips and slammed inside me.

"Ohhhhh... my... God..." I choked breathlessly, pleasure blazing through my veins.

"Your husband," he murmured against my mouth. "Not God. I'll kill him too."

My silly heartbeat tripped over itself. My breath shuddered. My tits rubbed against the material of his suit.

"Whatever you want," I breathed, my fingers frantically ripping his suit jacket off, then working on his shirt. The moment my palms felt his warm skin, I sighed. Touching Illias was a sin in itself. His warm skin smelled like home. My home. I licked it, tasting citrus and sandalwood.

My own personal heaven. My own personal hell. My purgatory.

"Remember those words." He leaned forward and took my bottom lip between his teeth. "Because I'm fucking you all night," he rasped against my mouth. He was so deep inside me—my body, my soul, and my brain—that I should be terrified. Yet, the only thing I could feel was excitement.

Our mouths molded together. I slid my tongue inside and a groan from deep in his chest vibrated against my own heart. His hands tightened on my hips and he started grinding them against his cock.

He broke the kiss just long enough to say, "Ride me, baby."

I did. His kiss turned rough, his tongue mimicked the rolling of my hips. My blood drummed in my ears, rushing through my veins. Fuel and flame ignited, consuming me. Just like this man. My husband.

I rolled my hips, at first slow and lazy but he wouldn't have it. So he took charge. His fingers dug into my flesh and he lifted me slightly, until his hard length almost slid out of me. Only to pull me harder down on his shaft, slamming my pussy against his pelvis. My clit ground against it. My head fell back. His harsh breathing and my moans filled the silence.

The sensation of him so deep inside me drove me closer to the edge. His grunts and groans echoed my moans. He repeated the movement and a shudder rolled through me. His rough hands held me tightly. I could feel the brush of his body against every inch of me. My breasts against his hard chest. Our heartbeats thundering hard in sync.

His teeth nipped my jaw, then he kissed me hard. Rough.

He moved me up and down, hitting a spot deep inside me. The pressure built. He swallowed my moans. I shuddered against him with each brush of my clit against his pelvis. He rocked me, controlling the speed.

Coiled pleasure exploded through me. My insides clenched, strangling his cock. My breathing hitched.

"Fuck!" He let out a deep masculine groan, burying his face in the crook of my neck. He inhaled deeply, then bit my neck, marking me. My own pleasure sent tremors through my body and slowly dissipated as he shuddered in my arms, following me over the edge.

His forehead came to mine. Our breaths came out heavy and erratic. My gaze drowned in his.

"You okay?" he murmured softly. My fingers threaded through his hair, my senses overtaken by him. His hard body molded against mine. Or mine molded to his.

"Yes."

His eyes were focused on me. A molten flame, sending lava through me. "Good, because we've just gotten started." He kissed the tip of my nose. "I missed you."

Bu-bum. Bu-bum. I could feel his heart as if it were my own.

Emotions danced through me. And a startling realization sunk in.

I'd fallen in love with my husband.

TWENTY-TWO

KONSTANTIN

"I'm going to bed," Tatiana yawned.

"No, you're not," I told her. "You're mine all night. Seven nights to make up for."

The hallway to our bedroom was empty and dark. Everyone dispersed once they learned I was home. Back to their positions. They shouldn't have been swarming around my wife and sister anyhow.

She glanced at me over her shoulder. "You left for seven nights, not me. I've been satisfied, so now I'm going to sleep." She swayed her hips as she walked, purposely giving me a perfect view of her ass. This was not the way she usually walked. Little temptress. "You can jerk off in the shower until you have your fill. Don't forget the lube."

The moment our bedroom door shut behind us, I smacked her ass. Her hair whipped through the air as she turned to glare at me.

"What the fuck?" she snapped, whirling around and putting her hand behind her.

"I told you; we're doing this all night," I growled.

She narrowed her eyes. "Well, use words, Illias. Not your hands on my ass."

I grinned.

"You liked it when you rode my cock downstairs." Her cheeks

flushed crimson and my dick instantly responded. I'd love to see her ass turn red too. "Now, get rid of your clothes and bend over the table."

Her eyes followed mine to the desk where I usually did some work, then returned to look at me.

She swallowed. "Don't you need to rest or something? At your age, it must—"

Her words faltered at my grim expression. I didn't like to be reminded of our age difference. Normal couples wish their spouses to continue their life in happiness. Fuck that! I wanted Tatiana in life and death. Always the two of us. Together.

"Clothes. Off. Now."

She rolled her eyes, but she obeyed. Probably more for her benefit than mine. Her clothes discarded on the hardwood, she stood in front of me naked. It turned me the fuck on. I was already semi-hard making my way up the stairs, watching her sway her hips up the stairs.

But seeing her like this, there was no turning back. No sleeping tonight.

"Bend over that desk."

"This is ridiculous," she protested as she turned around and jutted her ass as she bent over the table. "Hands above your head."

She shook her head. "I bet *you and your friends* never want to hear those words."

Ignoring her jabs, I leaned down and spread her arms wide, then bent her fingers over the edge of the table. "Hold on to that, moya luna, and don't move."

My hand trailed down her graceful spine, lower to the curve of her ass, then I swatted her bare ass again. Her hips bucked and her toes curled.

"Spread your legs wider."

To my surprise, she obeyed without a complaint. But the joke was on me because the moment she did, I could see she was wet. Her juices glistened, begging me to lick her clean. My cock turned painfully hard, tempting me to just slam inside her.

She was my home. Not just her body. Her heart. Her soul. Her wit.

Everything about her screamed home to me.

My hand came down on her ass again and a pleasured moan filled the room. Her pussy swelled in front of my eyes. I reached between her legs and spread them further. The scent of her arousal and roses seeped into my lungs. She turned her head and watched me with lust in her eyes.

"I want your cock," she hissed her demand.

I kicked off my shoes, then casually started disrobing. My suit jacket. My tie. My shirt. Pants. Socks.

My cock strained for her. It always wanted her, but it was better if I made her suffer. I wrapped my hand around my shaft, stroking the length from tip to base. With my other hand, I slide my hand over her lower back, then her round ass.

"I thought you wanted me to jerk off," I said, sliding my fingers down between her legs and over her slick pussy.

"I don't anymore," she rasped. "Now I want you to fuck me."

Smack.

"How do you ask for things?" I demanded, swirling my fingertip over her asshole. "What's the magic word?"

"Fuck. You." I pushed my finger gently past her tight dark hole and she gasped.

"Try again," I purred as I withdrew my finger.

"P-please?"

This woman. She was used to getting her way. God help me, I'd give her anything. She had me wrapped around her little finger and she probably knew it.

"That's right," I commended her. I slid my fingers over her slick pussy again and brought her juices back to her ass, pushing my finger inside. I stretched her asshole, in and out. In and out. "I'm going to claim this virgin ass."

"Yes," she whimpered. "I need more."

I pushed two fingers into her tight hole, stretching her. Her ass ground back against me, her moans louder by the second.

"Want my cock?"

"Yes," she whimpered, her voice breathy.

"Where?" I asked her. When she gave me a confused look, I asked, "In your ass or your pussy?"

Her eyes widened and her lips parted. Goddamn it. I wanted her mouth, her ass, her pussy. All of it.

"Ass."

A satisfied growl vibrated through my chest. I brought my cock, leaking with pre-cum, to her ass and smeared it over her hole. Her hips pushed back against it, her ass muscles clenching greedily. She panted, rocking her ass against my erect cock.

"Remember to breathe," I instructed. She nodded and watched me over her shoulder as I pushed my cock past her ring of muscle. She bucked and I placed my hand on her lower back, caressing her. I kept my thrusts slow and shallow, in and out.

Her gasps and pants somehow matched my own heavy breathing. My hips moved, thrusting against her ass, deeper into her. With one hand, I reached around between her thighs and stroked her clit. I smeared her juices, rubbing it harder and faster. I could feel her tighten, her ass clenching my cock.

Then she bucked, pushing my cock all the way in and that did it. Her body locked and she orgasmed with a cry, her juices gushing down my hand. I thrust into her harder, my mouth latched to the back of her neck.

I bit into her soft skin as I spilled inside her ass.

Her head fell back to rest against mine, and for a moment, the world was as it should be.

TWENTY-THREE
TATIANA

I woke up with a warm, heavy body at my back and strong arms cocooning mine.

My body was sore. My soul and my heart too. True to his words, Illias fucked me all night until I was so exhausted I had to beg him to stop. I shifted around to look at Illias as he slept. Even asleep, he looked like a force to reckon with.

His brows were furrowed. His expression was restless. His lips were pressed tightly.

Maybe he could sense what I was about to do. Or maybe even in sleep he thought about the secrets he would unravel.

Careful not to wake him, I shifted off the bed, then padded to our walk-in closet. I had set aside clothes to put on. My bag was already packed and stored in the vehicle I planned on taking. It had enough clothes for Isla and me, as well as money. While Konstantin kept my phone and personal belongings under lock and key, he gave me free rein of his black American Express and cash.

I took full advantage of it.

The dim lights Illias had installed in his walk-in came in handy as I got dressed. I slid on a bra and panties, then black Lou & Grey yoga pants—hello, comfort—and a loose white sweater. I padded across the closet to grab a pair of Uggs when a fancy black box caught my eyes.

Unable to resist my curiosity, I opened it carefully. *Maybe Illias got me some fancy gift during his travels,* I mused as it popped open.

A piece of paper fluttered out of it and danced through the air until it landed on the floor. I slowly crouched down and picked it up. A note. In my handwriting.

"What—" I whispered under my breath.

You ruined my opportunity to get laid.

Now it's up to you to satisfy those urges.

Meet me at the gazebo.

All these years, he saved the note. A shiver snaked down my spine as the memories of that night came rushing in.

The scent. The consumption. The words.

I should have never mistaken Adrian for Illias.

So many years were wasted. So many lives.

Adrian never wanted me. It was painful to realize it but it was the truth. The question remained why did he marry me. The clues he left behind were confusing. They just kept sending me in circles.

Maybe the chip that everyone wanted held the answers, but I doubted those would ever be shared with me. I was left with no choice.

I'd drag it out of these men.

"Wake up."

Isla swatted her arm and almost punched me in the face. That girl should be cut off from alcohol.

"Wake up," I hissed. When her hand rose through the air I caught it, then slapped her gently on her cheek.

"What—" She jolted up and butted me in the forehead. I saw stars.

Both our whimpers vibrated between us. "Ouch."

I rubbed my forehead as I blinked hard, chasing the stars away.

"What's going on?" she mumbled, alcohol on her breath so heavy I was certain I'd get drunk from a little whiff. I should have cut her off after she switched from wine to hard liquor.

I handed her a pair of her own Uggs. "Put these on. We have to leave."

She blinked her eyes. Then she blinked again. So I pulled on her. "Hurry up. Shit's about to go down."

"Where is Illias?" she asked, her eyes darting around the room as if she expected him to appear out of thin air.

"He's handling the situation," I whispered. Guilt swarmed me. I didn't like lying to her but we had to get our butts out of here. Marchetti killed my husband, so he'd give me answers. And they better be good answers, or I'd kill him.

Still confused, she pulled on her Uggs and I took her cell from the nightstand and put it into my pocket. Thank fuck Lou & Grey had yoga pants with pockets.

Taking her hand into mine, I pulled her along and headed out of the bedroom. My heart thundered as we were sneaking through the hallways. Over the six weeks, I knew every camera and every blind spot.

My brothers didn't raise no fool.

Left corner. Then the right corner. Secret, servant door. Thank God for those.

Ten minutes and we were in the garage. I headed for the Land Rover I designated for this little excursion. Opening the passenger door, I gently pushed Isla into the seat, then buckled her in.

"Stay here."

She stopped me before I could shut the door. "What's going on?"

I waved my hand. "Just safety measures," I assured her. "I'll be right back. Close your eyes." When it was clear she wouldn't, I handed her the phone. "Check the weather."

It was the first thing that came to mind. But I needed her eyes on anything but me. If she saw what I was about to do next, she might become suspicious. She did as I asked, so I quickly shut the door.

I headed to the closest car. Another SUV. I popped the hood, cut the battery wires, then shut it. I moved on to the next SUV. And next. And next. Once all fifteen SUVs were non-functional, I eyed all the sports cars. There was no way they'd make it on the winter roads in Russia even if Illias was crazy enough to drive it in this weather.

"Nah, he's not that crazy," I muttered under my breath.

So I rushed back to the only functioning SUV left and got behind the wheel.

Marchetti, here we come.

We drove away from the castle in silence.

My eyes flickered to the rearview mirror, the castle getting smaller and smaller. Images of burning flames played in my mind. I might not have set fire to Konstantin's castle but I might have burned a bridge.

The tension in my shoulders amplified. The little whisper in my mind told me I was going about it the wrong way. It didn't stop me. My plan was in motion. I'd get the answers or I'd never find peace.

I was doing this for me.

The first flicker of dawn came over the horizon. I had been driving for hours and no car, helicopter, or plane roamed around. Speaking of planes... I looked over to find Isla'd fallen asleep, her soft snores filling the enclosed space. She was beautiful and so damn trusting.

My chest tightened at the thought of anything happening to her. But even worse was this feeling that I'd betrayed her trust. I hoped she'd forgive me.

I reached for her phone, held it in front of her for face recognition.

"And we're in," I murmured, returning my attention to the road. My eyes flickered to her phone book and looked for the pilot listing. She told me she kept Konstantin's pilot in her phone book as "Pilot" since she never knew who was answering that line. Illias apparently had three on standby.

I scrolled to the letter "P" and found it. "Voilà."

Pressing the call button, I waited. Riiiing. Riiing. He answered on the third ring. "Hello?"

"Hello," I greeted him, keeping my voice soft to mirror Isla's. "It's Isla. Can you pick me up in South Africa? I'm in Johannesburg."

"I thought I dropped you off in Russia."

I groaned silently. It was his job to say "yes, ma'am" and get the plane going. Not to fucking question me. Or her. Whatever.

"It got boring and cold, so my friends and I went to Johannesburg."

"Does your brother know?"

"Hmm." I expected a simple acceptance of the assignment, not all these questions. "Yes, but he wants me to come home. You know, with Christmas approaching and all that."

I looked over to Isla and she seemed to still be asleep. Her head was resting on the window, her breaths slow and even, her wild, ginger-red hair covering half of her face.

"You're lucky, since I was just about to fly back to the States."

"Thank you."

I ended the call, then let out a breath.

"What are you doing, Tatiana?" I startled at hearing her voice, my hand jerking on the wheel. The car swayed into the opposite lane and I quickly took control, returning to my lane. Thank God there were no other crazy Russians on the road. Or we would have been toast.

"Jesus, you scared me," I breathed, my heart pounding against my chest.

She didn't seem fazed. "And you kidnapped me." Shit, she was smarter than I even gave her credit for. "Didn't you?"

My grip tightened on the steering wheel. I didn't want to upset her. I didn't want to lose the relationship we built over the last week. We just got to know each other.

Keeping my eyes on the road, I answered, "Kind of. I actually need your help."

She let out a sarcastic breath. "You could have asked, you know."

"I could have," I confirmed. "But I couldn't risk you saying no. Or your brother getting wind of my plan."

She shifted on her seat, her eyes narrowed on me. "Are you leaving him?"

I swallowed. Was I? No, I wasn't. Although I wasn't certain if he'd want me when all was said and done.

It was clear that Illias fell in the same category as my brothers.

Protect me at all costs. Keep the truth from me. I could see it in the way he protected his sister that Illias wouldn't change that. The same way that my brothers wouldn't change their stance in the protection of me. It was ingrained in them.

"No, but I need to find out something and your brother won't help me," I explained.

She raised a brow, studying me. Then she let out a sigh. "Tell me the plan, then," she said dryly. "Obviously, I'm a glutton for punishment because Illias will find us and then he'll lock us up."

I smiled.

"He'll have to catch us first."

And sports cars and Russian winter roads didn't go hand in hand.

TWENTY-FOUR
KONSTANTIN

I stood with my legs slightly parted and my fists behind my back.

It took all my willpower not to explode right now. Not to kill every single one of the men working for me. Lazy, incompetent motherfuckers.

She left me. Took off.

Reaching for my phone, I pulled up the app that tracked her. She was still on the move. By the speed she was going, she had to be in an airplane. Not my airplane. I couldn't envision her in a commercial airplane, so I called up Vasili.

"You got some nerve calling me." Vasili's greeting was so fucking heartwarming, its frostbite was worse than Russian winters. "Where is my bloody sister, and why isn't she answering her phone?"

Fuck.

That meant they didn't help her. I would have actually preferred to learn they did. Tatiana coming up with her escape plan on her own might not bode well for our future together. Jesus fucking Christ! She destroyed the entire fleet of my vehicles, leaving only the useless sports cars behind.

My phone chimed, signaling a text message. **The plane is out of pocket. The flight log shows him going to South Africa.**

What-the-fuck… South Africa?

"She's fine," I grumbled ready to hang up when Vasili's laugh boomed through the headset. "What the fuck is so funny?"

"She escaped you, didn't she?"

"You know?"

"No, but you just confirmed it. She did that a lot during her college years." The fucker could have warned me. "I'll give you one piece of advice, Konstantin. Only for the benefit of my future niece or nephew." If nothing else, I knew my brothers-in-law would protect Tatiana's and my children as if they were their own. Not that there would be the need for that. I was here and I'd burn this planet to the ground for my family. But there was something comforting in the knowledge that if something were to happen, they'd be there for our children. Just like they were for their sister. "The more you try to lock her down, the more she'll run. Let her be free, and she'll never leave her cage."

"You could have told me that before," I hissed.

He chuckled. I saw fucking nothing amusing in this scenario. My wife was out there, vulnerable and open to be attacked. With our babies in her belly.

"I told you Tatiana will never be forced to do anything," he retorted dryly. "She might have fooled you and went along with it, but all along, she's been scheming how to get out of it."

Perfect. Just fucking perfect.

"It was nice chatting with you." *Not.* "But I have my wife to find and ensure she's safe."

"I'd check your men's weapons. I'd bet you money she stole a gun. And not to worry, she knows how to shoot and defend herself. You can thank Sasha for that. And her escape routines."

I'm gonna kill Sasha Nikolaev.

"That doesn't make me feel better," I remarked dryly.

"Me either. If I hear from her, I'll call you, but I doubt she's coming back to New Orleans."

I stilled. It would be the first thing I'd thought she'd do. "Why not?"

"Because she's determined to find out who killed Adrian."

Click.

TWENTY-FIVE
TATIANA

P aris.

The City of Love. The City of Light.

Christmas lights glimmered. The Eiffel Tower lit up like a magical kingdom, pulling you into its charm with the ambience of love and holidays. The weather was cold and crisp, but the city didn't rest. It was in full swing, music on the streets, busy cafés and beautiful lights and decorations everywhere you looked.

And we could see it all from our hotel room at Triangle d'Or. Hotel Marignan Champs-Elysées was romantic. So freaking romantic that I actually regretted not having my husband here with me.

I sighed.

Twenty-four hours. I had done a good job of destroying his chances at following us because we had yet to see a single Russian man. Although Isla's phone had blown up with messages and calls from her brother demanding she call him.

She didn't.

"Let's go have fun," I squealed.

I didn't know what tomorrow would bring, but I'd be damned if I'd let our evening go to waste. We had at least several evening hours to burn.

189

"Yay! I'm ready."

Five minutes of digging through the clothes and we both settled for a dress. Although we'd freeze our butts off. But you cannot be in Paris and not dress accordingly. I opted for a dark blue knee-length dress that flared from my waist down and a pair of nude Louboutin Pigalle heels.

I twirled around. "How do I look?"

"Gorgeous." On the other side of the bed, Isla twirled around. Her nude dress was more subtle than my blue one, but it only accented her natural beauty. "And me?"

Her pink Louboutin Dolly pumps gave Isla an extra three inches and matched her wide belt around her slim waist. The accessory and color coordination were perfect. It was sophisticated but didn't make her look too young.

"You should wear this tomorrow," I remarked. "Marchetti will drool."

She grinned, her cheeks flushing. "I have something better for tomorrow. I bought it in the lobby earlier."

I shook my head. "No credit cards, right?"

"All cash, baby."

"Such a good accomplice," I commended her.

She bowed lightly. "I aim to please."

Ten minutes later, we roamed the streets of Paris. I'd been to Paris a long time ago with Vasili when I was barely ten. It was a vastly different experience now.

Hand in hand, we started walking down the sidewalk. Silence followed us but it was a comfortable one. I sucked in a deep breath, the cold invading my lungs. Compared to Russia, it wasn't as cold. Yet, compared to New Orleans, it was freezing. I wrapped my coat tightly around myself and glanced at Isla to ensure she wasn't cold. Both of us wore similar black dress coats and matching black French berets.

When I handed it to her, she protested but I insisted. I told her, "When in France, you wear a French hat."

"Hats were a good call." She smiled, fixing it so it was tilted fashionably and we continued down the sidewalk.

It didn't take long to get to the humble, slow-moving river, the

Seine. The river flowed through Troyes and through the heart of the city. My step halted and I watched the lights reflect across the surface of the river. The beauty of it hit me and a memory I had forgotten came rushing through.

"Adrian, why can't we stop in Paris on the way home?"

"I have work."

I let out a frustrated breath. "You took time to come to Russia. We can take an extra two days and stop in Paris."

Adrian had taken me to a parking lot in Russia before ending at the hotel room. Our honeymoon was frankly shitty and totally not what I had been expecting. Not even a dinner at a restaurant. Instead, he ordered room service. Yesterday and today.

"No. When I'm dead, go to Paris."

I blinked confused, then repeated slowly, "When you're dead…"

His gaze met mine. Unemotional. Cold. Leveled.

"Go to Paris," he finished the sentence.

Clenching my fists, I gritted, "Then let's go walk the streets of Moscow."

It was an understatement of the century to say I was pissed off. I deserved better than this. If I uttered a single word to Vasili that my honeymoon sucked, he'd handle it, but I didn't want to have to do that. I didn't want to hear "I told you not to date him" from my eldest brother.

Adrian returned his eyes to the screen and I stomped my foot, fury threatening to boil over.

"Adrian!"

The streets and sights of Moscow were better than staring at these four walls. If he'd devoured me and we'd spent them between the sheets, I could be convinced to stay in. But he hadn't even touched me.

"You can go," he retorted, never lifting his eyes off the screen. "I'll wait for you here."

Anger boiled deep inside me, but I refused to start an argument on my honeymoon. No matter how shitty it was. So I grabbed a coat and left without a backward glance.

And here I was. In Paris. Years too late. A life too short.

"Are you okay?" Isla's breath clouded the air, her eyes on me full of worry. I nodded, turning my attention to the Seine. I stared down the river, the sounds of soft, romantic music traveling on the breeze.

"It's ironic, you know," I started softly, something deep inside me aching. Somehow both of my marriages had ended up starting the same way. Elopement. Rushing to Russia. "Adrian, my first husband, took me to Russia for our honeymoon too." She frowned, watching me confused. I shook my head, then sighed. "It's a long story," I added.

She remained silent, waiting for me to continue. Except, I didn't know where this story would take me. Another disappointment? Another clue?

"I'm glad I got to come here with you," I said warmly.

"Me too." She squeezed my hand. "W-was he good to you?"

Bitterness could be like poison, slithering through your veins until you forgot everything but the wrongs. It was so easy to get lost in the wrongs. His. Mine. Ours. It didn't even matter. I remembered the boy who snuck ice cream to me when Vasili said no. The boy who beat up my bullies in high school when Sasha was in the service.

In recent weeks, or maybe even months, I had come to the realization that Adrian *had been* good to me. Until we got married.

Then instead of bringing us closer together, our marriage had torn us apart. And, with each discovery, the seeds of doubt grew and suspicion started to form. Adrian wasn't who I thought he was.

"Yes," I finally answered because anything else was too complicated. Adrian was gone, and now, I just wanted to learn the truth. Have him rest in peace. Find peace for myself. We had earned it. I turned to her and smiled. "We are in the most romantic city in the world. Let's enjoy it tonight."

And we did. We strolled through the centuries-old streets. Its stunning architecture shone in a completely different light.

A Paris night cruise along the Seine River. Drinks at a rooftop bar. We swung by an Art Déco pool. Then ate in Montmartre.

We even shopped. We drifted in and out of the stores. French sales women were more than eager to sell us anything and everything. They called us rich Russians. I didn't bother correcting them until we were leaving the store with bags of dresses and shoes.

"By the way, we're Americans," Isla told them, stealing the words out of my mouth.

The two of us giggled as the door shut behind us with a bell. She looped her hand through mine and we strutted down the sidewalk. Her steps halted and my eyes took in the lingerie store.

My eyes flicked to her, then back to the store. "Why are we standing here?"

"Maybe—"

I shook my head, not letting her finish. "No, no. If your brother learned I took you to a lingerie store and you bought shit to seduce Marchetti, it'd be my head."

She rolled her eyes. "I doubt it. According to the messages I got from my brother, it'll be my head if anything happens to you."

A beat skipped in my chest. Warmth erupted in my heart. So many feelings bloomed in my chest. Illias cared enough for me to threaten his sister. His baby sister. The pressure in my chest grew, and I couldn't wait to see him again.

Just as I opened my mouth, a feeling of being watched slid down my spine. I turned my head and a dark shadow turned his back to me. Familiar broad shoulders. Narrow waist. Muscular ass.

"Is that Nikita?" I asked, narrowing my eyes on the man walking away from us.

"If that was Nikita, he'd kick our asses," Isla remarked. She was right. And he certainly wouldn't be walking away from us.

My pulse sped up. It pounded in my throat. Buzzed in my ears.

Lingerie store forgotten, I rushed after the familiar figure.

He flickered a glance over his shoulder, giving me a glimpse of his profile. A tremor rolled through my body. Anxiety brewed in my chest and ran through me like frost in the winter. It swelled in my chest until it became hard to breathe.

I shook my head. *No, no, no.* It couldn't be him. Calm down. Breathe, Tatiana.

Inhaling a deep breath, I exhaled it slowly. Then repeated it, and all the while my steps never faltered.

"Tatiana," Isla called out. "Wait."

I didn't stop, my steps picking up speed and my Louboutin heels clicking against the pavement.

The familiar stranger turned the corner and disappeared from my view.

I started running, listening for Isla's heels behind me. *Click. Click. Click.* The sound of our heels hitting the sidewalk blended together as I chased the phantom who'd been watching me. I reached the street and turned the corner, then stopped abruptly.

"Jesus, what's that about?" Isla's breath was labored as she bent over and put her hands on her knees. "These heels are a bitch to run in."

She lifted her head, still half bent over, her eyes darting over the dark alley, then back to me.

"What is it?" she asked, still breathing heavily.

My eyes locked on the alley, I started to question myself. The man kept walking, although he wasn't running.

"Nikita?" I called out. His step never even faltered. No acknowledgment. The guy didn't even turn to see who called out.

I was just about to call out again when a bus cut off my view of the shadow man. Zoom. I barely blinked my eyes, the bus was gone and so was the man.

Nobody. There was nothing there. Gone just like that.

"Let's get back to the hotel," I rasped, staring down the empty street.

"Why?"

I swallowed, dread growing in the pit of my stomach.

Because I might be losing my mind.

TWENTY-SIX

KONSTANTIN

My gaze slid back to the monitor, reflecting Tatiana's movement.

Two days! Two fucking days and it felt like two goddamn years.

I attempted to take my Bugatti out to get to the city. Fucking piece of junk! The damn thing barely made it half a mile before it slid out of control. It crashed against the fountain and now sat there with the hood open and the whole driver side smashed.

Then, a snowstorm swept through. There was no way of getting out. My helicopter was unable to make it through the storm. Tatiana ensured my plane was in South Africa. Goddamn end of the world.

And my fucking vehicles were useless.

Fuck, fuck, fuck.

I kept watching the screen, as the little blue dot kept pacing. I was able to narrow down her and Isla's location to the hotel. I could call in a favor to Marchetti, but I didn't trust him. Not with Tatiana and not with my little sister.

Calling the Nikolaev lunatics was out of the question too. Sasha would start a war in the underworld.

Goddamn it!

All the men I trusted the most were stuck in this fucking house with me. I'd been racking my brain trying to figure out what Tatiana's angle was. Maybe she remembered the accident and kidnapped Isla to get back at me? Or maybe Tatiana told her what I had done to Isla's mother and I had lost both of them.

Fuckery all the way around.

I sent messages to Isla. No response, although she read them. I traced down any calls and texts she might have made. She was silent, non-responsive to any messages. Even from her best friends.

Until she reached out to Marchetti.

Except, who reached out to him—Tatiana or Isla? And why didn't that fucker alert me right away?

It made me want to burn his empire to the ground. Fuck it, I didn't even care if I went down with him.

But Tatiana and Isla—I couldn't risk them falling too.

I hacked into the public surveillance. I watched Tatiana and my sister act like tourists in Paris, both carefree like they were on vacation.

I slammed my fist against the table.

A red mist covered my vision. I wanted to protect her. Shield her from Adrian's shit. Instead of trusting me, Tatiana went right into the fire in her blind devotion to that fucker. Adrian.

If I could kill him again, I would. No hesitation.

I should have done that the moment he took Tatiana from me.

The overstimulation of my mind made me blind. It made it hard to think. I knew my control was slipping. My obsession with Tatiana made me blind. Now that I evaluated every single word and look since I came back, I was fucking positive she remembered the accident.

Leaving the table with the surveillance set up, I strode to the window, releasing a heavy breath as I stared at the vast white landscape.

"At least they're safe," Boris remarked, trying to be helpful. *He wasn't.*

I tapped my finger against my thigh. His observation didn't help. The need to protect and punish pulsed through my veins. When I get my hands on my wife, I'd spank her and then fuck her so hard, she'd not be able to walk for fucking months.

"Call Yan, Tatiana's bodyguard," I instructed him. "Have them fly to Paris tonight and watch over them. One or both, I don't give a shit, as long as someone's watching them."

Boris's brows bunched. "That's actually a good idea."

I should have thought of that the moment I realized we were stuck in Russia. "Remind me to never come back to Russia in the winter," I remarked dryly.

"Your wife will be happy about that," he mused.

Assuming I still had a wife when all this was over.

TWENTY-SEVEN
TATIANA

We didn't have much time before Illias caught up to us.

The smart thing would have been to meet Marchetti the moment we arrived. But we needed a few hours of fun and some sleep. Besides, we weren't going to meet him wearing yoga pants.

I was vain. Isla was vain. Fucking sue us.

However, today we were ready.

I wore a champagne-colored dress that came to my thighs and had a crisscrossed back. It hugged my curves perfectly, although it felt slightly tighter around my front. The babies were growing fast and steadily. I glanced at my feet. I paired the dress with Louboutin heels, figuring it might be one of the last times I'd get to wear heels for a while. I opted for no makeup and pulled up my hair in a slick, high ponytail.

I was ready for answers. I steeled my spine and prepared for the worst. Whatever that might be—Adrian's blackmail, betrayal, secret life. I didn't know anymore.

The magnificent view of the Eiffel Tower stretched in front of me. The city glimmered just as brightly under the rays of sun as it did under the lights and the moon last night.

The image of the shadowed man flickered in my mind. I thought about him last night as I drifted off to sleep. Maybe the moon played tricks on me. Or maybe stupid memories were haunting me.

My mind went over every second of that brief encounter. Was that Nikita? The man looked familiar. But then, there looked to be a mark on his cheek when he gave me his profile. Maybe a birthmark? But then, maybe there was nothing there. The profile could have been deceiving. The man didn't act like he knew me.

By the time I drifted off to sleep, I felt sure it was my imagination playing tricks on me. The memories of the past. Then fear of Illias coming after us. It was all catching up to me. Adrian's death. Learning about Illias. Our past that seemed to go further back than I originally thought.

Yes, that had to be it.

And still, my chest tightened. My throat squeezed. Waves rushed through me, erasing the progress I'd made over the last year.

I let out a slow breath, hoping to calm my racing heart. I couldn't think about it. I couldn't go there. It'd put me back to square one.

My hand came to rest on my slightly rounded stomach. I was doing all this so I could move on. For me, for my babies, and for their papa.

I glanced over my shoulder at Isla who still had her head buried in the pillow. My lips curved into a soft smile. She was amazing. I went over the plan with her, and to my amazement, she even added a little spin to it herself.

Take her to Marchetti with a gun pointed at her. I liked the plan. I didn't like the idea of pointing a gun at her. I reached for my purse and pulled out the handgun, then checked the magazine.

Empty. Good!

I didn't want any accidents, especially unplanned shootings. Not when it came to her. She was innocent in all this shit.

"Are you plotting world domination?" Isla mumbled from the bed.

I rolled my eyes, but couldn't stop smiling affectionately. "Not while you're in bed."

"You've got to relax."

I chuckled. I loved her attitude. I loved her personality. I couldn't wait to introduce her to Isabella and Aurora. Even my brothers. They'd adopt her as their own sister.

"I am relaxed," I retorted. Okay, tiny lie. "Did Marchetti confirm?" She smiled smugly and my attention perked. "What?"

"Nothing."

My shoulders tensed. "Then why the smugness?" I took two steps and put my palms on the bed, leaning over her. "You better tell me or I'll tickle you to death."

She rolled her eyes, then sighed dreamily. "Yeah, he confirmed."

I narrowed my eyes. "You're not telling me something."

"What?" she asked defensively. "It's not like you tell me everything."

"For your own good."

She blew a raspberry. "That's for me to decide."

Stubborn woman. It was another thing we had in common. Except, Isla hid it exceptionally well.

"Did you talk to him?" I asked suspiciously. We both went to bed at the same time, and as I drifted off to sleep, I thought she was asleep too. I eyed her and her blush betrayed her. "When?" I demanded to know.

"God, if you were my sister, I'd be a nun," she muttered. "Doesn't bode well if you have a daughter."

It was my turn to smile dreamily. Twins. I wouldn't mind two daughters. Or one of each. Actually, it didn't matter as long as they were both healthy. Then I remembered my question. Little minx almost distracted me.

"When did you talk to him?" I repeated.

"Last night," she mumbled, her cheeks turning an even darker shade of pink.

Then realization sunk in.

"Oh my gosh," I muttered. "Oh my gosh. Did you... Did you have phone sex with him?" Her answer was clear in the way her blush spread down her neck and disappeared under her pjs. "While I slept? In the bed next to you?"

"Well, I had to ease his worries," she mumbled. "I left him with a note that I never wanted to see him again. And now, I'm asking to see him. So—"

"So you played him," I concluded, impressed. "Are you sure we're not related?"

She let out a chuckle. "We are now."

Warmth spilled into my chest. For her. For my new family that had recently expanded and included her. Hopefully it'd include Illias too. It'd be up to him. But he waited for me for so long. Since that night in the gazebo! I hoped that meant he was in it for life.

I waved my hand, hiding the way my heart gushed.

"Go get ready. Make yourself gorgeous but not slutty. Kind of innocently beautiful." She rewarded me with an eye roll. "That way when I hold you at gunpoint, Marchetti will spill all the secrets in his attempt to save you."

She gave me a dubious look. "He might be suspicious."

"Why?"

She shrugged. "He's not a dumb man."

"Well, duh," I retorted wryly. "The man hid behind his luxury brand and somehow had time to run a large part of the underworld. Yeah, I'd say he wasn't dumb. But he's blind when it comes to you," I declared.

Her eyes bulged out of her head. "What makes you say that?"

I shrugged. "I saw the way he looked at you in the video at the fashion show."

"Goddamn it, you're scary," she grumbled, jumping out of bed. "If only we knew you—"

She cut herself off and her eyes glanced away from me. Her complexion paled and her bottom lip quivered for a fraction of a moment before she pulled herself together. There were secrets she harbored. And I didn't think it was anything trivial, but she didn't trust me enough to share those with me.

She padded toward the bathroom, her hand on the door. "Isla?"

Her eyes darted to me. "Hmmm."

I watched her, every fiber of me on high alert. I didn't know what she had done... actually, she said "we," so I'd wager it had something to do with her and her friends. But I knew that no matter what it was, I'd have her back. I'd murder anyone who tried to hurt her.

She was family. And a Nikolaev never turned their back on family.

"If you're ever in trouble or need anything," I said softly, holding her emerald gaze. A protective streak flared inside me. "And I seriously mean *anything*, I'm always here. No matter what."

She disappeared into the bathroom, shutting the door behind her, but not before I noticed her hands trembling.

"Tatiana?" Her muffled voice came through the closed door.

"Yes?"

"Thank you."

The corners of my lips tipped up. "I'll burn the world down for you, sestra."

"Ditto."

We were in this for life.

"This is his house?" I asked. Isla nodded. "Jesus."

The massive house in the city of Paris with a fence surrounding it had to be worth a fortune. It was like a mini-castle in the heart of the city.

"Who did it belong to?" I muttered under my breath. "Marie Antoinette?"

History wasn't my strength, but there was no way in hell this place didn't belong to royalty over the last ten centuries.

"No fucking clue," Isla answered, her tone tense. The two of us stood around the corner, keeping out of sight until we were ready for our three-act play. It was best to think of it as a theater drama.

Act one—The discovery of conflict. Act two—The obstacle or complication. I could go without this one. Act three—The resolution.

In fact, I'd prefer it to be a one-act play. *Just get it over with so we could all move on.*

I needed to get rid of the tension in my body. Shaking my hands and loosening my legs, I looked like I was getting ready to run a marathon. Or be in a fight. Fuck, I was nervous. I didn't know why. Something in the back of my head kept nagging at me but I couldn't quite pinpoint it.

"Nervous?" Isla's voice was a tad bit breathy. If I had to guess, she was nervous for an entirely different reason than me. She wore a pair of skinny jeans and a cropped green sweater top that revealed a sliver of her midriff. She paired it with a pair of heels and she looked gorgeous.

"Yeah." Deep breath in. Release. Deep breath in. Release. "Let's do this."

She nodded and I reached inside my purse for the empty weapon. God, I hope this didn't backfire. I needed Isla to come out of this unharmed. If she got laid in the process, it was a bonus.

Her words, not mine.

And who was I to argue? If Marchetti was a good lay, she should get it.

"Okay, I'm gonna put it against your lower back," I murmured low. "Hopefully, his guards don't notice anything until we're inside."

"He doesn't have any guards," she mumbled under her breath.

I tensed, confusion pouring into me. Everyone had guards in the underworld. It was unheard of to be completely unprotected. "Are you sure?"

She nodded. "Yeah, I was here before. There were no guards."

Bizarre.

"Okay, then. This should be easy."

The two of us came around the corner we were hiding behind, strode across the empty street and towards the iron gate. Sure as shit, there were no guards waiting for us. I still couldn't shake off the feeling of a trap. Pushing the iron gates open with a soft creak, Isla kept marching forward with me at her back.

I hated the idea of having her in front of me. It made her an easier target. But she insisted. In her words, "If I'm your captive, I can't be behind you," so we finally settled on the position.

We were at the mahogany front door and she pushed it open with both hands.

"We don't knock or ring a doorbell?" I muttered my question under my breath.

She barely moved her lips. "He said to come in. Trust me."

I trusted her. I didn't trust Marchetti.

We wandered into a gorgeously designed foyer. The crystal chandelier glittered. The marble floors had angel designs on them. The beige walls had valuable art dating back centuries on them.

Jesus Christ!

You'd never have to move past the foyer to rob this man and he didn't even have guards. There was something fundamentally wrong with Marchetti. I was certain.

She started for the staircase and I stiffened. "Please tell me he didn't instruct you to go to his bedroom."

She let out a soft groan and I watched in fascination as the back of her neck turned red. Good God, I didn't think I wanted to know what she and Marchetti got into. I might kill him myself. Yeah, he was hot as sin and had some serious hot daddy vibes, but Isla was too fucking young for him.

Goddamn it! I should have loaded bullets in my gun for him.

Fuck, fuck, fuck!

We made our way up the stairs, our heels clicking softly against the off-white marble floors. Our breathing mixed with the echo of our heels, projecting through the house.

We were both nervous. Perspiration ran down my back and my hand trembled, holding the gun pressed against my sister-in-law's back. I tried to apply the breathing technique Sasha taught me to keep me calm. Breathe in. Breathe out. Breathe in. Breathe out.

It was fucking nonsense.

It only fed my adrenaline. My ears buzzed. My stress kicked up a notch. This couldn't be good for my babies.

"Just a bit more, babies," I murmured softly. "Then it'll be all over."

"Are you talking to the twins?" Isla asked incredulously.

"Yeah."

"Now?" she hissed under her breath. "You couldn't have done that before we left the hotel?"

"I wasn't that nervous then." Deep breaths. Deep breaths. "I want them to know they're safe."

"Enrico won't hurt them," she assured softly, just as we reached the top of the first floor. "Or you. If he tries, I'll kill him."

I rolled my eyes. "Isla, you're scaring me."

She shot me a dark look. "I'm not that innocent," she remarked.

I knew it. It slipped in the moments she didn't keep her guard up. Except I didn't think she liked whatever plagued her. This secret that sat heavy in her heart.

"None of us are," I told her softly. "All of us make mistakes and fuck up. But we move on, make the best of it, and make peace with our mistakes. It's the reason I'm doing this."

She gave me a pensive look, both of our steps faltering. I wanted to tell her so much more, but the moment wasn't right. I needed to assure her that whatever it was she was harboring, I could help her. Her brother could help her. She'd be family, no matter what.

But I never had the chance.

"I must say, I didn't expect two of you here." A deep voice startled us and had us jumping out of our skin. My heart raced into overdrive and I tried to control my breathing.

Steeling my spine and evening my breaths, I shoved the barrel of the gun into Isla's back. Not hard, but enough that she'd feel it pressed on her back. On cue, she stumbled forward, as if I pushed her with all my strength.

"Ouch," she whimpered and I had to bite the inside of my cheek.

Marchetti's eyes darkened to midnight storms and a shiver ran down my neck. My heart faltered as he took a threatening step forward. I barely blinked and his own gun was pointed at me.

Suddenly, I understood why Marchetti didn't need guards. He'd easily kill anyone who threatened him. And I'd bet my life that he'd do it without a second thought.

I swallowed. Maybe we should have thought this plan through a bit more.

"I wouldn't," I said coolly. Thank fuck my voice didn't portray the turmoil inside me. "Not unless you want to see Isla's guts scattered all over your white marble."

Sasha would have been so fucking proud.

His movement stilled, something crossing his face. It was barely a flicker but I saw it. This guy had it hard for Isla. Good, we might get out of this alive yet.

"What do you want, Tatiana?" His voice was like a cold whip against my skin.

I met his gaze head-on, keeping my shoulders straight. I wasn't scared of him. If I whispered it silently enough, I'd give out that vibe.

"I told you I'd come after you when you killed my husband," I said grimly. "Here I am."

Marchetti didn't seem perturbed. He smiled, cold and cruel. "But your husband is alive. In fact, he just landed in Paris. My guess is he's headed here."

I should have known a storm wouldn't keep Illias away. The raging snowstorm has plagued Russia since we left the castle. Honestly, I was surprised he hadn't shown up sooner.

"I guess it means we only have a short time to get this over with, then," I drawled, pushing the gun against Isla's back. "Don't even try to move," I warned her, glaring at her.

Her green eyes flashed with humor but she quickly schooled it. Fuck, she was having too much fun with this.

"Now, Marchetti, unless you want to see your blood or Isla's stain on these floors, you're going to give me some answers," I started, hiding all my anxiety behind my bravado. Fake it till you make it. It was what Sasha always told me. Well, he actually said "Fake it until I come to save you," but I didn't think my brother could save me from this one.

"Are you a cold-blooded killer?" Marchetti drawled.

I shrugged. "Aren't all Nikolaevs?" I answered with my own question. "Kind of like you and the men you work with, huh?"

He put his gun away. I would have taken offense to it if my gun was loaded, but instead, I felt relieved. I couldn't shoot him with an empty gun. He slipped his hands into his pockets and leaned against the wall, looking like a picture of a bored businessman.

"Men?" he asked. "What men?"

I narrowed my eyes on him. They always thought they were so much smarter than women, but I didn't have time for this shit. Not with Illias on his way over.

"I don't give a shit about your men," I spat, glaring at him. "I want to know what happened."

"A lot of things happened," he retorted dryly. "You're going to have to be a bit more specific."

I narrowed my eyes in annoyance. "Why did you kill him?"

My heart clenched and my voice cracked slightly. It still fucking hurt to think of it. I'd known Adrian since I was five. Maybe we weren't the right lovers but we were friends before. For over two decades!

Compassion passed Isla's expression. It was exactly that which made her innocent in all this. She had a good heart. She cared about others. She fought for them. Defended them. Helped them.

"What had he done to put him on your hit list?" I asked.

He studied me, that dark expression reminding me of Illias. I could see these two men being either hardcore enemies or reluctant friends. I wondered what they'd be after today because the way Marchetti watched Isla told me the man would keep her.

I wasn't entirely sure how to feel about it. I guess if she was happy, so was I. Yet, I couldn't shake off the fear that his darkness would swallow her whole.

"You sure you want to know?" Marchetti asked, pulling me out of my worry for Isla's well-being.

"That's why I'm here," I retorted dryly.

"Fine." He extended his hand. "Please, enter."

"I'm not going into your bedroom," I sneered. "I'm not here to fulfill your fantasies. I'm here for answers."

A sardonic breath left him. "I'm starting to see why Konstantin is so obsessed with you."

I chose to ignore his comment. He was just trying to distract me.

Marchetti's eyes flickered to Isla, something dark and vehement flickering in them. His expression changed to mild disinterest when it returned back to me.

"Last chance, Tatiana," he said, his voice dipping to freezing temperatures. "Certain things are best left in the past."

I shot him a dark look. "Just tell me so we can be on our way."

Even as I said "we," I knew I'd be leaving this place alone.

"Fine, have it your way," he drawled in a tone that told me he knew he'd come out on top out of this conversation.

My heart thundered as I held my breath waiting for the answer. He ordered Adrian's execution. Illias wanted Adrian dead, but he defended me. I needed to know why. What had Adrian done that was so bad?

Although deep down I feared I already knew.

I just needed someone to say it out loud.

TWENTY-EIGHT
KONSTANTIN

Anger burned in the pit of my stomach.

I sat on the edge of my seat as the car fought the traffic to get us into the city. My screen showed Tatiana in Marchetti's home.

I ran my hands through my hair. Tatiana had no idea how goddamn crazy I could be. When it came to her, all my rules went to shit. My control was nonexistent. The Omertà would be too if Marchetti fucked me over and touched a single hair on her head.

"Is she moving?" Boris asked. I didn't respond, just watched my phone screen flashing with that little blue dot that represented my wife. "She's a smart woman. She probably remembered that night and went directly to Marchetti to demand answers."

I shot him a dark look, then returned my attention to the screen. As if scared that little blue dot that connected me to her would disappear. If Marchetti decided to take her, she would.

And I'd fucking send all the dirt on him to Interpol, CIA, FBI, DEA. Any and every agency that'd want to stop the underworld from existing.

Apparently Boris was unable to remain quiet today. "Nikita is in the city. Let him take her until you cool off."

My narrowed gaze found his.

"Why is he in the city?" I questioned. "He said he was staying behind."

Boris shrugged. "He said he had family in town and took a commercial flight." He grimaced. "It made no sense why he wouldn't hitch a ride with us, but—"

Something wasn't adding up. Nikita didn't have any family. It was the reason my father recruited him. It was the reason I kept him on.

I tapped my fingers against my thigh, faster and faster, then froze as a thought connected in my head. When I turned to face Boris, the idea was so clear in my mind that I couldn't believe I hadn't thought of it before.

"Pull out a backup server of the castle." When he gave me a questioning look, I continued, "Yes, it only covers one angle of the house." It was the reason we discontinued it. There were too many blind spots and the software was outdated. But it had one thing that updated software didn't.

Coverage of the old back gate.

"If I wanted to smuggle someone into our home, I'd use that old gate," Boris stated, reading my thoughts.

Boris was already retrieving images from the backup server. "It's been wiped," he muttered, locking eyes with me. It was a confirmation it was an inside job. Not too many people know about that server.

"Follow public surveillance from that side and out into the city."

It took two minutes. The familiar clothes. Familiar build. The two Yakuza men joined him, shaking hands.

"Nikita?" Boris's voice held a note of shock. He had been around for a long time. I'd never questioned him twice. "He betrayed us?"

"Yes." My voice was cold. "The question is why."

Boris's brows bunched. "Maybe this family—"

"Trace his family tree," I ordered, tapping my fingers on my thigh. "You have his blood sample?" He nodded. All my men were required to provide it. Boris and Nikita never had theirs run because they've been with me the longest. We just collected the sample and stored it away. I stilled the top of my forefinger on my thigh, remembering

Tatiana's words. That picture. "Have our guy run it against Adrian's blood sample."

He sent the request. The phone chimed, signaling it was being worked on. Five minutes passed in tense silence when the phone chimed again.

"He wants you to call him," he read his message.

I retrieved my phone. The old man picked up after two rings. "Da?"

I got straight to business. "I need answers."

"You're very much like your father in that regard," he retorted dryly. "Cutting straight to the chase."

I didn't have time to waste. "Now," I gritted. "What do you know?"

"You won't be happy," he started. That was never a good way to start a conversation. I clenched my teeth, keeping my fury at bay. "Nikita and Adrian are related. I ran autosomal DNA testing. They are biological first cousins, sharing approximately twelve point five percent DNA. On mother's side." *Motherfucker.* When I got my hands on him, I'd strangle the traitor with my bare hands.

"There's more," he added, his voice almost fearful. I bet the old man was happy to be thousands of miles away.

"What?" I barked.

Two quiet moments passed. "You share DNA with Adrian Morozov." That picture Tatiana told me about flickered through my mind, but before I could even form a thought, his next words confirmed Tatiana's suspicions. "You share twenty-five percent of your DNA with him, which makes you half-siblings."

I ended the call, staring at my phone. My cool tethered, ready to boil into a full, red rage.

"Get me the full file on Nikita and Adrian's family tree," I gritted, barking my demand. Boris nodded and got straight to work.

I clenched a fist, wishing I kept Adrian alive to beat the answers out of him. There was only one other person alive left who could give me the full story. Even if I had to torture him to get it.

It was time to find out the truth.

TWENTY-NINE
TATIANA

I'd like to think I wasn't a coward.

But at this very moment, a part of me battled. To know or not to know the truth.

A part of me wanted to remain in this state of ignorance. Whispers in my head warned there'd be no coming back from this. However, my eldest brother taught me to never back down. He said closing our eyes to the truth eventually hurt us more than helped us. After all, it was what made him lose five years with Isabella. He trusted our mother blindly and it burned him.

It was just another betrayal layering our distrustful Nikolaev nature.

Goose bumps erupted on my flesh. Images of that accident flickered through my mind.

Kill him.

Two little words that changed the course of my life.

Or possibly my life had taken on a different course the moment I hooked up with Adrian, believing him to be the man from the gazebo.

The shadows on Marchetti's sharp cheekbones gave him a darkened, lethal edge. It almost reminded me of an angry god.

But I came for answers. The truth would hurt as much as the lies, but I'd heal from it. I knew I would.

"Tell me why he had to die," I rasped, my heart thundering in my chest. My hands shook. *Fear,* I realized. I was scared. I had more to lose now than ever.

"He targeted our organization," he retorted.

"What organization?"

His eyes darted to Isla who stood still, her eyes on him. There was a flicker of fear in them and suddenly I worried whether I made a mistake. Did I pull her into something she wouldn't be able to get out of?

"Thorns of Omertà." *Too late.* I knew it was too late the moment those three words left Marchetti's lips. "And unknowingly he dragged you into it."

A gasp. Not mine, but Isla's, filled the room and her complexion paled, making her eyes appear darker than I'd ever seen them.

"Why?" I asked, while something ugly reared its head from the depths of my soul. Images played in my mind. The first time I met Adrian. *Hey, pipsqueak.* Playing hide-and-seek. *Why are you crying, pipsqueak?* The way he handled my bullies in school. *Don't cry, pipsqueak. Boys are not worth your tears.*

Did that apply here? Maybe Adrian knew all along this was where we'd end up, so he made sure I remembered those words. Tears filled my eyes. They stung, needing to let loose. I bit into my bottom lip, choking on a sob.

Never show them how you feel. Those were Sasha's words. Not Adrian's.

"He used you to pay back the Konstantins for killing his parents." Another gasp. Whose was it? Everything was distorted. My ears buzzed. Marchetti's voice sounded far away. "He blamed them and the organization for losing his parents. Adrian's father was a gardener to my old man. During his trip to New Orleans, he took him along. To study botany. It's where he met Adrian's mother."

I swallowed. "Illias's mother." My voice was barely above a whisper, yet the words traveled through the room like an echo in the church.

His brows scrunched. "Illias's mother?"

I waved my hand. "Never mind."

He studied me curiously, unwilling to let it go. "You think Illias's mother is the very same?"

My lips thinned. I didn't have proof to support that theory. The picture he left behind was hardly proof.

"Finish your story." Was that my voice?

To my surprise, Marchetti nodded.

"Anyhow, the gardener had a kid and left my father's employment. Years later, he attempted to make a run for it with Illias's mother. She tried to leave the old Pakhan, take the twins and go into hiding with Adrian's father. It didn't work out. They got caught and executed on the spot."

The parking lot. I choked on a sob, but I was determined not to fall apart here. Not now. Not in front of him. I clamped my lips together to prevent them from trembling or letting out a sound that I'd regret. No weakness.

"So Adrian made you all a target as revenge for his father's death?" Isla asked for me. Her voice was small. Her eyes shimmered like emeralds in the sun. Except they were unshed tears. Marchetti nodded. "How?"

I needed to know what was pinned on me. I needed to know how he used me. I needed to know how little I meant to him.

"He dug for information that could destroy us." The videos of my brothers flashed in my mind. As well as videos of many other men Adrian kept on his laptop.

I shook my head. "I went through the videos on that laptop." Bitter tears made their escape and rolled down my cheeks. I could taste them on my lips. On my tongue. "He had stuff on my brothers. Other men. But nothing on you. Or the Konstantins. Even the Yakuza."

I thought I saw a flicker of regret in his expression before it vanished. "It's on the chip."

The fucking chip. Always that goddamn chip.

"Where is the chip?" I asked, tasting those stupid tears on my tongue.

He let out a sardonic breath, his frigid façade terrifying. "We all hoped *you* could tell us."

So he didn't have it. Illias didn't have it. I didn't have it. Then who did?

"The Yakuza," I murmured. "Maybe—"

I trailed off when he shook his head. "If they had it, they'd come down demanding all our territories and give up on chasing you. They don't have it either."

There was no reason to hold the gun to Isla's back anymore, so I lowered my arm, letting it fall down my body.

I sighed, slumping my shoulders and meeting his gaze. "What's on that chip?"

He shook his head. "You really think I'd hand you information that could destroy my family?"

Destroy his family. Destroy Illias's family. Adrian was busy.

"What's on there that could destroy Illias?" Isla asked and my eyes widened. I shook my head. *No, no, no.* But before I could say a word or plead with Marchetti not to answer, the truth was already out there.

"Among other things, video of Illias killing your mother."

Deafening silence. Thundering of my heart. Aching in my soul.

Betrayal. Mine. Illias's. Ours.

"You knew." It wasn't a question but a clear statement. My betrayal cut her deep. My throat tightened. I gripped the handle of the gun, my heart twisting with regret. I should have told her, but it wasn't my story to tell.

It was at that very moment I knew I'd always choose Illias. Whether right or wrong, I'd always take his side. Although I'd give him a piece of my mind when alone.

"Isla—" My voice cracked.

"How could you not tell me?" she rasped, accusation clear in her voice. "I thought we were—" Friends. Sisters. Family.

"We are," I rasped, emotions choking me. She stood by me, let me kidnap her. Even helped me get to Marchetti.

And I betrayed her.

Straightening my shoulders, I held her gaze. I had known her for a short time, but I loved her and I cared about her. I couldn't just let her believe I did it on purpose. To hurt her.

"I can't give you your story. That's for your brother to tell. But I'll give you my story." A lump in my throat grew until it choked me and distorted my every word. "In recent months I found a video of my own mother when going through my husband's stuff. I knew she killed herself." I took a deep breath and then slowly exhaled. "What I didn't know was that she was going to kill me too. To get back at my father for not loving her. Sasha, my crazy brother, who was only ten, took me from her and saved me."

Isla's lips trembled and I'd give anything to take her pain away. By now, tears flowed freely down my face. I couldn't stop them if I wanted to. "My brothers still don't know I learned that truth. And I don't want them to. They're finally happy. They've earned it, and the last thing I want to do is give my mother more power. After all she had done."

By the expression on Isla's face, I hadn't gotten through to her. Her next words confirmed it.

"He should have told me."

The worst part was that I couldn't even argue.

"I'm sorry." It was the only thing I had left. "Let's go back to the hotel. I'm sure he's there waiting for us now and make him explain."

She shook her head. "No, I'm going to crash at my friend's house."

"I don't think so." Marchetti's voice had both of us turning our attention to him. He held a gun pointed at Isla. Both of our eyes widened.

"What are you doing?" I screeched. "Remove that gun before I shoot you."

But then I remembered. My gun wasn't loaded. Fuck!

He gave me a cold smile. "Before you even move, she'd be dead."

Jesus Christ! Did I misread him? My eyes darted to Isla, then back to Marchetti, only to end on Isla.

"I—I'm fine," she assured.

"No, you're not," I snapped. "That psycho daddy's holding you at gunpoint." My eyes narrowed on him, shooting deadly glares.

"Funny," Marchetti remarked unamused.

Isla waved her hand. "I'm used to it by now." I blinked my eyes. What the fuck was going on here? "Tatiana, you go and get my brother. Okay?"

My gaze flickered to Marchetti, but he was impossible to read. His expression was made out of granite. He didn't seem to be joking around though.

"You put even one scratch on her and what Adrian wanted to do to you will pale to what I'll do to you," I hissed my warning.

"Really?" he asked, amused. "Considering you married Illias, you're part of our organization too. And that means, you're required to protect Omertà interests. When he married you, he signaled to everyone you're off-limits and under our protection."

Huh? That sounded like a bunch of rubbish to me. It was so fucking clear I was way out of my element here, but I'd be damned if I'd show him that.

"Now see, he failed to mention that," I said, keeping my voice bored. "And I'm not much for one for all and all for one, you know. That shit has never been my thing, so I'm not gonna start now. Besides, if this means being under your organization's protection, please take it the fuck away."

He let out a sardonic breath. I was getting on his nerves.

"Go to your husband, Tatiana," he drawled. "I'll deal with Isla."

Shit, that didn't sound very good. Enrico Marchetti had lost his status as a hot daddy. He'd been demoted to... just daddy. Fuck, I didn't know.

My gaze found Isla's. Strangely, she didn't seem scared.

"I'm still mad at you," she muttered. "But I'll be okay. You go and find Illias." It sounded foolish leaving her here. Except, I didn't know what other options I had.

"Tatiana! Go. Now."

I had no idea Isla could be so bossy.

THIRTY
TATIANA

I stood in front of Marchetti's house, hesitant to leave.

My heart pounded at all the reckless images that played in my mind. Sasha would bust through this fucker's door and begin shooting. It sounded like a good plan. Except, I left all the bullets in the hotel room, worried I'd accidentally shoot Isla.

This fucking blows.

And I didn't even have a phone. It was in Isla's jeans pocket. Damn it! Maybe I'd finish Marchetti myself. Hot motherfucker.

A hand grabbed my arm from behind and I instinctively tried to jerk it. A sharp object dug into my ribs.

"Don't scream or I'll slice you open." A thick Russian accent. Definitely not Illias. Fuck, I just held a gun to Isla's back and now what… Was it my turn?

I swallowed. "My husband is Pakhan and he won't take kindly on you threatening me."

"I don't give a fuck."

Today was a bad day. Paris. The city of catastrophes.

I definitely regretted leaving the magazine of my gun blank. Stupid, stupid decision. If I had loaded it, I could have killed Marchetti and this damn fool behind me.

As it was, I was helpless.

A black car, an older-style Crown Victoria, pulled up in front of me and Nikita jumped out of the car. My eyes widened. My brain had to be slow because I exclaimed in relief. "Nikita, this guy—"

I never got to finish my sentence because the guy behind me shoved me forward.

"Get in," Nikita hissed, his gaze dark. Then he pulled out his gun. Jesus Christ.

"What are you doing? Illias will have your head."

Nikita grinned a cruel, twisted smile. "Don't worry, he'll be next."

Before I could say anything else, the guy behind me shoved me forward, the sharp object digging into my back. "Get into the car."

It was the worst thing I could do. Once in the car, my chances of escaping were slim to none. My adrenaline surged and I elbowed the guy behind me with all my might. I kicked at him, then screamed, yelling for anyone and everyone.

He let out a string of curses but his grip didn't lessen. The trunk popped open. I was lifted up in the air, my legs pushed against the frame of the car.

"Help!" I shouted and screamed as loud as my lungs would support me.

My strength didn't compare to my captor. He half carried, half dragged me forward and shoved me into the trunk.

"Cause any more trouble and I'll shoot you."

I twisted around, but before I could see who the voice belonged to, he shut the trunk and darkness came. I heard muffled voices, then slamming doors, screeching tires, and we were on the move.

I was locked inside the trunk. Like a goddamn package. Or an animal. Instead of letting panic swell inside me, I let anger overtake me. I was sick and tired of this shit and these Russian motherfuckers always kidnapping me.

I kicked at the trunk, putting all my strength on it. It did nothing but break a heel on my Louboutin shoes. Now that really pissed me off. I just couldn't catch a break. First Adrian. Then the damn chip. Yakuza. Being kidnapped, then married on the fly. Literally.

Jesus Christ.

There was only so much a girl could take.

My chest heaved as I inhaled a deep breath. My eyes stung. I brought my hands to my lower belly and murmured softly, "It's okay. Papa is going to save us."

I hope. Then I immediately corrected myself. *He will save us. If he doesn't, Uncle Sasha will.*

I had to believe it. Deep in the back of my mind I knew I'd lose my shit if I started to think anything else. I'd have to be prepared, if a window to escape happened, I'd seize it.

But not with these damn shoes. Sighing, I slid my shoes off.

I was as ready as I'd ever be. So I waited and waited.

Suddenly the car came to a stop and I tensed. The trunk opened and bright light flooded my eyes. Thinking on my feet, or on my back in this case, I kicked the guy, aiming for his balls. He hunched over and I climbed out of the trunk.

Before I could take a step, a hand wrapped around my ankle. My legs trembled and I almost toppled over.

"Let me go," I hissed.

"Stop it or I'll knock you out cold, Tatiana." I froze at that voice. I knew that voice.

My chest cracked. The ache burned through my heart and soul.

No, it couldn't be. My mind was playing tricks on me.

Slowly, as if in a dream, I turned around and came face-to-face with my dead husband.

"Hello, wife. Have you missed me?"

I opened my mouth, yet no words came out. Then I closed it and tried again. I couldn't find my voice. I couldn't find the words.

Anger and sadness coasted through me and dug into my chest with claws that would leave permanent marks.

"I take it you're not happy to see me, *pipsqueak.*"

"Adrian." My voice came out void of all emotions.

Just like the eyes staring at me.

THIRTY-ONE
KONSTANTIN

I knew something was wrong the moment I pulled in front of Marchetti's Paris home to find him and his men on the sidewalk. Marchetti preferred not to have his men around.

I jumped out of the car, leaving the door open behind me.

"Konstantin," he said in a cold voice.

"Where is she?" I barked, my eyes flicking to the house, then back to him. "Where are my wife and sister?"

Marchetti grimaced, knowing me well enough to understand that if a single hair was out of place on my wife, I'd go to war with him. I didn't give a shit that it was an open display of weakness or against the rules of the Omertà.

"Tatiana was kidnapped," he said. "I heard her screaming, being shoved into the trunk. By the time my men and I got here, the car pulled away."

My chest tightened and my gut clenched at the thought of my wife in harm's way. I pictured the terror in her eyes and instantly a red mist coated my brain and vision.

The anger, violent and consuming, rushed through me and I lost my shit. With a roar, I slammed my body against Marchetti's, gripping his collar.

225

"*Porca puttana!*" He wasted no time and shoved a Glock to my temple. "Fucking mad Russian."

"I'll show you fucking mad," I bellowed, my gun pointed at his head and pushing him back a foot. "Maybe you'll care about my warnings then."

"You better watch yourself, Konstantin," he snapped. "Calm down before you cross the line."

"Don't tell me to calm down," I roared, shaking him with force while blood rushed in my ears. "And I don't give a shit about the line." I had no idea how Marchetti shook me off, I went berserk, hell-bent on killing anyone in my path. "She's pregnant," I shouted. "All you had to do was keep her with you until I got here."

I shoved my hands in my hair and pulled hard on the strands. I wouldn't survive this fucking life without her. Without our babies. It'd destroy me losing her. Break me for good.

"I had a man follow them." Marchetti's voice came through the rush in my brain.

"We have her on the tracker," Boris reasoned. "We can find her."

I'd tear Nikita apart. Skin him alive. Then break every fucking bone in his body.

Fuck!

"There's something else," Marchetti said, his voice cool. Unperturbed while I was falling apart at the seams. "Either Adrian has a twin or he's not dead."

I stilled and met his gaze. "Adrian? Are you sure?"

"I'd stake my life on it," he retorted wryly. "Which makes sense now. The videos never stopped coming. Tatiana wasn't sending them."

The haze in my brain slowly began to clear. Adrian was alive. He had my wife.

I fixed my suit sleeves and straightened my cuffs. My hands shook for Christ's sake. I killed men. I killed Isla's mother. My hands never shook. But the thought of Tatiana being hurt had me shaking.

"Nikita is a traitor," I said, my voice hoarse. "And he's Adrian's cousin."

"Fuck," Marchetti muttered. "How long have they been planning this?"

Apparently a very long time. Years. Possibly decades. For fuck's sake, Nikita had been working for me for decades.

"Where is Isla?" I asked, trying to get myself together.

"She's locked in a safe room inside."

I nodded. She shouldn't be in Marchetti's house, but I'd be no good to her now. All I could think about was my wife in Adrian's clutches.

Or maybe she prefers it that way, my mind whispered.

If she did, she wouldn't be in a trunk. Jesus, I had to get a grip.

"Where does the tracker show her?" I snapped at Boris.

He turned the screen over my way. "That's the private airport," I said, recognizing the area. "Tell the pilot to have the plane fueled and ready. We'll follow them."

My phone buzzed. Unknown caller. It rang. Once. Twice. Three times.

Marchetti glanced at me. "You going to get that?"

I pressed the answer button on the fourth ring.

"Hello, brother." Adrian's snarling tone came over the line. "Miss me?"

"Adrian," I growled. "Where is my wife?"

He snickered. "She's sitting here next to me." He let out a heavy sigh. "It doesn't look like she missed me either. I feel so betrayed."

"I swear to God," I hissed. "You hurt her—"

"You're in no position to threaten me," he snarled. "She's going to meet the same end as my parents. Eye for an eye, brother."

My heart iced over. His parents. I remembered that night as if it were yesterday. His father. My mother. It turned out, it was *our* mother.

The look of pity Marchetti gave me set my teeth on edge. He knew that my odds of getting her back were slim. After all, he lost his wife and mother to a kidnapper. He'd know firsthand how these things end. I blamed him as much as Adrian. I wanted to punch him, beat him black and blue, for not keeping Tatiana inside.

"She has nothing to do with that," I gritted. "Let her go. You can have me."

"I don't think so," Adrian drawled. "I like this better. Want to see a video of her?" His taunting voice marred my vision with a red mist. The cell phone in my hand protested with a crack at my firm grip. Then it beeped, signaling an incoming message.

I opened the message and I froze. I fucking froze as I watched my wife tied up to a chair, her face covered in tears and her eyes full of terror. A Glock was pointed at her temple, the sheer fear in her blue eyes sending a shattering ache through my soul.

Pain, unlike ever before, exploded in my chest. It didn't compare to the feeling I felt when I learned she eloped. Or when I saw her utterly happy and in love with Adrian. This feeling tore through my soul with a raw blade and let it bleed.

I finally got her back. After years of waiting for her. And now, I might lose her and just the thought of it made my chest squeeze worse than anything. It had to be the way a heart attack felt.

"What goes around, comes around, little brother," Adrian purred, satisfied with himself.

Adrian used her. He fucking used her for all those years only to get to me. My father's words came back haunting me. Adrian should have died that night. Goddamn him!

"I swear to God, Adrian," I started, my voice cold and calm, despite the volcano ready to erupt inside me. "You hurt her and I'll hunt you down. I'll burn down any and all relatives you might have. Starting with your aunt in New Orleans. In fact, I have men on her already. One scratch on Tatiana, and Nikita's mother is dead."

He didn't think I'd find all his relatives. My contacts were very thorough when tracking family trees and digging information. The world was a lot smaller than I initially thought. I found the last members of his family and now I'd wipe them all from this fucking planet to keep my wife and family. Safe.

Click. He hung up. Fucker!

I breathed so harshly, my pulse roared in my ears. Each beat screamed "I cannot lose her" in my brain over and over again. Seven fucking years. I waited seven years. It was our time. She had always belonged to me.

"I know where they're going." I strode toward the car, the doors still wide open. "Boris, keep tracking them, but I believe the general direction is Russia. The same parking lot."

He perked up, already issuing orders to the driver and typing a message to the pilot.

"Take a few of my men," Marchetti offered.

It was on the tip of my tongue to refuse, but I didn't know what Adrian had planned. More men might come in handy. If Nikita had turned rogue, I could have other men who worked against me.

Boris and I shared a glance.

"Okay," I accepted.

THIRTY-TWO
TATIANA

The Adrian I had known growing up was gone. Truly dead.

In his place was this damaged, bitter, hateful man.

We were on a plane. A fucking cargo plane at that, and I swear to God, I could hear a dog barking on the opposite side of it. The below deck of this plane was illuminated, leaving us in semi-darkness.

I couldn't keep my eyes from flickering Adrian's way, afraid my brain and eyes were playing tricks on me. My gaze darted up to his face, then back to the gun he held pointed at me. His face was familiar, yet the expression was one I had never seen on him. I could see scarring on part of his cheek, but he kept that side of his face hidden from me.

I swallowed, that ache in my chest I felt since his death slowly returning.

"How are you alive? I saw you! You were dead. I tried to revive you." My brain was having a hard time making sense of this.

For a minute I didn't think he'd answer me. He wouldn't look at me, staring off as if his mind was somewhere else. "Nikita knew I was still alive even if you were too stupid to realize it. You actually did me a favor with all of your theatrics that night. You managed to convince them that they'd succeeded. You also distracted them enough that you gave Nikita the chance to pull me out of the way when the car was about to blow. He just didn't pull me far enough," he said bitterly.

Who was this man? Did I ever really know him? Did my brothers? I couldn't comprehend him hating us—me—so much that he'd leave me believing him dead. Mourning him. That he'd use me.

"I loved you," I murmured softly and at that moment I knew those words were true. I *loved* him. Maybe the illusion of him, but I did. However, it was all past tense. Loved, not love. Obviously, he didn't love me because nobody sane would ever do something like that to someone they loved.

An emotion flickered across his expression but he quickly masked it. I couldn't reconcile this man to the smiling and teasing Adrian I had known all my life. They were like two different men with the same face.

"What happened, Adrian?" I rasped with a lump in my throat. "How could you hate us so much?"

"What do you mean?" he snickered. "You were a way to get to him, that's all."

"Really? That's so comforting to know," I said, keeping the emotion out of my voice. "If I was your way to get to Illias, why target my brothers?" Surprise flashed across his expression, but he didn't answer. "I saw those videos." He kept staring away from me, ignoring me. Two decades of friendship. Two decades of love. All thrown away. "Don't you think I deserve to know?" His lips thinned, but I believed I was getting through to him. "My brothers are your friends."

"Were," he snapped.

"Are," I corrected him.

He spun around and crossed his arms over his chest, glaring at me. "Were, Tatiana. They were my friends as long as I was in line with their goals. As soon as I chased my own justice, they ganged up on me."

I sighed. I didn't know if it was the truth but it sounded like my brothers. "They always chose their baby sister," he scoffed.

I shook my head. "You must hate me so much to use me like that," I whispered.

Something shattered in his gaze and my chest clenched. I couldn't hate him. Even knowing all that had happened, I couldn't hate him. But I couldn't love him either.

"I didn't hate you," he finally said. "Not until that night at the gazebo."

"Gazebo," I murmured.

"Of all the men on this planet, you pick Illias Konstantin," he spat out.

"I didn't pick him that night!" I exclaimed. "That note was meant for you. I thought it was you that night. You *know* that!" His jaw clenched, but he refused to admit nor deny. But we both knew there was no way of denying it. I even told him I thought it was him back at The Den of Sin so many years ago. "You knew it wasn't you, and yet, you proceeded with the farce, making a fool out of me."

"I used it to my advantage," he continued as if he hadn't heard a word I'd said. "It was an opportunity I couldn't miss. So I started my plan."

I shook my head in disappointment. "What plan?" I asked tiredly. I might as well learn it all before my untimely death.

Adrian leaned back in his chair and stretched his legs. The move was so simple, yet it was his signature move I'd watched for years.

"I made sure Illias couldn't learn your identity," he answered. "I erased all surveillance of that night in the entire D.C. area so he couldn't find you. I bought you a few years of freedom." I stared at him in shock. "You're welcome," he retorted and I feared he actually believed he did me a favor. "It gave me time to line it all up."

Anger simmered in my veins and heat flushed through every pore of me. I scoffed. Adrian had lost his goddamn mind.

"You bought me a few years?" I asked incredulously. "I'm only twenty-seven and you're planning on killing me."

He remained silent, his expression dark. "How will that bring your parents back?" I tried to reason with him.

"It won't, but it will make his life hell," he hissed, glaring at me.

My eyes stung. Anger and ache mixed in my chest. How did we get here?

"How did you survive?" I rasped. "I saw you—" I licked my dry lips. I haven't had anything to drink or eat for hours, and it was starting to catch up. "I thought you died."

He retrieved his phone and started tapping on it. I thought he wouldn't answer, but after a few minutes, he started talking.

"Half of my body is burned." My eyes moved to his scarred cheek. My heart ached for him. He was so bitter and wrapped up in his thirst for revenge that he threw *us* away. The chance to be happy. "Do you know how fire feels against your skin?"

I shook my head, swallowing the lump in my throat. The terror of that night rushed to the forefront of my mind. The pain. My desperate attempts to revive him. Months of searching for something to keep me going.

And all along, he hid. From me. From the enemies he created.

"You left me wide open and vulnerable," I said, keeping my voice even. It'd do me no good to go into attack mode. "The Yakuza were particularly eager to get to me."

He chuckled. "Yeah, they've always been eager to take down the Omertà. The only problem is that they'd continue the tradition, but only in their own favor. Rather than eliminating all those fucking families."

"Why do you hate them all so much?"

He glared at me. "First, that old fucker Konstantin snatched my mother so he'd take her for himself. Then, he killed my father and my mother. In front of me. He destroyed my life. Killed my family. What should I do? Let him go?"

"But the old man is dead," I pointed out.

He snickered. "But his legacy isn't. I won't rest until they're all dead."

So much hatred. So many lies. So much hurt.

And for what? For something that neither one of them could control. They were both kids. They both suffered. They both lost a mother. Growing up under Illias's father wasn't easy. For Christ's sake, Illias killed his own father.

"You're taking this too far, Adrian."

He leapt to his feet and was in my face in my next breath. I had never seen so much rage and hate on his face. That beautiful face that I swooned over each time he saved me in high school. Each time he called me pipsqueak, regardless of how much I objected.

"Too far!" he shouted, his hot breath on my face. "I saw my parents murdered in front of me. I lost everything. EVERYTHING. I was abused, beaten, and starved under my foster parents. But you wouldn't understand that, would you? Spoiled little princess, sheltered by her big brothers."

My heart drummed fast in fear, cracking my rib cage with each beat. The man in front of me wasn't who I thought. It couldn't be. Then his scent registered.

I blinked, then stared at him wide-eyed. I even leaned in and inhaled deeply. He didn't smell how I remembered. There was no hint of his citrus and sandalwood scent. There was no hint of my old Adrian.

"We could have been happy, Adrian," I whispered, my heart thundering. "We could have had the world. Instead, you chose revenge over that. Revenge over us."

Something shattered in his eyes. Maybe my words hurt him. Maybe there was still a chance at saving him. Not for me. It was too late for that. There was no more us. But for himself.

It was one thing that the world got wrong about us, the Nikolaevs. They thought us unhinged, slightly mad, cruel even. But we had soft hearts. We cared too much.

"Adrian, please—"

I didn't get to finish my statement. He pushed me hard and I fell back against the dirty seat.

"It's too late," he spat, then stood up as if he couldn't stand to be around me.

Pain rushed through me. Not the physical kind but the one that you couldn't put a Band-Aid on. It was raw and real. My bottom lip trembled. Tremors shook my soul.

"I gave you a warning," he grumbled, his voice low.

My eyes widened. "What warning? You left me in the dark, stumbling through some clues that made no fucking sense," I accused.

"Memento mori," he uttered in Latin.

"Remember you must die," I translated in English, my heart cracking all over again. This time not for him, but for me. For the betrayal. For our tragedy.

"It's too late, Tatiana," he repeated softly.

I shook my head. It couldn't be too late. I had a future, my babies to think about. But I didn't want to tell him about my pregnancy. I didn't know if it'd set him off further or make him spare me.

"No, it's never too late," I rasped.

"My body is ruined, pipsqueak," he murmured, giving me a glimpse of the old Adrian. He misunderstood my comment thinking I wanted another chance with him. I didn't. But I didn't correct him. He stood up and started to remove his clothes. His jacket slid off his broad shoulders.

I tensed. What was he doing? I wouldn't sleep with him. The time for that has well past.

He pulled his shirt over his head and my gasp filled the shitty cargo airplane. Adrian's body was scarred. The skin on his back was all raw red sandpaper. It was the only way I could describe it. An ugly patch on his shoulder where the bullet must have pierced through him.

"Adrian," I whimpered. My hands were still bound, so I couldn't do anything. I couldn't hug him nor comfort him although I was sure he needed it. "D-does it hurt?"

He slid his shirt back on. "No, I lost most of the feeling on my back. It was a blessing really."

I gulped. What could I possibly say to make this better?

"Maybe we could take you to see a doctor," I murmured. "Isabella knows some excellent ones. I'm sure she—"

"I've crossed the line," he cut me off. "Your brothers are no longer part of my circle. They'll kill me the moment they can. There's no coming back. Not from this."

"No, no," I muttered, shaking my head. I didn't care about his scars, his past. "We can fix it. Just talk to Illias."

It was the wrong thing to say. Wrong way to appeal to him because his expression darkened and I could see him shut down his walls.

"Always so quick to forgive," he grumbled, almost as if he hated that. He wanted me to hate him. It'd make it easier for him to follow through with his plan. Whatever it was. Although I had a good idea that it ended with me dead. "Do you know I fucked with you the whole time you stayed at the penthouse? Konstantin thinks he protected you, but I hacked into his surveillance, played audio to freak you out. I even bypassed his men. Illias is not as good as he thinks he is."

I stilled, staring at him with wide eyes. Was that hate in his eyes?

"And then you rushed into Konstantin's arms," he added in a disgusted tone. "Like a moth to the flame. And now... now you're one of them."

One of them.

"Because I married him?" I questioned him. "Except, what did you expect me to do? You left me thinking you're dead. You LEFT me! Illias is ten times the man you are."

If he'd told me what he was up against, what happened to him, I would have helped him move past all of it. If he would have only let go and let me in. But he didn't. The whole time, I was never part of him.

He held his rage and hate in, letting his hate fester until he put me in the same group as his enemies. The enemies *he* created.

"You chose this," I screamed, fury getting the best of me. "You chose your hate over us. Over me."

He sneered. "You never loved me. You thought I was someone else and chased an illusion."

"Maybe," I hissed. "But you didn't even do that. You didn't love me. You used me. Made me believe I was mad. Fucking crazy out of my mind. And why?" He remained still, his eyes cold and cruel. "Fucking answer me. Why?" I screeched, my nails digging into my palms. The sharp pain of it grounded me. I had to keep my head, get it all out of him. "Did you hate me so much you had to make me believe I was crazy? Moving things around. Playing those voices at night. Scaring me out of my mind."

A shadow passed his eyes, but it disappeared in the next breath.

Then his lips curved into a cruel smile. The one I had never seen on his face.

"I needed you out of there, but you kept lingering. I played sounds at night to scare you. To convince you to leave."

My head shook, remembering those early months. The unbearable ache. Fear. Sadness. I questioned my sanity. And he was fucking with me. Literally torturing me.

"How could you?" I rasped in a voice I didn't recognize. "Why would you be so cruel?"

He let out a sardonic breath, full of bitterness. "Because your brothers tied up all my assets, attempting to transfer it all to you. It left me with nothing. I had to hide at my aunt's house."

"Aunt?" I repeated, dumbly. "I thought you were an orphan?"

"You actually met her," he remarked dryly. "Remember the super-intendent for New Orleans Municipal Cemeteries?" My eyes just about jumped out of my head. "Jane Ford. She's my mother's sister. It took me many years to find her."

Then it hit me. "The dedication message! It was never me. I didn't make that dedication for your plaque." He didn't need to confirm it. I knew it wasn't me. I wasn't crazy. This son of a bitch tried to make me believe I was losing my mind. "That's fucked up, Adrian. Truly! Even for a villain."

He shrugged.

"I couldn't have it written by me. So I had to assign it to you. My aunt assisted. She has quite a sense of humor."

I narrowed my eyes on him. There was zero humor in any of this. "And Nikita?" I demanded to know. "How did you get him to betray Illias?"

"He's my cousin. Nobody knows that. It was perfect. He's been on my side all along," he grumbled. "Biding our time until we could bring them all down."

And they say hell hath no fury like a woman scorned. Jesus Christ. That didn't scratch the surface on Adrian and Nikita.

"You'll fail," I said with conviction. I wasn't sure if I meant it or not, but I sure as hell faked it well.

He walked over to me, in that sure stride that I used to admire. His hand came to my neck, gripping lightly. Fear shot through me like adrenaline. I had never been scared of Adrian, but then it turned out I had never really known him.

I held my breath, getting lost in that familiar green gaze. "Thanks for keeping it always on you, pipsqueak."

Confusion swelled in me, and before I could question him on the meaning of it, he gripped the necklace and yanked it in one swift move. The key clinked against the ground and Adrian knelt to pick it up, while still gripping the emerald pendant.

"What are you doing?"

"The chip," he drawled, swinging the necklace around his index finger. Oh my gosh! That motherfucker. "You had it all along." Then he raised his other hand, holding the key I had found underneath that tile in our bathroom. "And you even held on to the key. Such a good girl."

I shook my head incredulously. "I never realized you're such a sadist, Adrian." He raised his brow as if shocked by that comment. "Tormenting me during all those months. Making me believe I was losing my mind. Making me the target of every fucking underworld family. How does that make you better than Illias's father?"

Slap.

The pain across my face was immediate. It whipped my head to the side and knocked the breath from my lungs. My cheek burned and the metallic taste of blood filled my mouth.

It was the first time *anyone* had raised their hand at me.

I swore it'd be the last.

THIRTY-THREE
KONSTANTIN

The image of my wife played on repeat in my brain.

Tied up. Scared. Did he torture her? Touch her?

A red mist covered my vision and the world around me turned to blood. I'd burn the entire fucking world down and tear Adrian limb from limb if there was a single red mark on her skin.

My control rattled the bars of the cage, ready to snap.

I couldn't handle anything happening to Tatiana.

Adrian hurt her. Because of me. I should have told her everything. I should have told her what had happened that night of the accident and what led us there. Instead, I kept it all in and pretty much sent her to search for answers.

I knew Tatiana wasn't the type to just accept half-truths. Fuck, I knew it and still I refused to tell her out of fear I'd lose her.

That was what it was. I feared losing her.

Somewhere deep down, I knew my own mother feared me. Maxim feared me. I didn't want to see that same fear in her eyes too. So I hid it all, and now, I could lose her.

I shoved my hands in my hair again, pulling at it. I felt like my sanity was hanging by a thread and it'd snap at any moment. I had to get her back. I *needed* her.

This world was safer with her in it. Without her in it, I'd make this fucking planet burn. Without her, neither I nor this world would survive. Losing her would break me.

She was the air I breathed. My reason for existence.

"You're right," Boris said, interrupting my dark thoughts. "They're headed to Russia. On a cargo plane."

No wonder we couldn't trace any commercial or private flights. We assumed he traveled the normal way.

"We can't be late," I rasped. Boris nodded. Marchetti's men hung in the front of the plane, checking their weapons.

I kept checking my phone. I didn't know whether calling her brothers was good or bad. Was calling her brothers admitting defeat or not? Then before I'd change my mind, I dialed up Vasili.

He answered on the second ring. "Found my sister?" His greeting was filled with humor.

If Adrian wasn't involved, I might have felt it too. Except I didn't. Adrian would give Tatiana the same treatment my father gave our mother. Only for the fact that I loved her. That was her only offense.

"I did." My voice was raspy. I gritted my teeth before adding, "Adrian has her."

Two heartbeats passed.

"Are you fucking kidding me?" He roared so hard that the static came through the headset. "What in the fuck is going on?"

"In short, Adrian isn't dead after all and is using Tatiana for revenge against me," I rasped. "He's my half brother and he's going to kill her unless I get to her in time to stop him."

"Fuck!" Vasili's voice portrayed rage. Anger. "And why didn't I know this?" he bellowed. "How the hell did he go from being dead to being alive? That's my baby sister he's taken. You're supposed to protect her, not put her in more danger."

"Maybe you should have checked into your friend a bit more," I snapped. I didn't need him to point out the obvious. "You should have never let him touch her."

"Do you even know your wife?" he spat, anger lacing his voice.

"Telling her to stop is like adding fuel to her fire and throwing her into it."

Yes, I fucking knew that. I fucking did that by withholding information. Except, I was so fucking pissed off, I needed an outlet.

"Where is Adrian?" he demanded. "I'm going there."

"You'll never make it in time," I said, resting my elbows on my knees and gripping my hair. "They're headed to Russia. Outside Moscow."

He was already barking orders. He'd go to Moscow either way.

"I'm going to tell you this, Konstantin," he growled. "If anything happens to my baby sister, Adrian will be the least of your worries."

He hung up. I clenched my jaw so hard that my molars protested. Before I knew it, the glass that sat on the table next to me flew across the cabin and hit the little round window. The liquid spilled over the seats and the glass that once held my drink shattered.

"We'll get her," Boris said in a low voice. "We're not far behind. If anything, we'll probably pass them. Cargo planes go through extra steps at the border."

I stared at Boris. The idea flickered to the surface and I immediately dialed my contact at the border. Five minutes later, I had it all lined up. Every single cargo plane in all of Russia would undergo additional inspection and scrutiny.

"Good thinking," I commended him. At least someone was able to think clearly since obviously I was out of my fucking mind.

"Illias?" he called out. "She might want to leave after—" He paused when I shot him a dark, murderous look. Apparently it wasn't scary enough because he continued talking. "After she learns about the connection and shit."

I let out a sardonic breath. "I think she knows." His brows furrowed. "She mentioned a picture she found of Adrian and his parents. She suspected it, but I thought it was too far-fetched."

"Nothing with your father was too far-fetched."

Wasn't that the goddamned truth?

It didn't matter. I wasn't my father. I'd never let Tatiana go. She was mine and I was hers. She was in this mess because of my father. Because of Adrian. I'd get her out and then I'd keep her forever.

She was my woman. For better or for worse. In sickness and health.

I meant every vow we spoke when I put that ring on her finger. It was more than just obsession or physical attraction. After all the shit with my mother, my father's bitterness changed him. He taught me that women are useless and good only for two things. Fucking and breeding.

My mother taught me that Maxim and I were unworthy of her love. She was unwilling to let go of her lover to stay with my father. She was willing to risk all our lives. Deep down, she must have known she'd get caught. Nothing ever escaped my father. And still she didn't care.

But when I met Tatiana, things in my chest shifted. I didn't notice it. Not at first. I spent years obsessing over the blonde angel until she strode through my L.A. restaurant. Only to learn weeks later she'd already eloped.

She was my nirvana. My chance at redemption. My chance at happiness.

Tatiana had touched parts of me that were dead from the moment I saw my mother shot in front of me. The parts of me I had forgotten. It was more than just a physical need. It was about the connection I felt with her. Whenever she fell apart under me, I felt her soul merge with mine. I felt that connection grow with each word and each gaze. There was no sating this thirst for her.

I wouldn't be able to live on without her. Just the idea of losing her had raw pain exploding in my chest, making it unbearable to breathe.

So I'd chase Adrian to that fucking parking lot where it all began.

I'd give him what he wanted. If it was my death he wanted; he'd get it. But he'd die too. It was the only thing that would protect Tatiana and our babies.

My father's voice from all those years ago echoed in my brain like a broken record.

Boys grow up to become men. They come back to find you, and suddenly, the hunter becomes the hunted.

No more second chances.
It was a hard lesson to learn.

THIRTY-FOUR

TATIANA

"Adrian, please."

My feet were frozen. Bare feet and Russian winters didn't mesh well. My feet hurt, the cold seeped into my bones, sending shivers up my body. The coat I wore did nothing to keep me warm.

I was dressed for the French Riviera, not fucking Russia.

"Adrian." I tried to pull away as Nikita dragged me further away from the car.

"Where are the fucking Yakuza?" Nikita hissed, ignoring me. Panic swelled inside me, my eyes darting around. Adrian was typing furiously on the phone, his brows furrowing each time he looked at me.

"You're working with Yakuza?" I accused, glaring at them both. "They've been trying to kill me."

"They're going to buy the chip," Nikita answered.

"Actually, they're out," Adrian remarked. "They tried to bypass me and go straight for Tatiana. I have another buyer."

Nikita whipped around, his grip on me slightly loosening.

"Who? You didn't say anything." Adrian kept his eyes on his phone, not acknowledging him. "Goddamn it, Adrian! Who?"

Adrian didn't miss a beat. "Sofia Volkov."

I tensed. I'd heard my brother and Illias discuss Sofia Volkov. The lunatic. Jesus fucking Christ. Why was this world so goddamn small?

"Well, where in the fuck is she?" Nikita growled.

With each of Adrian's answers, Nikita's grip lessened. Not wasting a single minute, I elbowed Nikita with all my strength, then sprinted forward, ignoring the probable frostbite on my feet. Adrian shouted at me to stop, but I ignored him. I kept going, putting my all into it.

It was stupid, I knew it. There was nothing around for miles. But I had to try. I had to get away.

Suddenly, I was lifted off my feet. "Let me go!" I screamed, trying to wrestle free and kicking my bare feet.

"Stop it." Adrian's voice suffocated me, his grip firm on me. I swung my head back and headbutted him. Stars swam in my vision. Pain shot through my brain, but I ignored it. "Stop it, or I'll shoot you right now," Adrian hissed, his tone furious.

I inhaled a deep breath, then exhaled, trying to calm my racing heart and adrenaline ringing in my ears.

"You calm?" he gritted. I was anything but calm, but I nodded nonetheless. He put me down and I turned around to see Adrian rubbing his nose. "Fuck, Tatiana. I think you broke my nose."

I narrowed my eyes on him. "And you fucking broke my heart. I doubt that we are remotely close to even."

He rolled his eyes. "Stop being dramatic."

Now that my heart rate slowed, the cold rushed through me. Goddamn it! Maybe I should have jogged a bit more.

"Adrian, I don't have any shoes." I shot Adrian pleading glances.

Nikita jerked my arm hard and I heard a pop in my shoulder. I clenched my teeth to stop a whimper from escaping me.

"You won't need them," Nikita gritted. "This road leads you to a cold, dark grave anyhow."

"You fucking—"

"Don't make this harder, Tatiana." Adrian's voice was deceptively calm and soft, but a vein thundered in his temple. He was pissed off, although it remained to be seen whether it was at me, Nikita, or the mysterious Sofia Volkov.

"Welcome to your gravesite," Nikita drawled. "Same place where Adrian's parents were murdered."

My eyes flickered to Adrian. He avoided looking at me, his gaze trailing over the white landscape. White as far as your eye could see. Nothing but snow surrounded us, tainted only by our feet. But it was unmistakable where we were. The same howling wind. The same barren landscape. The same ghosts.

Goose bumps rose on my skin.

I bit my lip as I watched with horror the same parking lot he brought me to dance all those years ago. For our fucking honeymoon.

It was a different time. Different man. Different life.

"I'm sorry it couldn't be different," Adrian muttered and he looked like he meant it. "I mean it. I love you."

Fury shot through me, warming my insides. It was better than cold fear. "I mean it too, Adrian. This is the final line. You shouldn't cross it," I hissed.

"We'll make it fast," Nikita spat, shoving me to my knees. The cold snow soaked through the hem of my dress and into my knees. The chill in my bones sent shudders through me. "You won't feel... much."

My gaze fleeted from Adrian to Nikita, then back to Adrian. *No, no, no.*

I couldn't die this way.

There was so much left to do, say, see. I was too young. My babies needed to see the light. Their mama and papa. Have a beautiful, happy life. They deserved that.

"Or maybe we should drag it out," Nikita snickered.

"Shut up," Adrian snapped at him. His gaze darted to me and darkened. Maybe a flicker of regret stared back at me. So I tried to appeal to his good sense. For anything he might have felt for me. He said he loved me.

"Adrian, please, don't do this," I begged, my eyes burning from tears and the cold. My nose tingled and I brought my tied wrists up my front to rub it. I sniffled, a lonely tear escaping and rolling down my icy cheek. The cold froze my skin to the point of numbness. "Please," I sniffled. "I've known you my whole life."

"You fucked Konstantin," he snapped, his voice worse than a whip against the sensitive skin. "I even used that fucking cologne you raved about. Overpriced and smelly." I stared at him, gritting my teeth. *Fake.* Everything with him was fake. "Any last words?"

"You're not going to win," I told him defiantly, although deep down I shook with fear. "Illias will find you and he'll end you. Once and for all."

Without a doubt, I knew my words were true. I might not live long enough to see it, but Adrian wouldn't come out of this alive.

The cold barrel of Adrian's gun pressed against my temple.

"By the end of this, someone's going to hurt," Adrian said, his voice whipping through the air. "But it won't be me."

My body trembled and tears sprung free. My head swam with emotions and memories. Images of Illias flashed in front of my eyes. The night he dragged me out of the burning car. His words ordering me to remain alive. Our fleeting moment in L.A. before I realized who he even was to me. Gazebo.

We had barely gotten started. I wanted to tell him I loved him. I *needed* to tell him that I was his, just as he told me he was mine.

I swallowed hard and closed my eyes. Tears refused to stop falling. They found a way out, freezing on my eyelashes. Some made it down my cheeks and onto my tongue. My lips trembled as I tasted salt.

My ears buzzed, drowning out the howl of the wind. Numbness took over. My skin was so frozen I no longer felt the cold. Nor the pain. I was too late. I'd run out of time.

Did I tell my brothers I loved them?

I hoped they knew. I should have told them more often. God, my little nephews and niece. They wouldn't remember me. *I'll miss them growing up. I'll miss it all.*

The lump in my throat grew bigger and bigger. Something clawed at my chest and my breathing hitched, the freezing temperatures invading my lungs.

I tried to remember a prayer. Just one before my last breath. I couldn't remember a single prayer.

I'm going to hell, I thought with horror. *My babies and I are going to hell.*

Screeching tires came through my scattering throughs.

Pop. Pop.

Absolute terror consumed me. I could no longer feel the barrel against my temple. The nails dug painfully into the palm of my hands. My head swam like I was in the clouds. Was I dead? *Thud.* A cold, soft powder splashed against me. Warm liquid splashed over my face.

I could feel its warmth. I could feel the pain. I couldn't be dead.

I opened my eyes. Shouting. The loud heartbeat in my ears made it hard to make out any words. More bullets. I sat frozen on my knees. The commotion around me was real, but something inside me went deadly silent for a beat.

Then I heard it.

"Tatiana!" The familiar voice. My chest warmed. Eyes wide, I stared at men, my roaring heartbeat increasing its staccato rhythm.

"If she's hurt, I'm killing you, Konstantin." Another familiar voice.

A sob raced up my throat, but I kept it muffled. My husband was here. Relief flooded through me, followed by a whimper. I stumbled onto my feet, my limbs stiff from the cold and my feet frozen. But I Ignored it all.

I ran towards him and collided into his warm chest, smelling of citrus and sandalwood. *Home. Heart.* It was all here.

Illias immediately lifted me into his arms, my legs circling his waist. I buried my face into his chest, heaving and sobbing. This brush with death was too real. Too close. My bones rattled with the intensity of my cries.

A warm touch. "I'm here, moya luna," he rasped. Then he repeated it. Over and over again. As if he needed to assure himself as well as me. "Look at me."

I lifted my head, my eyes meeting his dark consuming gaze. He squeezed me against his chest, keeping me in his arms. I buried my face in his neck, inhaling that familiar scent.

"You came for me," I croaked.

"Always," he murmured. "I'll always come for you," he chanted. "I'll always save you."

Just as he promised.

Pieces of me crumbled, only for him to put them back together. "You're safe," he murmured. "Never again. He'll never hurt us again."

He fell down onto his knees, as if he were overpowered by relief, while holding me tightly like a god of vengeance. He drew in a deep breath, then slowly exhaled.

"Fuck, you're so cold." His voice cracked, his hands roaming over my body, almost as if he hoped his touch would warm me up. It did. I needed it.

"You came for me," I whispered again, while he placed soft but urgent kisses over my face. My forehead. My snotty nose. My cheeks, My ears.

"Let's get you out of here," Illias urged softly. "Somewhere warm."

"Move out of the fucking way." My brother's voice came through. Sasha. "You're lucky I didn't accidentally shoot you. Get your hands off my sister, you goddamn Konstantin."

"Don't push me, Sasha." My husband didn't even spare him a glance. "Or I'll stab you by accident."

It was affectionate bickering. Right? I could hear the pounding pulse in my ears. It was slowly easing. My body trembled. I sucked in a deep breath as I watched the scene in front of me.

Men roaming this snowy wasteland. Black SUVs surrounding us. Men with guns everywhere.

Illias's eyes turned coal black and colder than the temperatures here, but they weren't aimed at me. They were aimed at the two men behind me. My gaze followed his to find Nikita lying dead, blood slowly tainting the white snow. Dead eyes staring into oblivion.

And Adrian. Alive.

His green eyes locked on me and I stared at him paralyzed. He was shot in the leg, blood seeping out of his wound. And my heart ached for him. Not because I loved him as my husband or a lover anymore. My heart ached for my friend. The boy who was there almost as long as my brothers. For the man who could have had so much more but chose hate and revenge over his future.

His eyes, those dark greens watched me with so much hate that it hurt to breathe. He didn't move. He didn't try to fight them. He just stared at me like it was me who had betrayed him.

"Tatiana." The plea in his voice hurt. It spoke of childhood and memories that turned sour. The thing was that he twisted it all.

Konstantin growled, kicking the gun out of his reach, then scooping me up into his arms. My feet dangled and his chest pressed against mine. "Don't fucking talk to her. Don't look at her. Not unless you want a long and painful death."

Adrian's bitter laugh filled the air. "So typical of a Konstantin. They always take what doesn't belong to them."

Illias stiffened. "Are you fucking kidding me?" He took a step forward, towering over Adrian's form. "Your hate blinds you, asshole. She was never yours."

"I've known her since she was a kid," Adrian spat, shifting to his knees. "She knows me inside and out. You'll never have that. I married her first."

Illias's eyes turned dark. Cruel. He trained his gun on Adrian, and I placed my palm on my husband's chest. His gaze flickered to my face. This was the Pakhan people feared. Ruthless. Merciless. Deadly.

A shiver went through me but I wasn't scared. No, it wasn't that which had my insides quivering. It was my husband's heartbeat drumming strongly under my palm. It was his warmth. How he made me feel alive.

And each time I doubted my mind, I roamed my hands over his chest. I could touch him. A mere few minutes ago, I was saying goodbye in my mind.

"Do you want me to spare him?" Illias asked.

My breath hitched and my eyes widened. Something flashed on my husband's face, but he kept his composure. He kept a firm mask over his expression. He was giving me a choice.

He didn't even know how much that choice meant. My gaze found Adrian. He was perfectly still, his eyes burning but not with love. They burned with the maddening need for revenge. Hate had swallowed him whole. He just used me.

Yet, I had the power to save him. To spare him.

"When did you decide to use me?" I asked him, holding his gaze. That green that used to fascinate me. The same green eyes I hoped our children would have one day. When he didn't answer, I did it for him. "In D.C.?"

Adrian's jaw tightened. "At first, I erased all traces of you from the surveillance so he—" He tilted his chin at Illias, pure hate filling those emerald eyes. " —so he couldn't find you. He kept searching, but came up empty." It finally made sense why he refused to touch me for so long. I thought it was him in the gazebo. It wasn't. He used my assumption to his advantage. "When you ran into him in the L.A. restaurant, I knew I had to move quickly. Vasili was busy with Isabella. It left you wide open."

"Because he trusted you," I hissed. "**I** trusted you."

He used me. Like I was nothing. Like he hadn't known me my whole life.

As I stared at my not-so-late husband who had been seconds from pulling the trigger and killing me for something I had never been a part of, I knew my answer. Adrian knew it too. He might have been lying to us all, but he knew me well enough to recognize my decision. My choice.

On his knees, he met my gaze. Sadness lurked in his green depths. "Spare me, pipsqueak. Take me back and I can fix us." I shook my head. He must be out of his mind if he thought I'd just look over the shit he'd done to me. "Please," he pleaded, hope lighting up his eyes.

I scoffed. "You don't know me at all, do you?"

I was a Nikolaev through and through. We didn't give second chances, and we always settled a score. "Nikolaevs always settle the score," I said out loud.

The statement reverberated in the silence of the parking lot, making its way through the ghosts of our pasts.

"I love you, Tatiana," he rasped, attempting to appeal to my heart. He couldn't. Not anymore. My heart clenched but I ignored it. He was manipulating me. These were the words he had never given me before, and yet, in the span of a day, he had uttered them twice. "I loved you. Always, pipsqueak. My love and hate know no limits."

It was his final goodbye. His final warning.

"I'm sorry you loved me," I rasped as my heartbeat trembled in my chest. The man I loved died in the car crash, maybe even before. The man I loved didn't inflict pain. The Adrian I loved was a figment of my imagination. "It was your mistake. Not mine." He crossed the line. And we both knew if I spared him, he'd be back. "I want a man who will ruin my lipstick, not my mascara. And you've done that one too many times even before the accident, Adrian."

Adrian's gaze darted behind me and I followed his eyes to find my big brother striding towards us with Alexei. My family. They were all here. For me.

Vasili stormed over to Adrian and punched him in the face. His head snapped sideways, spitting blood all over the snow. And all the while, Alexei dried my feet and slipped a pair of Uggs onto them.

I didn't know where to look—at Vasili punching Adrian or Alexei actually touching me. He despised touching people, siblings or not, and avoided it at all cost.

"You were supposed to take care of her," Vasili roared, pulling my attention away from Alexei. "Protect her." Then he punched Adrian again. "You were like a brother to me."

Adrian chuckled darkly. Bitterly. "Like a brother, but I'm not your brother." His face was a mess already, his lip split. He spat on the ground at Vasili's feet, the blood stark on the white snow.

"That's a huge difference, Vasili."

My eyes burned. My throat squeezed. The raw ache in my chest swelled. Even though he used me and his hatred outweighed all the years of our history, he was a victim of circumstances. He was the boy who lost both his parents due to passion and hatred. His parents were taken from him just because they loved each other.

But Adrian festered in his own pain, forgetting that Illias lost a mother too. He was so consumed with his hatred and need for vengeance that he forgot he was hurting innocents in his path to revenge.

Vasili turned his back to Adrian and came up to me, pressing a kiss to my forehead.

"*Ty v poryadke?*" he asked in Russian. Are you okay?

I nodded.

"Always protecting the princess," Adrian sneered. "God forbid a scratch marks that pretty face."

The hateful words etched into my soul. I'd be lying if I said it didn't hurt. Part of me still remembered the Adrian who protected me.

The lines of Illias's face sharpened. All warmth drained out of his eyes and the already cold temperatures plummeted into negative triple digits.

"You're damn straight," he snarled at Adrian. "Not a single scratch on my wife and the mother of my children."

Surprise flashed in Adrian's expression and his eyes flickered to my stomach where my hand subconsciously protectively covered my lower belly. His left eye twitched, and I knew he thought back to all our arguments when I begged him for a baby.

"You always get what you want, don't you, Tatiana?" It was the last stab to my heart he'd be allowed to make.

I turned my head and met Illias's gaze. "He has the chip," I told him. "It was in the pendant of my necklace. It's in his right pocket along with the key you need to unlock the pendant. He was going to sell it to Sofia Volkov."

"What the fuck?" Vasili and Illias cursed at the same time. "That looney bitch?"

I nodded. Sasha took two steps toward Adrian and dug it out of his pocket. Then he punched him in the face. "For holding a gun to my sister's head." Then he kicked him in the gut, Adrian's body folding over. "It's time for you to pray to every god known to man. Tick. Tock. Tick. Tock. Time to die, motherfucker."

Jesus Christ.

My brothers were a bit nuts. But then so was I because my next words had everyone's eyes shift to me in shock. "No more reincarnations." I slid out of Illias's arms and my feet crunched the snow beneath them. "I don't want him coming for my family ever again."

The words burned in my throat. The ache throbbed through my chest. But it wouldn't break me.

"Your wish is my command, wife," Illias responded.

Something glinted under the bright sun. My eyes widened as I saw the knife in Adrian's hands. Illias noticed it too. He pulled me back but it was too late.

The blade zipped through the air. My hands covered my lower abdomen. I shrieked as piercing pain shot through me.

Bang! Bang! Bang!

Three bullets rang through the air.

By the end of this, someone's going to hurt.

Adrian's words rang in my ears, mocking me, as darkness pulled me under.

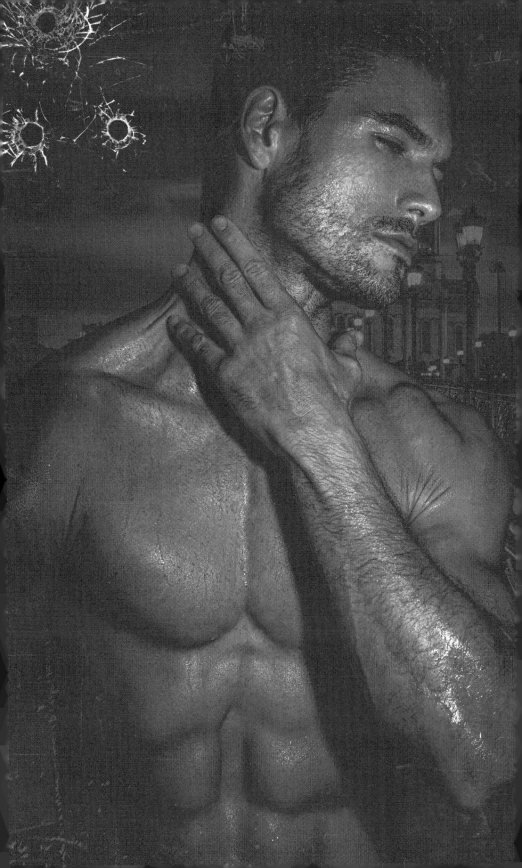

THIRTY-FIVE
KONSTANTIN

I'd tasted death three times.

The first time was when I saw my mother murdered in front of my eyes. The second time when I saw Tatiana in the rolled-up vehicle, bloody and bruised, while her piece-of-shit husband tried to flee.

The third one was now. And it just about brought me to my knees.

The world turned in slow motion as that fucking knife flew through the air. I pushed her out of the way but gravity worked against me. I watched with horror as blood spread over her dress, like a nightmare determined to swallow me whole.

Bullets flew. I didn't hear them.

Panic unlike any I'd ever felt before froze me in place. My hands gripped my fragile wife, pressing her to my chest. Pain tightened through my chest, making it hard to breathe. I couldn't breathe without her.

She's my air. She's my life.

Fuck no!

This wasn't how our story would end. We had just barely gotten started.

I put my fingers on her slim neck and waited for the pulse.

There! It was there.

The knife was lodged in her abdomen. My heart lodged in my throat, I held her gently, my mouth skimming over her cheeks.

"Don't you fucking dare leave me," I murmured. Her light strands of hair shone like gold against the white background. She needed medical help. Now!

"We can't pull the knife out. It may cause her to bleed out," Alexei said, his voice monotone but I caught a slight tremble of his hand as his fingers wrapped around the handle of the knife.

I stared at him. Sasha and Vasili behind him, falling to their knees. Boris shot another bullet into Adrian's corpse. Straight between his eyes. No reincarnations.

Except none of it meant shit without her.

"I'll keep it steady while you move her to the SUV," Alexei said. Fuck, my eyes burned. My throat hurt. My chest constricted with the kind of fear I hadn't felt since I saw my mother die in front of my eyes.

"Konstantin, you hear me?" Alexei snapped.

I nodded.

Alexei's cold composure fed me strength. It kept panic out of my head and dread out of my heart. I have waited too long to have her to let anyone, even God, take her from me. She was mine—my future, my heart, my life.

I touched my hand around the knife wound, tracing the flesh lightly while the warm liquid drenched my fingers. The scent of copper and roses thickened the air.

Just like that night!

No fucking way. She couldn't die. She *wouldn't* die. Our story wasn't done yet. It had barely begun.

"She needs a doctor!" I shouted, keeping my hand on the knife and getting to my feet. Carrying her to the car, Alexei's hand steady on the knife, I barked, "The hospital. Now!"

Her beautiful red lips paled a shade. Life was leaving her.

It wouldn't be. It couldn't be.

She's mine. Death can't have her.

I made a promise. I'd always come for her and save her and I meant to keep it. She was fucking mine, and if I had to kill Death itself, I would.

Because the two of us had a future to look forward to.

Beep. Beep. Beep.

Back at the hospital. A year ago, our story started back up in the hospital, but fuck if I'd let it end here too.

That annoying machine was what kept me going. Each *beep* meant she was alive. Each *beep* brought her closer to me. Each *beep* during the last two days kept my promise to keep her alive.

She was strong and stubborn. Fierce. She'd never let Adrian win. She'd pull through. She had to—for me, for our own happily-ever-after. Sasha couldn't stop talking over the last two days, filling my head with all the shit Tatiana made him do when they were kids. Playing fairy tales was one of them. He said she insisted on having happily-ever-afters.

Because anything else was unacceptable, she'd tell him.

The doctor came back to check on the monitors and Tatiana's vitals. His gaze flickered hesitantly my way. He suggested I shower or change. I refused. Dr. Sergei at the Moscow hospital used to be on my father's payroll. Now he was on mine. However, after Nikita's betrayal, I didn't trust anyone. Not with my wife's life. So I refused to leave Tatiana's side.

I watched the doctor and nurses work efficiently as they stitched her up. No internal organs were harmed. And by some miracle, the babies were safe. *Healthy and strong,* the doctor said. But I couldn't find any peace, not as long as their mama's eyes remained closed.

"I can't believe she's having twins," Sasha blurted out, sitting in the corner of the hospital room while Dr. Sergei performed another sonogram. Sasha tried to hide it but he was worried. Vasili and Alexei too.

"Not that shocking," Isla muttered. "After all, my brothers were twins. Unless you've forgotten."

"We didn't forget," Sasha retorted. "He tried to kill my wife."

"He needed help," she snapped back. "Not a bullet in his skull. Which one of you did it? Maybe you'd like a bullet in your little brain?"

Sasha glared at her. Vasili shook his head, glaring at his younger brother. Alexei did nothing. I was too exhausted to tell them all to fuck off.

Needless to say, Isla had found out all my secrets. It went over like a ton of bricks. But she had a soft heart and it was the reason she flew back as soon as she learned of Tatiana's condition.

She forgave her. She didn't forgive me.

"Twins are usually from the mother's side," Dr. Sergei chimed in, writing down his prognosis. "But as you can see, it's possible to have surprises."

"Maybe we get to beat those Morrellis who breed like rabbits after all," Sasha remarked, although his humor was wasted on everyone. Including himself. At this point, it was probably a habit to drop ridiculous comments.

"Don't you have a wife to go back to?" I snapped. He had to get out of here or I'd lose my mind. "You know, the one you kidnapped."

Sasha glared at me. "She's at the hotel. I'm not leaving until Tatiana wakes up."

Until. Not if.

And just like that, I liked Sasha a bit more. We were moving in the right direction, I guess. After all, we were brothers-in-law.

Silence followed again. Broken only by the doctor's shuffling of the equipment.

Beep. Beep. Beep.

And the beeping. He pushed the equipment to the left and the sound went off. All of our heads snapped in his direction, our breaths cut off.

"Oops, too far," Dr. Sergei grumbled, quickly fixing the wires. A round of relieved breaths followed. Jesus, this fucking doctor was supposed to save lives not fucking end them by giving us heart attacks.

"When a body is chopped up into pieces, can you identify its

DNA?" Isla broke the silence. She said it as if she were asking if aspirin was better than ibuprofen.

All the Nikolaev eyes as well as my own shifted to my sister. I thought Alexei's mouth might have parted in shock before he shut it. Probably mine too.

"I don't know if that's an appropriate question," Dr. Sergei responded when the rest of us were at a loss for words. "I will give you all some privacy." His eyes met mine. "No changes. Babies are good. Mother's vitals are good. Now we just wait for your wife to wake up."

Dr. Sergei headed out of the room. Silence followed, while I ran my thumb over the soft flesh of my wife's wrist. I couldn't deal with cut-up bodies and Isla's questions right now. I'd give her a lesson on how to kill someone—hopefully Marchetti—and dispose of a body some other time.

Right now, I wasn't in the right frame of mind.

I wanted to make the entire world pay for shit going wrong at that fucking parking lot. After I ensured the cargo inspection would take extra-long and would require them laying over for an extra day, I coordinated the plan with Vasili.

It was supposed to be easy. Kill Adrian. Kill Nikita. Save Tatiana.

Goddamn it! She was never supposed to get hurt. It was my job to protect her.

Vasili broke the silence. "I'm not a DNA expert, but chopping up the body won't remove his or her identity. Not unless you burned it to ashes."

Jesus H. Christ. Was this conversation really happening in my wife's hospital room?

Isla tilted her head studying Vasili. "Burn the body, huh?" Why in the fuck was she even asking this question? Vasili, Alexei, and Sasha nodded in unison. "Hmm, that's good to know."

"Just make sure there's nothing left of the body," Sasha chimed in. "Burn it to ashes, then get rid of the ash."

"Are you fucking kidding me?" I snapped at him. "She's twenty-three." My eyes narrowed on him, hoping I could kill him with just a look. Of course, I'd resurrect him eventually. "You don't tell my sister shit like that."

Sasha shrugged. "Seems she needs to know. After all, she is a Konstantin."

Isla let out a sardonic breath. "Killing is in our blood, isn't it, brother?"

Vasili's eyebrow shot up. Alexei's lip twitched. And Sasha put his hands up in the air. "I sense a conflict."

You think, motherfucker!

"Why don't you all go get lunch?" I suggested tiredly. I needed them all to leave. Or I'd lose my cool and say something that would be impossible to take back. My wife needed me to stay calm. Not go killing her brothers.

"You'll call us if she wakes. *Da*?" Alexei said, more than asked. I nodded, then watched them all disburse out of the hospital room.

Vasili was the last one to leave. "I'll keep an eye on your sister."

"Thank you."

The door shut with a soft click and I let out a breath. My eyes found my wife, the rising of her chest barely visible but it was there. The touch of her hand against mine kept me sane.

"Come back to me, *moya luna*," I murmured, pressing a kiss on the soft flesh of her wrist, where her pulse drummed.

It had been two whole fucking days. *Beep.*

Two whole days since I saw her blue eyes. *Beep. Beep.*

Two whole days of holding her hand in mine, whispering all the things I should have told her a long time ago.

Beep. Beep. Beep.

There were so many things I had yet to tell her. There was so much we left unsaid and unresolved.

"I love you, *moya luna*," I murmured softly. I had to tell her now. Maybe she'd hear me, wherever she was, and she'd come back. For me. "I have loved you from the first moment I saw you. I'll give you the moon. The stars. The fucking world. Anything you ask, it's yours. I'm yours. I've always been yours."

Beep. Beep. Beep.

The memory flashed in my mind. That naughty smile on her lips. The way her eyes twinkled with mischief even as those two boys were escorted out of the house. But the deal was sealed the second I touched her soft skin.

"Your note was a temptation I couldn't resist." It led to a chain reaction. Adrian hid her identity from me for years. A chance meeting with Tatiana's brother brought her my way. I should have snatched her right then and there. Married her. Instead, I focused on Maxim's mess and Adrian married her.

"Your moan was game over for me. I dreamt of you. I stalked you. I waited for our time because I knew deep down, you were mine. You were always meant to be mine." I brushed my lips over her skin, the scent of roses filling my nostrils. "Don't you fucking leave me." I put my hand on her stomach. "Don't leave us," I rasped.

I released a long, harsh breath. Years wasted. What I wouldn't give to get them back. Once I learned who Adrian was, everything I'd done was to protect her.

"I thought you were happy," I murmured. "Not a day went by where you didn't cross my mind since the moment I spotted you at that party. Then when I finally learned your identity, Adrian snatched you away from me. You looked so fucking happy, so goddamn in love that I convinced myself you were better off."

It fucking hurt to think of it, never mind say it. I didn't know who Adrian really was. I didn't recognize the boy who had become the man. "But make no mistake, Tatiana, I would have ended him a long time ago if I'd known who he was. If I knew his intentions weren't pure."

Skimming my lips over her cheek, I murmured against her ear. "I love you. I'll kill anyone who tries to hurt you. Just come back to me."

The door opened and Boris came in. My second-in-command.

My eyes darted his way with the unspoken question. I couldn't leave Tatiana, otherwise I would have done it myself. "She's in the dungeon," he spoke softly, his eyes flickering over Tatiana. "How is she? Babies?"

I trusted Boris. He had proven his loyalty. Over and over again. Nikita's traitorous ass at least didn't destroy that.

"She'll pull through," I said. *She has to.* "Babies are healthy."

He nodded, then turned around, his hand on the door. "I'll keep Jane Ford alive until you can deal with her."

I nodded. She was the last link to my mother's side of the family. The last threat to be eliminated. No more loose ends.

Boys grow up to become men. They come back to find you, and suddenly, the hunter becomes the hunted.

There were no more boys left to hunt us. But there was one aunt, Jane Ford. My mother's sister; Nikita's mother.

Then when all threats were eliminated, Tatiana and I would write our story. Our future.

A shift of the hospital bed pulled my attention. Tatiana's fingers twitched in my hand and her eyelids opened.

"Tatiana?" She blinked, her gaze disoriented. I leaned forward, stroking her chin and cheeks. Her brows scrunched and our gazes met.

"Hey," I whispered, emotion thick in my voice. I stroked her cheek. "You gave us a scare. How are you feeling?"

She stared at me, blinking slowly. I watched life slowly creeping back into her gaze, as if she was trying to process everything. Seconds turned into minutes. My heart rate slowed as I waited to hear her voice like my life depended on it.

"*Moya luna*," I called, worry creeping into my expression.

"I'm okay," she rasped and a relieved breath instantly filled my lungs. The tightness in my chest eased just a fraction. "I thought I was dreaming but I wasn't."

I frowned "Dreaming what?"

"All the crap with—" *Adrian.* The name remained unspoken. My mood blackened, worried about her feelings for my half brother. I fucking hated that word. *Half brother.* He had stolen her, taken years from our lives and for what. In some pursuit of revenge for something I couldn't have stopped if I wanted to.

There was nothing nobody could say or do to stop him from

bestowing revenge on our mother and her lover. Nothing short of his own death before he killed them.

"Is he dead?" Her voice was soft. I nodded and her brows knitted for a fraction before determination entered her expression. "Good."

I studied her expression, worried maybe she didn't mean it. Or blamed herself. There was one thing Adrian was right about. She had known him for most of her life. She had loved him for most of her life. It wasn't something that could be switched off.

It was the only reason I was willing to spare Adrian's life. If she'd asked me not to kill him, I'd have thrown him in one of the dungeons and kept him there.

Thankfully, she didn't ask for his life to be spared. *No reincarnations.* It reflected my wife's strength. She'd always come through and do what needs to be done. For her family. For *our* family.

"I heard what you said," she murmured. "I heard my brothers. Isla."

Tension rippled through my shoulders. How long has she been awake exactly?

"You were awake the whole time?" I asked.

"Not fully awake." Her palm came to rest on her lower belly and I put my own over her hand. I'd always keep them all safe. "The babies are safe," she said, relief coloring her voice.

"They are," I confirmed. "Healthy and strong."

She smiled, her expression softening. I knew, right there and then, she'd be the most amazing mother. Protective and fierce. The queen would tear down this world to protect our prince and princess.

My hand over hers, I squeezed it softly. "They're fighters like their mama."

A smile cracked on her face. Her eyes twinkled. "Really? I was gonna say, like their papa. Stubborn, too."

I snorted dryly. "My stubbornness doesn't scratch the surface of yours."

A full-blown grin stretched her lips. "Remember that the next time you keep shit from me." Fuck, I was so in love with her. I loved every single part of her—stubbornness, poutiness, sassiness, her bravery.

"Duly noted."

She snorted, rolling her eyes. "Somehow I have a feeling you'll always try to hide bad shit from me."

She glanced at me through her thick, pale lashes and I couldn't resist leaning over and pressing my lips against hers. Her mouth parted slightly and she moaned in my mouth. Fuck, I loved that sound. I loved everything about her.

She pulled back, ending the kiss way too soon as a small, satisfying sigh left her lips. Thank heavens nobody was in the room, because I'd have to kill them for hearing that sound. It was mine, and mine alone.

"Then you remind me to tell you everything," I said, keeping my face close to hers.

"Partners, then?" That glimmer in her eyes fascinated me. It was the same one I saw in her eyes that first night I saw her. Full of mischief and trouble. "Because that's the only way this is going to work, Illias. No hiding shit from me. You can hide it from our kids, but not me."

"Partners, moya luna."

She stared at me, seemingly shocked by my easy acceptance. But she couldn't hide her grin. "So does that make me a Pakhan?" she asked sassily.

I bit my lip, tempted to take her even in her condition. But I didn't. Her health and our babies were more important than my hard dick.

"Give them a finger and they'll take the whole hand," I remarked with a sound of abhorrence but I couldn't keep a smile off my face.

She groaned and shoved me, and I laughed. For the first time in years, my chest felt lighter. I loved the playful side of my wife. Our start was rocky but we'd pull through and we'd be even stronger for it.

She took my face in her palms, her eyes turning the deepest shade of blue that would pull me into their depths and I would happily drown in them.

"I love you, Illias," she murmured softly, our gazes locked. Three simple words and the world stopped turning. Three words and they had the power to change our lives. "Adrian wasn't who I thought he was.

He was a figment of my imagination. I didn't know him. But I know *you* and I love *you*."

Fuck, my head buzzed with adrenaline that rushed through me.

She loves me.

My heart had been lost to her seven years ago. I had felt empty without it. Without *her*. But life had blown her my way again. Life had given *us* another chance, and she had kept my heart safe.

"Say it again," I demanded. I could never tire hearing those words leave her lips. For the remainder of my days.

"I love you, Illias Konstantin." The certainty in her voice and her eyes had my heart racing. She wrapped her arms around my neck and brought me closer. "You realize we'll probably drive each other bananas. Possibly even kill each other." Her smile was weak but it was there.

My breaths turned harsh and my lungs burned. But it was a good kind of burn. It was a good kind of pain.

"Never," I scolded her softly. "I'll let you kill me before I'd ever lay a finger on you." Her lips tugged up more, and I couldn't help but to cup her face. "My moon. My entire world. It's all wrapped up in you."

"I'll kill and burn the world down for you, Illias," she murmured softly. "I'm sorry it took me so long to realize it."

"It's my job to burn down this world for you, moya luna." I stroked a stray lock of hair out of her face, her hair like a soft glow around my fingers. "It's my job to protect you and our family."

"Our job," she murmured, brushing the tip of her nose against mine. "We'll do it together."

THIRTY-SIX

TATIANA

"I can't wait to get home," I murmured.

Illias was helping me get dressed, fumbling with my hospital gown.

"I'm sorry we can't go back to the States yet," he stated, regret clear in his voice. I held on to his shoulders as he slid it down my body. I didn't bother telling him there was a button in the back he missed. It was clear that hospital gowns and Illias just didn't mesh. For all I cared, he could have ripped it off.

"That's okay." His eyes flicked up to my face as he threw the gown on the hospital bed.

"Is it?"

I nodded. "Yes. You can't exactly drag your aunt—" *Prisoner.* But I didn't want to call her that. It turned out my husband had Boris drag his aunt to Russia. She was so certain of Adrian's plan she didn't even bother going into hiding. "—back to the States. Besides, as long as you're with me, I'm home."

Satisfied with my answer, he continued with the task of getting me ready. Isla was back in France, Vasili was outside my hospital room, and my other two brothers went to fetch the car.

"Lift your foot," Illias instructed. I did and he slipped one white

271

legging on, then repeated the motion with the next one. He rose up to his full height, pulling my pants up and ensuring the waistband didn't rest on the stab wound. While it didn't hurt, it was sensitive to the touch.

"Okay, hands up," he ordered softly.

I grinned. "Now we're talking, Pakhan. Are you going to pat me down?"

He shook his head, amusement passing his expression, as he slid on a long off-the-shoulder pink sweater dress over me. The dress came down to my thighs. I'd been trying to convince him I was good enough to have sex by tempting him into my hospital bed, asking him to help me take a bath, flashing him. It all backfired. Turns out, Illias had a will of steel.

He'd lie with me; he'd bathe me; he'd kiss me. But he resisted my wiles, refusing to take it a step further. Regardless of the hunger that burned in his gaze. Much to my dismay.

I had to step up my game.

He reached for my pink Uggs next. If I had to guess, Branka helped him pick out my clothes. For some reason, she seemed obsessed with seeing me wear pink. She said it reminded her of the time we met.

"Illias?"

"Hmm."

"What did I wear the first time we met?" I questioned him.

"At the gazebo or the restaurant?"

"Both."

"At the gazebo, you wore a black strapless minidress. At the restaurant, you wore a long pink Valentino dress with the slit that showed your thigh each time you took a step closer to me."

"Wow, that's a memory," I muttered impressed. My shoes on, we stood chest to chest. "I think you wore a suit."

His eyes found mine, sparkling like black diamonds, while his lips tugged into a half-smile. He cupped my face with a palm running a thumb over my lip. "I did wear a suit. I remember everything about you, *moya luna*. Every word you uttered, what you wore, who you talked to." My throat tightened at the intensity of his voice and stare. "I loved you from the moment I saw that sparkle in your eyes and became obsessed."

Happiness and love burst through my body, leaving me feeling raw. He pulled me closer, his arms around my waist, until his heartbeat thundered against my ear.

"That doesn't sound very healthy," I teased softly.

A half-smile pulled on his beautiful lips. "I disagree. You're the best thing for my health. The best thing that happened to me."

I rose to my tiptoes and brushed my lips against his. "I'm going to take care of you tonight, husband. No more platonic shit."

A rough chuckle rumbled in his chest. "You really know how to rattle my good intentions."

I grinned. "I want your bad intentions tonight, Mr. Konstantin. Give it all to me."

"God, woman." His voice was coarse. "It's too soon. We have to make sure you're healed completely."

I scoffed. *Too soon!* He must have lost his mind. Three weeks without his dick in my pussy. I needed it. Stat. Tonight!

"Tatiana, I see trouble on your face," he groaned.

I rolled my eyes. "If you don't give me your cock, you can watch me get off," I retorted dryly. "I'll make sure you get the full view of what you could have."

He let out a sardonic breath. "Are you only using me for my dick?"

I shrugged, my eyes crinkling. "What else?" Playing it cool with Illias was too hard. I wanted him too much.

"For my wealth. My good looks. My heart."

I waved my hand nonchalantly. "I got all that. I *need* your dick."

There was no stopping my lips from curving into a smile.

He shook his head, though it didn't escape me the way his eyes shone with humor.

"What am I going to do with you?" he sighed exaggeratedly.

"Fuck me?" I murmured suggestively.

Just as he was about to answer, and probably cave in, his phone vibrated in his pocket. He retrieved it, and when he saw Sasha's name flash on the screen, he frowned.

"What is it?"

He rejected the call, shaking his head. "Your brother being a pain."

It started vibrating again and Illias's body instantly went into alert mode. "Yes?"

I could hear gunshots echoing through his headset. Tension filled the room and the temperature turned icy. My eyes widened as I leaned closer to my husband, trying to hear what was going on.

"The Volkov bitch is here…" That was all I heard.

"Which exit?" Illias barked. Another second and he hung up, then slid the phone into his pocket. He retrieved two earpieces, strapped one to his ear, then called out, "Vasili!"

My brother was in the room in the next breath. He must have gotten an update too. Illias handed him the second earpiece, and while my brother put it on, my husband grabbed his gun, then scooped me up.

"You can't run," he explained. "It'll be faster this way."

I nodded, my heart thundering wildly. "What exits are safe?" Vasili asked.

"A and D," Illias answered. "Which one do you want?"

Vasili thought for a moment, then retrieved his phone, typing quickly on his phone. "You take exit A. Exits C and D are connected. I'll take that one."

"Maybe we should all take exit A?" I offered.

Both of them shook their heads. "No, I'll draw them out." My big brother bent his head and pressed a kiss on my cheek. "I'll meet you back at Konstantin's place."

I swallowed. "Promise?"

"I do." Vasili always kept his promises.

Pulling out his own gun, Vasili wordlessly slipped out of the room.

"You hold on to me," Illias ordered, all his soft edges gone. He was in boss mode now. Killer mode. I wrapped my arms around his neck and held on to him. "Boris will lead us out of here." He tapped his intercom. "And Vasili is hooked into the network. I'll know if anything happens." I gasped and he quickly added, "But we won't let anything happen. To any of your brothers. We'll get out of this."

A terse nod, and with that, he left the room, then took a back exit to the staircase "A" where Sasha met us. My fingers trembled, but I trusted him. I trusted my brothers. We'd get out of here.

"Alexei is downstairs with the car," Sasha hissed. "Boris is getting Vasili."

"Branka?" I breathed.

"She's already waiting for us at Konstantin's fancy palace," he said. "She's the safest one right now."

We rushed down the stairs. Every so often, one of the enemies obstructed our view. They wore masks. Sasha and Illias aimed and shot at the same time, each time putting two bullets into masked men.

"That fucking bitch, Sofia Volkov, has to be terminated," Sasha muttered as we reached the parking lot. "There's the car."

Sasha pointed to the black Land Rover. Just as we approached, a few armed men tried to intercept us. As if one person, Sasha and Illias shot them both dead. The last one was shot by Alexei, behind the wheel.

"Get in the fucking car," Alexei hissed.

"What do you think we're doing?" Sasha growled. "Stopping for ice cream?"

I caught Illias rolling his eyes, but he wordlessly slid into the back seat, while Sasha covered him. Then once the door shut behind him, he got into the passenger seat and we were on the move even before my brother shut his door.

"Have you heard from Vasili?" Illias demanded.

"They've made it," Alexei answered, relief instantly washing over me.

I was cradled on Illias's lap, while Alexei drove like a madman through the streets of Moscow. The tires screeched each time the car turned, the wheels coming off the ground. I feared we'd eventually end up in a ditch on the side of the road. Upside down.

The memory of the last car chase flashed through my mind. A tremor rolled down my body, fear wrapping its hand around my throat.

"I'm guessing the cops don't enforce traffic laws here," I rasped, breaking the tense silence. My voice shook, and with each second that passed by, so did my whole body. My ears buzzed.

"Tatiana." My husband called out my name, but his voice sounded faint through the bubble of panic. Slowly the world started to fade, taking me back to that night. Images of Adrian's dead eyes were replaced with Illias's and my heart sliced. It hurt to breathe. I wouldn't survive losing him.

The buzzing in my ears increased.

"Look at me." A clear demand. Firm fingers took my chin and our gazes met. "Breathe." I gasped for air, my lungs squeezing tightly. My husband took my hand and pressed the palm against his chest. "Focus on my heartbeat." *Bu-bum. Bu-bum. Bu-bum.* "That's right. Hear it. Steady. We're safe."

The ringing in my ears slowly receded. The world came back into focus. I could hear my brother's voice.

"What's the matter with her?" Sasha growled.

"That's right, moya luna," Illias purred, ignoring Sasha's glares. "Breathe. You're doing good."

I took a lungful of air, then slowly exhaled. Again. Then again.

Bu-bum. Bu-bum. Bu-bum.

And the whole time, Illias's heartbeat drummed steady against my palm.

"What the fuck is happening to her?" Sasha hissed, worry etched in his voice and face. But I couldn't focus on him now. I needed Illias's steady heartbeat and the assurance in his eyes.

"Panic attack," Alexei said in a flat voice. "Us being chased is probably not helping."

"Well, get us the fuck out of here," Sasha barked.

Alexei did exactly that.

And all the while, my husband's heart beat steadily under my palm, holding me together.

My villain had turned into my king. My hero.

THIRTY-SEVEN
KONSTANTIN

Fierce. Fearless. My queen.

It wouldn't be easy, but then nothing worth having was. Sofia Volkov, our enemy, would pay for this. I was many things, but forgiving wasn't one of them.

Alexei lost the men following us, but we remained on high alert until we got home. Vasili and Boris already waited for us there. They must have just arrived themselves. The moment we pulled up, Branka appeared at the entrance too.

She ran into Sasha's arms. "God, I was so worried."

"Ah, kotyonok. Didn't we talk about useless worries?" The slightly psychotic brother became a kitten under his wife's gaze. She should call him *kotyonok*, not the other way around. Honestly, it would be comical if we weren't just attacked while getting discharged from the hospital.

Leaving them all behind, I took the stairs two at a time until I reached our bedroom. A fire already burned, I noted, satisfied. The staff learned Tatiana's likes and dislikes in the matter of a day. While they were barely ever seen, they were efficient as fuck.

Just the way I liked it.

I carefully placed my wife on the bed, then covered her up. Her tremors subsided, but she was still pale.

"Are you okay?" I asked, crouching beside her and holding her hand in mine.

She nodded. "Yes. The car chase... It freaked me out. If you get hurt, I couldn't—"

Her neck bobbed as she swallowed. "I'm not hurt. *We* are not hurt."

She let out a heavy sigh. "It's so stupid. Suddenly, I was back at that accident, and it felt like déjà vu." Her eyes shimmered like the surface of the clear blue sea. "I won't survive losing you, Illias. Just make sure you always come back to me. Okay?"

I groaned, her words hardening my dick. She was all I ever wanted and more. There was nothing I wanted to do more than slide between the sheets and stay in bed with her.

"I promise you," I vowed. "I will always come back to you."

But there were answers I needed. Threats I had to eliminate. Starting with my aunt. I needed to know what agreement Adrian had with Sofia Volkov. The chip was destroyed. There were no chances of resurrecting it.

Then why did Sofia Volkov attack today?

"Should I send Branka to sit with you?" I didn't like the idea of leaving her alone. Not now.

But my queen smiled, her strength shining through. "No, let her be with Sasha. I'm going to take a nap with our twins."

Another kiss on her forehead.

"I'm going to be back."

An eye for an eye. Blood for blood.

The moment I stepped into my dungeon and saw my aunt, Jane Ford, hanging from the ceiling with her wrists tied, my gut clenched.

I didn't like seeing women in pain. In fact, I fucking hated it. My father was crazy about Mama, and as far as I knew, he never hurt a woman. Until the night she betrayed him and he put a bullet in her head.

It was his undoing and things went downhill from there.

I swore I'd never become him. Yet as the years passed, I found myself in the same fucking situations as him. I put a bullet into Isla's mother. Now, I'd have another woman's blood on my hands.

My aunt's.

Fuck, I had never tortured a woman. Every fiber in me revolted at the thought. But if it came down to this woman or *my* family, it'd always be my family. Jane Ford could have been my family, but she chose to work against me.

So if I must, I'd torture the information out of her. There was a first time for everything—even this. As despicable as it might be.

My knuckles hurt from clenching. Slicing her throat would have been a better way to go, but it wouldn't give me any information I needed.

Her eyes, green like my mother's, met my gaze. Instantly something resembling disgust flickered in them.

"I take it you recognize me," I said coldly.

"You look just like the devil who snatched my sister," she spat out.

I ignored that comment. The past didn't matter to me. Not anymore. I wanted to focus on the future. My children's future. My wife's future.

Slowly, I walked to the table where all the instruments of torture sat and I started going through them. There was a reason we kept them in plain view. It was psychological more than anything. The captives usually saw the assortment and they spilled their life story.

I picked up a pair of pliers. "We use this to pull out nails," I stated, conversationally.

Glancing at her, she met my gaze and her expression turned ashen, matching her silver hair.

"And this one—" I picked up a small-sized saw that truthfully, we never fucking used. " —we use to saw off fingers. One by one."

A whimper filled the room and I grinned savagely.

"My dear aunt Jane, I make the devil look like a saint," I remarked wryly. "But then, I'm sure you knew that already."

She bit into her lip to prevent another whimper from traveling through the air. I couldn't help but wonder if my mother would look like her if she lived. Minus the fear and the dungeon, the woman looked to be in good health.

Pathetic how little I knew about my mother. It took Adrian slamming into my life and threatening my woman for me to dig into her life. This woman was the last link to my mother's side of the family. Possibly the last link to my humanity.

However, as we watched each other, I knew—just fucking knew—she'd rather die than give me what I want. Answers. Still, I'd give her a chance. Everyone breaks eventually.

"What do you want?" Her voice shook like a leaf.

Smart woman.

I had to get to Sofia Volkov and learn her endgame. It was clear that she wanted power and was a threat. You didn't make a deal to obtain a chip that contained secrets against people so you could destroy it. You went after it to gain something from it.

"I want to know how Adrian made contact with Sofia Volkov."

I saw the exact moment her eyes flickered with recognition of that name. But she still decided to fight me on it.

"I don't know who that is." She stared at me unblinkingly.

I stepped in front of her, the little saw still in my hands. I tapped it pensively against the palm of my hand.

"See, my dear aunt, I don't believe you," I drawled. *Tap. Tap. Tap.* Her eyes bounced up and down, following the saw movement. "I think you helped Adrian come up with the plan. He might have had the ideas, but you had to have helped him. To recover. To taunt my wife. To play games."

She shook her head frantically. "No, no, no."

I slammed my fist against the table, the tools on the table rattling. "Stop fucking lying."

"It's the truth."

"It's a lie." I put the saw down and reached for the gun. "We both know it's a lie. But luckily for you, I'm feeling generous today." Perspiration shone on her forehead. "I'll give you one more try to tell the truth. To help your nephew out."

Hatred flickered in her eyes, green as those of a poisonous snake, and she snickered.

"You killed my son, my real nephew," she spat out. "Adrian was the son my sister loved." Okay, that jab hit the spot, but I refused to let it show. "Why would I help you with anything?"

I offered her one of my coldest smiles. "Because you'll want at least a fraction of your family's legacy to carry on through my children."

Her eyes widened. Harsh breathing and silence mixed with the dampness in the air, until her lips thinned.

"I hope she gets them," she said, her eyes shooting poison at me. "And I hope she ends your children before they take their first breath."

It took a fraction of a second to pull the trigger. The bullet hit her knee and her shriek echoed through the dungeon, traveling down the dungeon hallways.

I flicked a glance at Boris. "Patch up her knee. Just enough so she doesn't bleed out on me. We're far from done."

Then I left her to think about her options while I went back to my wife.

But first I made a stop. I needed a stiff one.

I climbed the stairs two floors up and headed for the library. I had a fully stocked bar in there for emergencies. This was one of them. It was obvious my newfound aunt knew something about Adrian's deal with Sofia Volkov. The question was how far I'd have to go to find out what that was.

The library used to be one of my favorite rooms when I was a kid. Ironically, I'd come here because my mother usually spent her time here. She said she loved the quiet here. So did I. The fire in the fireplace threw shadows over the room, and I didn't bother with turning the lights on.

Heading straight for the minibar, I pulled out a tumbler, threw in three jumbo-sized ice cubes and then poured myself some cognac.

"You willing to share some of that?" Vasili's voice came from the corner of the room and my gaze found him. That was how much all this with the woman in my dungeon fucked with me. I could have been shot in the back of the head, and I'd never see it coming.

I fixed another identical tumbler and headed towards the couch, handed him the drink, then sat in the leather chair opposite him.

I took a big gulp, then let the brown liquid burn its way down my throat and my chest.

"That bad, huh?" Vasili questioned.

I took another gulp and swallowed it down. "It could be better."

He nodded in understanding. "I'm guessing she wasn't willing to share information."

"Affirmative." The ice rattled in my tumbler.

"Want me to take over?" he offered.

I shook my head. "No, you don't need this family shitshow on you."

Vasili chuckled. "Trust me, we've had plenty of our own family shitshows. Starting with my own mother."

I nodded in understanding. Everyone knew Vasili's mother was a slightly psychotic and excessively jealous bitch. She was willing to sacrifice a little boy for her vendetta.

"Did you know that Adrian was gathering up evidence against you too?" I asked him.

Vasili was too smart not to pick up on stuff like that.

His gaze, the same shade as Tatiana's eyes, met mine. "I suspected it. It was the reason I started to look into his company, but he beat me to it. He falsified Tatiana's signature, had it all transferred to his name, and then the accident happened. I thought it didn't matter after that. But here we are."

"Here we are," I agreed.

"Did you destroy the chip?" he asked.

I let out a sardonic breath. "Such a small thing wreaking so much havoc," I remarked dryly.

"Did you see what's on it?" he asked.

Did I fucking ever! In Sofia Volkov's hands, that chip would have been disastrous. For many families, including mine. It would have given her or the Yakuza leverage over every single member in the underworld.

"I did, but it doesn't matter. It's all gone. Nobody is getting any of that data."

"I guess Adrian had been busy for a long time," he remarked. I nodded. "Does it bother you that Sofia Volkov didn't show up to that meeting with Adrian?"

"Yes," I admitted. "It's making me paranoid."

"Ditto." Vasili pushed his hand through his hair. "Tatiana said not even Nikita knew that Adrian changed the deal from the Yakuza to Sofia Volkov."

"No surprise," I retorted dryly. "No honor among thieves."

Silence followed, both of us lost in our thoughts.

My mind was on my wife. I ached for her, my balls turning blue, demanding her pussy. But she was still healing and I couldn't be that bastard. So I jacked off a lot since the stabbing, thinking about her. God knew I'd had enough practice with it over the last several years. Except, it wasn't the same. She was so fucking close to me. The scent of roses even lingered in here and she hadn't stepped into this room in weeks.

"Do you have a plan for Sofia Volkov?" Vasili asked, breaking the silence.

"Find her. Kill her." My tone was slightly aloof, recognizing it wasn't much of a plan. The woman had become an expert at hiding. She had years of experience with it. "Maybe her niece or her niece's husband could get their hands on Sofia and do the job for us."

The expression on Vasili's face told me he didn't believe they would.

"So what's the deal with your sister?" He changed the subject and I immediately went on alert. It'd be hard to change that reaction. I was so used to killing anyone who learned about our connection. Now it fucking seemed to be common knowledge.

Isla went back to her friends, still pissed off at me. There were still words left unsaid, except I didn't know how to say them. Maybe it was better to let her continue to hate me than crush her ideal of her mother's love.

Fuck if I knew. Tatiana thought I should tell her exactly what happened. I didn't want to see the pain on my little sister's face when she learned the truth.

I let out a heavy sigh. "She's mad," I settled for a half-answer.

"So she's preparing to kill you? Cut you up and burn you so she can hide your DNA?" Vasili asked half-amused.

"Maybe," I grumbled. I still didn't know what the fuck that was about. Isla was one of the softest, most gentle souls ever. You heard it in her music. You heard it in her laugh. The words murder and her shouldn't be part of the sentence.

Though after that comment in the hospital, I wondered. When I asked her about it, she just shrugged and turned her back to me. My little sister detested me at the moment.

"She said she stayed with Marchetti when you followed Adrian from Paris?" he questioned.

I nodded. It was another thing that bothered me. At that time, I thought it was the safest decision. Now I wasn't so certain. I kept getting vague answers from the fucker too. Jesus, maybe I'd turn a not so new leaf and kill everyone for a fresh start.

"Yes."

"You don't like it," Vasili remarked.

"Would you like to leave your daughter with Marchetti?" I responded wryly.

"Considering his wife and mistresses turn up dead, no."

Done with this conversation, I stood up. "I'm off to bed."

My hand on the door handle, Vasili's voice stopped me. "Konstantin."

I glanced over my shoulder. "Yes."

"My offer stands," he said seriously. "It might be easier if I torture the woman."

I shook my head. "Thank you for offering."

THIRTY-EIGHT
TATIANA

I lay naked on the bed, waiting for my husband. The stitched mark on my lower abdomen was still red, and I kept trying to adjust my body so it wouldn't be so visible. I wanted Illias to lose his head and fuck me, not remind him of what happened.

Just as I was putting a pillow next to me, then shifted to my side, propping my leg on it like I was a seductress, the door opened. I stilled, pushing my knee slightly higher, giving him a glimpse of my ass.

It felt a bit awkward, but the moment Illias's dark eyes landed on me, I reveled in his darkened gaze. And so did my pussy, because I felt a trickle of arousal between my legs. God, help me. The man just glimpsed me and I was ready for the final act.

Slowly, like a predator stalking his prey, he walked into the room, his gaze never wavering from my nakedness. He loosened his tie, discarding it carelessly on the plush rug. His jacket followed.

He was only a step away from me. "Take off your pants too," I rasped. "Give a girl something to admire. I'm completely naked."

"Maybe I'm shy," he retorted dryly.

I smiled, shifting slightly up, and reaching for his belt. "Don't be," I purred, looking at him through my lashes. "I'm here to serve you and all your fantasies."

A dark chuckle vibrated through his chest. "That's tempting, moya luna." He pressed a kiss on my forehead. "But you're still recovering."

A frustrated noise left my throat. "Illias—" I whined.

He shook his head. "Your health is more important. Think of the babies."

"The babies want their mama to be pleased," I groaned. "If their papa won't do it, I guess I'm taking matters into my own hands." I blinked my eyes innocently as I slid my hand between my thighs. I adjusted slightly to ensure he could see exactly how wet I was for him. "You can watch," I breathed. "I don't mind."

My knees parted, and the moment my finger touched my clit, a moan slipped through my lips and my hips bucked.

"Fuck." I had no idea who said it, Illias or me, but I knew the second his control snapped. He straddled me, his mouth slamming against my lips, kissing me roughly.

"You like to torment me," he groaned. "I swear, Tatiana, you'll be the death of me."

I licked his lips, my hips grinding against his shaft. "If you die, I die. So you better stay alive, husband."

The promises in his dark gaze had me quivering with need. Still straddling me, Illias reached for the nightstand and retrieved some silky black ropes.

"You better not have used them on anyone else," I growled, jealousy slithering through me.

"Nobody else, outside my family, has ever been here," he admitted, never ceasing his movements. "I've thought about nobody else since I got that note asking me to pleasure you. Since I fucked you in the gazebo." His nose brushed against mine. His mouth skimmed over mine, then trailed down my jaw and on my neck. "You've had me since the first moment I saw you, Tatiana. I needed you like a rose needs its thorns. I've been obsessed with you."

Happiness ping-ponged off my chest. There was something so seductive about knowing this gorgeous, powerful man was obsessed with me.

I tilted my neck to the side, giving him better access to my neck.

"I'm obsessed with you too," I murmured my own admission. "I promise, I'll be making it all up to you. For the rest of my life."

He grabbed both my wrists with one hand, then slammed them over my head. "I'll hold you to it, wife."

He used one of the black silky ropes and wrapped it around my wrists, then tied them to the bedpost. My heart trembled with excitement, my lips parting while I watched him through half-lidded eyes. It started with lust for me but it ended with love. I loved him so fucking much that it scared me.

"Illias," I murmured softly.

His eyes locked on my face. "Yes, love?"

I smiled softly. "I don't want you to think I love you any less because I wasn't obsessed with you from the start." Reaching up with my lips, I took his mouth for a kiss. "I love you so much that sometimes it makes it hard to breathe." He watched me while his eyes glimmered like a dark night with stars shining in their depths. "It scares me. But I want you to know, it's always been you. I was confused, maybe even childish. But your scent, your obsession, your love... it was what I always wanted. It has been part of me, my heart and soul, from the moment you touched me."

Bu-bum. Bu-bum. Bu-bum.

"Fuck, Tatiana. I was born for you."

"And I was born for you," I murmured. "Now for the love of God, please fuck me."

"Oh, *moya luna*," he rasped, hooking his big hands under my thighs and wrapping them around his waist. "God has nothing to do with this fucking."

He poised himself at my hot entrance and I almost whimpered with frustration as the tip of his hard shaft put pressure against me.

"More," I begged.

He paused, his whole body rigid as he held himself back. "The moment it hurts, you tell me."

"Yes, yes, yes. Just fucking do it," I pleaded. "I need you."

"Promise me," he groaned, a grimace marring his expression. I arched my hips. "Promise me, Tatiana." He hissed when his cock slid further inside me. A bead of sweat formed on his forehead, his muscles straining with self-control.

"I promise. Right now, you not fucking me hurts like hell," I moaned. "I'm aching so fucking much for you."

He pushed in, slowly. Deeper and deeper. My head thrashed, the sensation of fullness overwhelming me. His thrusts were slow and shallow, his pelvis grinding against my clit. It was different, but so perfect. Every time with Illias was perfect.

"Whose pussy is this?" he rasped against my ear, keeping my hips immobile with both his hands, and all the while, he kept thrusting. Each time he hit that sweet spot and a shudder rolled through me. "Whose pussy is this?" he gritted, repeating the question I forgot to answer.

Every cell in my body trembled with the need to tumble over the cliff. I was almost there, another brush of my clit and I'd fly. I didn't think, just answered. "Mine," I breathed.

He stilled and I blinked in confusion, searching his gaze. "Illias," I whimpered. "Please—"

I licked my lips, and his gaze darkened as he followed the motion.

"Whose pussy is this?" he growled, his hand reaching between our bodies. His finger rubbed my clit, in slow, lazy circles. "Tell me, wife. Whose?"

"Yours," I answered as I leaned upward, needing his lips. "Always yours."

"You sure?"

"Yes, yours."

A groan came from deep in his chest and his hands tightened on my hips. "Good. Now, I'm going to ride this pussy of mine." He thrust. Harder this time.

"Yes, yes, yes." My voice was too enthusiastic. My eyes rolled to the back of my head.

"Don't move your hips," he grunted. Another thrust. I could feel him deep in my womb. "God, Tatiana. I can feel you clenching me. Strangling my cock."

I rolled my hips. It was a moot point. He refused to give me an inch. I reached for his lips and kissed him. Urgent. Wet. His tongue thrust into my mouth. He pulled out of me, until his tip was at my entrance, only to ram deep inside me once more. The sensation of him deep inside me, his pelvis against my clit, and his mouth on me. It was all too much after not having him for weeks.

He swallowed my next moan. Another thrust. His hands held me roughly in place. He kissed my mouth wild and rough. Sweet, hot pressure built and built.

"I love you," he groaned against my mouth with another thrust. His body tensed, then shuddered, right as the pleasure burst through me, rattling my bones.

He trailed kisses from my mouth, over my whole face, until he buried his head into my hair, letting out a masculine groan that sent a shiver down my body.

Both of us breathed hard, holding each other. His love soaked through my skin until it became part of my DNA. He inhaled deeply and murmured soft words against my lips.

"Tatiana Nikolaev, would you do me the honor of becoming my wife?" His voice was hoarse, his heart beat hard in sync with mine. He lifted his head, our gazes meeting.

I stared at him in confusion as he reached over to the nightstand and retrieved a little black box. Then he slid down the bed and onto his knees.

"Please be my wife because you want to be," he said, his voice dark, full of reverence and love. "I should have done it right the first time."

Tears stung my eyes and one rolled down my cheek.

"Yes," I muttered, then cleared my throat, emotions stuck in my throat. "Yes, yes, yes. Always yes." He jumped to his feet, his glorious, naked body in full view and wrapped his arms around me.

"Untie me so I can hug you back, damn it," I croaked, blinking the happy tears away. I'd cling to him like my second skin. In one swift move, my hands were unbound and I wrapped them around his neck.

"You're mine and I'm yours," I whispered. "Forever."

I had found my happily-ever-after. It'd be with him.

My brothers could be so overbearing.

It had been three weeks since Adrian held the gun to my head. Three days since I'd been released from the hospital but my brothers refused to leave. Considering their wives and children were still in the States, it was downright odd. It showed how much Adrian's betrayal had shaken them.

Vasili kept muttering it was his fault. I assured him it wasn't. Truthfully, if they all didn't leave soon, I'd end up guilty of murdering them.

I sighed, looking at them all sitting around my living room in a semi-loving, semi-murderous way.

The fire in the fireplace kept crackling. Christmas was only three weeks away. Alexei leaned against the wall by the floor-to-ceiling windows, his arms folded and his gaze traveling outside every so often. Sasha sat on the sofa chair, while Vasili and I sat on the couch.

My legs were folded, as I watched my family and thought about Illias.

I knew everyone was eager to get back home and get ready for the holidays. Especially with all my nieces and nephews. I had been utilizing my "Buy Now" button like it was going out of style. I wasn't sure whether Amazon was a godsend or a curse.

"Let's put it behind us and y'all go back to your wives," I suggested hopefully. Branka was here with Sasha, but Aurora and Isabella were still back in the States. It was unheard of for my brothers to be away for that long. "I need rest and lots of food to feed my own babies. You guys are not helping. Every time I turn around, all my ice cream is gone."

Vasili stifled his grin. "That might be Branka's doing. She's crazy about ice cream. Go figure."

Sasha's gaze turned murderous at the mention of my babies. He really couldn't handle the idea that I'd been having sex. Somehow with Adrian it never registered, not that I had much sex with him, but now that I had two little buns in the oven, so to speak, my brothers couldn't pretend to be oblivious.

"Your husband is lucky you ordered me not to kill him," Sasha grumbled. "Knocking up my sister. How dare he touch you?"

I rolled my eyes. "How dare you touch your wife?" I retorted wryly.

"That's different," he mumbled under his breath.

"I'm sure Alessio wouldn't agree," I snapped, a bit cranky. God, they really had to go back home. "But if it makes you feel better, feel free to think of the holy spirit filling me with twins. Whatever works for you."

"Let her be, Sasha," Alexei came to the rescue. "She's still recovering."

I shook my head. "I'm not. I'm all good. Honestly, y'all can go home." I picked up my cell phone. "See this device?" I waved it in the air. "It means we can FaceTime and talk every day. Via this magical device called a *cell phone.*" Accentuating the last two words like I was trying to teach them a new language. The fact that I managed to keep my eyes from rolling was a miracle.

Sasha feigned hurt feelings. Even went as far as his lip trembling, but the twinkle in his eyes ruined it all. "I feel unwanted."

Branka strode into the room at that moment and I jumped at the opportunity. "Branka, guess what? Sasha was just saying how he might surprise you and take you to visit your brother." Alessio, her brother, lived in Toronto. They were on slightly better terms. *I think.* "Since Canada's practically our neighbor."

She snorted, but the moment our eyes met, she got the message. "I think that's a great idea," she agreed. "I want to see my nephew. I heard Aurora has been trying to take over my 'best aunt' status."

Alexei's eyebrow shot up. "Trying? It's already done. She got the boy a drone."

"What?" Branka squealed, her eyes darting between her husband and Alexei. "Why am I only now finding this out? Goddamn it. What is better than a drone?"

I grinned. "Get him a helicopter or an airplane. You'll totally win."

"A real one?" she gasped.

"Or one of those remote-control ones," I suggested. "With the camera installed in it. They're better than drones."

"Aha," she exclaimed. "Sasha, pack it up. We're going to be there at the same time as the plane. I want to see his face when he gets it and then we'll FaceTime Aurora."

Her grin and smug expression matched my brother's. No wonder the two got along.

"Shouldn't we get him that for Christmas?" Sasha questioned, reluctantly getting to his feet.

She snickered. "Are you kidding me?" Her hand waved at Alexei, then back to Sasha. "He'll tell Aurora. He's her husband and she's got him wrapped around her little finger."

And just like that, I got rid of Sasha.

Vasili's gaze softened on me, then he kissed both of my cheeks. "Are you happy, Tatiana?"

"I am," I murmured. "Deliriously. Crazy happy."

Or I would be, when my brothers went back to their families, and I'd spend some quiet time with my husband.

My lips curved thinking of my husband. It had been three nights since he proposed. The ruthless Pakhan seemed to be a romantic at heart. Okay, that might be going too far but I appreciated the gesture. He gave me the choice. He wanted me to choose him.

And I did. I would. Always.

For the rest of that night, Illias couldn't stop touching me. As if he had to convince himself that I was alive. I slept cuddled into him, holding on to him. To this. To our happiness. But then the next morning Illias pecked me on the cheek and said he had some work to do. He kept tight-lipped about the type of work and then I hadn't seen him since.

My brothers kept me busy for the three days following our first day back. But tonight, I'd get rid of them. Vasili insisted on ensuring I went to sleep. So he sat on the couch in my bedroom, reading something on his phone. Knowing him, probably a contract for a real estate deal.

I lay on the bed, with my hands tucked under my cheek and my eyelids heavy. He was never much of a talker. It was the reason he used to put me to bed when I was a kid. When Sasha tucked me in, he'd talk and then I'd talk, next thing you knew, it was midnight and Vasili would lose his shit on us. When Vasili tucked me in, it was efficient and quiet.

"You still sleep in the same position," Vasili remarked, his eyes still reading the screen of his phone. The man was efficient and quiet. He was lucky Isabella fell for him, because I honestly didn't know another woman who'd put up with such a workaholic.

"I'm a creature of habit," I admitted softly.

"Where is Illias?" I questioned.

He shrugged. "Somewhere downstairs."

"That's helpful," I noted wryly. "This place is huge. Any chance you could narrow it down for me?"

"No."

I let out a frustrated breath. So typical. Men always stuck together. But they could never outsmart me. I'd find him one way or another.

Silence followed, full of past ghosts and memories. For me, most memories of my childhood were happy. Thanks to my brothers. But I knew Sasha and Vasili weren't as lucky. He finally put the phone down, guilt crossing his face.

"Fuck, Tatiana," he rasped. "I failed you. I let Adrian, that asshole—"

I sat up suddenly, the mattress shifting under my weight.

"No, Vasili." My voice was firm. Sharp. "You didn't fail me. You have never failed me. Thanks to you and Sasha, I had a good life. I was loved." My voice cracked at the last word. "So don't you ever apologize."

My big, fierce brother shouldn't apologize to anyone. My throat squeezed and a tear rolled down my cheek. My darn hormones and emotions working overtime. I slid out of the bed and padded across the floor to the couch where he sat. I lowered myself on the floor and hugged his knees.

"I don't want you to be my father and mother anymore," I rasped. "Just my brother. You have little ones and enough things to worry about. And I'll worry for them alongside you. But no more gray hair for you because of me."

Our gazes held. "I love you, brother."

He let out an affectionate breath.

"God, you grew up." He brushed my cheek affectionately. "I love you too. And I can't help but worry about you. Always."

I grinned. "Well, you don't have to anymore."

He let out a sigh. "I know, sestra." Two, no, three favorite words in Russian. Sestra and moya luna.

"Promise me, you'll try not to worry," I insisted. "Isabella would have my head if my actions caused you to have a heart attack." The look on his face was the one I knew well. The stubborn man. "Let Illias worry about me," I suggested playfully. "Let him get gray hair."

That drew a big smile out of my brother.

"I like that," he said, chuckling deeply. I loved hearing my big brother laugh. Sasha and I gave him plenty to worry about, even before he learned the truth about our mother. His expression turned serious. "You are safer with Konstantin than you ever were with Adrian. It makes it easier not to worry as much."

"It's time you and Alexei go back to your wives," I told him seriously. "They're starting to nag me. I know they're nagging you."

The knock on the door interrupted. "Come in."

My heart did a flip, but I knew it wouldn't be Illias. He wouldn't knock on our bedroom door. Alexei strolled in and I smiled.

"Exactly my other favorite brother I wanted to see," I exclaimed softly, then rose to my feet.

"I thought Sasha is your favorite," he remarked flatly.

I grinned mischievously. "All three of you are my favorite brothers. Some days more than others."

He rolled his eyes. Legit rolled his eyes. I wouldn't have believed it if I hadn't seen it myself.

"Alexei, did you just do an eye roll?" I teased. He shrugged, the ghost of a smile on his lips. It was good seeing my brothers happy. Content. They deserved it. They'd suffered enough in life and earned their happiness. Their families. "Okay, now. I just told Vasili and I'm going to tell you. Both of your wives are driving me nuts. My cell phone beeps all the time asking me what you're doing. You have to go home."

Alexei folded his arms, leaning against the doorframe. He always liked to have an exit strategy. It was part of his DNA now. It was what years of being caged and abused did to a human being.

"Sofia Volkov has to be found," Alexei answered.

"Moy brat, that could take years," I murmured. "She held you and Aurora prisoners. She got away. She attacked her own great-grand-daughter and got away. I know Illias can keep me protected. Just as both of you can protect *your* families."

The two of them shared a look, and I knew they could see my reasoning made sense. So I waited, holding my breath.

"You'll see me for Christmas," I murmured softly. "Nothing can keep me away from my nephews and niece. Even though Kostya is a tad bit judgmental."

Alexei cocked his brow and I shrugged. "He told me I stunk the last time I saw him," I added.

"Umm, he can't talk yet," Vasili remarked, suspicion in his eyes about my clear head.

I grinned. "Well, he talks to me."

"Impossible," Alexei protested matter-of-factly. "He'd talk to his papa first."

"Go home and find out," I uttered, half-jokingly and half-seriously.

"She's really eager to get rid of us. Isn't she, brother?" Alexei asked calmly.

"I think you might be right," Vasili agreed, letting out a sardonic breath. He stood up, then straightened his impeccable suit, the move reminding me of my husband. "Shall we, then?" he asked Alexei as he joined him by the door.

"Yes, yes, he shall," I answered on his behalf.

Then without any warning, I ran to both of them and hugged them. Alexei stiffened slightly, but then relaxed. I didn't take it personally. It was his instinct.

"Okay, no more hugging," I announced after a short moment. I didn't want to torture Alexei, but I needed him to know he was as important to me as Vasili. We were family. "Now, get lost. Get lots of sleep, and catch your flight out."

Both of my brothers disappeared through the door and my eyes glanced at the clock. I let out a small breath, then counted to one hundred before I headed out. I walked out of my room, my eyes darting to the end of the hallway, before I headed downstairs.

My pulse fluttered with each step I took. I missed Illias. It was so goddamn easy to get used to him and his presence. Maybe I had an addictive personality and never noticed it until that man slammed into my life. Or maybe it was all about this man who was part of me before I even knew about him.

The first floor was empty. The entrance hall was so quiet that I thought I'd heard footsteps of old ghosts roaming the halls. I held my breath, listening. It almost sounded like an echo of moans. I frowned, or maybe they sounded more like cries.

I followed the sound. The closer I got, the easier it was to distinguish the cries of pain. They carried up from below and made me shiver. I took another flight of stairs, this one made of old stone that looked to be part of the castle when it was built.

My fingernails dug into the palms of my hands and my chest squeezed. I paused for a moment, wondering if it was wise to see what was going on. Clearly, neither Illias nor my brothers wanted me to see it if they all feigned oblivion.

I pushed a heavy steel door open, then peered down another long, dark staircase. Jesus, how far down did this castle go? I held my breath as I crept down the remaining steps.

Another cry of pain carried through the hall. It was close. I was almost there. A heavy wooden door with iron bars was just a few steps away. I swallowed and took a step closer, scared of what I might see but I knew I couldn't stop. Not when I was so close.

One more step and I leaned forward, coming face-to-face with the reality of what my husband had been doing for the past few days. A woman, drenched in blood, hung off the ceiling, her cries of pain traveling through the room and passing me right along the hallway.

From the looks of it, her fingers were broken. Black, purple, and bloody. Nails, if there were any left, were covered in crusty blood. Her knees were broken.

Bile shot up my throat.

Alexei leaned against the dark wall, his complexion stone cold, but there were beads of sweat forming on his forehead. He hated basements. He hated enclosed basements. But it was the sight of Illias that shocked me.

I knew he was ruthless. I knew it was required to survive in our world. But it was different seeing it like this. His white shirt was covered in blood. His rolled-up sleeves revealed those strong hands that held me. That loved me. Except now, they were drenched in blood.

And my husband's face was pure terror. There was no pity, no mercy. Absolutely zero emotion. Just a granite mask. Judging from his expression, he didn't feel anything.

"Give me information on Sofia Volkov," he snarled, holding the pliers against her wrist.

"It can be over," Alexei said, his voice so cold that goose bumps rose on my skin. "You aligned yourself with the wrong person. She kidnaps, tortures, and traffics children. Just tell us and this is all over."

She laughed. "Go. To. Hell."

Illias's lips curled. Cruel and cold. "Lady, I've been there. And they didn't want me."

He clamped the pliers together, the sound of bones crunching filling the air.

My eyes widened. The dinner I ate made its way up my throat. I hunched over just in time to throw up all over the stone floor.

"Tatiana!" Illias's voice registered, but I was too busy emptying the contents of my stomach. "Fuck, Alexei, get her out of here."

I straightened up, wiping my mouth with the back of my hand. Alexei advanced on me, imposing and cold. The arctic look in his eyes froze me down to my soul.

"A-Alexei," I rasped, feeling a semblance of fear in my brother's company. Not of him. But of the past that lurked in his eyes that gave me a glimpse of the shit he had to endure. It was all there, staring back at me.

"Go to bed, Tatiana." He didn't touch me, however this time it was because he feared I'd reject his closeness. I wouldn't. I couldn't.

I swallowed another flood of bile threatening to come up, my eyes darting to the battered woman hanging from the ceiling. Her eyes met mine, green like Adrian's, and recognition washed over me.

"You!" I said.

She smiled, a batshit-crazy smile. "She's gonna come for you all," she murmured. "All of you. There's no stopping it. I can't wait to see her burn your babies alive."

"Shut her up!" Alexei growled, his eyes never wavering from me. "This bitch won't tell us anything tonight."

Illias took tentative steps towards me, still covered in blood. The coppery scent hung like fog in the air, clogging my throat and I couldn't stop it. Another round of vomit came up and I hunched over.

And the whole time the woman cackled and cackled. Like she had lost her mind.

Maybe she had. Maybe I had.

Because I felt no remorse or pity for her.

THIRTY-NINE
TATIANA

Illias lowered himself into the chair with a tired sigh.

Blood smeared his clothes and his hands. Exhaustion marred his face, but there was a hardness there too. The shadows on his face seemed darker. More drawn, somehow.

Another day had passed since I witnessed the torture. I still loved him. I still trusted him. But I'd be lying if I said I wasn't worried. For our future. For our babies. For our family.

"Are you okay?" I asked softly.

"She's dead," he answered flatly. "She wouldn't break." I nodded understandingly. If the woman refused to break after days of torture, nothing would break her. "If Nikita was alive, I could have gotten answers. But with him and Adrian dead, she lost her will to live."

God, I wished I could do something for him. Anything.

I slid out of the bed and padded barefoot to him, wearing nothing but my silky, pink baby doll nightgown with my belly barely visible with each step I made. Taking his hand in mine, I wordlessly pulled him to his feet and over to the bathroom.

"Sit down," I told him softly, nudging him down. "Let me take care of you."

He eyed me tiredly as I turned on the sink and grabbed a cloth. I put it under the running water and began to clean his face, wiping away the speckles of his aunt's blood still clinging to his face.

"You shouldn't do this in your condition," he said in a strangled voice. "It made you sick yesterday." I swallowed, remembering how my throat burned as I puked my guts out last night. "I made a mess. I should clean myself up."

I shook my head, chasing the memory of last night away. "You're lucky. I have nothing to throw up," I teased, wiping blood off his forehead. Each time I put the cloth under the running water, it ran red, staining the white sink pink.

"Besides, we're partners. Remember?" I reminded him with a soft smile, moving on to softly wiping his knuckles. His hands. "You did that for us. For *this*." I put my hand on my belly, his gaze darkening. "To keep us all protected. So the least I can do is help my husband clean up."

His eyes met mine. "You shouldn't have seen it. You shouldn't have seen me like that."

I threw the cloth into the sink and turned off the water, then cupped his face. I pressed my lips against his and my chest fluttered in that familiar way when he kissed me. Deep and raw.

When he finally pulled back, we were breathing heavily.

"I want all of you, Illias," I rasped bluntly, my left palm against his cheek. Then I ran my fingers over his dark stubble. "I want your darkness. Your light. Your struggles. Your successes. All of it. You save me; I save you. We're in this together."

He took my free hand into his, our fingers intertwining. Both of us watched his tanned skin against my pale skin. His big hand against my small one. Yet, we fit perfectly.

"Together," he rasped.

I smiled and reluctantly let go of his hand, then turned on the shower. The sound of water running filled the bathroom, the constant rush vibrating through the air.

I returned to my husband and put both my hands on his shoulders, straddling him. I wasn't queasy from the blood, nor of the knowledge he had just killed someone. She wasn't innocent. She might have been once upon a time, but now she was a threat. She planned my death along with Adrian and Nikita. She almost cost us our babies.

His sins were my sins. The blood on his hands was blood on my hands.

I pushed his suit jacket off him and tossed it to the floor. The white dress shirt, stained by the blood of his aunt, fit him like a second skin. I'd never have enough of this man. His strength. His masculinity. I loved every inch of him.

My fingers fumbled with his buttons, one by one, until I was able to touch his skin. I slid my hand down his chest and down his stomach, his warm skin searing through my palm. Fisting my pink baby doll top, he ripped the material. The shredding sound filled the bathroom. Then fisting the string of my thong, he ripped that flimsy material off too, leaving a sharp sting behind.

His gaze grew half-lidded as his eyes roamed my body. My breathing grew shallow at the reverence in those dark pools.

He ran his hand over my little bump. "Our babies," he said, his voice hoarse.

A smile touched my lips. "Our babies," I repeated, meeting his eyes. "Safe because of you."

A groan vibrated through his chest and he wrapped his hand around my nape and kissed me, then slipped his tongue into my mouth. He pulled my bottom lip between his teeth, sucking on it. Nipping it.

That familiar, hazy lust pooled in my stomach, but it was so much more than just that. It was lust and love, without any thorns. They no longer hurt nor pricked. Those once painful thorns now bound us together. Forever.

"I love you," I murmured, our lips inches apart and his eyes deep, dark pools keeping me a willing captive.

Pushing the shirt off his shoulders and letting it fall soundlessly to the tile, I let my hands travel over his hot skin. I ran my fingers through the hard ridges of his muscles, scraping my nails over his skin. I shifted to his erection, rocking my hips and grinding against his pants, needing to feel him, skin to skin. Moans and whimpers escaped me as I ground against him completely naked.

He let out a few Russian curses, his fingers pushing into my hair and yanking my head back.

"I love you too," he admitted. "So fucking much that it terrifies me," he rasped, the look in his eyes owning the words. Vulnerability lingered there.

A shaky breath escaped me as my hands reached for his belt. "Ditto," I whispered.

His hands slid under my butt as he stood up. My legs wrapped tightly around his waist. His pants fell down his muscular legs with a quiet *thunk* and he kicked them off.

For a moment, we just watched each other. His mouth was barely an inch from mine. His minty breath mixed with citrus and sandalwood, clouding all my senses. The tip of his tongue traced the corner of my lips, licking a trail over my cheek and to my ear.

"Ready to be fucked, wife?" he whispered darkly into my ear.

"Yes," I breathed. I'd been born ready for him, but he swallowed those words as his mouth latched on to mine. His hot skin seared mine, my nipples hardening under his touch.

A shiver rolled through me and my heart thundered wildly.

He walked us into the shower, the water trickling down our bodies like rain. He pressed me against the wall, my legs still wrapped around his waist and he captured a nipple in his mouth. He licked and sucked, while his hands kneaded my other breast. Then he switched, giving his mouth to the other. My hips rolled against him, and with each arch of my back, the tip of his hard cock brushed against my hot, greedy entrance.

My pussy clenched, a pulse throbbing between my legs. "Please," I begged, feeling his hard length against my entrance.

In one powerful thrust, he pushed deep inside me, filling me to the hilt. I moaned. He groaned. His hand slipped between our bodies, tracing down my pussy until he found my clit. He circled it, again and again. My eyes rolled back into my head. I arched my back, my nipples brushing against his chest.

"*Fuck.* You take my cock so good, *moya luna*," he praised, my thighs quivering. He lowered his gaze, looking down at where we were connected. "I love seeing my cock disappear into your pussy."

His hold tightened on me, his fingers digging into my ass. Our heartbeats thundered as one. He gripped my hips, grinding them harder against him and making me bounce with each slam against his length. He filled me so perfectly.

Bobbing me on his erection, I held on to him like he was my lifeline. No, not like. He *was* my lifeline. His gaze trailed over my breasts, the water cascading down over my pregnant belly and further down to where he slid in and out of me. His gaze caught fire watching as our bodies connected.

My moans grew with each thrust. His groans turned harsher, matching the force of his groin slapping against my flesh. The savage power of his hips as he rammed into me, pushed my pleasure higher.

"My dirty little wife." His voice was like velvet, his ruthless thrusts sending shudders through my body. "Your cunt is strangling my cock, greedy for more."

My back arched against the tile as I thrashed against it. My core tingled. The world started to spin. My whimpers grew louder, my pants harder.

"Oh... God... Yes, yes, yes." My walls clenched around his shaft as his rhythm took on a whole new level. He fucked me like he owned me. Scratch like. He did own me. My body, heart, and soul. Just as I owned him.

"So close," I moaned. Each thrust stretched me further, accommodating his hard length.

"Fuck, you're so perfect." He strained, his speed increasing. My heartbeat roared in my ears as he hit that sweet spot. His rhythm turned animalistic, feral, uncontrollable, as he rammed inside me. Each thrust rattled my teeth and my insides.

"Ahhh... Illias... Oh, fuck." I screamed as the pleasure detonated. I came so hard that spots swam in my vision. My husband powered into me, over and over again, fucking me through my orgasm so that, just as I reached my peak, another one rolled right behind it. He drove into me with such force that I was certain I was falling apart.

Our gazes met. His sparked like black diamonds, the lust and love in his gaze mirroring my own.

He crashed his mouth to my lips, plunging his tongue inside. He swallowed my moans, and with a punishing last thrust, he spilled inside me.

My hands wrapped around him, I buried my face into my husband's neck. Our breathing harsh and our hearts beating as one, we remained like that as the water showered down our bodies. This was heaven. This was happiness. This was—

"Thorns of love," he muttered, breathing heavily. I shifted to seek out his gaze, furrowing my brows.

"What do you mean?" I questioned.

"The two of us fit perfectly together, like roses and thorns," he explained softly as he slowly lowered me to my feet, then started to lather my body. "It has to be the thorns of love."

I smiled softly. "I like that, husband."

The two of us were bound by thorns of love.

***

Ten minutes later, after we washed each other's bodies, shampooed each other's hair, and rinsed off, we exited the shower.

He patted me dry with a soft towel, but I quickly took over.

Wrapping the towel around my breasts, I dried my husband down with a towel. I ran it down his broad back, down his waist and that perfect ass, all the way down to his calves. I stood up tall, but before I turned him around, I pressed a kiss to his upper back, on his tattoo.

"See no evil. Hear no evil. Speak no evil," I murmured softly. I was starting to get the meaning of the tattoo. He didn't like to talk about the lengths he went to protect.

"Except we do," he rasped, tension vibrating through every inch of him.

I turned him around and started drying the front side of him, starting at his biceps.

"No, you don't. *They* do," I growled softly, focusing on the task at hand. "*She* did."

She, being his aunt Jane.

Once we were both dried, I discarded my towel, took his hand, and led him into our bedroom. We both crawled under the covers naked. My husband insisted we sleep naked. He said he needed my skin and my pussy easily accessible.

"You know, once the babies are here, we won't be able to sleep naked," I remarked amused.

His hand was already trailing my belly, his fingers tracing the scar left behind by Adrian. His skin against mine, our bodies pressed together and my ear over his heart, I had never felt warmer. Even being in Russia, in the middle of the winter nonetheless.

"I'll insist on getting you naked every chance we have." Amusement colored his voice but also a worry.

Over the last month, we'd fallen into a routine. We'd eat breakfast together, then he usually had some work to do. If there was anything I could help with, he'd let me. If there wasn't, I'd work on helping Isla and her friends with their endeavors.

And those were quite... eventful. But I was intent on keeping my word to my sister-in-law. I'd always be there for her. No matter what she needed. I just didn't realize at the time, my vow would apply to her little circle of friends as well.

"You're still worried," I noted, as his fingers traced circles over my lower belly. Raising my head off his chest so I could look at his face, I took his hand and stilled it. "Talk to me, love."

The corner of his lips lifted and he pressed his palm against my stomach.

"She's the second woman I killed." The unspoken words "*but not the last*" spun their dark web through the air. Sofia Volkov would be the last. They hadn't been able to find her, but they would. I had no doubt about it. "At least with the first one, it was quick. This—"

The anguish in his voice was unmistakable and I wished I could take his pain away. He knew the torture was necessary to get any information we could to get an advantage over Sofia Volkov. She was the last threat to our family. To any family in the underworld, really.

I cupped his face and brought it close to mine. "Isla's mother was broken. We don't know what she went through, but she was dead long before your father brought her home. You probably ended her suffering and saved your sister's life."

It was hard to penetrate the guilt. Words didn't erase it, but maybe with time he'd see that it was for the best.

"Sofia Volkov is a threat. She supports child trafficking. Human trafficking. She partnered with the man who made my brother's life hell. So whatever she gets, she has had it coming for a long time.

"And your aunt," I started, sighing heavily. "Well, she made her choice. She wanted you dead. *Us* dead. Even with Nikita and Adrian gone, she would have kept coming back. I heard what she said. She was crazy, Illias. You're smart enough to have recognized it. Her hate blinded her and she passed that on to her son and eventually Adrian."

His shoulders stiffened at the mention of Adrian. It was still a sore subject, but I refused to let that ghost linger between us. I pressed my lips against his chest, inhaling his scent deep into my lungs. My heart did that fluttery thing and my stomach somersaulted. No matter how many times he'd have me, I'd never tire of him.

"It's you, Illias," I murmured against his skin, taking his nipple and biting it. Hard. Just the way he seemed to love to bite mine. I grinned, noting his body's jolt, so I licked it, easing the sting.

"It's always been you," I murmured. "The way I loved Adrian is completely different from the way I love you." I lifted my head and our gazes met. "He was something between a brother and…" I scrunched my brows, looking for the right word. "…a brother and a first crush. But you, my husband, *you* are the man who saved my life, stole my heart, and gave me purpose. You gave *us a future*."

I gasped when in one swift move Illias flipped us over, his body on top of mine.

"I stole your heart?" he growled.

I nodded. "Either that or I have given it unknowingly."

"Do you want it back?"

Our breaths filled the silence. Our gazes caught and time lagged. Ten lifetimes wouldn't tire me of this man. His body hovered over mine. His heat seeped into my bones. Russia in the winter wasn't bad after all. At least not when I was with my husband. He kept my body, heart, and soul warm.

"No. My heart's the safest with you."

Without warning, he thrust inside me and my body welcomed his intrusion. "That's the right fucking answer," he growled, keeping his body still while his cock grew bigger and harder inside me. It made every cell of my body quiver with anticipation.

"I aim to please," I murmured.

He nuzzled against my hair, inhaling me in. "Fuck, I love your scent. I can't think of roses without getting hard anymore. Just smelling them and I'm ready to come."

I chuckled. "I'll be sure to fill the house with roses tomorrow," I teased.

The truth was that for the past month, he had brought me flowers every single day. Red roses. And I gushed over them every single time.

"None of the flowers compare to you though." With his biceps on each side of me, his forehead came to rest against mine. He thrust inside of me, deep and slow, with the intimacy that brought tears to my eyes. "Your body's my temple, moya luna," he rasped thickly, his Russian accent lacing every word. "But *you... you* are my home."

"And you're mine," I whispered, emotions thick in my voice. I put a palm to his cheek and he leaned into it, making my chest expand with so much love I thought it'd explode. "Just keep our babies safe, Illias. Use all your resources. Omertà, Kingpins, Cassio and his gang, Yakuza. Use them all. It's not only our battle. Sofia Volkov is a threat to all of us—all of our children and all of our families."

Was it ridiculous to have this conversation while he was buried deep inside me? Maybe. I didn't care. This was our family we were talking about. This was our future.

I knew he needed a release after the torture and ultimate death of his aunt. And I'd give it to him, in any way—my body, my heart, my soul. Even my advice, regardless if he asked for it or not. He felt more relaxed now than when he first came upstairs. His muscles weren't as tense and the lines of his face were full of tenderness.

"You don't mind the Omertà?" he questioned. "Marchetti?"

"The hot daddy?" I mused, unable to hide my grin as his eyes turned stormy. "Why would I mind the hot daddy?"

He pulled out almost completely only to thrust back in. Rough. Hard. Savage. I gasped, my back arching off the bed and ready for another round of pleasure. Needing him to own my body.

"The only hot daddy you're allowed to think about is me," he growled with a dangerous tilt to his voice. "I'm your hot daddy, your god, your husband, your partner. Your fucking *everything*." His hot, dark whisper brushed my ear. He thrust deep inside me again, this time each ram harsher. "I'm the only right man for you. Is that understood?"

"Yes, daddy," I breathed, attempting to joke but it came out all wrong. Needy. Hoarse.

He let out an animalistic groan, then started fucking me with deep, long thrusts.

"Now, let me show you how right *you* are for me, moya luna."

And oh my God. Did he ever!

FORTY
KONSTANTIN

"Who thought a Christmas wedding was a good idea?"

Of course, it was my favorite brother-in-law. Sasha Nikolaev would drive me fucking bananas. I was too old for his shit. Fuck, he was too old for this shit.

"Shut up, Sasha," Alexei said, his voice flat. He might as well be telling his brother to get a drink of water. "Nobody whined when you had a Halloween wedding."

"Doesn't it bother you that he's marrying your baby sister?" Sasha asked nobody in particular. "First he knocked her up, then he kidnapped her, married her on the fly." His eyes darted around the room only to land on me and slitted to a glare. "Literally on the fly. He took her to Russia and my baby sister doesn't like Russia in the winter. And now, here we are."

Massaging my temple, I let out a tired sigh. Our airplane wedding was so much better. Easier. Quieter.

But I wanted this for Tatiana. For her memories. For the stories we'd tell our children.

St. Patrick's Church was filled to capacity. Family. Friends. Members of the Omertà. Kingpins. Billionaire Kings. Liam Brennan

309

with his family. Cassio King and his gang. My wife was right. We were stronger together than fighting this battle on our own.

Sofia Volkov was an enemy to us all.

She had disappeared. We didn't know where she was, but we knew she was alive. The frustration clawed at my chest. It pissed me off to no end that I couldn't find her. Nico Morrelli and I built a facial recognition app that we'd attached to every known database. The fact that the program hadn't spotted her anywhere in the whole fucking world had me on edge. The crazy bitch knew how to hide though. She had been doing it for so long, it was probably part of her DNA. Just like Alexei always strategically placed himself by the nearest exit, Sofia Catalano Volkov's instinct was to always hide.

But I refused to let that ruin my day. My wife's day.

The sound of "Canon in D" began, and without prompting, Sasha and Alexei took their spot behind me. The first bridesmaid came out. Isla. My baby sister. She avoided looking in my direction and I gritted my teeth. It turns out, my sweet baby sister was as stubborn as me.

Isabella Nikolaev followed behind Isla and my eyes drifted to the back of the church, waiting to see my bride. I waited, holding my breath until I caught a glimpse of her. Our eyes connected and Tatiana's lips curved into a wide smile. The light shone through the church windows, making her hair glow like spun gold. At this very moment, she looked like an angel coming to meet her devil.

The white Valentino dress hugged her curves, her little baby bump visible. I fucking loved that she didn't hide it. She wore it proudly, like a badge of honor. And she'd slay anyone who threatened our babies. Just as I would.

My chest grew warm, watching her take every step closer to me. Willingly.

Her steps were in sync with Vasili's until they both reached me. Her big brother gave me a small nod and handed me his sister.

"Take care of her."

I nodded, my eyes locked on my bride. The way her eyes sparkled. The way she watched me like I was her whole world, just as she was mine. If the whole church erupted into gunfire, I didn't think I'd be able to peel my eyes away from her.

This time she gave me her words with conviction and with love. This time she looked at me the way I felt about her.

This time, I knew she was in it like I was.

"I love you, Tatiana Konstantin." Pure devotion shone in her pale blue gaze. There were no words needed to know she loved me. "You are my future. My love. My life."

"And I love you, Illias Konstantin," she murmured softly.

Forever.

EPILOGUE—KONSTANTIN

TWELVE MONTHS LATER

Our twins were born on the first day of summer. Healthy and beautiful. Anushka and Astor.

The pregnancy was easy. At least Tatiana kept claiming it was, despite the many nights when our babies kept her awake while kicking in her belly. I'd massage her back, her calves, and talk to our babies. Those nights were long, but we got through them.

Together. Always partners.

Watching my fearless queen, my wife, give birth to our children was the single most beautiful moment of my entire life. It brought me to my knees. When our little bundles of joy entered the world, screaming at the top of their lungs, I knew I'd burn down the world for them. By the expression on my wife's face, she felt the same.

She looked at them with so much love that it stole my breath away. Emotion wrapped around my throat and lungs, and when Tatiana turned her dazed expression to me, the love and devotion in her eyes threatened to bring me to my knees.

Thank you, she mouthed soundlessly, tears shining in her eyes. She was thanking me when she did all the work. When she gave me a gift that I'd never be able to repay.

To everyone's shock, Anushka had my coloring and her mother's eyes. Astor had his mother's coloring and my eyes.

I watched my babies and my wife. They were perfection. They held the power to disarm me with just a simple look or a simple smile. The moment my wife and I held our children, the world around us ceased to exist. It was just the four of us, lost in each other.

I had stopped breathing. And when my wife's eyes found mine, I knew she felt exactly the same.

"We did good," Tatiana said, smiling down at our babies.

"We did good, moya luna," I agreed, watching my little family.

My endgame.

As the weeks and months went by, I realized how wrong I was about everything. My parents' life story taught me love stuck you with thorns. That love made you weak.

They were wrong. I was wrong.

My family had taught me that. My wife. My children. My sister. Love was strength.

Marriage with Tatiana was full of laughter and love. Full of love. It all bound us together. It took a lot of sacrifices and pain, but we got here. We got our fairy tale. Our own happily-ever-after. Anything for my wife.

After much debate, we settled our life in New Orleans with a lot of traveling to California and Russia. The truth was, there wasn't much I could deny my wife and her family was important to her.

Since the twins' birth, we fell into a routine. We'd wake up in the morning, each handling one twin. We always had breakfast together. Then Mama took it from there. She'd work some or meet her sisters-in-law while the twins were napping. Dinners, bath, and bedtime we tag-teamed.

Currently, my wife was putting Astor to bed, while I held Anushka. They shared a room, although I wondered whether it was wise. If one woke up, the other did too.

But Tatiana claimed it would let the twins connect. All the books she'd read said it was important; as if they hadn't spent nine months on top of each other while in their mother's belly. Who knew if it was real or not? At times like these, I wished I knew whether Maxim and I shared a room when we were born. Probably not but it'd be nice to know for sure.

"Vasili said they'll be a handful," she whispered, smiling. "He said they are as loud as I was."

I chuckled.

My brothers-in-law claimed our twins would be hellions. I feared they might be right. Even at the tender age of three months, they frequently had little tantrums.

Of course, our twins took after the Nikolaevs. God help me.

"Nothing we can't handle," I murmured softly. "My partner and I. Together."

My wife's eyes shimmered like pale sapphires. "Together."

My wife leaned over, our fingers interlocking. "I love you, Illias Konstantin."

"I love you, Tatiana Nikolaev Konstantin. In this life and next."

She and our children were my everything.

My sun, moon, and stars.

EPILOGUE—TATIANA

THREE YEARS LATER

I played with the devil and the result was a fairy tale. It wasn't all roses, there were thorns too, but I loved every single moment with him and our children.

It turned out the devil was exactly what I needed in my life. My villain became my hero. My husband. My lover. And most importantly my friend.

True to his word, Illias and I were partners. Sometimes he still liked to protect me and keep stressful things from me, but I cut that shit right off. He was demanding, so was I. He needed a lot of love. So did I.

Turns out my gazebo man was a romantic at heart. He had purchased the property that brought us together, and every now and then, when we needed time alone, we'd fly there and he'd show me exactly how good we fit. Not that I doubted it. Never again would I doubt my husband. He owned me, but I owned him too.

That was how marriage worked.

Placing the pregnancy test on the bathroom sink, I washed my hands. I couldn't help flickering my eyes to the little window on the stick. I just celebrated my thirtieth birthday last week. Illias took me to Paris—just the two of us. It was our first trip alone since we'd had the twins.

It was magical. Everything with my husband felt like a fairy-tale dream come true.

He booked the Eiffel Tower, just for the two of us. We wined and dined, then took a stroll, enjoying the magnificent views as he whispered the world was at our feet. I grew up not seeing love, at least not the kind between a man and woman, but somehow the idea of it always lingered in my heart. It wasn't until I tasted it myself that I saw the power of it.

"How does it feel having Paris at your feet, Mrs. Konstantin?" my husband had asked with his strong arms wrapped around my waist.

I'd turned my face to the side, so I could drown in my devil's eyes. "Nothing beats the feeling of having you, Illias." I loved him so much that sometimes I swore I could feel thorns pricking my skin. "As long as you're with me, I wouldn't care if we were in the middle of a jungle. But Paris at my feet is nice too."

I'd leaned back against his strong body, letting his heat seep through my skin. "Now, please touch me," I'd pleaded half-teasingly. "I've never been fucked on top of the Eiffel Tower. Show me how good it feels."

He did. The noise of Paris couldn't reach us, but my heart thundered just the same as he touched me, owning my heart, soul, and body. I screamed his name, letting it carry over the wind while he whispered how much he loved me. How happy I made him. And how we'd make more babies.

It was bound to happen again when we both ignored protection and fooled around day and night. I was just surprised that it had taken this long, if I was indeed pregnant again. He'd made it no secret he wanted more children. It was fine by me because I wanted a big family. A happy family.

Leaving Paris in my memories and bringing reality into our bathroom at our manor in New Orleans, I returned to the original reason I was hanging in the bathroom while my little ones threw Legos all over my bedroom.

The pregnancy test.

Two pink lines stared back at me and I smiled. "Daddy's gonna be happy," I murmured softly.

My twins busted through the door, ignoring my need for privacy and Astor reached for the used pregnancy test.

"No, no, no," I scolded. Luckily, I was fast enough and I snatched it out of his reach, tutting him softly.

"What that?" he asked, that determined look that reminded me so much of his father, staring at the unfamiliar device. "That mine."

I rolled my eyes. "Astor, that's not yours. It's in Mommy's bathroom. It's Mommy's."

He watched me pensively, contemplating my words. "Papa's bathroom too. That Papa's."

I shook my head. If I said it was Daddy's, he'd reverse it. "You're too smart for your own good," I muttered. He didn't seem impressed, his attention still on the pregnancy test. I didn't want to throw it away. First, I'd take a picture and send it to Illias. Maybe it'd bring him home faster.

He and my brothers had some business in L.A. to tend to. It had only been two days, but I hated sleeping without him next to me.

Anushka giggled and I turned to find my daughter's face white as a ghost. She applied a shit ton of concealer. A chuckle tore from my throat. "Anushka, you're supposed to use just a tiny bit, not the entire tube on your face."

Her toothy grin flashed. My two babies might be twins but they were like night and day. Even at his tender age of three, Astor could be overwhelming. A force to be reckoned with. Much like his father. Anushka, while definitely not meek, worked in a slightly different way. She observed until she was ready to pounce like a wrecking ball to achieve her goal.

Neither boded well for our peace in the future.

Yet, I wouldn't change it for anything. It was our family. Our children. Our happiness.

I pulled both of my babies into a hug. "Mama loves you so much," I murmured. It was something I said to my children every day. My brothers told me every day. They didn't hear it every day, but they made sure I didn't feel neglected like they had. It made a difference in my life. I'd be sure to make an even bigger difference in our children's lives.

"Should we take a picture to send Papa?" I asked. "He's missing us and it'll make him happy. Maybe he'll hurry home?"

Astor and Anushka eagerly nodded and I snapped the photo in the next breath. You never knew when children would change their mind. Anushka's dark curls framed her face and those blue eyes hid her strength while Astor's dark eyes hid the little mischievous devil of his soul under his light blond hair that made him appear like an angel.

Typing in my husband's number, I sent off the photo of his children with a simple message. *We miss you.*

The pregnancy test could wait. For now.

Beep. The reply was instant.

MY MAN: **I miss my prince and princess too. Thank you for the photo. Now send me a photo of my world.**

I grinned, lifting my eyes to the twins. "How about one more photo for Papa? He wants one with Mama in the picture."

They both rushed over and I grabbed the pregnancy test. If he wanted his world, this was it—pink lines, twins, and I. "Everyone say selfie," I announced.

The twins mumbled something that was nothing like "selfie" but I snapped the picture, then studied the photo. The same face stared back at me, yet so different. Maybe it was all in my head, but happiness stared back at me. My cheeks were flushed. My eyes shone.

I was at peace.

Sending off the picture to the love of my life, I shifted towards the sink. "Okay, my beautiful Anushka. Let's clean up your face. Mama wants to kiss your cheeks, not foundation."

She giggled, looking behind me.

A pair of strong arms came around my waist and I squealed in surprise.

"Hello, Mama." The scent of citrus and sandalwood drifted around me and I twirled around, coming face-to-face with my husband.

"You're home," I exclaimed, my lips widening into a large smile.

Illias's eyes were warm on our little family. "Right on time too," he murmured, his warm mouth skimming over my skin. The twins pushed their little bodies between us, but my husband didn't let me go. Instead, he lifted Anushka while I lifted Astor up and the four of us stood in the middle of our bathroom. Together.

He pressed his free hand to my belly, our eyes drowning in each other. Stars shone in his dark-as-night eyes, trapping us in our own universe.

"I am such a lucky man." Our noses brushed together. "The luckiest man alive."

"You made me the luckiest woman alive," I rasped.

This man had taken me on a journey that I wouldn't have missed for all of the treasures in the world. It was a different kind of chaos—the one born out of love.

"You and me," I murmured. "Together."

"Together. Forever."

THE END

For a preview to the Thorns of Omertà Series, Book Two, Thorns of Death, make sure to keep reading.

PREVIEW OF THORNS OF DEATH: PROLOGUE

Isla

I caught him looking at me before the show started.

Dark eyes. A sprinkling of silver in his jet-black hair. A thin layer of stubble.

The air caught in my lungs, feeling his eyes on me like a cool breeze against my heated skin. Usually men watched me with a single purpose. To get me into bed. But this guy looked at me like he wanted to consume me.

And I'd let him.

He was older, but definitely not old. Maybe double my age or so.

I inhaled deeply, but there wasn't oxygen to loosen up this knot in my chest. His black eyes burned through me, tracing down my body and studying my every curve. Did he like what he saw? Arousal shot through me, sending a shiver down my spine.

I should look away. I should turn my back on him. But I didn't.

Instead, with a thundering heart against my ribs, I blew him a kiss and winked playfully.

"Isla, are you ready?"

Athena's voice pulled my attention away from the stranger. I turned to find her staring at me, right along with Phoenix.

"Ready for what?" I asked, confused.

"We agreed you'd play before Reina's fashion show starts," she muttered. "I swear, is everyone losing their minds?" I didn't get to answer because she continued with her ranting. "I know I have good organizational skills, but the least you could do is follow directions."

I bit the inside of my cheek. Athena was a control freak. She hated any mess. And broken schedules sent her over the edge. It had to be part of her disorder but it worked well for all of us because the rest of our group was a mess.

"Where is your violin?" she squealed, snapping her fingers to get my attention.

I lowered my eyes and realized it wasn't in my hand. Then I remembered. I never grabbed it. The handsome stranger captured my attention and I'd completely forgotten about it.

"Let me grab it," I said, rushing to where I had left my violin.

As if pulled by a force, my eyes flickered to the spot where the dark stranger had stood, but he was no longer there. Disappointment washed over me, which made no sense. I didn't even know him. He could be a complete douche for all I know.

"Okay, I'm ready. What was the first song we're playing?" I asked, signing in ASL at the same time so Phoenix would understand me too. Phoenix was deaf. When I first ran into her in my music class, I marveled at the thought of someone playing the piano while not being able to hear a single note. Yet, she taught me so much.

And her dedication put mine to shame. Her sister, Reina, and Phoenix were super close. Two years apart, Reina took extra classes in high school to graduate alongside her older sister. Whenever a professor argued about having a deaf child in their music class, Reina stepped in like a little firecracker and argued until they accepted Phoenix, even at the cost of sacrificing her own time.

It was how we all ended up in the same college. Reina wanted Phoenix to get everything she wanted—namely, the best music college in the world. But none of us were ready to let Reina give up her passion. Fashion design. So we all settled for the best of both worlds.

The Royal College of Arts and Music.

After all, it allowed us all to remain together.

"Okay, let's get this party started!" I exclaimed enthusiastically, taking my violin out of its case. "Reina Romero, mere human today. Fashion goddess tomorrow."

We rushed around the large podium. It was hectic, everyone making last-minute changes to arrange for everything to be perfect. The venue was magnificent. I had no idea how Reina got so lucky to have Enrico freaking Marchetti let us use it. He even extended an invitation to some of his key contacts.

Yikes! More pressure.

It was important that it all went well. For all of us. It would open the world of fashion to Reina, the world of top musicians to Phoenix and me, and expose Athena to artists and buyers.

I found Reina running around like a chicken with her head cut off in the back room, getting all the models ready. Shoes for this one. Ribbon for that one. Fix makeup on that one.

Geez. I'd just kill them all. Much easier.

"Where have you been?" she exclaimed in her over-the-top "mother" voice. The girls and I shared a look, rolling our eyes. "Stop rolling your eyes," she grumbled. "Get to your spots," she ordered in her most stern voice.

The three of us snapped to attention, stifling our grins. "Aye aye, Captain." The salute we gave almost made me lose it and burst into laughter.

⁂

Three hours later, we clinked out glasses, alcohol swishing, and drops spilling over the table.

"To us," we exclaimed in unison. "Today Paris, tomorrow the world."

We found our way back to the dance floor, swaying our hips and laughing. For the first time in over two years, we felt lighter. The murder we committed didn't feel as heavy on our souls tonight.

It was then that I spotted him again. A few feet away from me. Oh my gosh, he was coming my way. My friends forgotten, I took a step towards him and the scent of chocolate and sin wafted into my nostrils.

Fuck, I always loved chocolate so much.

The corner of his lips tugged up. "Ciao."

Oh my wet panties. Italian accent. Smooth and raspy. God, yes. Take me. Ravish me. Do something.

"Hello," I greeted him, appearing cool and sophisticated, at least in my mind. All the while, my heart bounced within the walls of my rib cage like it was on steroids. Jesus Christ, so much hotness couldn't be healthy.

"Celebrating?" he asked, his eyebrows arching in mild interest. "By the looks of it, the fashion show went well."

"Yeah," I breathed, wondering what exactly he wanted. Somehow, it struck me that I wasn't his type. My eyes flickered behind him to where he'd left his date. Thirties. Blonde hair. Legs that went on and on, almost reaching the sky, while mine stopped too close to the earth. God, what was she? Like six feet tall, while little ol' me was barely pushing five foot four.

Yeah, something was fishy here. Why was this guy talking to me?

He closed the rest of the distance between us and stole the air from my lungs. I could feel the heat radiating from beneath his sophisticated, tailored suit. He kind of reminded me of my brothers. Dark, brooding, intimidating.

None of which I cared for very much. Luckily for my brothers, I loved them anyway. This guy, however, had some crazy magnetic pull on me that I definitely didn't need. Just a look his way could steal the breath from my lungs.

I was S. C. R. E. W. E. D.

This was what all the stupid Disney movies were all about. Handsome men who swooped in, made you do dumb stuff, and then left you. Except Disney decided not to cover the last part.

As if he read my thoughts, his beautiful—oh so kissable—lips curved into a smile and every part of me melted into a puddle.

"Isla, we're gonna go to the next bar," Athena shouted. "You coming?"

I waved my hand noncommittally, drowning in the dark gaze of this stranger. "Yeah, I'll meet you there."

I didn't bother sparing her a look. I feared if I tore my eyes off this man, he'd disappear and I'd miss my chance. For some dumb reason, it felt like I *needed* to keep him in my vicinity.

To keep his heat. To keep his darkness. Just for a little while longer.

He studied me with the same interest and I wondered what he saw. A drip of darkness that slithered through my light, slowly suffocating it? Or was it the sins I'd committed? A ghost of a smile passed his lips and his dimples turned my stomach into warm goo. God, I had never been much into anatomy but there was something so bewitching about his sharp jawline. The curves and edges of his face were ruthless. Between those cutthroat cheekbones and square chin was a mouth that must have been made for saying filthy things in the language of romance. Even his straight nose was attractive.

Leisurely, I let my gaze travel down the tall, strong frame of him. I couldn't find a single flaw. His navy suit made him look severe. He cocked his head to the side, as if waiting for me to render my judgment.

I remained silent. Because really, what could I say? The man looked like a Roman god.

I averted my gaze to his fingers to check for a wedding band. No wedding band. Silent relief washed over me. I'd never get involved with a married man. It was a hard pass for me.

He cocked his head to the side. "Did I pass the test?" he mused, the accent alone sending tremors through me. I was a sad case if the accent alone was turning me on.

"I haven't decided yet," I quipped, lying through my teeth.

He jerked his arm, allowing the sleeve of his blazer to slide up as he glanced at his vintage Rolex.

"Better hurry up, little one," he mused, confident that he could make any woman's dreams come true. He probably could. "The sooner we get started, the sooner we both get pleasure."

Oh. My. Freaking. God.

This man was all business and serious about pleasure. That was an Italian man for you. God, I needed to get laid. My first boyfriend was a disaster. I swore he almost shoved his penis in the wrong hole and scarred me forever. Obviously since then, I didn't venture to second or third base with a boy. I'd been busy with shit and trying not to make the same mistake again.

Either way, I'd bet my violin—my most precious possession—that this man knew exactly how to give and take pleasure.

My eyes darted around him to where the blonde bombshell stood. "Aren't you on a date?" I asked him, narrowing my eyes. "The last thing I need is a scene with a scorned woman screaming at me. God forbid, it's in Italian. I wouldn't even know how to respond."

He offered me his hand. His poise unnerved and fascinated me at the same time. "She didn't come with me, and she won't leave with me," he responded.

Fuck it. I wasn't the impulsive type, but tonight, the stars were aligning. This was meant to be, I was certain.

So I slid my hand into his, his warmth instantly seeping into me and spreading all the way down to my toes. He leaned toward me, entering my personal space and brushed his thumb along the column of my throat. A simple touch, yet it sent my body into overdrive. Shudders rolled through me and my entire body broke out in goose bumps.

His smile was predatory, my insides clenching on nothing and my panties dampening between my thighs. He leaned forward, his lips close to my ear, and whispered, "I'll make it good for you."

Without a single doubt in my mind, I knew he would.

Ten minutes later, we entered a fancy home. No, not a home. A mansion in the middle of Paris. Knowing the real estate of this city, I couldn't believe anyone aside from the government could afford something like this in the heart of Paris.

"What do you do exactly?" I asked as my heels clicked against the marble. The whole house was dimly lit and soft Italian music drifted through the air.

The moon glimmered in the sky, probably witnessing many one-night stands and laughing at the ridiculous people looking for pleasure. Well, let the moon laugh. I'd be laughing in the morning when the sun came up.

We climbed the stairs silently while my heart screamed, nearly bursting from my chest. My phone buzzed, or maybe it was his, but neither one of us paid it any mind. My knees trembled under my flirty yellow dress that Reina had designed for me.

Last night she handed it to me with the words, "I think it'll bring you good luck."

Oh my gosh, I was doing this. I was really having a one-night stand. I was twenty-three, and there was nothing unusual about a twenty-three-year-old having a one-night stand at least once in her lifetime.

We entered the large dimly lit bedroom with accents of black and white everywhere. The door glided shut with a soft click, and before my next breath, the man stalked towards me, his eyes cool and detached.

He cornered me against the wall, every step more eager than the last. My back pressed against the wall and a thought pushed through my desire.

"Hold on," I breathed nervously. He instantly stilled and somehow that assured me. He wouldn't force me to do anything I didn't want to. My pulse wrestled inside my throat, while he watched me with that dark gaze that made me feel like I was drowning in deep waters. "I—I don't know your name," I murmured.

He considered me with those eyes. "Enrico."

Was he—

No, it couldn't be. Enrico was a very common Italian name.

"Any other questions before we get started?" he asked in that deep, accented voice.

My nostrils flared. He probably considered me a chick that flirted and had sex with strangers all the time. I wasn't but it didn't really matter. I'd probably never see him again.

"No more questions," I answered. "You may proceed, Enrico."

Dark amusement flashed in his eyes and something about seeing his mouth curved into a half-smile made my insides clench. Maybe I waited way too long to give sex another try and now everything about this man made me want to orgasm.

He cupped me through my dress, and I whimpered, my body arching against the wall behind me. His thumb found my clit and dug its way through the fabric, pressing hard and massaging it in lazy circles.

A moan climbed up my throat and filled the space between us.

"Fuck, you're eager, dolcezza," he murmured, his lips skimming my throat.

"My name is Isla," I snapped back. "Not dolce-whatever."

A dark chuckle vibrated in his chest. "It means sweetheart in Italian."

"Oh." He pulled away, studying my face as he removed his blazer.

He kicked off his shoes next and I eagerly waited for his shirt and pants to come off. They didn't. Not yet anyhow and his next move made me forget everything.

His body slammed against mine and his lips fused to mine. He was so much taller than me that it felt like I'd be swallowed whole by him. My eyes rolled into the back of my head from the pleasure that shot through me. Stars exploded behind my eyelids, and I wrapped my hands around his neck, clutching the collar of his shirt, pulling him closer. Needing more of him.

He hoisted me up in his arms, his fingers digging into my ass. My legs wrapped around his waist, my heeled shoes falling against the hardwood floor with a thump. I ground against him, lust igniting in my lower belly. But when he rubbed against me, I lost all control. I moaned, sinking my claws into him, needing so much more from him.

His body was hard as marble and his lips were as soft as velvet. Enrico slipped his tongue into my mouth and another moan bubbled in my throat. He swallowed it, his hips rolling against my hot core. And by the feel of a hard—very hard—cock, he was very well endowed.

Each roll of his hips against my slit sent shots of pleasure through me. We kissed like two needy humans. Maybe he'd been just as starved for touch as I had been. Or maybe he just gave it his all when he fucked. Right now, it didn't matter to me. Like a greedy woman, I took it all.

He bit my lower lip, hard, then sucked the pain away. I cried out for more, grinding my body shamelessly against his. He slipped his hand between us and under my dress. He nudged my panties aside, then slipped two fingers into me and my head fell back against the wall. I was so wet that an obscenely erotic noise filled the room. A noise that came from me.

He growled, murmuring something in Italian. I was so far gone that I couldn't have cared less what he said. I just needed him to see this through. An involuntary groan escaped my lips when he dug his fingers deep into me. Each time he thrust them in, he curled them and hit my G-spot.

He pulled his fingers out and a whimper escaped me. My eyes shot open to find him staring at me. He looked put together, almost unaffected, but there was a dark gleam in his eyes that had my soul shaking with dark promises.

His other hand traveled up to my breasts, twisting one nipple roughly, through the thin fabric of my dress. "Isla," he drawled, bringing his fingers up and smearing my desire over my bottom lip. "Is that Russian?"

"Yes," I breathed. "No." I couldn't think straight. My brothers always insisted on keeping my Russian heritage a secret. "I grew up in California."

He returned his fingers to my pussy while he tasted me on my lips. "You taste like dolcezza."

He skimmed his mouth over my lips, then my jawline down to my neck. Ignoring my inexperience, I brought my hand down to his zipper and pushed my palm against his huge hard-on. Jesus H. Christ.

There was no way he'd fit. He was built like one of those dicks in my favorite alien romance novels.

He must have sensed my panic, because he purred, "I set the pace, but you get the pleasure first."

It sounded like a good deal. Fuck if I knew. I was still hung up on his huge alien cock.

He slipped two more fingers into me—most of his hand—and I was so full I thought I was going to explode. He swallowed another moan with our filthy kiss, as he kept thrusting his fingers into me and pleasure shot through me like a lightning bolt. I came all over his fingers, shudders rolling down my spine and my body quickly turning into mush.

Enrico lifted me back up, taking my chin between his fingers and holding our gazes locked. "We have barely gotten started," he growled. "Are you ready for the next round?"

I watched him through my half-lidded eyes. "I was born ready," I murmured, my voice hoarse.

"Bene." He seemed pleased with my answer, his eyes lasering in on me. "Now, I'm going to taste you. You better taste as good as you look."

Before I could even process his words, he slid to his knees. Effortless and agile, like he was in his prime. Well, duh. The man was in his prime. In one swift movement, he flipped my dress up and threw one of my legs over his shoulder. He ripped my panties with one swift move and his tongue drove into me.

"Holy shit," I breathed, my eyes squeezing shut. He licked and sucked, then rolled his tongue around my clit like it was a lollipop. "Oh my... God!"

A rumbled chuckle vibrated to my core as my hips arched of their own will into his mouth. Then he started fucking me with his tongue. I threaded my fingers through his hair and gripped it like both of our sanities depended on it. It was my first experience with oral sex, and I swore to God, it wouldn't be the last.

I have been missing-the-fuck-out.

My head rolled against the wall as Enrico's mouth devoured me and every noise from his throat brought me closer and closer to another orgasm. I clamped my thighs around his face, grinding against him like a wanton hussy. The sounds he made vibrated through me, making me think he actually enjoyed eating my pussy.

And that thought alone, pushed me over the edge. I felt it from my toes to the tips of my hair. It was like an electric shock, sending waves through my body and sending me to heaven.

This man was a walking, talking orgasm.

He closed his lips over my swollen clit and sucked it with force.

"Enrico!" I cried out, my entire body shaking violently as waves of pleasure smashed through me. This had to be heaven.

My feet met the cold hardwood, a stark contrast against my heated skin. With a seductive zipping sound, my dress loosened and fell down my legs, pooling around my feet. I forewent a bra since the dress had a built-in one and now I stood naked in front of him while he was still dressed.

Then, as I watched him under my lashes and with labored breathing, he stood up, then rid himself of his socks, followed by his dress pants and shirt. God, he'd been commando this whole time! My mouth watered at the sight of him naked. Olive skin covered every hard plane of his muscles, making me salivate. I wanted to lick every inch of him.

I had no idea from where he produced a condom, but I was grateful at least one of us was thinking. The damn thing didn't even cross my mind. I watched him rip the condom wrapper with his teeth and then roll it onto his length and just the act of it was a whole new brand of porn.

"You know, if you record yourself rolling on a condom, I bet you'd make millions on an Only Fans page," I rasped, my eyes locked on his shaft. "Or TikTok," I noted reluctantly.

I hated the idea of anyone seeing this man's naked body. I wanted to claim it as my own. Claw any bitch's eyes out if they dared look his way.

Jesus, that's kind of violent for a one-night stand, I mused in my head.

His finger trailed over my breasts, twisting one nipple, then the other. My back arched into his touch. His musky scent overwhelmed me, and I realized, I'd never be able to eat chocolate without thinking about this. *Him!*

"Get on the chair," he ordered. The sound of his low, gravelly voice made my heart stutter.

My gaze flicked around the room until I saw the chair he was referring to. It was close to the window and my heart hammered against my rib cage. I opened my mouth to question him whether he really wanted me there, but the intense look in his eyes told me everything.

With my heartbeat drumming, I padded across the room and lowered myself onto the chair, its cool material like ice against my searing hot skin. Never wavering my gaze from him, I scooted backwards, watching him approach me like a predator ready to devour its prey.

"Open your legs."

A trickle of arousal made its way down my inner thighs. Good God. The man had made me climax twice already and my pussy was still greedy for more.

"Don't make me repeat myself, dolcezza," he purred with a dark warning.

Fuck it. He wanted evidence of my arousal, he'd get it. I spread my legs open, leaning against the soft back of the chair.

"You going to get down on your knees for me, Enrico," I drawled lazily, my voice huskier than I'd like it to be. "You ready for the next round?"

Enrico's lips tugged up and he actually seemed to like my temper. Lovely. I, Isla, had officially lost my mind.

Despite being naked, he looked like a king as he walked towards me, and to my shock, he got down on his knees.

"Anything for my queen," he purred, then buried his face into my pussy.

He ate my pussy like a starved man who knew this was his last meal.

When we finally collapsed into bed five hours later, I was thoroughly fucked. My lips were swollen and stubble marks covered every inch of my fair skin. Not to mention bite marks. I'm sure the look on my face was a testament to the fact that I had been to sex heaven and back.

I woke up to dark eyes staring me down, five inches from my face. I screeched. She didn't. I scooted away like she was a plague, pulling the sheets up to my chin.

"What the fuck?" I hissed.

She didn't answer. In fact, she didn't even flinch. My eyes darted next to me to find the bed empty. Jesus, where in the hell was Enrico?

"Who are you?" I spat, glaring at the woman. She was pretty. Dark hair. Even darker eyes. Petite. Olive skin that made you jealous. It was easier to hide your emotions with that kind of skin complexion.

Again, no answer. "Where is Enrico?" I asked, tiredly.

She reached over to the nightstand and all the wrong scenarios twisted in my mind. She'd kill me. She was a psycho. I could see the front page already—Jealous ex-lover kills a one-night stand.

Get yourself together, Isla, I scolded myself mentally.

I startled, jumping out of my skin, when she pulled out a photograph. So fucking weird.

She flipped it over and my heart stopped.

It was Enrico's wedding photo. And this woman… she was his wife.

Oh. My. Fucking. God.

TO BE CONTINUED

WHAT'S NEXT?

*Thank you so much for reading **Thorns of Love**! If you liked it, please leave a review. Your support means the world to me.*

*If you're thirsty for more discussions with other readers of the series, you can join the Facebook group, Eva's Soulmates group (*https://bit.ly/3gHEe0e*).*

*Next up in the series is Marchetti and Isla's book, Thorns of Death (*https://amzn.to/3yaJ0h2*).*

ABOUT THE AUTHOR

Curious about Eva's other books? You can check them out here. Eva Winners's Books https://bit.ly/3SMMsrN

Eva Winners writes anything and everything romance, from enemies to lovers to books with all the feels. Her heroes are sometimes villains because they need love too. Right? Her books are sprinkled with a touch of suspense, mystery, a healthy dose of angst, a hint of violence and darkness, and lots of steamy passion.

When she's not working and writing, she spends her days either in Croatia or Maryland daydreaming about the next story.

Find Eva below:

Visit www.evawinners.com and subscribe to my newsletter.
    FB group: https://bit.ly/3gHEe0e
    FB page: https://bit.ly/30DzP8Q
    Insta: http://Instagram.com/evawinners
    BookBub: https://www.bookbub.com/authors/eva-winners
    Amazon: http://amazon.com/author/evawinners
    Goodreads: http://goodreads.com/evawinners
    TikTok: https://vm.tiktok.com/ZMeETK7pq/

Made in the USA
Las Vegas, NV
12 November 2024

11649989R10206